RUINOUS ENDS

By I. V. Marie

RUINOUS ENDS

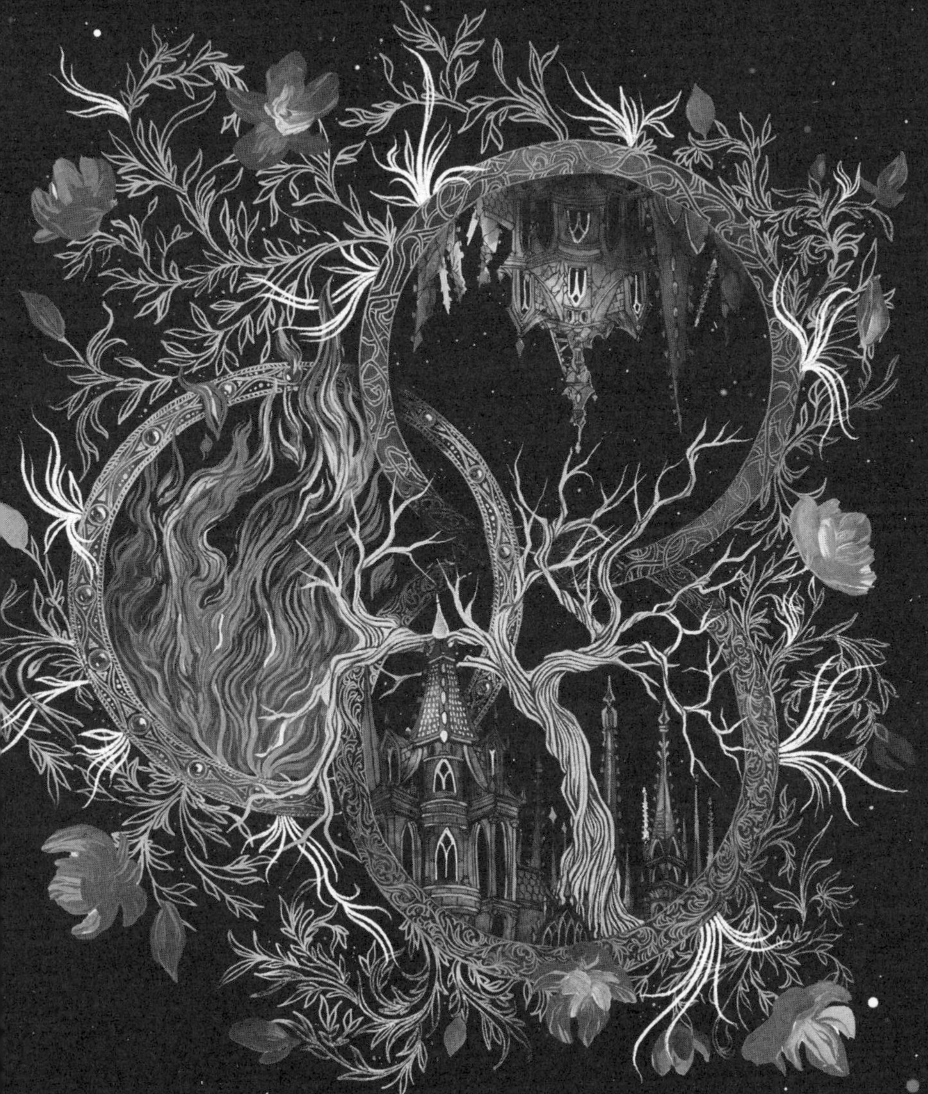

I. V. MARIE

DELACORTE PRESS

Delacorte Press
An imprint of Random House Children's Books
A division of Penguin Random House LLC
1745 Broadway, New York, NY 10019
penguinrandomhouse.com
getunderlined.com

Editor: Lydia Gregovic
Cover Designer: Liz Dresner
Interior Designer: Cathy Bobak
Production Editor: Colleen Fellingham
Managing Editor: Tamar Schwartz
Production Manager: Tracy Heydweiller

Library of Congress Cataloging-in-Publication Data is available upon request.
ISBN 978-0-593-89884-0 (hardcover) — ISBN 978-0-593-89886-4 (ebook)

The text of this book is set in 10.6-point Warnock Pro.

Manufactured in China
10 9 8 7 6 5 4 3 2 1

The authorized representative in the EU for product safety and compliance is Penguin Random House Ireland, Morrison Chambers, 32 Nassau Street, Dublin D02 YH68, Ireland, https://eu-contact.penguin.ie.

For Camila,
Super sibs forever

BLACKWOOD ACADEMY
ASPHODEL HALL
PETTYWORTH
LITTERMAN
MAIN YARD
HOLSTERD
CHAMBERS & FIDDLE
IVORY
ASCENDED QUARTERS
MEMORIUM
LIBRARY
GAZEBO
SHED
ELYSIUM HALL
BONESTROD HALL
DALEMONT HALL

PART I

IT IS WRITTEN

BETWEEN WORLDS

In the shadows of night, slithering between the folds of time, he waited. Starved for retribution. A hollow ache blossoming in the empty cavern where his soul had once resided. He had waited centuries for her. For the one who could unlock the usurper's heart. The one branded by his hatred, marked by the hands of the reaper.

His sweet catalyst. His fated destroyer.

And he would have waited an eternity for her. He would have slumbered in the shadows, patient and willing.

But Wren Loughty had arrived.

And now . . . now the time for waiting was over.

1

AUGUST

Augustine Hughes was losing his mind.

Time had become a fickle and unstable thing; it drifted through his fingers like the remnants of a bad dream. There were moments of clarity—breaths of hope among the rot filling his lungs—but it was never enough to drag him back to reality. The darkness was too hungry. The poison too thick.

It was almost comical, the absurdity of it all. Losing his mind in the afterlife. He would have thought the worst of his troubles were behind him once he had died. Yet there he was, wandering the outskirts of purgatory, mind fragmented, whispering to the darkness like a madman.

He *was* mad, wasn't he?

August laughed and the sound grated against his skin. He was fairly certain he was lying on the dirt floor, though it was impossible to tell. The only thing he was truly certain of was the agony. It filled every crevice of his soul. Every ligament and bone. Every atom of his being.

How long had he been like this?

The last thing he could remember was Wren's voice dripping into his mind, warm and inviting, and then . . . *fury*. An anger he had never known possible. Everything blurred after that, twisting together until all semblance of reality had lost its meaning. And now all he knew was this torture . . . this suffering.

Old memories flickered through his vision like a sun-damaged film reel, vignettes of a life that was no longer his.

August watched as a group of strangers slowly lowered his mother's body into the ground. Next to him, his sister sobbed. She gripped August's wrist as though she might float away if she let go. As if he were the only thing tethering her to the earth. Behind them, their father remained silent. He had not wept for his wife, and August was certain he never would.

Why would he?

He was the one who'd killed her, after all.

The memory fluttered away, drifting like morning fog, replaced by another.

"We must do something," Edith pleaded, red-rimmed eyes brimming with desperation. They were standing in the garden, hidden beneath the shadows of night. Above them, their father's study window glowed amber.

"What are you suggesting?" August asked, fearing her answer.

Edith's gaze drifted to the window, her face torn between sorrow and rage.

"We can make it look like an accident."

"Edith," August whispered. "You mustn't say things like that—" But his sister interjected, cutting him off.

"Her death was no accident, Augustine. We both know this." Edith stepped closer, her dark eyes blazing beneath the light of her lantern. "Do you truly believe she simply fell down the stairs? After everything we've seen? Everything we've heard?"

"How will we be any different if we do to him what he did to her?" August challenged.

"What he did was murder." The word spoken out loud, with such candor, sent a chill down August's spine. "This . . . this is vengeance."

"But . . . what if something happens?" he asked, voice shaking. "What about your soul?"

"My soul?" Edith chuckled, though her smile dropped when she saw the sincerity in her brother's eyes. "Oh, Augustine. Do not fear for my soul. It is in nobody's hands but mine." When August didn't budge, Edith let out a long and weighted sigh. "I'm sorry. I shouldn't say these things out loud. I just need some rest."

August stepped closer, carefully inspecting his sister. "Are you certain?"

"Yes, little brother." Clearly sensing August's apprehension, Edith reached out and wrapped him in an embrace, whispering the next words into his ear. "I promise."

But when she hugged August, he felt her heart hammering in her chest, her pulse beating like the frenetic wings of a hummingbird. And though he could not see his sister's face . . . he knew exactly what she was staring at.

He knew her eyes were locked on that study window.

August tried desperately to cling to the memory, but it faded before he could watch what happened next, drifting within the invisible current. A new one took its place from one breath to the next.

The one he had tried so desperately to forget.

The door to the kitchen was ajar. August took a step inside, peering around the corner. His sister didn't notice him at first, her lips lifted into a serene and placid smile as she poured a cup of tea. When he stepped forward, the old wood creaked beneath his weight and his sister's head snapped up in surprise.

"Augustine. I thought you were asleep."

"I was." He approached the counter, rubbing the exhaustion from his eyes. "But I heard you down here."

"Go back to bed." Edith set the teacup on a tray, stirring the liquid inside with a silver spoon. "Father is in one of his moods. It is best you stay in your room and out of his way."

"Is that for him?"

"Chamomile tea with a splash of rye and valerian." She winked, stepping around the counter. "I am hopeful it will be enough to calm his nerves and send him to sleep."

"Let me come with you—"

"No," Edith interjected, pausing beneath the doorway. "If he lashes out, I'd rather it be me than you." She offered him an apologetic smile. "Please, Augustine. Just go to bed."

August conceded with a nod and watched as Edith made her way upstairs, her footsteps receding. He was moments away from walking back to his bedroom when he noticed the empty glass vial on the counter.

He picked it up, lifting it toward one of the iron sconces lining the walls. The label had been partially scratched off, but he could just make out the writing. Squinting, he read what was written upon the vial.

Arsenic.

And Edith had poured the entire bottle into their father's tea.

August scrambled out of the kitchen, running up the stairs so fast he nearly slipped, barely catching himself on the railing. He gasped, picking up his pace, panic clouding his judgment. And before he could stop himself, before he could even decipher what he was about to do, he stumbled into his father's study.

Edith stood next to their father, a hand on his shoulder. He had lifted the teacup to his lips and begun to take a sip when August first stepped into the room. Upon seeing August, their father froze, the edge of the teacup pressed against his mouth.

"Augustine . . ." Edith's face contorted in confusion. "I thought I said to—" Her voice caught in her throat when she noticed the glass vial in her brother's hand. She tried to hide her reaction, quickly averting her gaze, but it was too late.

Their father had noticed.

"Come here," he instructed, motioning August forward. "Hand me that."

What happened next, August couldn't quite remember. The memory sped up and slowed down, warping like a fun-house mirror. The scene jolted, staccato, each moment flashing from one heartbeat to the next.

His father realizing what had been poured into his tea.

His hands gripping Edith's neck.

August slamming his fists against their father's back.

The unfathomable pain as his father threw him to the floor and snapped his leg in half.

Edith removing the knife in her waistcoat and plunging it into their father's back.

Their father screaming like a wild animal as he ripped the knife out.

The look on Edith's face when her own father brought the same knife down upon her.

In that moment, the memory came rushing back in with unwavering clarity. The knife had sliced clean through Edith's abdomen. She fell to the floor, hands clutching her stomach, blood seeping through her fingers. August's reaction was instinctual. Primal. He tackled his father, pushing him onto his desk, sending a candle tumbling to the floor.

The curtain closest to the desk caught fire. The flames ate away at the fabric, inch by inch. Beneath August, his father had hardened into stone. Mouth agape. Eyes wide.

August pushed himself away from his father, collapsing as the pain from his leg took hold. Next to him on the floor, Edith lay motionless, her vacant eyes staring up at the ceiling, the ghost of a smile on her lips. August dragged himself toward her, screaming out in agony as his broken leg arched unnaturally behind him. Around him, the fire grew. It devoured everything in its path—the bookcases, the piles of notebooks, the old wallpaper.

Black smoke rushed into August's lungs. He coughed, sputtering, choking helplessly.

There were two options. Two conclusions to his story. He could attempt to pull himself out of the study, to somehow drag himself down the stairs and out of the house. Or . . . he could stay there. He could end their story, once and for all, and burn.

The decision, however, was never truly his to make.

It was in that moment that a dizziness came over him. Whether it was from shock or his wound, he didn't know. All he knew was that he was unable to move. His head slammed against the floorboards, as though he had been knocked to the floor by an invisible weight.

Smoke clouded his vision. Through the haze, he swore he saw someone standing on the other side of the room . . . watching. But before he could properly understand what he was looking at, the flames swallowed him whole.

And then . . . darkness.

August opened his eyes and found he was lying in a cave. He blinked, attempting to make sense of where he was. Beneath him, streaks of blood glistened against the rocky floor. It wasn't until he glanced down at his hands, the raw blisters scattered across his palms healing at a rapid speed, that he understood the blood must be his own. That he must have dragged himself into the cave, crawling on his hands and knees in the throes of delirium, until he found a place to rest his eyes. But now that he had clawed his way back to reality, the weight of his situation fell upon him like a guillotine.

"My humanity . . ." August croaked, his voice rough from days spent screaming, drowning under memories.

Now he remembered.

He had carved out his humanity. He had opened the locked door and invited the shadows inside, sealing his fate. The tidal wave of memories made sense now—he could remember hearing about this happening to others within the Order . . . a sort of purging. Days spent writhing in pain, subjected to horrifying hallucinations after removing their humanity. But just to be certain, August reached a trembling hand toward his chest, slowly unbuttoning his shirt until his bare torso was visible. Even shrouded in the darkness of the cave, there was no avoiding what now swam through his veins like venom.

Shadows.

August cursed and pressed his head back against the cave wall. His chest shuddered with every panicked breath, terror sinking into his bones. This was exactly what he had tried so hard to avoid . . . what he had been desperate to shield himself from. The shadows had poisoned his sister, turning her into something unrecognizable, into a monster.

And now he would meet the same fate.

With his humanity gone, August would never be able to cross over to the Other Side. And if he allowed himself to use the shadow magic he now had access to—if he *truly* succumbed to the shadows—he'd lose himself. Just like Edith. The more shadow magic he used, the less *him* he would be.

More shadow than human.

But he would do it again. He would do it ten times over if it meant saving Wren.

If it meant keeping his promise.

Find me. Wherever you are, wherever we end up, don't stop looking for me.

August gathered himself onto his feet, bracing himself against the walls of the cave. Next to him, a shadow coiled around his wrist, its movement almost shy. Despite the nausea wrapping around his throat, August didn't push it away. He welcomed it, letting it travel across his palm, slithering up and down his arm in delight. Instantly, a coldness swept through his body. An unnerving chill.

August knew the truth now, the inescapable verity sowed into his soul. He had thought he could run from it, that he could somehow trick the hand of fate into believing he was worth loving, into believing he was worth *something*. But August wasn't the hero. He was broken and tarnished and wretched.

And Wren . . . Wren was the cosmos. She was the very stars themselves.

So—he would do anything to save her from the destruction he had caused. Even if it pained him. Even if it destroyed him.

He would save her . . . even if it cost him his soul.

2

IRENE

"Your exam begins . . . *now*."

The boy standing at the center of the room let out a shaky breath. His eyes scanned the rest of the classroom, terror etched onto his face as he took in the rows upon rows of students looming in front of him, waiting. A cloud of tension permeated the air. A heaviness that seemed to linger over the anxiety-riddled students like a storm cloud. Some of them wanted him to succeed. Most wanted him to fail.

Irene Manette Bamford, however, mainly wanted him to hurry the fuck up.

She glanced over at the grandfather clock on the other side of the room. *Tick. Tick. Tick.* She shifted uncomfortably in her seat next to Housemaster Marigold, crossing her legs with an impatient huff. The boy was moving at a glacial pace, hands shaking as he raised his palms in front of him.

Irene groaned.

Honestly, Marigold should just fail him now and get it over with.

The boy shut his eyes, grimacing, and the faintest gust of wind flickered in his palm, an almost indiscernible vortex materializing in his hands. He gritted his teeth, sweat dampening his temples, and the swirling gust of wind grew in intensity, transforming into what almost appeared to be a miniature tornado.

Irene snorted. Marigold shot her a quick glance, clearly biting back her own smile.

The boy's eyes snapped open and the swirling air in his palms vanished. A few students seated in the front row snickered into their notes. Others looked on with palpable pity, faces pulled into apologetic smiles.

Marigold cleared her throat.

"That'll do, Tao."

A deep blush bloomed on the boy's pale cheeks. He tugged at the hem of his olive wool sweater, feet still firmly planted on the ground.

"Wait . . . I—I can do it again." He peered over his shoulder, looking between Irene and Marigold with pleading eyes. "Let me try again. Please."

Marigold pushed the sleeves of her lace blouse over her elbows.

"That won't be necessary."

"I can do better. I can prove it to you." He raised his hands once more and the air around him barely moved—just the faintest flicker of wind, which sent a pathetic little wisp of air floating over his palm.

"Tao." Marigold spoke his name with a bit more force this time. "I said that's enough. You know you cannot retake an exam. Your grade is final."

But Tao was proving to be a bit more stubborn than either of them had anticipated.

"*No,*" he choked out, desperate, face turning beet red from effort. "I can—I can do this. I just need . . . a few more . . . seconds." The veins running along his neck bulged as he pushed harder, his entire body trembling as the faint wisp of air began to swirl faster.

Jesus Christ. He's going to knock himself out cold.

Marigold leaned in toward Irene, dipping her voice lower. "Do you mind taking care of this?"

Irene smirked. "Oh . . . it would be my *pleasure*."

As Tao continued to ignore Marigold's instructions, resolute about making an absolute fool of himself, Irene stood up from her chair, dusting her hands along the sides of her silk dress. She stepped forward, her heeled boots echoing against the floorboards. As soon as she stood up, the other students straightened in their chairs, clearly sensing what would happen next. Some of their faces blanched in fear. Others leaned in closer, eager to see how the scene would unfold. Tao, however, was too busy casting the world's most pathetic air manipulation spell to notice Irene standing behind him.

That was, of course, until she'd sent him flying across the room with nothing but a flick of her wrist.

Tao hit the eastern wall of the classroom with a loud and echoing thud. He let out a strangled cry of surprise, the noise garbling in his throat as he scrambled to push himself onto his feet.

"Your time is up." Irene's lips curved into a smile. "You can leave now. Unless you'd like to spend the next month locked in reformatory."

Tao hesitated for a moment, eyes flitting across the other students. But nobody was coming to his rescue. He dragged his gaze back to Irene, sheepishly nodding his head before skulking out of the classroom.

Honestly, the boy should be thanking her for not snapping his neck out of sheer annoyance.

"Thank you, Irene." Marigold turned to address the rest of the class. "And a reminder to all of you that there are no redos in this classroom. You have one chance to take your exam. No exceptions."

Irene was about to gesture for the next student to take her

place—a trembling girl who had gone three shades of green during Tao's exam—when a sudden knock at the door interrupted her. It creaked open, revealing another Ascended that Irene vaguely recognized. Samira Heydari stood at the doorway, an annoyed look in her dark chestnut eyes.

"I apologize for the interruption, Housemaster, but I need to speak with Irene for a brief moment."

Marigold let out a sigh of understanding. "Yes, yes. Go on. But make it quick."

Irene fixed Samira with a perplexed look before walking across the room and following the other Ascended out into the hallway.

"What's this about?" Irene asked once the door had closed behind them.

Samira spun on her heels, her berry lips lifting into a smirk. An array of freckles dotted her dark brown skin, traveling across the bridge of her nose and down her cheeks. Her wavy black hair, which she had braided and secured with a ruby ribbon, had a silver streak that slithered over her shoulder. She was offensively pretty and a monstrous bitch, a combination that Irene couldn't help but respect.

"I have a gift for you."

Irene raised a brow in suspicion. "A gift?"

Samira reached into her coat pocket and produced a black envelope, dangling it between them. Irene rolled her eyes, snatching the envelope from the other girl's hand, and ripped it open. Inside, she found a letter.

Pleasure awaits at the heart of Blackwood.
This evening, celebrate a new round of Council initiates.
Bring your most depraved desires and feast upon the forbidden.

A rush of excitement burst through Irene as the letter's message echoed in her mind, though it had less to do with the ridiculous party she'd been invited to and more to do with what the party represented.

The Council—Blackwood's enigmatic secret society in charge of all the school's defenses—was about to select a new group of potential initiates in a tapping ceremony, which was *exactly* what Irene had been waiting for. What she and Mateo had been planning for since the beginning.

Join the Ascended.

Infiltrate the Council.

And take Blackwood Academy down.

"Well?"

Samira's voice drew Irene back to the present.

"Well *what*?" Irene asked, clearing her throat.

"Are you going to go?"

Irene managed a nonchalant shrug. "I'll consider it."

Samira chuckled, as if she saw right through Irene's feigned indifference.

"Well, if you ask me, I think you should go," she said, slowly sauntering away from Irene, a coy smile on her lips. "Who knows . . . you might even enjoy yourself."

Enjoy myself? Irene doubted it. But before she could snap back with a rebuttal, Samira was gone, waltzing around the corner and vanishing deeper into Elysium Hall.

Irene detested how the other Ascended had been treating her ever since she'd joined them. As if she were beneath them simply because she was new. As if they knew something she didn't. Samira was no different—always watching Irene with a smug grin. Speaking to her with purposeful condescension.

Not that it mattered. There was business Irene needed to attend to.

And—more specifically—someone she needed to speak with.

Despite the circumstances, Irene had grown rather accustomed to the sight of a Demien sprawled across her bed.

When she finally made it back to her bedroom after her Ascended duties, she opened the door to find Mateo lying there, scribbling in a red leather-bound journal marked with the Demien Order's sigil—three interconnecting circles bathed in black flames. He was always jotting things down in there . . . writing late into the evening. On most nights since she'd joined the Ascended, Irene had fallen asleep to the sound of pen scraping against parchment, the faint crackle of a burning wick echoing from Mateo's side of the room.

"How was your day?" the Demien asked now, eyes still glued to the pages of his journal.

Irene let out a snort, slamming the door closed with a flick of her wrist. "Riveting."

She stalked across her room and paused by the arched window overlooking the grounds. The dormitories of Blackwood Academy loomed in the distance, a sprawling maze of pointed towers and stained-glass windows. Late afternoon gave way to the familiar silver glow of night, mist coiling around the ground in thin rivulets, welcoming the haze of dusk. Far across the other side of campus lay Ivory House, the dormitory Irene had once called home. She could barely see it from where she stood now, a dark and foreboding skeleton wrapped in a web of vines, but even so . . . she missed it.

Though it had been weeks since Irene had been forced to move out of Ivory House and into her new room within the Ascended Quarters, she still hadn't entirely settled in. Perhaps she could admit that it wasn't Ivory House she missed, but something else.

Someone else.

A memory sliced through her mind, sharp and sudden.

Masika staring back at her in the clearing. The disbelief in her eyes as Irene turned away from her and tore their friendship in two.

Irene flinched as the present came rushing back in. Thinking back on what had happened was useless. She couldn't change what fate had already carved into stone. Masika, her only friend—if she could even call her that anymore—had gone missing after the third Decennial trial, buried under rubble and devoured by rock and ice. And after nearly two weeks of searching, two weeks of scouring the outskirts of purgatory, her body had yet to be found.

None of them had been found.

Wren. August. Emilio. Olivier. Masika. All of them—*gone.* As though their souls had been obliterated, sucked out of existence. They should have been marked as sacrifices for the Ether's insatiable hunger, just like the other six eliminated nominees, but they had disappeared at the end of the final trial.

Grief prickled at Irene's chest as she thought back on the other unlucky nominees. Nick. Liza. Georgia. Carter. Jocelyn. Tristan. All of them devoured by the Ether. But even with their sacrifice, it wasn't enough. There should have been *eleven* souls sacrificed. Irene could feel the Ether's discontent with every breath, the gaping hole demanding to be filled, scraping at her insides like a petulant child.

"What happened?"

Irene hadn't heard Mateo walk over. He was standing beside her, blue eyes blazing with concern. He often moved like a shadow, silent and undetectable. A ribbon of silver light shone across his tanned skin, illuminating the webbed black veins on his neck.

She curled her trembling hands into fists, flexing her fingers back and forth.

"The tapping ceremony," she whispered. "I think it's happening tonight. There's some stupid party to celebrate it . . . I have a feeling they'll choose the initiates there."

"Good." Mateo nodded, eyes still anchored on Irene. He cocked his head, as if assessing her. "What is it? Are you nervous you won't be selected?"

Irene shrugged. Even if she was—she'd never admit it out loud.

Her eyes traveled to the journal in his hands. "What were you doing?" she asked, quick to change the subject.

"I've been considering the possibility of a third coalition forming on the outskirts. A new faction, separate from both Blackwood and the Demien Order. I'm afraid my suspicions might be right," Mateo muttered, tapping the journal against his arm. He wandered back over to the bed and sat down. "I thought it might just be rumors at first . . . fearmongering from Silas to keep us distracted. But a recent string of disappearances within the Order had me questioning the validity of these claims."

Irene arched a brow in surprise. This was the first she'd heard of this. "What disappearances?"

"They've happened for a while now . . . sporadic. Not frequent enough to pose an actual threat, but consistent enough that we've noticed a pattern."

"And what does this third coalition want?" Irene asked.

"To stop us."

"From doing what, exactly?" As Irene asked the question, she made note of the tension in Mateo's shoulders. The slight crack in his stoic expression. "I know we want to take down Blackwood and stop Silas, but you still haven't told me *how*."

But Mateo didn't answer her. He simply began flipping through the notebook, gnawing on the inside of his cheek. *Of course.* More unanswered questions. More secrecy. Irene should have been used to it by now, but she still found herself bristling at his silence.

"Oh, come on." She let out a groan. "Seriously? I'm tired of being kept in the dark. I deserve to know!"

Mateo sighed and glanced up at Irene as though she were a child throwing a tantrum.

"You *know* I can't tell you." His voice was hoarse, clipped with impatience. "Not yet. You should be concentrating on the party tonight, anyway."

Irene scoffed. "I think I'm capable of deciding what I *should* and *shouldn't* be concentrating on."

She hadn't meant to snap back, but his reluctance had set something off inside her. She had done everything to earn his favor—sacrificed more than she was willing to admit—and yet she was still being kept at arm's length. Secrets piling up between them.

At the sound of her outburst, Mateo's expression shifted.

Irene often found herself forgetting the power lurking under Mateo's seemingly benign mask. It was in these moments, silence reverberating between them, tension twisting the air, that she was unwillingly reminded of the danger lurking beneath the surface. But instead of backing away, of cowering under that realization, Irene simply straightened her shoulders, looked him squarely in the eyes and asked, "Do you want me to trust you?"

Mateo flinched, taken aback. When he looked at her, it was almost as if he were seeing through her, examining every inch of her soul with nothing but his gaze. And then he inhaled a quivering breath and lowered his eyes in surrender.

"There's a prophecy . . ." he began, his voice barely a whisper. "The Soulless One spoke it with his first breath. He carved it into his soul, branding it within the heart of the Demien Order. *From my blood she will drink, a debt for a price. A promise of darkness, a last sacrifice. Rotten and broken, his lie comes undone; when the two meet their maker . . . the two become one.*"

"I don't understand." Irene shook her head, desperate to make sense of his words. "What does that mean?"

"*She* . . . is the catalyst," Mateo explained. Something unsettling blazed behind his eyes, an intensity Irene had never seen before. "The harbinger of destruction. The one who will lead the Order in battle and destroy Blackwood, once and for all. *That's* our how. We find the catalyst . . . and she ushers in the clean slate."

"And how are we supposed to figure out who *she* is?" Irene asked.

Mateo dropped Irene's hand, opening the notebook once again.

"We don't need to. We already know"—Mateo turned to the final page and angled it toward Irene—"and so do you."

At first, the page appeared entirely blank, whatever was written upon it concealed by a privacy enchantment. But as the seconds passed, something began to form upon the surface. Bloodred ink swirling into shapes . . . a pair of eyes . . . a nose . . . a mouth . . . until a perfectly drawn figure emerged, sketched in red ink and shimmering speckles of magic.

Irene couldn't contain the gasp that sprang out of her.

She took a step backward, hoping and praying that what she had seen, what she was looking at, wasn't real. That this was all some sadistic, twisted joke. Because the face sketched in red ink, the face staring back at her . . . was none other than Wren Loughty.

3

MASIKA

Masika Sallow had mastered the art of subtlety. Dipping in and out of shadows undetected, plastering on an inconspicuous smile—*nothing to see here, keep it moving.* It was for this reason that people tended to underestimate her, to see her as nothing more than the meek and unassuming friend. But she had learned that, sometimes, being invisible was *exactly* what she needed.

As Masika made her way through the winding corridors of the Resistance's manor, eyes lowered and mouth curved into a placid smile, she was silently thankful for this keen ability of hers. Members of the Resistance scurried past her, clearly running late for the meeting, but nobody batted an eye. Nobody even spared her a passing glance.

Which was fine by Masika—given what she was about to do.

Sneaking around the Resistance's manor had posed a bit of a problem the first few days. Masika had attempted to explore the various Wings, though she'd somehow ended up getting inexplicably lost. Similar to the Ascended Quarters back at Blackwood, the Resistance's manor appeared to be enchanted on the inside, almost as if it magically expanded to fit the roughly one hundred members roaming inside. There were multiple floors and basement levels, a maze of hallways that had been nearly impossible for her to navigate when she'd first arrived. Now, after a couple of weeks—*and some trial and error*—Masika had gotten the hang of it.

For the most part.

As the corridor began to clear, Masika summoned a cloaking enchantment, the defensive magic washing over her skin in a haze of pale blue and golden threads.

Her window of opportunity was small. The last person was entering the Battle Room, the door slowly closing behind them. Masika beelined for the closing door, slipping into the room with barely a second to spare.

As she stumbled forward, she looked up, surveying the scene.

A large oval table stood at the center of the room, made from dark oak and embellished with intricate carvings. A chandelier dangled a few feet above the center of the table, though each arm appeared to be made from bark and the bulbs shaped like crystallized droplets of water. Instead of the usual amber glow of a flame, each bulb gave off a pale cerulean sheen, washing the room in a bluish glow.

The table itself was massive, large enough to fit all twenty-one Leaders of the Resistance. The Leaders were divided into three subgroups—combat trainers, healers and strategists. It was their job to train the rest of the Resistance, to prepare them for the inevitable battle looming on the horizon.

It's their job to make sure we stand a chance, Masika thought with a shudder.

There were only two faces Masika properly recognized—Birdie and Russo. Birdie sat on the right side of the table, among the strategists, while Russo sat on the left, at the head of the combat trainers. It still felt odd to see the pair without their Housemaster's cloak. Like the other Leaders of the Resistance, Birdie and

Russo appeared to be perpetually poised for battle; their shoulders covered with shimmering chain-mail spaulders, ruby-encrusted chokers protecting their necks. Leather armor sat snuggly around their torsos; a set of corporeally infused daggers rested upon Birdie's waist, while Russo kept a glowing spear strapped to her back.

And sitting at the far end of the table, arms draped over her chair as she waited for the others to settle, was Catherine.

For a terrible, prolonged moment, Masika could do nothing but stare. After all this time, after all the years spent waiting and clinging to the stubborn hope that she might one day see her again—Catherine was *here*. But there was no room in Masika's heart for joy, not when the truth stung more than losing her ever did.

Because Catherine had escaped the Demien Order years ago to join the Resistance.

Which meant she hadn't been forced to stay away from Masika . . . she'd *chosen* to.

Despite the anger and resentment seizing her heart, Masika couldn't help but briefly marvel at the sheer beauty that was Catherine. The years had hardened her, her features alight with an intensity that wasn't there before, but she was still undeniably breathtaking. Her tawny hair was tied into multiple braids that fell down her leather-clad shoulders, the tips brushing against her waist. An armored corset covered the curves of her torso, ruby buckles adorning the front. She donned the Resistance red in her bracers, the armguards fitted around her forearms.

It was excruciating, being this close to her again. A tirade of memories threatened to overtake Masika—late nights spent hidden beneath the winding corridors of Blackwood, whispering secrets and sharing parts of themselves that nobody had seen before. Trading kisses beneath candlelight. Holding hands as they walked through the mist-shrouded grounds.

Masika shut her eyes, pushing the thoughts away. She wasn't here for Catherine.

She was here to listen.

As Masika made her way around the room, passing by a small oval mirror, she caught a glimpse of her reflection. She startled for a moment, afraid the others could see her, before quickly remembering the cloaking enchantment concealing her from the rest of the Battle Room. Her chest tightened at the sight of the unfamiliar scar marring her deep brown skin, slicing down from her eyebrow to her neck. The healers had done what they could to mend her injuries, though they were unsure why they hadn't been able to heal the scar completely.

But Masika didn't mind it anymore.

The scar was proof that she had crawled her way out of the Decennial. That she had beat Silas at his own game.

And if she had beat the game . . . then perhaps she could win the war.

Masika shifted her gaze away from the mirror and back toward the table when a voice cut through the restless murmurs of the room.

"I think we've endured enough waiting," said a girl with cropped silver hair seated among the combat trainers. Floral tattoos adorned her brown skin, traveling up her forearms and onto her shoulders. Her eyes were locked in on Catherine. "What's this about, Cat?"

Cat? Masika couldn't help but feel a slight sting at hearing the nickname.

An unwelcome memory fluttered through her mind.

Masika had just finished classes for the evening. She'd found Catherine sitting by the hearth in Ivory House, legs crossed and hands extended toward the crackling flames. She crossed the room, slowly sinking down next to her on the floor.

"You okay?"

Catherine blinked, as if she'd just realized Masika was next to her. She'd been acting strange the past few days. More distant. Masika would often catch her staring out of a window, a sort of vacant look in her eyes.

"Just tired," Catherine murmured softly beneath her breath, mustering up a small smile, though the light didn't quite reach her eyes.

Masika reached out her hand, gently tucking a strand of tawny hair behind Catherine's ear. Her fingers briefly grazed the other girl's cheek, and Masika watched as a blanket of goose bumps fluttered up and down Catherine's neck.

"There's something on your mind, Cat. I can tell."

Catherine gnawed on her cheek. Masika held her breath, waiting. But then Catherine simply laced her hand through Masika's, bringing the back of her hand up toward her lips, brushing a featherlight kiss upon her knuckles.

"I'm fine, my little dove. Promise."

Masika shuddered, pushing the memory away, forcing herself back to the present. In front of her, Catherine inhaled a deep breath, leaning forward. She focused her attention on the silver-haired girl.

"Dina . . . settle down."

Dina slumped back into her chair, though she kept her gaze fixed on Catherine. The others watched intently as Catherine stood from her chair, hands splayed over the table.

Masika made a mental note of the key dangling at Catherine's hip. Though they were allowed to roam freely throughout the Resistance's base, there was one area that was explicitly forbidden to enter. One area that only the Leaders themselves ever stepped foot in.

The Southern Wing.

Whatever Catherine was hiding in there was *clearly* valuable . . . and Masika had every intention of figuring out what it was.

"I understand you're all eager to know why we've called this meeting, so I'll cut to the chase." Catherine's tone was calm and level, though Masika could sense the underlying wariness peeking at the edges. "As you all know, our latest tracking crew left the base three days ago. They were meant to return tomorrow, however . . . there's been a problem."

Masika had heard of these tracking crews . . . and the danger of being part of them.

Despite the Resistance being partially made up of ex-Demiens, none of them were able to pinpoint the location of the Demien Order's encampment. It was enchanted to be hidden . . . even from memory. Every ex-Demien who tried to recollect where they had come from—who tried to trace their way back to the encampment—couldn't remember a single thing. It was as if the memory had been carved out of their mind, replaced with a murky haze. Which meant that every few weeks, a new group of Resistance members would venture out into purgatory in the hopes of tracking down the Demien Order's location.

Not a single crew had been successful.

If they even made it back at all.

"What kind of problem?" asked Dina, pulling Masika out of her thoughts.

Catherine's jaw twitched, the faintest crack in her stoic mask.

"They've been taken."

Tension swept through the room in a wave of harrowing silence.

"By who?" whispered a boy to the left of Catherine. He had a lean frame with a sharp jaw and copper hair that fell to his shoulders. Masika had seen him before, during her mandatory training sessions with Russo. *Brayden,* Masika thought to herself. She remembered hearing Russo call out his name in warning when he'd nearly rendered another boy unconscious during a combat match.

"There's something else," Catherine whispered, ignoring his question. "Before their positioning was lost, Thalia was able to record a final message. She . . . well . . . I suppose it's best if you take a look for yourselves."

Catherine lifted her hand and a swirling pool of darkness trickled out from her fingers.

From one blink to the next, the darkness began to shift and bend, creating eyes and a mouth and ears—until a fully formed face stared back at them, a projection made of smoke and magic hovering over the surface of the table. *A girl.* Recognition prickled at Masika's consciousness—she was certain she knew her from somewhere.

Through the projection, Masika could vaguely make out a dark and foreboding forest looming behind the girl, but the image was too blurry to pinpoint any details.

And then the girl began to speak.

"This . . . this is Thalia Greevson . . ." Her voice was strained with exertion, her breaths labored and heavy. "We . . . we were able to make it to the border of Widow's Forest—" *Widow's Forest.* That was the forest that the Resistance believed hid the Demien

Order's location. Not that it helped much in their hunt. Widow's Forest was massive—stretching far enough that it even bordered the edge of Blackwood's perimeter.

The girl's face warped momentarily, static disrupting the sound. A deathly hush had fallen upon the meeting room as everyone listened, enraptured. "—a group of them attacked us. They knew our coordinates. I don't know how, but . . . there's no fighting our way out of this. I've already lost half the crew. You have to avoid the arrows . . ." Again, the message glitched, a garbled mess of static and sound: "—if you find this, don't bother sending a search party . . . it's not . . . I don't think it's worth—"

Static cut through the message once again as Thalia tumbled out of view, shoved aside by an invisible force.

A struggle echoed in the distance.

A bloodcurdling scream.

And then . . . silence.

The image of Thalia melted, the swirling mass of darkness slowly evaporating.

A terrible, piercing emptiness enveloped the room. Everybody seemed equally stunned by what they had just heard, a sort of haunted look in their eyes.

Catherine clasped her hands firmly over the table and let out a sigh.

"We haven't heard from them since."

Russo drummed her fingers against the table.

"When are we sending a search party?"

Catherine's face hardened.

"We're not."

It was Brayden who spoke next. He slammed his hand against the table, rising from his seat with a jolt.

"Bullshit!" he cried, brows furrowed. Masika hadn't noticed

before, but he appeared to be even more distraught than the others. His skin had gone splotchy and pink, the whites of his eyes glassy with tears.

"Easy," whispered a girl next to Brayden. She attempted to place a comforting hand on his arm, but he brushed her off, turning his attention back toward Catherine.

"You truly expect us to do *nothing*?" he spat out. "To let them be taken—"

"Everything has changed," Catherine interjected. "You know just as well as I do that we cannot afford to send out a search party. Hell, we can't even waste any more time trying to look for the Demiens' location! We *have* to prepare for the expedition—" Masika leaned in closer, suddenly alert. *Expedition?* What was Catherine talking about? "—and that will be five bodies at the very least. Who will protect the base if we all leave? We'd be left exposed. Vulnerable."

A million questions ricocheted in Masika's mind—*what expedition is Catherine talking about? What changed? And what can possibly be more valuable than the lives of their fellow Resistance members?* Before anybody could offer further clarity, Dina's voice echoed around the room once more.

"So, what?" Dina leaned back against her chair. She crossed her arms and lifted her lips into a sardonic smirk. "We just condemn them to what might likely be an eternity of torture in the hopes that this expedition will work? An expedition that—might I add—is solely based off of *these two's* word." Dina gestured toward Birdie and Russo, both of whom rolled their eyes at the not-so-subtle dig.

"It's more complicated than that and you know it," whispered Birdie, shooting Dina a glare. "And it's not just some guess. We saw it with our own eyes. We brought Catherine a copy."

"Right. Leave it to the bloody strategist to argue semantics," Dina chuckled, rolling her eyes. "Plus, not to mention that a copy can be forged. How do we know you haven't simply made the whole thing—"

"Enough."

Catherine's voice sucked the air out of the room, quickly silencing Dina. For a moment, nobody said a word. And then Catherine was standing, pushing herself away from the table.

"Let's take the night to sleep on it." She cleared her throat. "We'll reconvene tomorrow morning and discuss the possibility of a search party."

This seemed to be enough to appease everyone . . . well, *mostly* everyone.

Brayden rose from his seat and stormed out of the room, severing Catherine with a poisonous glare before slamming the door closed behind him. The others trickled out shortly after, whispering among themselves as they funneled into the corridor. Masika knew her best chance at exiting the room undetected would be to wait for everybody to leave, but Catherine continued to linger. Even once the last few members drifted out of the room, plunging them into silence, Catherine remained rooted behind her chair, a faraway look in her eyes.

Masika took a cautious step toward the meeting room door, hoping and praying that her cloaking enchantment would hold despite the anxiety coursing through her limbs. She took another step forward, hand outstretched, fingers trembling as she reached for the doorknob—

"It's not polite to eavesdrop, little dove."

Shit. Shit, shit, shit.

Well, she supposed there was no point in keeping the façade

any longer. She dropped the cloaking enchantment, the haze of golden light vanishing with a flicker.

Catherine's eyes met hers, not a hint of surprise in her expression.

Masika let out an exasperated breath.

"What the hell are you trying to find out there? What is this expedition about?"

Catherine smirked.

"Do I need to put locks on your door? Have a guard follow your every move?"

"Right." Masika crossed her arms. "Deflecting. Shouldn't be surprised, should I? You're just as secretive as always."

Catherine's expression hardened as she took a step forward. When she spoke next, the teasing lilt in her voice had vanished, taking on that authoritative edge she'd put on during the meeting.

"You shouldn't have been in here."

"Why?" Masika shot back without hesitation. "What are you keeping from us?"

Catherine shrugged.

"Nothing."

"Oh, don't *nothing* me." Masika scoffed. "I heard every word." She stepped forward, unflinching beneath Catherine's narrowed gaze. "So . . . answer the question."

"We're . . ." Catherine looked up at the ceiling, biting the inside of her cheek as she searched for the right words. ". . . looking for something. Something that has the potential to shift the tides of this war. That could save the afterlife."

"What?"

Catherine cocked her head with a teasing grin.

"That's classified."

Masika blinked, cheeks burning with anger.

"You think this is *funny*?"

Catherine stepped closer, reaching a tentative hand out.

"Oh, come on—"

"You left me!" Masika bellowed. She hadn't meant for the words to come tumbling out, but she couldn't restrain herself. Not anymore. Not when the dormant pain had fully ruptured, bringing with it the unforgiving sting of old wounds.

Catherine's hand dropped to her side, her mouth opening and closing in surprise.

"Ah." She awkwardly shifted from one foot to the other. "So that's what this is really about."

"You could have talked to me about it," Masika whispered, ashamed of her own desperation. "Given me a chance to reason with you. Dammit, Catherine . . . you could have at least *tried* to take me with you."

Catherine's face fell as Masika's words echoed between them. She stepped closer, close enough that an unwanted wisp of longing coiled around Masika's stomach. She could imagine that in another life, in another version of their story, she'd reach out and brush her fingertips against Catherine and destroy the space between them.

But not in this one. In this version, Masika remained motionless, her expression cold and controlled.

"Come on, little dove." Catherine looked up at her with pleading eyes. "What will it take for you to forgive me?"

An idea sparked in Masika's mind. Something wildly out of character. It would be a risk, but given the circumstances . . . one she was willing to make.

"Why?" Masika inched closer. With that single step, the space between them was nearly nonexistent, *begging* to be closed.

Catherine must have sensed it, too. Her gaze darted between Masika's eyes and lips. "Did you miss me?"

When Catherine spoke next, her voice was low and hoarse, a sound that Masika wanted to drink in.

"More than you know."

"Is it difficult to see me again?" Masika reached her hand out, tentatively tucking a loose strand of hair behind Catherine's ear. The second Masika's fingertips brushed the delicate skin of Catherine's neck, Catherine's eyes fluttered, a deep sigh escaping her lips. "To be so close to me, yet . . . unable to have me?"

Catherine shut her eyes.

"It's torture," she whispered.

Masika let the moment linger, the anticipation building as Catherine leaned in closer, nearly melting in her palms. It was exactly what Masika wanted . . . what she had envisioned on so many lonely nights.

But then Masika stepped backward, snatching the moment away with a smug grin.

"Perfect," she chirped, sauntering toward the door. "A few decades of agonizing torture, and we can call it even." She glanced over her shoulder, delighted to see Catherine staring back at her, jaw slack. "See you around, *Cat*."

On any other day, Masika might have felt a sting of remorse for her little performance. She might have even been tempted to follow through with it, unable to temper her desire to close the space between them. But she couldn't dwell on any of that now . . . not when her plan had worked.

Because as Masika exited the room, victory swirling in her chest, Catherine was too stunned to notice the empty key ring dangling at her hip . . . and the key tucked within Masika's palm.

4

WREN

Wren Loughty succumbed to the darkness and

fell

back

into

time . . .

The patter of rain. Tires against asphalt. Static as an old folk song drifted through the radio. The sweet scent of vanilla perfume and the remnants of liquor lingering on minty breath.

Wren opened her eyes.

She was sitting in the passenger seat of her mother's old Jeep Wrangler, looking down at her hands. The world around her tilted momentarily, blurring and refocusing as she came back to her senses.

"Mom is gonna kill us."

Wren blinked, dazed. She turned to her left and spotted her sister in the driver's seat, fingers drumming against the steering wheel. Maeve's strawberry-blond hair fell over her shoulders in tousled waves, her recently cut bangs fluffed right above her brows. Freckles dotted her sun-kissed skin, tan lines etched into the curve of her shoulders. They'd spent the entire summer lying by the lake. Wishing. Dreaming.

"What did you say?" Wren heard herself ask. She had the sense that she was missing something . . . that there was something she was meant to do. But no matter how hard she racked her brain, how carefully she tried to think back and recall what it was that was nagging at her subconscious, she couldn't remember.

"Mom," Maeve repeated over the sound of the rain hitting the roof. "She's gonna have our heads for this. There's no way she didn't wake up."

Right . . . the party. They had snuck out once their mom had fallen asleep, slipping out of Wren's bedroom window, giggling under their breaths as they tiptoed across the lawn and scurried into the car.

Thunder rumbled in the distance now, streaks of lightning zigzagging across the black storm clouds dotting the sky. Humid air trickled in from the window closest to Wren, the smell of damp earth and brine filling her lungs.

"Maybe we should pull over." Wren lowered the radio. A nagging worry was burrowing into her chest, an unmistakable sense of panic she couldn't shake off. She was forgetting something . . . what was she forgetting?

Maeve chuckled, brushing Wren's words off with a wave. "What for? I told you I didn't drink. I'm fine. I promise."

Something in Wren snapped like a blaring alarm.

There was something about the car. Something about the slate-black road stretching out before them . . . the headlights illuminating the yellow lines . . . the dense forest flanking them, whipping by in a blur.

"Maeve . . ." Wren's voice trailed off as her heart pounded against her chest, her pulse racing, thrumming in her throat. Something

about it was wrong. Unnatural. She lifted her trembling hand to her throat, her heartbeat thrashing against her fingertips. Her heartbeat . . . her heartbeat . . .

Her heart.

I shouldn't have a heart.

The thought sliced through her mind, sharp and sudden.

"Stop the car," Wren blurted out, panicked. Time seemed to bend at the edges, warping and fragmenting. Around her, the forest began to disintegrate. Faces emerged in the darkness, staring at her, glowing sapphire eyes watching her between the crooked branches. She tried to look through the swirling haze, to find who those eyes belonged to, but everything was moving too fast.

"What are you talking about?" Maeve asked, but her voice had grown distorted, twisted and wrong.

Wren wanted to scream.

They weren't meant to be here. This night. This car. This moment.

It was all wrong, it was all wrong, it was all—

Maeve gasped as something materialized on the road in front of them. Beady dark eyes stared back at them—a deer. Wren didn't even see it jump onto the road. One second it wasn't there, and the next . . .

The car swerved left.

Maeve screamed.

Wren reached for her sister.

Metal screeched, bent, twisted, ruptured.

Wren's neck snapped forward, head slamming against the dashboard, blood filling her mouth. Gravity shifted. The car tilted and flipped and—

. . .

. . .

Wren woke up screaming.

Her eyelids snapped open, throat raw and cheeks damp with tears. She was sitting on a wooden chair, her limbs frozen by some sort of enchantment. She couldn't move a muscle. Her mind trapped within the prison of her own body.

And standing before her, an indecipherable expression on her face, was Edith Hughes.

Despite the shadows running through her veins and the feathered darkness swirling behind the whites of her eyes, the High General of the Demien Order looked painfully human. Just a girl. Perhaps only a year or two older than Wren.

But she was the farthest thing from *human.*

As Wren came to her senses, the reality of her situation dawned on her. She remembered now. *She remembered it all.* Her abduction during the final trial of the Decennial. Edith's confession that Wren was somehow the key to destroying Blackwood. The look of glistening pride in Edith's eyes when she'd shown Wren the Demien Order encampment.

But now . . . she was here. Wherever *here* was.

After bringing Wren to the encampment, Edith had promptly relocated her into a large tent hidden deep within the Demien Order's winding caverns, torturing her with a magic Wren had never known possible.

Somehow, with the help of some dark and perverse magic, Edith was forcing Wren to relive her death.

Over and over and over.

The same night. The same car.

The same mistake.

For what purpose? Wren hadn't the faintest clue. Before she could even get a word out and beg Edith for more information, the High General would place her hands upon Wren's temples and the process would begin again. The only respite she got was a few hours at night when Edith would relocate her to another tent to sleep, though even then, Wren couldn't shake off the memory. It was as if it were burned into her retinas. Branded into her mind.

Now, Edith dropped her hands from Wren's face, the shadows retreating with her, slithering over her arms and sinking back into her skin. Wren let out a strangled cough. The acrid taste of blood flooded her mouth.

"Please." Wren's voice was hoarse, almost unrecognizable. *"Enough."*

But if the other girl felt any inkling of pity, she didn't show it. Edith's face remained expressionless, her dark eyes anchored on Wren's face as though she were attempting to look *inside* her.

"How do you feel?"

"How do I—" Wren couldn't help but let out a shock of laughter. "How do I *feel*?"

Edith's lip twitched.

"Answer the question."

"I feel like ripping you apart limb from limb," Wren snapped. She attempted to move her hands, to move *anything*, but her body remained frozen. She was nothing but a puppet. A plaything for Edith's whims.

"Pity," Edith huffed. "I suppose we'll just have to keep going."

Terror laced through Wren, sudden and violent.

"No," she choked out. "Please. Just—just *stop*. Haven't you had enough?"

"It's not up to me," Edith replied, voice cold.

"What does that mean?" Wren asked, hating the raw desperation in her voice. "I'm begging you. Just tell me what it is you want."

Edith tilted her head, her eyes raking up and down Wren's face.

"Funny. I never thought the catalyst of destruction would be one to *beg*."

Wren groaned, fighting against the paralysis that had taken hold of her body.

"Has it perhaps occurred to you that you're wrong, then? That I'm *not* the catalyst of destruction? That I'm not the one you've been looking for?"

Edith stepped closer and the whites of her eyes bled to black. "Oh, but you are, Wren Loughty. You will sever the link. Cleanse the threads of corruption. Because the Soulless One demands it." When she spoke next, her voice was not her own. It was dark, distorted . . . like rusted nails scraping against Wren's skin. *"Because it is written."*

Wren wanted to scream. The voice that slipped out of Edith's mouth felt like poison dripping into her ears, a shooting pain blossoming at the base of her spine. She was tired of hearing about the damn prophecy. Of being told there was nothing she could do to stop what had been written. *Screw* the prophecy. Wren was nobody's pawn. Her body might be under Edith's curse, but her mind and her soul were entirely her own. But before Wren could even open her mouth to retort, a jumble of noise echoed from beyond the tent, stealing their attention.

Edith blinked, the whites of her eyes returning. She whipped her head around, listening intently. It was a muffled commotion; the voices in the distance rose, a chorus of shouts and mumbled words of confusion.

"Come with me," Edith commanded, her voice back to its normal rasp. "And don't try anything—not that it would work, anyway."

With a jolt, Wren rose from the chair, her limbs moving with rigid precision as she followed Edith out of the tent. She winced, frustration welling in her chest. Edith was right. Even if Wren wanted to attempt an escape, her efforts would be futile.

Wren glared down at the silver band fused around her wrist.

It had appeared the first morning, right when Wren had awoken after her initial round of torture. *A security cuff*, according to Edith. Forged by the metalworkers in the encampment, the metal cuff was imbued with magic that prevented Wren from crossing the perimeter of the Demien Order encampment.

As Wren walked out of the tent and exited the dark tunnel that led to the heart of the cavern, she stumbled upon a chaotic scene. A crowd had formed, a congregation of Demiens staring at something emerging from the other side of the cavern. Wren craned her neck, desperate to get a better look, but her vision was blocked by the dozens upon dozens of Demiens crammed into the space around her.

But then the crowd shifted . . . and a figure emerged.

Tall, broad shoulders cloaked in shadows. Dark, disheveled curls. Eyes forged from steel and ice.

The realization hit her like a shotgun straight to the heart.

It's him.

August stepped forward, parting the crowd with nothing but his presence, his steps slow and methodical. And despite what had happened to her, despite the torture and pain and confusion, Wren couldn't help but break out into a smile.

Ever since she'd been taken to the Demien Order, Wren had tried desperately to push August out of her mind. To pretend he had never even existed. But still . . . the memory of him had haunted her.

The past few weeks had been agonizing. Every time she was alone, every time she closed her eyes . . . there she was—back in the Ether. The image of August crawling to her, writhing in pain, *screaming,* was seared into her memory. She could still hear the truth he had struggled to tell her through bouts of pain: how he had been assigned to get close to her, how their entire relationship, from the very beginning, had been carefully orchestrated by the Demien Order.

And now he was here.

But he wasn't alone.

Shadows.

As August stalked forward, a halo of shadows trailed after him, clinging to him like hungry parasites. They traveled up and down his limbs, coating the very ground he walked on. His white shirt was partially unbuttoned, torn and shredded, that same ravenous darkness running beneath his skin, a steady stream of shadows slinking up and down his veins.

No.

Wren's smile fell.

Whatever brief joy she had felt at seeing him again was immediately squashed by the sight of him shrouded in shadows. Because if August could access shadow magic, that could only mean one thing.

Wren sucked in a breath.

He's given up his humanity.

"Augustine," Edith called out to her brother, her voice eerily steady given the circumstances. "I had assumed you'd succumbed to your cowardice after our last encounter, but showing up *here*? With no protection? No army?" She motioned to one of the shadows curled around August's arm, a tight-lipped smile on her face. "And with some new friends, I see."

"What can I say?" August lifted his hand, a shadow swirling against his palm. "I like to make an entrance."

"That you do." Edith stepped forward, angling herself in front of Wren. It wasn't so much a stance of protection as that of a greedy child unwilling to share her toys. "Now . . . perhaps you don't mind explaining what the *hell* you're doing here?"

"Isn't it obvious, sister?" August stretched out his hand and a shadow sprang from his fingertips without warning, instantly coiling itself around Edith's crown. He snapped his fingers and the shadow came flying back like a boomerang, tossing the crown straight into his hand. He caught it with ease, twirling the crown between his fingers as his lips curled into a smirk.

His eyes trailed to Wren, a wickedness in his stare.

A darkness.

"I've come to take back what is rightfully mine."

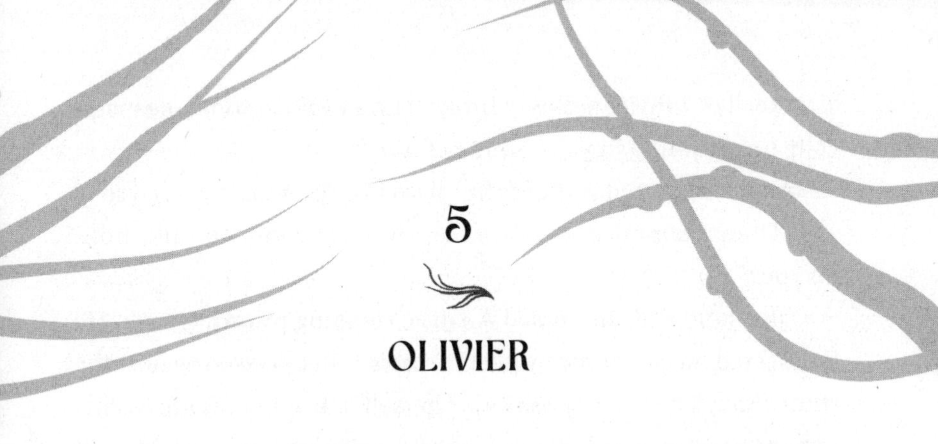

5

OLIVIER

Olivier Dupont was beginning to think he hated magic. What good was it to him, anyway? All it ever seemed to do was get him into trouble. If it wasn't an angry horde of shadow monsters hell-bent on eating him alive or a bloodthirsty replica of himself nearly destroying the love of his life, it was something equally horrific and traumatizing. Sure, magic had its perks—*mainly when it came to enchanted liquors and magically induced highs*—but in the grand scheme of things, magic was a monstrous pain in his ass.

Of course, his judgment on the matter was perhaps a bit clouded.

"I need you to stop fidgeting," said Analisa, a rather impatient groan in her voice. Ever since the Resistance had been made aware of Olivier's . . . *condition* . . . he'd been seen by numerous healers nearly every day, a never-ending stream of forced smiles and apologetic murmurs. Analisa, however, had been a constant presence throughout each mortifying healing session. Of all the healers in the Resistance, she seemed to be the one most obsessed with unraveling the chaos happening inside Olivier's mind.

"Apologies," Olivier muttered in a tone that was *far* from apologetic. "It tickles."

"It does not."

"Really?" Olivier arched a brow. "Have you had someone magically poke around in your mind before?"

Analisa frowned, crossing her arms in irritation. "No. I haven't."

"Then I suppose you don't really have room to talk, now, do you?"

"Just hold still," mumbled Analisa, stepping toward Olivier. He was seated on one of the inspection tables, feet pressed against the stone floor. The healer positioned herself in front of his knees, lifting her hands toward Olivier's head. Christ, he hated this part. It made him feel nauseatingly vulnerable—as though he were carving himself open and offering his organs for dissection.

But it was also his only hope . . . and *that*, perhaps, hurt more than anything.

Despite having found a loophole, a way out of the Decennial, that had saved Emilio, Olivier hadn't managed to find a way to save himself. *The Forgetting.* It was still corroding his brain, stripping him of memories with each passing day, preparing him for the inevitable conclusion to his duty as a reaper of lost souls. The healers within the Resistance had spent nearly every waking hour attempting to find a solution. They'd never encountered anybody with Olivier's condition. All the members of the Resistance had left Blackwood before the Forgetting could take over.

The healers had discovered that the source of the Forgetting wasn't just Silas's betrayal, but the school itself. If you managed to escape Blackwood before the Forgetting's corrosive effects took over, you'd be spared. Safe. But if the process had already begun, even leaving the school's perimeter wasn't enough to stop it.

They were trying to help—Olivier knew that. But it was hard to feel grateful when he spent most of his time locked up in the Healing Bay, getting poked and prodded like some science experiment.

Nothing seemed to stop the memories from fading. In fact,

with each passing day, he *swore* his mind was quite literally unraveling. He'd been having strange dreams. Hearing things in the night.

Honestly, losing his mind was proving to be a *major* inconvenience.

"Go easy on me," Olivier whispered through a half-hearted chuckle.

"I'll try."

Analisa shut her eyes and began her work.

Olivier felt it instantly. His mind became sluggish and cold, as though the world around him were moving in slow motion, time bending and warping at the edges. Shimmering silver threads slithered out of his head, connecting with the healer's fingertips, which she began to twist and move around into varying patterns.

Each thread was a different memory. Olivier wasn't entirely certain how he knew, but it was a subconscious understanding. He could *feel* the memories nestled inside him—*his father teaching him how to ride horseback, his mother reading him a children's book by candlelight, the feeling of tall grass slipping between his fingers as he walked around his family's farm.* But there was also an unmistakable rot leaking into the memories, a dark *nothingness* slowly engulfing them.

"It's getting worse, isn't it?" Olivier choked out.

Analisa said nothing, continuing her work in silence. Beads of sweat gathered at her forehead, veins rising at her temples. Healing magic was new to Olivier, but he was constantly amazed at the sheer strength radiating from the healers he had encountered. There was something profoundly powerful in having the ability to mend a soul, rather than destroy it. And despite Olivier's disdain for the whole routine of these healing sessions, he couldn't help but secretly admire Analisa's work.

Learning the art of healing magic wasn't as simple as reading an instruction manual. It took *centuries* to master. Which meant the sanctioned healers of the Resistance also happened to be some of its founding members. They had been a part of the Resistance before it even had a purpose. When it had been nothing but a few lost souls floating aimlessly in purgatory, refusing to pick a side in the afterlife's looming war.

Analisa dropped her hands. The silver threads connecting her to Olivier slowly dissolved.

"There hasn't been a lot of progress," she admitted with a sigh. "I've delayed it slightly . . . slowed the corrosion temporarily . . . but no matter what I do, I can't seem to restore the memories. They just—" She let out a breath, frustration lacing her words. "They just keep fading."

"So," Olivier said, resting his hands upon the inspection table and leaning back. "In layman's terms . . . I'm screwed?"

Analisa frowned. "I wouldn't put it that way."

"Well, I'd hope not. That would be *terrible* bedside manner."

Analisa crossed her arms, unamused. "Olivier. I think it's time we talk about the possibility that—" But her words were cut off as the door swung open, revealing two familiar faces. Emilio and Masika were standing side by side, waiting in the doorway. There was a sort of frantic look in Masika's eyes, an infectious eagerness that made Olivier want to leap from the table.

Emilio, on the other hand, looked as though he'd rather be anywhere else.

Despite Emilio's clear annoyance over whatever Masika had dragged him in here for, Olivier felt a rush of relief upon seeing him. They'd barely spent any time alone together since arriving at the Resistance's manor, sharing fleeting conversations during brief moments of respite. It wasn't their fault. Emilio had been swept up by the rigorous training routine that every Resistance member was forced to participate in, while Olivier had been unwillingly crowned the Healing Bay's most fascinating medical anomaly.

Which meant these moments, brief as they might have been, meant everything to Olivier.

"Can I help you?" Analisa asked, brow quirked.

"We . . . uh—" Masika cleared her throat. "We need to take Olivier to a mandatory combat session."

Analisa crossed her arms. "His training isn't for another hour."

Olivier squinted at Masika, a silent communication passing between the two of them.

Play along.

Olivier didn't hesitate. He jumped to his feet and placed a comforting hand on Analisa's shoulder. "She's right," he chimed in. "I forgot to tell you. It got moved up." When Analisa opened her mouth to say something, Olivier gently patted her shoulder, interjecting before she could get a word out, "I promise I'll be on time tomorrow. And then you can tear open my mind to your heart's content, okay?"

Analisa frowned.

"Do not be late."

Olivier lifted his hand into a mocking salute.

"Yes, Sergeant."

He walked past Analisa, offering one final wink before sauntering out of the room, Emilio and Masika on his heels. The trio scurried down the hallway, putting distance between them and the Healing Bay. As they walked, Olivier spared Emilio a fleeting look, which instantly caused the other boy to blush.

Olivier bit back a smile.

"Hello, my love."

The tips of Emilio's ears reddened.

"Hi, Olivier."

Masika rolled her eyes, grabbing the two boys by their wrists and tugging them in closer.

"Look, you two will have plenty of time to stare into each other's eyes and marvel at each other's beauty, but right now, we have something we need to do."

Olivier sighed. "I'm listening."

Masika glanced cautiously over her shoulder, as though waiting to hear if anybody was approaching. After a few seconds, she reached into her waistcoat, revealing a large iron key dangling between her fingers. "Want to join me in doing something unequivocally dangerous and stupid?"

"Masika, dear . . ." Olivier smirked, placing his arm over Emilio's shoulder. "I'm offended you'd even ask."

6

EMILIO

As far as terrible ideas went, this one was *particularly* terrible. Emilio Córdova was already mentally rehearsing his apology as he reluctantly followed Masika and Olivier out of the Healing Bay and into the seemingly never-ending corridors of the Resistance's manor. *Just act natural,* he told himself, nervously tugging at the hem of his shirt. *The plan is simple. We're just going to waltz right into the most guarded area of the manor. What's the worst that can happen?*

"Emilio," Masika whispered through gritted teeth. "Stop breathing like that."

"Like what?" Emilio whispered back, awkwardly nodding at a passing scholar who regarded him with suspicious eyes.

"Like you're about to have a panic attack," muttered Olivier through a nervous chuckle.

Emilio whimpered. "I *am* about to have a panic attack."

Members of the Resistance swarmed the corridors. The Healing Bay sat at the heart of the Resistance's base, the connecting hub for all the various wings that made up the large and expansive manor. Emilio hadn't explored the entire base. It wasn't just that he'd spent most of his time forced to participate in the rigorous training routine imposed on all Resistance members, but it was nearly *impossible* to explore the entire base with its magically expanding corridors. The place was *massive.* Emilio hadn't the faintest idea how many floors there actually were. He'd attempted counting once and had accidentally ended up stumbling into a supply closet and locking himself inside.

He hadn't tried again.

"How did you manage to get the key to Catherine's office, again?" Olivier asked in a hushed whisper. A pair of combat trainers stalked by, shooting the trio a puzzled look. Olivier simply bowed his head, tipping an invisible hat. "Good evening, comrades! Lovely day for a stroll, isn't it?"

The combat trainers rolled their eyes and kept walking.

Masika cleared her throat. "How I got the key isn't important."

Not exactly a surprising response. Masika had been awfully secretive about Catherine since they joined the Resistance, never once broaching the subject of their tangled past. Though it didn't take a genius to deduce that whatever had happened between the two of them had clearly left a scar far deeper than the one Masika now wore on her face.

Emilio didn't blame her. He understood the feeling well. He'd spent months at Blackwood yearning for a crumb of Olivier's attention. Longing for the day the other boy might turn around and confess he felt the same. And though they'd expressed their feelings to one another near the end of the Decennial, Emilio still couldn't help but feel . . . wounded.

Olivier's worsening condition was an ever-present storm cloud dampening their blossoming romance. How could Emilio even begin to think about kissing Olivier when he might lose him? Olivier had sworn up and down that the healers were making progress, but Emilio wasn't quite sure he believed him. It was something about the way Olivier looked at him. A sadness in his eyes.

And Emilio couldn't quite decipher whether kissing him would make that sadness disappear, or simply tear their hearts in two.

Because the truth was simple: Emilio was embarrassingly, pathetically, *desperately* in love with Olivier.

Which was an absolute problem.

"All right, wait." Masika came to an abrupt halt, reaching her arm out to stop them in their tracks. Emilio fumbled, flushing as he pushed the thoughts of kissing Olivier out of his mind for the time being.

"What is it?" Olivier whispered, glancing around.

Masika pointed farther down the corridor. "The entrance to the Southern Wing is coming up."

"What exactly is our strategy here?" Emilio craned his neck to get a better look. As anticipated, two guards were patrolling in front of the arched double doors that led to the Southern Wing, each of them carrying corporeally infused weaponry. "Beguile them with our charm?"

"You mean *my* charm," Olivier corrected.

Emilio scoffed. "You don't think I'm charming enough?"

"Oh, you have *plenty* of charm, my love, but I just happen to be an expert on the subject."

"Hey," Masika snapped. "There will be no *charming* of any kind, all right?"

"Then what is your grand plan?" Olivier asked. When Masika hesitated, Olivier's face fell. "You *do* have a plan, right?"

"Well . . ." Masika gnawed on the inside of her cheek, clearing her throat. "Yes. Kind of."

Olivier pinched the bridge of his nose. "We're doomed."

Emilio couldn't lie—he was starting to panic as well.

"Just give me a second." Masika inhaled a deep breath, shaking her arms out. "I've been doing some research. Practicing. And there's something that might work."

"Have you done it successfully before?" Olivier asked.

"Do you want the real answer?"

Olivier sighed. "No. Probably not."

"Then yes." Masika beamed.

And with that, she closed her eyes and called upon her magic. Streams of amethyst light whirled out of her palms, trickling down to the floor in thin wisps. *Illusionary magic,* Emilio noted as the familiar sweet, syrupy smell flooded his senses. Something was forming inside the light, a hazy mass of limbs and fur. It was difficult to discern what it was at first, as though Olivier were staring at it through a warped mirror. But after a few more seconds, the features began to solidify, the purple mist clearing.

"Is that"—Emilio blinked in astonishment—"a puppy?"

It certainly looked like one. The creature had the shape of a small dog, its fur a mismatch of different shades—browns and blacks intermingling with white tufts. But something about it seemed a bit . . . off. Its ears were pointy, almost batlike, and its eyes were a startling shade of red.

"Not *technically,*" Masika said, staring down at her work in satisfaction. "It's a type of illusion. I've essentially infused it with something else . . . hidden it within." She looked between the two of them with a sigh. "Think of it like a nesting doll. The outer layer is an illusion, but the inner layer is what's really important." She rubbed one of the creature's pointy ears and frowned. "Though . . . I'm not so sure what happened to its ears and eyes. I think I might have slightly messed up the spell."

"What *exactly* is the inner layer?" asked Olivier warily, flinching as the puppy tried to nip at his ankles.

"An immobilizing powder. When inhaled, it freezes both your

mind and body. You're essentially an unconscious statue for about . . . oh, I don't know . . . thirty minutes?" Masika must have noticed their twin looks of confusion, shrugging as she added, "I stole the powder from the strategist's archives."

"How does it release the immobilizing powder?" Emilio asked, bending down to pet the strange creature, which was currently attempting to chase its own tail.

"It's on a timer."

Olivier blinked, horrified. "Oh my God. You've created a bomb. A slobbery little bomb."

"And on that note . . ." Masika picked the puppy up, bringing it to eye level. "It's time to see if you work."

The second she set it back down on the floor, the little creature sauntered toward the entrance to the Southern Wing with surprising confidence. As expected, it didn't take long for the two guards to notice the puppy prowling down the hall. The pair glanced up in bewilderment, heads tilting in sync.

"What the hell—" The guard to the right unsheathed her saber, sparks of corporeal magic flashing in warning. But before she could even make a move, the puppy let out a high-pitched bark. It was in that exact moment that a sparkling pall drifted out of its mouth, the dark cloud instantly shooting toward the two guards.

The second they inhaled the pall, both guards became expressionless and rigid, their eyes glazing over.

Emilio let out a shuddering breath. "Did it . . . did it work?"

Masika straightened her shoulders. "Only one way to find out."

She stepped forward and charged down the corridor. The puppy, which was currently nibbling at its own paw, turned to look at her with a crooked grin. It yelped in delight when she approached it.

"Good dog." Masika gently scooped the creature into her arms. She glanced over her shoulder and called out to them. "All right, boys! You can come out!"

Emilio and Olivier joined Masika at the entrance to the Southern Wing, awkwardly sidestepping the frozen guards. The immobilizing powder had done its job. From a distance, the guards simply appeared composed and attentive. But up close, there was a *nothingness* behind their eyes . . . a void.

"Ready?" Masika asked.

He supposed they had no other choice. Emilio looked over at Olivier, who managed a feeble nod.

"Ready."

As soon as Masika opened the door, the trio cocked their heads in unison. It was clear they had all been expecting the same thing. Every other wing in the base consisted of expansive corridors—rooms upon rooms that were scattered upon multiple floors. But on the other side of the door to the Southern Wing, there wasn't a corridor. There wasn't even a hallway.

It was just a single room.

An office.

They stepped inside, the double doors shutting behind them.

A shimmering candelabra illuminated the room, the warm flicker of candlelight casting hazy shadows across the walls. The mutant puppy barked in Masika's arms, squirming to break free. She placed him gently on the floor, allowing the creature to roam beside them.

As they ventured farther into the room, taking in the dimly lit space, Emilio noted that it was rather desolate, containing nothing but a wooden desk with some journals stacked atop it. The walls were made of stone, sparsely decorated with a couple of sconces and a wide blueprint of the manor's various halls.

"I don't understand . . ." Olivier rubbed at his forehead. "I thought the key was for Catherine's office."

"It is," Masika whispered. "Or, at least, it should be."

"But . . ." Emilio dragged his finger along the wall. "Isn't *this* her office?"

"The key must be for something else, then . . ." Masika scurried deeper into the room, beelining toward the desk. "To open something hidden in here."

"You mean this mysterious, unknown thing that Birdie and Russo *may or may not have* found?" Olivier asked warily.

Masika pierced him with a glare and Olivier instantly raised a hand in surrender.

"Sorry," he mumbled.

Masika rolled her eyes and continued to riffle through the papers strewn across the desk, digging through the various drawers.

"This is the most heavily guarded area in the base for a reason," she muttered. "Why else would Catherine keep this key on her at all times?"

Emilio hadn't the faintest clue. He rested against the nearest wall, crossing his arms as he peered over at Masika. "See anything?"

She let out a frustrated groan, anxiously tucking a curl behind her ear. "No. Nothing. But it has to be here. I know it. It's just this *feeling*—" Masika was abruptly cut off when something shifted behind Emilio. The wall he was leaning against quite literally *moved*, a deep grumble echoing in the air as the stone slid behind him. Emilio yelped, nearly falling backward, though he quickly righted himself. When he swiveled on his heels, he realized the stone wall behind him had parted to reveal a hidden door.

"Uh . . ." Olivier chuckled nervously. "It appears our darling Emilio has found something."

Masika's eyes widened. "What did you do?"

Emilio raised his hands in surrender. "I just leaned!"

"This must be what the key is for . . ." Olivier whispered, cautiously peering over Emilio's shoulder.

Masika quickly scurried over, placing the key inside the lock. She jiggled the knob, fidgeting slightly with the key, teeth worrying at her bottom lip. Emilio held his breath, waiting . . .

Click.

The trio let out a breath of relief as the door swung open.

Inside, there was only a single piece of parchment floating in the air, dangling as though it were suspended by an invisible string. Masika wasted no time. She snatched it from the air, angling it toward one of the iron sconces. Emilio noticed words etched onto its aged surface . . . symbols and shapes.

The three of them leaned in closer, staring down in wonder.

"What is it?" Olivier asked, squinting.

Masika snapped her fingers and a sphere of light appeared, illuminating the air around them. With the help of Masika's magic, Emilio could now see that it wasn't just symbols and shapes drawn upon the piece of parchment . . .

"It's a map," said Masika, tracing her fingers over the mountains and valleys drawn upon its surface.

"Of what?" Olivier asked.

"Purgatory," Emilio whispered. Of course. He recognized it now. "I think these are the areas that the Resistance has successfully mapped out so far. I've seen some similar copies hung in archives in the Western Wing."

A clear outline of Blackwood loomed at the center of the map, surrounded by a dense forest. To the west was a craggy landscape dotted with mountains and canyons, with the Resistance's manor concealed at the farthest end. The manor had been crafted through an enchantment, created by the founding members of the Resistance. It was completely invisible on the outside, its location ever-changing. The eastern side of the map was mainly uncharted, though there was a general perimeter for where the Resistance believed the Demien Order's encampment was hidden. Similar to the Resistance's manor, the Demien Order's location was a mystery, their base hidden by layers upon layers of cloaking enchantments and defensive wards.

But there was something different about this copy. It wasn't just a map of purgatory . . . it was a map *to* something. An obvious path had been laid out, instructions detailing a straight route out of the base.

"It's leading us somewhere," whispered Masika, clearly coming to the same realization.

Olivier and Emilio watched intently as Masika placed her fingertip delicately against the map and traced the path written upon it—a straight line from the Resistance's base to what appeared to be a large tree deep within the surrounding forest.

Emilio cocked his head in confusion. Olivier matched his puzzled expression.

"A tree," Olivier muttered with a lilt of annoyance. "The map leads to a tree . . . surrounded by other trees."

"Hold on." Masika brought the map closer. "There's a signature. Some sort of writing . . ."

She was right. A small inscription and a set of initials were inked at the bottom.

Masika cleared her throat and read the words out loud. "Follow the path. The keys are the answer. This is not my end."

"It's signed *TH*," Emilio noted, his fingers brushing against the ink.

"TH?" Olivier muttered. "Who the hell is TH?"

The words had barely left his lips when Masika let out a gasp, nearly dropping the map to the floor. Olivier reached out, steadying her, placing a hand on her arm before the parchment could slip out of her grasp.

"Masika . . . what is it?" he asked. "What's wrong?"

"When Birdie and Russo first found me in the mountain during the third trial . . . they told me about Blackwood's history." Masika's eyes darted between the two boys as she spoke, her fingers trembling. "How Silas was a Corrupted Soul who learned to harness his power when he was thrown into the Shadow Lands—"

"We know this already, Masika," Olivier interjected softly. "Silas destroyed the original Headmaster of Blackwood and took over. It's why the Ether has been so off-balance. It senses his corruption. It knows he's not meant to be there."

"I know. But . . ." Masika inhaled a shaky breath, hands tracing the map. "When they told me . . . they didn't just call him the original Headmaster of Blackwood. They called him something else."

"What?" Emilio whispered.

Masika glanced up, amber eyes burning.

"The *True Headmaster*."

There was a tense beat of silence. The weight of her words fell upon them like a sudden gust of wind.

"What are you saying?" Olivier asked, a haunted strain in his voice.

"*This is not my end.* Don't you get it?" Masika let out a shuddering breath. "The True Headmaster is still out there . . . and the Resistance intends to find him."

It couldn't be true.

It *couldn't.*

But there was no denying what was written upon these pages. No erasing what they had just learned.

It was at that exact moment that the office door swung open with a flourish, revealing Catherine on the other side, a glowing spear clutched in her right hand. Her expression was lethal, her eyes narrowed on them like two finely sharpened blades.

"The three of you . . ." Catherine said, seething, her voice ringing with authority. "Come with me . . . *now.*"

7

IRENE

Mateo had attempted to stop her, calling after her, but Irene had ignored his desperate pleas as she stormed out of her room and burst into the corridor. She needed a moment to think. A moment to wrap her head around what she had just learned.

Wren Loughty is the prophesized destroyer of Blackwood? The mere thought made Irene want to bend over in a fit of laughter. That pious, self-righteous little princess could barely stomach cheating on an exam, let alone disrupting the entire balance of the afterlife. There was no possible way. No conceivable world in which—

"Irene."

At the sound of her name, Irene nearly tumbled to the floor as she abruptly came to a halt, spinning on her heels to find Samira standing behind her. What was with this girl? Couldn't she simply let Irene be?

"Samira." Irene cleared her throat. "Hi."

"Are you all right?" Samira slinked closer, hands tucked behind her back. "You seem a bit . . . flustered."

"I'm fine."

"Actually, I'm glad I ran into you." Samira dipped her voice lower, a mischievous grin lifting onto her berry lips. "I'm about to head to the bacchanal. Care to join me?"

Irene groaned internally. *Dammit.* She'd been hoping to go alone. Use the solitude to mentally prepare herself for what she might find at the party. But given the fact that the last thing she wanted to do was raise Samira's suspicions . . .

"You know what?" Irene sighed, feigning a tight-lipped smile. "Screw it."

Samira squealed, clapping in delight. She hooked her arm over the crook of Irene's elbow, tugging her close.

"You are *so* going to thank me later."

Irene didn't even have time to register the relocation spell. One moment they had been standing in the middle of one of the Ascended Quarters' swirling corridors, and the next they were outside, enveloped by the darkness of night.

Irene blinked, adjusting her vision, and tried to make sense of where the other girl had taken her. They appeared to be standing in front of the rusted metal gazebo that sat a few yards from Elysium Hall, the first few steps shrouded in ribbons of mist. A web of slithering vines and tree roots shrouded the ground, crawling their way around the metal structure.

"Here we are." Samira motioned toward the gazebo. "Go on."

With a sigh, Irene walked up the steps. Samira trailed right behind her, whistling softly beneath her breath. Once the two of them were standing on the gazebo's main platform, Samira snapped her fingers and a small crimson flame sprouted from her fingertips.

"This is always my favorite part."

Irene cocked her head in confusion. "What is—"

A low, hissing sound cut her off. The noise seemed to echo all around them, consuming every particle of air. And then something shifted beneath her, a figure moving within the shadows . . . and that was when Irene saw it.

A snake.

She yelped, staggering away from it in horror. The snake was a deep umber color, about five feet long and covered in intricate symbols. Its eyes glowed, a golden sheen breaking through the darkness.

Samira giggled. "Oh, relax. It's not real. It's just an enchantment."

The snake slithered between their feet, gold eyes flicking between them.

"The passsssword . . ."

"It spoke," Irene whispered, swallowing hard. "The magical snake spoke."

Samira rolled her eyes, bending down toward the snake.

"Heavenly heretical."

As soon as she spoke the password, the snake curled into itself, disappearing in a puff of golden sparks. Moments later, one of the stone slabs beneath them shifted, sinking into the ground, revealing what appeared to be the top of a steep, narrow staircase. Irene could only see the first couple of steps.

The rest were completely swallowed by darkness.

Irene placed the bottom heel of her boot upon the first step and ventured forward. Samira followed after her, extinguishing her flame with a snap of her fingers.

As they began to walk down the stairs, a muffled noise echoed in the distance, a rhythmic pounding reverberating in the air. After a few more seconds, Irene realized that it wasn't just noise . . . but *music*.

The deeper they descended, the louder the music became, a deep resounding bass thumping in her chest. Seconds dragged into minutes, and just as Irene was beginning to lose the last shred of patience she had left, her foot hit something solid.

Behind her, Samira snapped her fingers, illuminating the narrow space with a soft flame and revealing the arched door in front of them. She stepped ahead of Irene and glanced over her shoulder, pearlescent teeth gleaming in the darkness as she opened the door.

"Welcome to the world of the Ascended."

Irene stepped through the doorway . . . and entered a debaucherous hellscape.

The entire party was engulfed in a greenish hue, strobe lights flickering in time with the pounding music, the air redolent with the nauseating scent of illusionary magic. Sweat-slicked bodies congregating at the center of the room danced along to the music, swaying together, arms draped over shoulders and lips grazing hungrily from one person to the next. Dozens of enchanted trays floated around the room, a crooked mountain of glass flutes overflowing with various liquors and elixirs. Emerald-velvet couches lined a seating area to the left of Irene, in which she spotted a trio of Ascended dipping their fingers into a fine black powder before sprinkling it into each other's mouths, licking the remnants from each other's lips.

"Come on," Samira said, signaling Irene forward. "Keep up."

Irene reluctantly followed after Samira, pushing through the sea of drunken bodies filling the room. Irene's vision warped under the flickering strobe lights dangling from the rafters, her senses overwhelmed by the noxious fumes filling the air.

Eventually, they broke free of the crowd and stepped into a less congested area of the room. There were a few leather couches and chaise lounges, an array of bodies sprawled upon them, drinking under candlelight and whispering between fits of drunken giggles.

"Here. Take this." Samira handed Irene a glass flute with a shimmering amethyst liquid inside. Truthfully, Irene hadn't even noticed her grabbing it, too fixated on the chaotic scene in front of her. "It's just a light euphoric."

Irene sniffed the drink and—*oh.* An array of scents washed over her like springtime mist.

Honeysuckle. Lavender. Gardenia. Mint.

As Irene took a sip and the drink trickled down her throat, a weightlessness flooded through her limbs, an all-consuming bliss. She blinked sluggishly, taking in the room around her. What had once been a claustrophobic cesspool of inebriated idiots had now transformed into Irene's personal Eden. A shimmering light engulfed her vision, a dazzling prismatic ray of colors. Even the air tasted of lavender, of sweet syrup coating her tongue. *Are the walls sparkling?* Irene looked around, dazed and delighted, a dreamlike sensation in her movements.

"Well . . ." Samira's face came into view and—*wow.* Had she always been this lovely? Her features seemed almost regal, her skin petal soft. ". . . I suppose it was a *tiny* bit stronger than a light euphoric. I think Petra might have spiked the glass with some Angel's Breath."

"*Angel's Breath . . .*" Irene echoed, adoring the way the words tasted in her mouth. She was touching something unbelievably soft. Featherlight. It wasn't until Samira giggled in front of her that Irene realized she had reached out and begun to stroke Samira's face.

"You're so *soft.*"

Samira laughed and a prism of color trickled out of her lips. "Oh dear. You're going to have a fun night."

And she most certainly did.

Time fragmented as Irene lost all sense of reality. She was dancing, swaying in time with the music, hands greedily roaming the bodies around her. How long had she been like this? *Minutes?*

Hours? Days? It was impossible to tell. She no longer cared. Not when everything felt this wonderfully, perfectly *good*. Not when all the pain, all the suffocating grief, had seemingly vanished with nothing but a single drink. She only existed in that moment, in that song, in that feeling of euphoria.

But then something hurled her back to reality. A flicker in her peripheral vision. A *face*.

Irene froze. The bodies around her continued to dance, moving against her, but Irene couldn't tear her gaze away from what—no . . . *who* she saw at the far end of the room. She kept her eyes glued on the face staring back at her as she pushed through the crowd, desperately shoving anybody who stood in her way. As the strobe lights flickered, the face moved farther away, as though every flicker were carving a rift between them, an invisible set of strings pulling them apart.

"Wait!" Irene shouted, her voice hoarse, lost within the music. "Please . . . *Masika*—"

Her words were cut short as someone rammed straight into her, sending her toppling to the floor. Irene fell onto her hands and knees, a dizzying wave clouding her senses. When she got back onto her feet, legs shaking, she frantically searched the sea of dancing bodies, but Masika was gone.

Of course she's gone.

Irene felt sick. Everything was too loud, too bright, too *wrong*. She staggered through the crowd, shoving her way forward, ignoring the hands attempting to pull her back. But before she could make it to the entrance, someone stepped into her path.

Irene blinked, dazed, trying to make sense of what she was looking at.

In front of her stood a figure shrouded in a gauzy white fabric. Was it another hallucination? The others around her didn't seem to notice the figure, their revelry undisturbed by the ominous presence. The euphoric still had its hold on her, its dizzying effects coursing through her body, but there was something *solid* about the figure in front of her.

Something real.

This isn't a hallucination.

Just as the thought shot through Irene's mind, the figure reached out, gripping her by the wrist before she could pull away.

And then, from one blink to the next, Irene was no longer at the Ascended party.

Her eyes shot open and she found herself standing at the center of a dimly lit room. Twelve figures shrouded in that same gauzy white fabric surrounded her, heads bowed and faces obscured, all standing in a perfect circle. A reverent silence engulfed the space, the feeling of it washing over Irene's skin like warm water. Beneath her feet, right at the center of the circle, was a symbol carved into the wooden floors: the Blackwood emblem, the carcass of an oak tree surrounded by bone fragments.

As Irene's heeled boots settled on top of the grooves, it was as though a simmering current coursed through the soles of her feet and up her legs, traveling through her limbs until she found she could not move, even if she'd wanted to.

And then one of the figures spoke.

"Irene Manette Bamford." She couldn't tell who had said her name, the voice reverberating around the circle, as if somehow all twelve figures had spoken at once. Irene's head pounded. Her vision blurred and refocused. "The Council has seen promise in you. The possibility of greatness. Therefore, you have been selected as a potential initiate. If you pass the test period . . . you will be initiated into the Council—an honor few will ever get." A deep hum echoed around the room, and Irene swore it was somehow coming from inside her.

"The test period ends in three days' time. Do you accept?"

She had done it. She had *actually* been chosen. A surge of relief rushed through Irene's chest, though it was quickly snipped by the reality of the challenge. *Three days.* Irene had no idea how she was meant to prove her worth in three days, but she'd have to worry about that later.

She gave a single nod in response. "I accept."

Her voice resounded unfamiliarly in her ears. As the two words left her lips, one of the figures stepped forward, revealing a small knife resting atop their gloved hand. Irene stared at it, blinking.

"What is that for?" she asked, eyes darting around the room.

"With an offering of blood, you seal the covenant. Let it fall upon the emblem."

Irene stepped forward, grabbing the knife from the figure's hand, and retreated to the circle. She lowered the blade onto her palm, slicing clean through, and squeezed her fist closed. The blood gathered within her palm, a steady stream dripping onto the emblem carved beneath her.

Instantly, the floor began to tremble. The blood on the ground simmered and moved, drifting like a current, until the entire emblem was drenched in it, a crimson river beneath her feet.

And then, as if lit by an invisible match, the emblem caught fire.

And so did Irene.

The fire shot up toward her, engulfing her, the towering flames covering every inch of her skin.

But even though the blood burned—*Irene did not.*

Her skin remained unharmed. Her body untarnished by the raging fire around her.

Something rose up within her . . . a hunger. It was a fleeting moment of power, the slightest taste, but Irene was *starved,* and the feeling washed over her in an irresistible high. She would do anything to prolong the moment—to seize the power and claim it as her own.

"Congratulations," whispered a voice somewhere beyond the flames. "And we wish you luck."

With those words spoken, the flames dissipated, snuffed out as if swept away by a sharp breeze. And when Irene's vision cleared—the figures had vanished, disappearing from one blink to the next.

Irene looked around the room, chest rising and falling as she let in shallow breaths.

The laughter started off as a wavering chuckle. But it wasn't long before Irene was practically doubled over, overcome with a hysterical fit. It was a torrential downpour—a sweet release.

Because Irene Manette Bamford had done it . . . she had been chosen.

And now she'd burn them from the inside out.

PART II

A PROMISE OF DARKNESS

8

EMILIO

Emilio had a notorious habit of getting into trouble—though, in his defense, it was almost never his fault.

Shortly after finding Emilio, Masika and Olivier sneaking around her office, Catherine had dragged the three of them to the Battle Room, flanked by two guards armed with corporeally infused swords. Nobody uttered a single word, nothing to keep them company but the echo of their footsteps resounding in the narrow corridor as they made their way out of the Southern Wing. And now here they sat, awkwardly shifting in their seats, while Catherine simply looked at them and waited for someone to speak. She sat on the other side of the oval table, hands clasped in front of her. The cerulean sheen of the chandelier washed her features in an icy breath; her narrowed hazel eyes were cold and unfeeling, her petal-shaped lips pulled into a withering frown.

But it wasn't any of them who broke the tension.

The little creature curled on Emilio's lap let out a sudden bark, shattering the silence.

Catherine's eyes snapped in its direction. "What is that thing?"

Emilio should probably have left the puppy behind, but he couldn't bring himself to let Masika destroy him—even if he really was just a product of magic.

He wrapped his arms protectively around the puppy's neck, tucking him in closer. "Benji."

Catherine blinked. "Pardon?"

Olivier groaned. "I believe he means that infernal creature's name is Benji." Olivier's gaze skated to Emilio before he added a softly whispered, "When on earth did you name it?"

Emilio shrugged. "On the walk over."

Catherine rubbed her face in exasperation. "You do realize the three of you broke the *one* rule you were meant to follow, right?"

"It's really not our fault," Olivier remarked with feigned innocence. "We have a terrible aversion to rules."

Masika rolled her eyes. "And either way, we wouldn't have had to break in if *you* had simply been honest with me." She pressed her hands upon the table, leaning forward. "The True Headmaster is still out there. *That's* what Birdie and Russo discovered, isn't it?"

To Catherine's credit, she didn't deny it. "Yes."

Even though they'd already found the truth hidden in the Southern Wing, hearing it spoken out loud was something else entirely. A cold shudder ran through Emilio, an electric current igniting the air. Even Masika and Olivier seemed to sink deeper into their chairs, as though the weight of the truth had fallen upon them in a sudden blow.

"All right, then." Olivier cleared his throat, drumming his fingers against his thighs. "If this *True Headmaster* is still out there . . . well, where the hell have they been?" He tossed his hands in frustration. "Why don't they simply come out of hiding and help us?"

Catherine sucked her teeth. "It's not that simple."

Emilio whimpered. "Of course it isn't . . ."

"When Silas took over Blackwood, he *thought* he'd destroyed the True Headmaster," Catherine explained, eyes drifting over the trio. "But the True Headmaster had prepared for this . . . for the day someone might try to usurp his power. He harbored a fraction of his soul and hid it deep within the farthest reaches of purgatory, leaving behind a clue to its location for his followers. A way to find that piece of his soul and resurrect him."

"The map," Emilio whispered.

Catherine nodded. "It leads to the first clue. The first step in finding what remains of his soul."

"But I don't understand," Masika interjected, leaning her elbows against the table. "Why did it take so long for someone to find the map?"

"Because . . ." Catherine let out a sigh. "Silas found it first."

A weighted silence settled over the room.

Catherine pushed herself away from the table, standing.

"He hid it within the halls of Blackwood. Years went by . . . centuries. All the while, the followers of the True Headmaster who had been banished to the outskirts of purgatory corrupted under the Soulless One's shadows. It wasn't until the Resistance began to form and we gained members who had access to Blackwood's halls that we were able to even learn of this map in the first place."

"Birdie and Russo," Masika commented under her breath.

Catherine nodded, solemn.

"We'd been secretly working with the two of them for a while. They would feed us information that they'd learn about both the Demien Order and Blackwood and report back. But then . . . they discovered something in the restricted section of the Library."

Emilio snapped his gaze toward Olivier, who stared at him with wide eyes. He must have been thinking the same thing. They had seen Birdie and Russo wandering about the Library before the Decennial Ball . . . the two of them sneaking around the restricted Housemasters' section.

"Does Silas know the map is gone?" asked Masika.

Catherine nodded. "That's precisely why Birdie and Russo had to leave Blackwood in a rush. They knew once they stole the map, it wouldn't take long for Silas to put the pieces together." Catherine gestured to Olivier and Emilio. "And that's when they took you two here."

"But is there any other proof that the True Headmaster's soul is really out there?" asked Emilio. "Other than this map, I mean."

Catherine shook her head. "No."

Olivier placed his elbows upon the table, burrowing his hands in his hair. "Okay. So what you're saying is that we have a way to save the afterlife, but it involves resurrecting an ancient powerful entity using a sliver of his soul that could very well not even exist?"

Catherine sighed. "Pretty much."

Olivier slid his hands over his face. "Delightful."

"When will you send the expedition crew out?" Masika asked, straightening in her chair.

"Tomorrow morning," Catherine replied.

"Seems a bit soon," muttered Emilio. "Didn't you just lose an entire group? Masika told us nearly a dozen members went missing on a tracking mission."

"There's no time to mourn," Catherine shot back defensively. "Not anymore. The entire balance of the afterlife is in our hands. And we've received word that the Demien Order has begun to plan their attack on Blackwood. That it could happen any day now."

Olivier snorted, dismissively waving his hand. "Oh, please. I've been hearing about the Order's big plan of attack for centuries—"

Centuries? Masika mouthed to Emilio, who flushed a deep crimson and shrugged.

"—and nothing ever happens," Olivier continued. "They follow their make-believe God and wait for a prophecy that will never come to fruition. What makes you so certain that anything has changed?"

"Because of Augustine Hughes."

The entire room seemed to go taut as soon as the words left Catherine's lips.

Emilio still couldn't quite wrap his head around the fact that August was a part of the Demien Order. When Masika had revealed to them what she had learned—that August had been an undercover member of the Demien Order from the very start—a part of him had been unwilling to accept the betrayal.

The August that Emilio had known had been many things—stoic, callous, intimidatingly beautiful. Yet, despite all that, it had never occurred to Emilio that August might have been harboring something darker.

And, truthfully, it wasn't even August being a Demien that stung.

It was the fact that he had lied to them.

That he had been planning their destruction all along.

When Olivier spoke next, his words came out slow and rough. "What does August have to do with this?"

Emilio shivered at the ire in Olivier's voice. They hadn't talked about it much, but Emilio could tell that August's betrayal had badly wounded the other boy. That Olivier had, in his own strange way, grown to trust August.

"He has *everything* to do with this," Catherine shot back. "His sister, Edith, is the High General of the Order. He allowed her to infiltrate the gates of Blackwood. We don't know what the particular goal of her mission was, but we can only assume she was successful. Which means that if we want to have any chance of stripping Silas's power and stopping the Demien Order before they destroy Blackwood and everyone inside it, then we need to act fast. We *need* the True Headmaster."

"I want to go," Masika blurted out, standing.

Catherine blinked. "Excuse me?"

"On the expedition," Masika clarified, slightly out of breath. "I want to be a part of the expedition crew."

"It's dangerous," Catherine replied, voice level, though Emilio swore he saw a flicker of panic in her eyes. "The outskirts of purgatory are . . . perilous. We have the path mapped out, but there's so much of it that remains uncharted. There's no way to guarantee your safety. I already had a group in mind—"

Masika shook her head, interjecting. "I don't care. Plus, I heard what you said in the Battle Room. You need as many people as possible to stay behind. To defend the base. Well, let me go on the expedition, then. That's one less body you have to worry about."

"Masika . . ." Olivier warned, bracing himself against the table. "Hold on a minute—"

"If this is truly the only way to stop Silas and the Demien Order, then I want to be a part of it," Masika said, looking among the group. "I can't just sit here anymore. I need to act. To do *something.* If not for myself, then for all the other souls that have been lost. For Josie. Carter. Tristan. Liza. Nick. Wren."

Emilio's heart sank at the memory of the sacrificed nominees. He couldn't quite believe they were all gone. Nothing but *sacrifices.* And though the memory of their collective loss was heartbreaking, Emilio had to admit that it was Wren's destruction, out of all of them, that pained him the most.

The last they'd heard, Wren had participated in the final trial. And though her fate wasn't clear, given the fact that Irene had come out crowned as an Ascended, they could only assume she hadn't made it.

It was unfathomable—an afterlife without Wren Loughty. Emilio had always seen her as a brilliant, indomitable force. Indestructible.

And now she was gone.

Just like that.

Olivier stirred uncomfortably, the sound of his voice pulling Emilio back into focus. "But you heard what Catherine said. You could . . . you could be destroyed. Or taken hostage—"

"It doesn't matter," Masika interjected.

Olivier scoffed. "Well, have you perhaps thought to consider, for even a fraction of a second, the possibility that you might matter to other people?"

The hardness in Masika's stare melted a fraction. Her lips curled into a sad smile. "Don't go soft on me now, Olivier."

He shook his head and let out a bitter chuckle. "I won't let you do this."

"Well, good thing I'm not asking for your permission," Masika shot back.

Olivier jolted from his seat, mouth open as he prepared to protest, but then something snapped inside Emilio. He found himself standing, his own voice carrying across the room as he spoke five words that he knew would solidify their fate.

"I want to go too."

Olivier had gone impossibly still. His hands were splayed upon the table, his green eyes locked on Emilio, wide and unyielding.

"Don't." Olivier held his breath as though he were bracing for impact. "Emilio. I am *begging* you—"

"Masika is right," Emilio interjected softly. "We came here to help, didn't we? To save the afterlife?" He looked among the three of them, shrugging. "Well . . . this is our chance."

Olivier swallowed. He hadn't moved a muscle. "You . . . you

have other skills." His voice was low. Hoarse. "Talents that are better suited to the archives—" But Emilio cut him off, silencing Olivier with an unfamiliar spark of frustration.

"I want to *fight*."

Olivier blinked, startled. Emilio had to admit . . . he had even surprised himself. But he couldn't stop the idea now that it had solidified in his mind.

He wanted to fight. He wanted to make a difference.

For once . . . he didn't want to be afraid.

Olivier must have sensed it too. The indignation in his stare softened into something tender and anguished, a quiet understanding stretching between them. He let out a sigh, running a hand through his hair.

"Well, I suppose that settles it, then." He slid his gaze toward Catherine. "All three of us are going."

Catherine hesitated. Her right hand rested upon the pommel of her sword, fingers drumming the handle. For a brief moment, Emilio wondered if she'd decline their offer.

But then she gave a single nod in response, striding toward the Battle Room doors.

"Tomorrow morning, meet me back here before the first bell." She didn't bother glancing back at them as she spoke, swinging open the double doors with a flourish. "Don't be late."

She was gone before any of them could utter another word.

9

AUGUST

His sister had not taken kindly to his arrival. August hadn't exactly been expecting a warm welcome, but locking him inside a tent, shackled and bound, seemed a bit excessive.

Mere seconds after he had made his grand entrance, a pair of guards had apprehended him, tossing him into a nearby tent before tying him to a chair and binding his wrists with fire-infused shackles. Every time he so much as flinched, a searing heat scorched his wrists, traveling down his arm as though his veins were dripping with fire. It was funny, having more power than he'd had at Blackwood yet still feeling pain. But that was the one advantage Silas and his Ascended had. Numbed pain receptors granted by the Headmaster himself. And though August could now heal faster than a regular student—he still felt pain. Which made for an unwelcome weakness.

Not that it mattered. August wasn't going to put up a fight. He simply sat, waiting. Because a moment alone with Edith was *precisely* what he had been hoping for.

And he had known exactly what buttons to press to get what he needed.

August glanced around the tent, shifting uncomfortably in his seat. Inevitably, his mind began to wander. He couldn't stop himself from latching onto the moment he had walked back into the encampment . . . the image of Wren staring back at him. He had expected to see the *tiniest* glimmer of joy, some indication that she was relieved to see him again, but all he had found reflected in those blue eyes of hers was abject terror at what he had done. A heartbreaking disappointment.

He had tried to explain. To whisper into her mind using their psychic connection: *I have a plan. Just play along. I promise we'll speak later.* At first he had assumed she was ignoring him, or perhaps hadn't heard him, because she'd said nothing back. But the closer he'd gotten to Wren, the more he'd felt a strange disconnect in her soul. An emptiness. It had dawned on him only a second later.

Her magic. Edith has blocked her magic.

He'd have to find a moment alone with her—and quickly. He couldn't bear the thought of Wren believing he had decided to give up his humanity for the Order. That he was truly willing to betray her.

Yes . . . he had given up his humanity. That much was true. His soul was ruined. He had tethered himself to purgatory—*permanently*—and welcomed in the shadows. But he still had time before the shadows completely took over.

The Quarterly Equinox was approaching, a sacred ritual meant to honor the Soulless One and his prophecy. But it was more than just a simple ritual. Every new recruit within the Order—all the Demiens who had yet to succumb to the shadows—would be brought upon the altar and tasked with performing the Reaper's Kiss. An ancient shadow magic spell that would push them over the edge. Once the spell was complete, those new recruits would officially succumb to the shadows and become fully formed Demiens.

Nothing but weapons for the Soulless One's game.

Nothing but *monsters.*

Just like his sister.

A seething voice cut through August's thoughts and dragged him back to the present.

"What the hell do you think you're doing?"

Edith strode into the tent without warning, beelining toward August. He tried not to flinch when she shot her hand out, commanding her shadows to wrap their tendrils around his throat. They answered with pleasure, crashing down upon August, enclosing themselves hungrily around his neck.

His own shadows screamed inside him: ***Use us, use us, use us, use us.*** But he wouldn't answer their pleas. He had to restrain himself. He had to be strategic about how much shadow magic he used.

He forced a tight-lipped smile, wheezing through the suffocating pressure. "Is this . . . how you greet . . . family?"

Edith's lips lifted into a snarl. "You dare step into this encampment after your betrayal? After you tried to *leave* us, abandon us—"

"Just . . ." August croaked, fighting to speak against the serpentine shadow squeezing his windpipe. "Hear me . . . out." And just when he thought he might actually black out from the shadows' vise grip, Edith let out a frustrated groan and released the shadows from his neck.

"What do you want, Augustine?" She spoke his full name like a curse. Bitter and sharp.

He kept his response simple. "I've come to join you."

Edith snorted, unamused. "Bullshit."

"I'm telling you the truth."

"You expect me to believe this . . . this *performance*?" Edith practically spat the last word, sneering with disgust.

"I gave up my humanity, Edith. The one thing I swore never to part with. The one thing I was desperate to cling to—"

"And what of taking what is rightfully yours?" she interjected. "You took my crown. In front of everyone. Questioned my authority."

"Come now, sister." August chuckled softly. "I have no genuine intention of taking your position as High General. I just knew I needed to get your attention. But . . . I *would* like to take my rightful place by your side. To honor the Soulless One's prophecy." He let the weight of his words linger before tilting his head to the side. "If you'll have me."

"And what of the girl?" Edith asked without hesitation.

The question took August off guard. He swallowed, his jaw reflexively tensing. The mere thought of Wren sent a searing pain through his chest. A terrible anguish. But if he was to truly get back in his sister's good graces, he needed to do everything in his power to push Wren out of his mind.

He shrugged. "What about her?"

Edith let out a cackle, head thrown back. "I'm not a fool, Augustine. *You love her.*" August flinched at the accusation. "Did you really think this would work? Waltzing into the encampment under false pretenses? Tricking me into thinking you give a damn about the prophecy?"

August bit down on his cheek, hard, tasting blood, though it didn't last long. His wounds healed faster now, another swift and stark reminder of the irreparable damage he'd done to his soul.

"You're right," he breathed out, a trembling agony in his voice. "I love her. I do. And it hurts, Edith. It fucking *hurts*. Because I see it now . . . the inevitability of our ending. You've won. There is no future for me and Wren. And as sad and pathetic as it might seem—I can't stomach the rest of eternity like this. With all these . . . these *feelings*. This pain." August grimaced and a choked sob escaped his throat. "I can't do it anymore. And the Reaper's Kiss . . . it's the only way. The only way to make it stop."

Silence flooded the tent. Edith stepped closer, analyzing him with narrowed eyes.

"So . . ." she mused out loud, eyes raking his face. "You intend to succumb to the shadows on Equinox to free yourself of these pesky little . . . *feelings*?"

"If I let the shadows take me . . . if I bend to the Soulless One's control . . . I won't be in pain anymore. I won't have this . . . this *weakness*. It'll all go away," August explained in a shallow whisper. When he spoke the next sentence, he made sure to stare directly into his sister's eyes. "That's why *you* did it . . . isn't it?"

And there it was.

The faint crack in her mask.

Because as soon as the question left August's lips, he swore he saw a tiny glimpse of the sister he had once known. The sister who would hold his hand when he was too scared to cross the nearby creek on his own. The sister who would vehemently defend their mother during their father's nightly outbursts.

The sister who, despite everything, he had loved.

But then shadows swarmed the whites of Edith's eyes and the moment vanished.

"Why should I offer you this mercy?" she spat out, staring down at him as though he were nothing but a bug to squash beneath her palm. "I should banish you from the encampment and let you wither away in your torment for the rest of eternity."

"Because . . ." August lifted his chin, meeting his sister's scornful gaze. "Despite the fact that you utterly detest me . . . you know that the two of us are stronger together. Imagine what we would be capable of once I'm free of Wren. Once I'm rid of the guilt and shame. Once the love I feel for her is ripped away from me." August's voice trembled as the words tumbled out of him. "The two of us . . . together . . . we could be Silas's undoing."

Edith hummed. The crown hovering over her head darkened, the shadows swirling around her with a fervent hunger. August sensed his own shadows purring in delight, slinking up and down his chest eagerly.

Yes, yes, yes, they cried inside him. ***Together. Together. Together.***

Edith straightened her shoulders and crossed her arms.

"I will permit you to stay"—a rush of relief coursed through August as soon as the words left Edith's lips, though the feeling was quickly squashed as she finished the rest of her sentence—"under one condition."

August let out a sigh. "I wouldn't expect anything less."

Edith's white teeth gleamed in the darkness as she lifted her lips into a vicious grin.

"You can stay and participate in Equinox . . . as long as you are stationed with Onyx Unit."

August's heart sank. Some retaliation from his sister had been expected. He had assumed she might keep him confined. Force him to participate in practice duels and push his shadow magic to the limits. But placing him in Onyx Unit as a new recruit?

That was a cruelty no soul deserved.

The Demien Order was organized like a military base—separated into four distinct quadrants. There was Silver Unit, the quadrant that housed all the new recruits, the Demiens who had given up their humanity but had yet to succumb to the shadows.

New recruits still had some control over their emotions. Some semblance of morality. Mostly . . . they were just assholes looking to cause a bit of trouble.

Once those new recruits participated in Equinox, once they underwent the Reaper's Kiss, they'd move into Emerald Unit. The Demiens in this quadrant were volatile, lacking total control over their shadows' hunger. They were unpredictable. Erratic. Like ticking time bombs. With enough training, those Demiens would eventually learn to tame their shadows, honing their skills and cruelty into a finely sharpened blade. Once they reached that level of control, they would transfer into Sapphire Unit. This was where most Demiens would end up—where they would spend the rest of their time training and preparing for the lingering battle ahead.

But there was one more quadrant.

One group of Demiens who were . . . different.

All fully formed Demiens were cruel. Emotionless soldiers for the Soulless One's bidding. But those within Onyx Unit possessed a darkness—*a hunger*—that made other Demiens look like bloody angels. They were ruthless. They didn't simply want to please the Soulless One.

They *craved* carnage.

And now Edith was going to force August not only to live with those Demiens . . . but to train with them. Because she knew that if there was any risk that August would not succumb to the shadows on Equinox, placing him in Onyx Unit was her next-best bet. He couldn't completely lose himself until he cast the Reaper's Kiss, but he could come pretty damn close.

As if sensing August's realization in his silence, Edith sucked her teeth, smiling.

"Why the long face?" she teased. "I thought this would please you. You know, considering how *eager* you are to succumb to the shadows."

August inhaled a sharp breath. He wouldn't let himself shrink under his sister's cruelty. "Fine." He conceded. "I accept."

"Good." Edith snapped her fingers and the chains shackling August's wrists snapped open, falling to the ground. "Because, let's be honest with ourselves, little brother . . . it's not like you ever really had a choice."

10

WREN

Wren paced around her tent and daydreamed of setting the whole thing ablaze.

And she would have by now, had her magic not been stolen. She'd have laid waste to every inch of this godforsaken encampment and danced upon its ashes. It was bad enough to have her magic stripped. To be forced to endure days upon days of endless torture. But now . . . *this*?

The mere memory of August covered in shadows was enough to make her sick. Nausea coiled itself around her throat, threatening to rise inside her, but Wren pushed the sensation down with a steady exhale.

I've come to take back what is rightfully mine.

She'd never heard such vengeance in his voice . . . had never even known he was capable of it. But there was no denying what she had seen with her own eyes.

August has ripped his humanity out of his soul.

The thought alone was enough to eviscerate the last shred of energy Wren had left, and soon she found herself slumping down onto her bed, the exhaustion of the day settling upon her bones. She blew out the candle at her bedside table, crawling under the sheets. It wasn't just the emotional toll of seeing August again. The torture sessions had left her feeling carved out and hollow. It was violating, being forced to relive her death over and over, being compelled to witness her sister's untimely end without reprieve. Her mind felt unsteady. As though it were on the brink of shattering into a thousand infinitesimal pieces, and all Wren could do was sit back and watch.

If only she had her magic.

Ever since Edith had stripped Wren of her magic, a persistent ache had lingered in her chest, as though a vital organ had been cut out. She had grown to find comfort in her magic. A source of joy in the bleak existence she'd been handed.

Without her magic . . . she had nothing.

She *was* nothing.

Wren had begun to close her eyes and drift into the inviting oblivion of sleep when a rustle echoed at the tent's entrance. Her eyes shot open. She sat up, scanning her surroundings, but all she saw was darkness.

Instinctively, she lifted her hand as if to summon a shard of light, cursing under her breath when nothing happened. *Right. No magic.* She blinked twice, attempting to adjust her vision to the dimness of the room.

"Is someone there?" Wren called out.

But the only response was a thick silence.

Despite the stillness that lingered, Wren couldn't shake the feeling that she was no longer alone. Somebody was watching her. She felt a presence in the darkness. A heaviness that wasn't there before.

Weapon, Wren thought, panicked. *You need a weapon.*

But what could she use? She didn't have magic, and her trusty dagger had been taken from her upon her arrival at the encampment. All she had was this bed and these sheets and a damn nightstand—

Wren muffled a gasp.

Of course.

She quickly reached her hand out, blindly searching the top of the nightstand, until she felt the sharp metal edge of the candleholder resting upon the surface. She flinched as the recently melted wax stung the tips of her fingers, and let the candle topple to the floor, though she kept a firm grip on the heavy metal holder.

Slowly, Wren slid out of bed. Her chest rose and fell with panicked breaths.

"Whoever you are . . . you shouldn't be here. Edith wouldn't be happy to know you messed with her favorite new toy."

Wren held her breath. She waited for a response.

At first . . . there was nothing. Only that weighted, tangible silence.

But then came a noise. A deep rumble.

Laughter.

Before Wren could process what was happening, a bright glowing light appeared a few feet in front of her, revealing a set of silver eyes staring back at her.

Augustine Hughes had one hand lifted between them, a swirling vortex of flames hovering in his palm. The other hand was firmly shoved into the pocket of his black trousers, a casual arrogance in his stance.

"You're right," August mused. The right corner of his mouth lifted a fraction. "She's never been fond of sharing."

Wren's response was instinctual. She lifted the candleholder higher, tightening her grip, though she didn't strike. Not yet.

If August was at all concerned with the blunt metal object, he didn't show it. He simply dragged his smoke-filled eyes up toward the holder before sliding them back down onto Wren's face.

He lifted a brow. "And what, exactly, do you intend to do with that?"

"What does it look like?" Wren seethed, ignoring the heat rising to her cheeks.

"Well." August cleared his throat. "It appears as though you intend to bludgeon me with a candleholder. And though I have to admit the weapon of choice is . . . *creative* . . . I can't imagine it would be very effective."

Asshole.

Wren didn't even bother with a response. She simply lunged forward, swinging the candleholder with all her might, though August's hand was gripping her wrist before the blunt edge could make contact with the side of his face. She groaned through gritted teeth, attempting to rip herself free of his grasp, but August was strong. Even more so than he had been back at Blackwood. Something had changed inside him. Wren could tell that he was barely putting any effort into holding her back.

That *he* was holding back.

"Screw you," Wren spat out.

"Oh, come on, Loughty." August let out a low chuckle, inching closer. "I'm sure you can come up with something a bit more clever than that."

"What the hell do you want?"

The teasing smirk on August's lips faded. "I want to talk," he whispered. "To explain."

"Explain what?" Wren scoffed. "How you lied to me from the moment we met at Blackwood? How our relationship was just some . . . some *ploy*. Some Demien Order tactic—" But August cut her off before she could continue, tugging her closer. And though his grip was firm, Wren could tell he was restraining his strength, never once pressing down hard enough to actually hurt her.

"Don't." The word slipped out of him, hoarse and desperate. His face was inches away from hers now, close enough that Wren could make out the small line of scar tissue beneath his right eye. The soft curve of his lips. "We're not doing this. We're not playing right into Edith's game. You know just as well as I do that what we had—what we *have*—is real."

Wren flinched. "You gave up your humanity."

"I did," August replied with a nod. "And I'd do it again. I'd do it ten times over."

"Why?"

August's brows creased together. He tilted his head, eyes snaking up and down her face.

The next words he spoke were a breathless confession.

"You know why."

The words were enough to knock the breath from her lungs. She knew the threaded meaning behind them. The truth echoing in the silence. But could she truly trust him? After everything she had learned? After everything she had seen?

"You expect me to believe that all of *this*"—Wren gestured to the shadows swimming beneath the veins of August's exposed forearms—"is for my benefit?"

"I made a promise," August whispered. "And I keep my promises."

Wren didn't need him to elaborate. She knew *exactly* what promise he was referring to.

Find me. Wherever you are, wherever we end up, don't stop looking for me.

August let out a disgruntled sigh. He released Wren's wrist, stepping away from her. Wren blinked, taken aback by the sudden distance. She was free to attack him now. To run. But something in the way he looked at her had her frozen in place, unable to tear her gaze away from him.

"Look." August rubbed the back of his neck. "I knew Edith wouldn't even entertain the idea of letting me back into the Order if I didn't do something dramatic. Something to catch her attention."

Wren snorted. "Well, congratulations. I'd say removing your humanity and condemning your soul to an eternity trapped in purgatory is pretty fucking dramatic."

August's jaw clenched. "I did what I had to do."

"You know what this means for you, don't you?" Wren stepped closer. She found her hand reflexively reaching for his face, though she stopped herself. She was terrified to cross that line between them again. To allow herself to touch him. "You can never move on, August. You can never cross over to the Other Side."

August smiled, but there was a sadness reflected in his gray eyes. "That was never in the cards for me."

"According to who?"

August had opened his mouth to answer when a sudden noise stole their attention. Footsteps echoed in the distance. The muffled rumble of voices. August raised his index finger to his mouth, and Wren held her breath, listening. Luckily, whoever they were, they didn't seem to be getting any closer, and a few seconds later, the footsteps receded.

August cursed under his breath, running his hand through his dark curls.

A thought occurred to Wren.

"How the hell did you even get in here, anyway? Edith relocates me here every night, but I know for a fact she keeps a guard on duty outside while I'm sleeping," Wren muttered. "I can hear them pacing back and forth all night."

August rubbed at his jaw. "Best if you don't know."

Wren chest tightened. "Are they . . . did you . . ."

Sensing the terror etched upon her face, August shook his head.

"I didn't rip his soul out of existence, if that's what you're asking." He let out a bitter chuckle, craning his neck from side to side. At the subtle movement, Wren noticed a slithering shadow trailing up and down the veins of his neck, disappearing beneath the collar of his white shirt. "But . . . I did have to use a bit of shadow magic to sedate him. More than I wanted to, if I'm honest."

Wren shivered. "How much?"

August opened and closed his mouth. For a second, she thought he might actually answer her honestly, but then he simply shook his head and said, "It doesn't matter. Look. We have to hurry. I don't have much time. And if someone notices I'm gone . . ." He glanced over his shoulder before turning his attention back to Wren. "Whether or not you choose to believe my intentions doesn't matter. I came here for *you*. I came here to get you out of the mess that I caused."

"But how can I trust you?" Wren asked. And though the question had been rhetorical, a part of her prayed he had an answer. *Help me trust you,* she begged silently. *Help me believe you're still the boy I knew back at Blackwood.* "The more shadow magic you use, the more it'll consume you. What if you end up like *them* before the two of us can make it out of here? What if you succumb to the shadows and then turn on me?"

"I won't," August shot back. But then he sighed and added a whispered, ". . . at least, not yet."

Terror coursed through Wren. "Not *yet*?"

"Edith put me in Onyx Unit," August told her. "They're the most ruthless and corrupt of all the Demiens. She knows they'll push me to my limits. Force me to use more shadow magic than I want to. But . . . I won't *fully* succumb to the shadows. Not until Equinox."

Wren scrunched her brows in confusion. "Equinox?"

"It a quarterly gathering that's happening in three days," August explained in a hurried whisper. "All new recruits are forced to cast the Reaper's Kiss. It's an offering of sorts. A way of fully tethering yourself to the Soulless One. But once performed—that's it. You succumb to the shadows. If we don't get out of here by the night of Equinox . . . if we don't find a way out—"

"You'll lose yourself," Wren whispered, the realization sinking its claws into her chest.

"I won't have a choice."

Wren stretched her arm out, flexing her wrist. The silver cuff secured around her wrist glinted in the darkness.

"Even if we find a way to sneak out of the encampment . . . there's no way I'm making it past the outer perimeter with this thing still on." Wren gestured to the silver band. "It keeps me bound to the encampment. I'm trapped."

"Those security cuffs are made by Demiens." August stared down at the silver band with narrowed eyes. "Which means that if someone in this encampment made it . . . they can also destroy it." He reached out, fingers brushing the metal band. "We just need to figure out who it was by Equinox."

Three days. Could they really come up with a way out in *three days*?

A terrifying thought occurred to Wren.

"I might not make it until then."

At this, August's expression hardened. He inched closer, the intensity in his gaze sending a surge of warmth into Wren's stomach. "What do you mean?"

"Edith . . ." Wren flinched as she whispered the High General's name. "She's been torturing me. Forcing me to relive my death. I have no idea why, or for what purpose . . ." Wren had tried to make sense of it the first few days, though she'd quickly given up once she realized her theorizing was pointless. "I assume it has something to do with that damned prophecy. It's all she talks about."

August had gone silent, as though he was calculating something in his head, teeth worrying at his bottom lip. Wren was moments away from asking if he was okay when August glanced up, a sudden determination in his gaze.

"Tomorrow," he whispered. "I'll have a talk with Edith. I can find a way to convince her to stop. Or at least pause the sessions until Equinox."

"And if she doesn't?" Wren asked.

August stepped closer. He reached out, gently cupping Wren's face in his hands.

"I will find a way." A burning resolve echoed in his words. "I promise."

And somehow, despite everything she had learned, despite the lies and secrets and betrayal . . . Wren believed him. But she still wouldn't allow herself to fully tear down the wall between them. To fall headfirst without thinking.

As if hearing Wren's thoughts, August lowered his hands and took a rigid step backward. "I should go."

Wren swallowed and willed her body to settle. "That's probably a good idea."

August hesitated, awkwardly shifting from one foot to the other as he flexed his hand by his side. For a moment, Wren thought he might reach out again . . . that he might even close the distance between them. But then he was turning away from her, striding back to the entrance of the tent.

He paused at the threshold, his voice echoing out once more. "One more thing."

August kept his back to her. Around him, the shadows seemed to bend and warp, *his* shadows and the shadows of the room twisting together, until it was impossible to know where August began and the shadows ended.

"If we find a way out of here, but it's too late . . ." He paused, as if attempting to find the right words. "What I mean to say is . . . if I lose myself to the shadows before we can make it out of here . . . I need you to promise me that you'll run. That you'll leave me behind and save yourself."

Wren let out a soft breath. "August . . ."

He glanced over his shoulder. Agonizing desperation creased his face.

"Please."

Wren sucked in a sharp breath. She knew there was no point in fighting him on it.

"Okay." She crossed her arms over her chest. "I promise."

A sad smile lifted onto August's lips, and then he was striding out of the tent without a glance back. As the darkness of the tent swallowed Wren once more, August's words echoed in her head, following her into sleep.

I made a promise. And I keep my promises.

August was right. He *was* a boy who kept his promises.

But that doesn't mean I have to be a girl who does.

11

MASIKA

Masika was thinking about her father when the first bell rang out. She wasn't fixated on a particular memory, though she had plenty of those to reminisce on. It was simply *him*. The deep rumble of his laughter. The scent that clung to him—warm amber cologne mixed with cigarette smoke. The rough texture of his callused hands, hardened from years of manual labor. She rarely let herself think of the past anymore; she'd closed the door to that life long ago. But as she waited, standing at the entrance to the Southern Wing, the familiar traces of panic building inside her, she couldn't help but let her mind wander, to indulge in the memory of him, no matter how painful.

Anxiety is a trickster. It'll convince you that you're not the one in charge . . . that you don't have control over your mind, he'd whisper to her. *You gotta look it in the eyes and prove it wrong. Because you are the one in charge, my darling girl. And you are far stronger than you realize.*

Masika wrapped her arms across her chest, if just to still her trembling hands, and groaned in frustration. It had been her idea, after all. She had been the first one to speak out, to volunteer to be a part of the expedition crew. And she wanted to. It beckoned her—the hunger for adventure, the call demanding to be answered. But that didn't stop the anxiety from rising inside her, sneaking into the darkest parts of her mind, planting seeds of doubt. *You'll fail,* it seemed to whisper. *You'll disappoint them all.*

Masika shut her eyes, willing the thoughts to stop, to leave her alone. Somewhere behind her, footsteps echoed, growing louder and louder. Two familiar voices rose, cutting through the panic, drowning out the doubt filling her skull. And then Masika opened her eyes and Olivier and Emilio were there, standing next to her. The moment she saw their faces, it was like she could breathe again. All the panic, all the doubt—*gone.*

The boys were both dressed in their training uniform: black shirt with black pants, a leather armored vest over the torso and a backpack slung over the shoulders—though Emilio, of course, had also slipped his wool sweater over the top. He was holding the little creature from before, Benji; he was tucked snugly in Emilio's arms. The mutant puppy began to wag his tail the moment he spotted Masika.

"You guys came," she said.

"Of course." Emilio scrunched his face in confusion. "Did you think we wouldn't?"

Masika shook her head. She hadn't known what to think. Perhaps she simply wasn't used to having friends who followed through with their promises, who told her they'd be there for her and actually meant it.

"You're stuck with us," said Olivier with a smirk. He wrapped his arm around Masika's shoulders. "For better or for worse."

Masika smiled and looked between the two of them. "Thank you."

The trio turned to face the large double doors of the Battle Room. Muffled voices echoed just beyond. A collective realization seemed to wash over the trio, an understanding that if they walked through those doors, if they truly decided to do this, there would be no going back.

"Are we ready?" whispered Olivier. His usual bravado had faded, replaced by a tentative look of apprehension that made Masika's chest tighten. If Olivier, of all people, was frightened, then perhaps they all should be.

Emilio clutched Benji in his arms, and the little creature shivered, as if even he understood the gravity of the situation.

"Ready," muttered Emilio.

Masika let out a shuddering breath.

"Ready."

And then Olivier pushed open the doors and the three of them walked inside.

Even though Masika had been anticipating a small group, it still unnerved her to see their crew in person. They weren't exactly the most intimidating bunch.

Can we really do this on our own? Masika wondered, glancing around the table as she took in the faces of the others within the crew.

There was Dina, the silver-haired girl from the meeting. Masika wasn't sure what it was about the girl, but she didn't entirely trust her. She had a flighty, restless look in her eyes . . . like she was always itching for a fight. And then there was Analisa, the healer with a particular fascination with Olivier's fading memories. Masika noted the look of pure annoyance on Olivier's face when he spotted the healer standing in the room, his eyes rolling so far back into his head that she truly wondered if they might get stuck there.

There were Emilio and Olivier, of course. Out of everybody there, Masika trusted them the most. Not just for their talents, but for their loyalty as well. Masika knew she could rely on them if things went south—that they wouldn't leave her behind to save their own skins. She couldn't say the same for the others in the room.

And then there was Catherine.

Masika hadn't expected her to join the expedition crew, especially given her leadership position among the Resistance, but it appeared that time was truly of the essence, and Catherine had ostensibly decided to take matters into her own hands.

"Any questions?" Catherine asked now, seated at the head of the table. Silver spaulders adorned her shoulders, her entire torso covered in leather armor, an array of blades strapped to her waist and thighs.

She looked lethally beautiful. It made Masika loathe her that much more.

"What if we don't return?" asked Dina, a curl of amusement on her lips. She lay slumped in her chair, legs spread wide, twirling a knife against the surface of the table. "I suppose what I mean is . . . what happens if we fail? What if, despite everything, we don't find the True Headmaster?"

Catherine didn't so much as flinch. "Then someone else will try."

"And if we run out of time?" muttered Analisa. Her brows were pinched together, a weary look on her face. "You said it yourself—it's only a matter of time before the Demien Order attacks."

"If they attack before we locate the True Headmaster, then the others will fight them on their own until we can make it back to them. Birdie and Russo have been prepped."

Olivier scoffed, muttering something under his breath. At his reaction, Catherine rolled her eyes.

"Have something to say?" she asked with a sigh.

"No," Olivier shot back. "I just highly doubt we have what it takes to fight both Silas and the Demien Order without the True Headmaster's assistance. We're kind of outnumbered. Blackwood has *hundreds* of students—not to mention the *literal* Headmaster of the afterlife. God knows how many recruits the Demien Order has, though they've clearly had enough time to prepare their ranks. And then there's us with . . . what . . . a hundred? Maybe a tiny bit more?" Olivier rapped his fingers against the table and sighed. "I don't mean to be a downer, but . . . we're kind of screwed without the True Headmaster."

"Then I reckon we better find him," muttered Dina with a wink.

Catherine stood up from the table, the silver tip of her spear glinting as the blue sheen of the chandelier fell upon her. "Well, I suppose that settles it, then . . ." When nobody stirred, she scraped her chair back and turned to face the other side of the room. The group rose from their seats, and Masika followed suit, the panic from earlier slowly taking hold once again.

"Follow me," Catherine instructed, walking toward the southernmost wall. She paused when she reached the perimeter, glancing over her shoulder. "Everyone ready?"

The crew nodded. A hallowed silence had filled the air, and nobody seemed to want to be the one to break it. Catherine pressed her hand against the stone wall. One by one the stone slabs began to shift, spreading open, until a large archway stood before them.

Masika felt it first—the cold gust of wind brushing against her shoulders, a sudden chill running down her spine. And then came the smell—thick pine swirling in the air, a warm earthy musk filling her lungs. Catherine stepped forward and walked through the arch. Masika could see what lay beyond—a seemingly endless prairie stretching out before them, dotted with tall grass and wildflowers, the horizon blanketed by jagged snowcapped mountains in the distance. Dina and Analisa walked through, following Catherine, though Emilio and Olivier lingered behind, standing by Masika's side. The trio looked at one another.

One final glance.

One last chance to change their minds.

But nobody said a word; and then the three of them walked through the arch, out into the darkness, and sealed their fate.

PART III

THE CATALYST

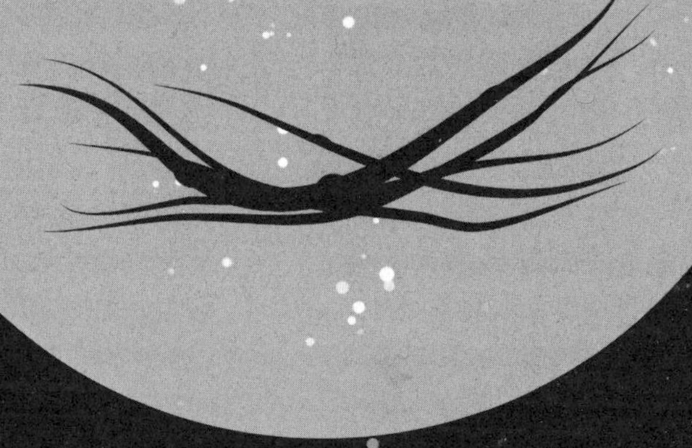

12

IRENE

It wasn't that Irene didn't have the stomach for torture, but there was something particularly uncouth about doing it first thing in the morning.

The girl let out another broken cry, the sound echoing against the narrow stone walls. This time, the strangled scream was accompanied by the lightning *crack* of corporeal magic as Samira thrust the glowing spear into the girl's side.

Though Irene had expected her Council trial period to begin shortly after the tapping ceremony, she'd still been caught off guard when she'd awoken earlier that morning to find Samira Heydari and Everly Hawthorne standing over her bed, the pair looming like a set of snickering specters.

"Surprise!" Samira had said, yanking the sheets away from Irene's body. "We're Council buddies!"

For a brief moment, Irene had assumed she was still hallucinating. At least, she'd *hoped* she was still hallucinating. But much to her dismay, Samira and Everly were not figments of her imagination, nor the product of some magically induced hangover. And their presence was very much real.

Instantly, panic had flooded through Irene. *Mateo.* But as she glanced around, the Demien was nowhere to be seen, so she could only assume he'd managed to sneak out when he'd sensed the two Ascended approaching. Though Irene had told him about her initiation into the Council the previous night, she'd been hoping to discuss their strategy further, but it appeared any alone time with Mateo would have to wait.

Irene blinked in confusion, drawing her attention back to Samira and Everly. "Excuse me?"

Everly rolled her eyes. "What Samira means to say is . . . we're the other potential initiates." She gestured among the three of them. "For the Council."

Irene couldn't contain her disbelief. "You've got to be fucking kidding me."

She wasn't even trying to be a dick about it, but *what in the actual hell?* The two girls hadn't been Irene's first guess for who else might be chosen. She supposed Everly had her merits—she was ruthless and cold and had sent more students to reformatory than most Ascended combined—but she was sloppy. Easily swayed by her whims and emotions. And Samira . . . well, Samira was a notorious party animal who spent more time concocting hallucinogenic elixirs than doing anything of value. But maybe Irene had been underestimating the two of them.

Maybe they were more dangerous than she realized.

"Okay, well . . ." Irene had sighed, sitting up. She'd reached beneath her bed, grabbing her boots and sliding them on. "I'm assuming you're not here to chitchat and braid each other's hair, so what the hell *are* you here for?"

Before either Samira or Everly could respond, a deep purple cloud had billowed between them, and then Housemaster Violet was materializing within the smoke. Her raven-black curls were pinned away from her angular face, dark brown eyes narrowed in assessment.

"They came to fetch you under my instruction," Violet had

said, wrapping her tweed coat tightly across her chest. "It's time for the Council test period to officially begin."

And now here they were. Learning the mechanisms and intricacies of torture.

Irene steeled herself against the sour odor emitting from the cell they were in. When Housemaster Violet had initially relocated them, Irene had been struck by a wave of disorientation. She hadn't recognized the strange corridor they'd been transported to. The air was damp and thick, with a mildewy scent that made her nose itch. But there was another scent in the air—something bitter and metallic, with a pungent undercurrent that reminded her of rotten meat.

Blood.

Housemaster Wesley had been waiting for them, leaning against one of the stone walls, nervously fidgeting with his glasses. When he'd spotted them, his head had popped up in attention.

"H-hello, girls." His lips curled into an apprehensive grin. "Follow me."

They'd walked through the narrow corridor in silence. As they ventured forward, the stone walls flanking their path slowly shifted into a seemingly never-ending line of cages. Most of the ones near the entrance were empty, though the floors were stained with oxidized blood.

"What the hell is this place?" Irene had asked out loud.

"These are our dungeons," Violet had said matter-of-factly. "We are deep beneath the Ascended Quarters."

Dungeons? Irene had shivered as the word echoed in her mind.

As they journeyed deeper through the corridor, a faint shuffle began to echo in the distance, a collection of weak and brittle breaths rattling in the air. And a few seconds later . . . Irene saw the first body.

They were lying in the fetal position, clothes torn and shredded, skin covered in gruesome lacerations. With every cage they passed, Irene was faced with another prisoner, each one more battered than the next. They were barely conscious. Their souls hanging by a thin, fraying thread.

How long have they been here? Irene had thought. *Right beneath our feet.*

Eventually, they had stopped in front of one of the cages. The girl inside was curled inward, arms wrapped tightly around her bony knees. Blood stained her tangled hair, a thousand jagged cuts marring the skin of her arms and legs. She was shaking. Teeth chattering so loudly it sounded as though they might break in half. When they'd approached the cage, the girl's eyes had snapped up like those of a wild and frightened animal caught in a trap.

Thalia.

Irene barely recognized her. Thalia Greevson had been a fellow student, long ago, though she'd disappeared a few years back. But the Thalia that Irene could remember was prim and poised, always impeccably dressed, with a serene expression on her face. Now she looked hollowed. An empty shell of the girl she had once been.

Wesley and Violet had explained their interrogation tactics.

Violence first, questions later.

Apparently, Thalia was part of that same mysterious third coalition Mateo had mentioned the previous afternoon, the one forming in the outskirts of purgatory. According to Wesley and Violet, Thalia had information that could lead them to their base.

"Notice how her defenses have grown weaker?" Violet asked now, looking between Irene, Samira and Everly. Samira pulled the spear away from Thalia, who whimpered and clutched her side with a trembling hand.

Irene cautiously dipped into Thalia's mind, feeling her way through her mental wards. Violet was right. When they'd first arrived, Thalia's wards had felt solid and resolute. Like an impenetrable fortress. But now, after enduring Samira's torture, they felt pliable . . . more susceptible to moving and bending.

"But I still can't cross through them," muttered Irene. Samira and Everly must have sensed it too. Samira looked merely disappointed, while Everly looked positively enraged, her arms crossed indignantly over her chest.

Wesley pushed his glasses up the bridge of his nose. He leaned in toward the bars of the cage, staring down at Thalia with a detached pragmatism that made him look as though he were staring at the results of a lab experiment, as opposed to the aftermath of invasive torture.

"In most cases, with this level of pain, you'd be able to successfully dismantle those mental wards and access her memories. But . . . Thalia here is different." Wesley closed his eyes, humming in fascination. "She hasn't just placed the wards around her mind . . . but threaded them *through* it. Think of it almost like a maze. And in my professional opinion, even if we weaken her further . . . the maze will hold."

"There has to be a way to solve it, then." Everly huffed in annoyance. "I mean, if it's a maze or whatever."

Wesley slowly slid off his glasses, wiping them against the hem of his wrinkled shirt.

"Magic of the mind is far more complex than that of the body. With something this elaborate, I'm afraid the best we can hope for is her physical form breaking before her mind. If we can cause enough physical pain . . . perhaps she'll simply tell us." As he spoke the words, Thalia's eyes flitted to him. Irene had expected to see fear reflected inside them—a sense of panic at knowing what awaited her . . . but instead, there was nothing but stone-cold resolve blazing there.

"She's not going to break," Irene whispered. She was certain of it. But Everly seemed undeterred, shoving Irene out of the way with her elbow.

"We'll see about that," she sneered, snatching the corporeally infused spear from Samira's hand. The Housemasters made no attempt to stop her, merely taking a step back as they silently observed.

Everly approached the iron bars of the cage slowly, head tilted.

"How about you play nice, Thalia. Tell us what you know and I won't have to use this."

But Thalia's response was simple and straight to the point. She lifted her head an inch off the floor, clearly using all the energy she had left to look Everly in the eye, and spat blood directly onto the other girl's feet.

Samira stifled a cackle of laughter. Irene sucked in a sharp breath.

And then, with a feral scream, Everly thrust the tip of the spear straight through Thalia's ribs. The crackle of corporeal magic was instantaneous—bright silver flashes lighting up the room as Thalia's entire body began to violently convulse, white foam sputtering from her lips, and her eyes rolling back into her head.

"BREAK!" Everly bellowed over the crackling magic. "Tell us what you know!"

After a few more seconds, she yanked the spear out, chest heaving. Irene held her breath, waiting to hear what Thalia would say, but the other girl simply lay there . . . motionless. Her limbs had gone unnaturally stiff, her skin pallid, almost translucent, as if her form was slowly fading away.

Violet sucked her teeth. "And here we have a lesson on

limitations . . ." She walked closer to the cage, snatching the spear out of Everly's hand before the girl could protest. She used the end of the spear to poke at Thalia's unmoving body. "If you push the pain too far . . . if you accidentally enter the core of a soul . . . you can destroy it."

Irene's chest tightened. "Are you saying . . . Did she just—"

"Shatter the core of Thalia's soul?" muttered Violet with a defeated sigh. "That would be correct."

Everly flushed. She staggered backward.

"I didn't mean to . . . I just . . . I thought maybe I could . . ." Her voice trailed off as she stepped away from the cage.

Samira snorted. "Way to go, Everly. Now all our interrogation was useless."

"It's quite all right," Wesley said, peering down at Thalia's fading body with a deflated frown. "It happens every now and then. Truthfully, I doubt we could have gotten anything out of her. Headmaster Silas might not be too pleased, though—he was really hoping this one would give us something concrete."

"What happens to her now?" Irene heard herself ask.

"I can already sense her soul fading," Violet said matter-of-factly. "I'd give it a few minutes. And then the fragments of her soul will disintegrate. She'll simply . . . cease to exist."

A shiver ran down Irene's spine. As wrong as it might seem, Irene couldn't help but feel as though this was a merciful ending compared to what might have awaited Thalia.

"Anyway!" Wesley clapped, an almost comical grin on his face. "Let's keep moving, shall we? Plenty of other souls to interrogate. Next up, we'll be attempting what I call a Mind Loop. It's essentially a form of mind alteration that allows you to infiltrate their memories and force them into a living nightmare. It's quite fun, actually . . ." Wesley's voice faded as he ushered them forward, making his way deeper into the dungeons. The others followed, vanishing around the corner. Irene was moments from scurrying after them when she heard a breathy whisper behind her.

"Catherine . . ."

Irene froze. Her breath caught in her throat.

She turned, slowly. Thalia was still lying on the floor, her physical form fading, but her eyes had fluttered open . . . and she was staring straight at Irene.

"What did you say?"

The girl drew a shaky breath. It rattled in her chest.

"She'll come . . ." Another breath. Thready and barely there. "They will . . . find you."

Irene cursed. She didn't have time for this. She squatted next to the iron bars, leaning in closer.

"That name," she whispered. "What name did you just say?"

Thalia smiled and wheezed through cracked lips.

"I see . . . the war in you. Your heart . . . is split. Two sides . . ." Thalia's eyes began to flutter closed as she whispered her last words. "I wonder . . . which . . . you will choose." And then she was slipping away, the tiny sliver of life inside her extinguishing. Her body came apart, disintegrating piece by piece, breaking into swirling speckles of ash.

"No, no, no." Irene lunged forward, trying to grab Thalia, to piece her back together, but it was too late. One second the girl was there, withering away in the cage, and the next, her entire self had come undone, nothing but a mass of swirling particles drifting in the air. Just like the other eliminated nominees.

Gone.

Destroyed.

Irene scrambled backward, nausea coiling around her throat, pushing herself away from the cage until her back hit the stone wall behind her. She let out a groan, rubbing her face with her palms.

Catherine.

The girl had said the name. She was sure of it.

But what were the odds that she was talking about the same Catherine who Masika had lost to the Demien Order all those years ago? The same Catherine who Masika had finally told Irene about during the second trial? But if it *was* the same person, that meant Catherine had left the Demien Order to join whatever this third coalition was that Thalia had been a part of.

And maybe . . .

No.

It was pointless to indulge in a future with Masika in it. To pretend that she'd ever see her friend again. It was nothing but a useless fantasy. A silly dream. And either way, what good would it be if Masika was around? She'd only admonish Irene for joining the Order. Hell, she'd probably despise her for it.

Wherever Masika was, it was best for her to stay as far away from Irene as possible.

13

OLIVIER

For a journey riddled with danger, Olivier had found the first few hours to be rather boring.

They'd walked for what felt like an eternity, trekking through the seemingly endless prairie, eyes set eastward. As dawn bled into early morning, Olivier could make out the dusty purple mountains in the distance, the barbed horizon of snowcapped peaks and craggy canyons. Every once in a while, a warm scent washed over him—crisp apples mixed with woodsmoke—but it would vanish before he could trace its origin, swirling away in the wind.

Eventually, a dense landscape of dark green materialized in the distance. Towering pine trees made up the looming forest ahead—the large expanse stretching as far as the eye could see. As soon as they entered the mouth of the forest, a strange chill trickled down Olivier's limbs, a tingling in his spine.

Something was changing.

Whether it was him or the atmosphere, it was hard to tell.

His mind felt . . . fractured. It had been unraveling since he had been dragged to the Resistance's manor, but *this* feeling was different. The disorienting presence he'd been experiencing since the Forgetting had first sunk its claws into his mind had seemingly doubled in size since he had set foot outside the manor's walls. There was a heaviness pressing upon his skull. A dullness in his memories that terrified him to his core. He didn't even bother attempting to recollect a memory from his past—from his old life. It would only solidify what he already knew.

Your time is running out.

He shivered as the thought bounced around in his head. Was it his own voice? Or the voice of a ghost clinging to his consciousness, beckoning him into oblivion? It was impossible to tell anymore.

Olivier refocused his attention on the woods. There was no obvious path, so they weaved between trees, the crudely drawn map their only guide. Olivier's fingers brushed against damp earth and gnarled branches, little tufts of moss clinging to brittle bark. He noticed that the leaves had morphed from a dark green to a morose palette of deep burgundy and charred black. Above them, what sky he could see through the canopy of interconnected trees burned a strange umber, a swirling vortex of smoke-gray clouds moving with the wind.

A few steps ahead, Emilio walked beside Masika, that terrifying little creature snuggled in his arms. Dina and Catherine trudged along at the head of the group, their eyes locked forward, a silent determination in their movements. Analisa, of course, had decided to plant herself right beside Olivier, her eyes drifting over to him every few seconds.

Ugh.

Can't she just let me rot and wither away in peace?

Analisa snorted, biting back a smile. Olivier narrowed his gaze in confusion.

"What's so funny?"

Her eyes widened as a sudden flush burned behind her cheeks. "Nothing," she muttered, rubbing away her smile with the back of her hand.

Olivier stared at her. And stared at her. And—

He gasped as the realization dawned on him.

"Oh my God!" he shriek-whispered, grabbing her firmly by the arm and tugging her in closer. "Were you just . . . *in* my mind?"

"No," Analisa replied, though she shrugged and added, "I mean . . . not *technically*. I was just . . . feeling around. And for the record—*no*. I'm not going to simply let you rot and wither away, despite your death wish."

"Analisa!" Olivier hissed, lowering his voice. His eyes darted to Emilio, but the other boy was too preoccupied with scratching the puppy in his arms to notice the conversation happening a few yards behind him. "You cannot just poke and prod in my mind without asking. We're not even in a healing session—"

"It's getting worse," she muttered abruptly. Her expression grew solemn. "Changing. I've felt it ever since we left the base. Something about purgatory's atmosphere . . ." Her voice trailed off as she took in Olivier's growing alarm. "You feel it too . . . don't you?"

Olivier swallowed. "How long?"

Analisa nervously rubbed her wrist. "It wouldn't be an accurate guess—"

Olivier cut her off, voice grave. "How. Long."

Analisa fussed with the golden bangle on her arm. "Without the manor's protection and our daily healing sessions?" She sucked in a breath, gnawing on the inside of her cheek. "A week. Maybe less."

Olivier's heart sank in his chest.

He tried to muster up something useful to say. Something meaningful. But all he could manage to utter in reply was a pathetic and defeated *"Shit."*

Analisa reached out and squeezed his arm.

"I could be wrong," she offered, though they both knew she wasn't. "It could be longer."

"Right." Olivier snorted. "Or it could be less."

A weighted silence fell between them. Analisa's eyes traveled to Emilio. He was chatting with Masika, the puppy in his arms happily staring between the two of them as he dangled his head back in Emilio's embrace.

"You should tell him," Analisa muttered softly.

Panic surged through Olivier's chest. He dragged his eyes away from Emilio. "And give him something else to worry about?" He shook his head. "No, thanks."

"Right." Analisa let out a dry chuckle. "Because lying to him about your imminent doom is *super* healthy. I'm sure that purposeful miscommunication won't cause *any* problems whatsoever."

"Okay, cut the sarcasm." Olivier lifted a hand between them. "It's weird."

Analisa shrugged. "I learned from the best."

Olivier groaned in frustration. She was right. He *hated* that she was right. He should tell Emilio. He deserved to know. Nothing good would come of withholding the truth from him. He would find out eventually. But why distract Emilio when they were already in a dangerous situation? Why cause him even more pain?

"Look." Olivier rubbed at his temples. "I'll tell him . . . *eventually*. But we need to focus on finding this clue first."

Analisa hummed. "I never figured you for a martyr."

"I'm not," Olivier muttered defensively, shooting her a frown. "And either way, I'm hardly religious enough to be branded a martyr."

"Religion is about faith. And you believe in *him* with enough holy reverence to happily sacrifice your own soul at his altar."

Analisa stared at Olivier pointedly. "So. Like I previously stated. *Martyr.*" And with that, she sauntered off, catching up to the rest of the group, but not before glancing over her shoulder and striking Olivier with one of her vexing all-knowing smiles.

Olivier groaned and rolled his eyes.

This is going to be a painfully long journey.

14

WREN

Wake up, my sweet catalyst.

The voice yanked Wren out of her dreams and into the murky haze of morning. She gasped, clutching her chest, eyes skating around her dimly lit tent. But there was nobody speaking to her . . . nobody in the room.

Wait.

Nobody is here.

The sudden awareness washed over Wren as she slid her legs out of the sheets and pressed her feet upon the cold floor. Every morning since she had arrived at the Demien Order's encampment, she'd awoken to find Edith looming over her, ready to drag her into another endless day of torture. But this morning . . . nothing. No one.

Without thinking, Wren slid her boots on and beelined for the entrance, but when she tried to part the edges of the tent's canvas, she noticed there was no entryway. As if the tent had hardened into a concrete wall. She furrowed her brow in confusion and searched, desperate to find some sort of opening, but there was *nothing.* The entrance to the tent had seemingly vanished, trapping her inside.

Wren groaned in irritation. *It must be some sort of protective barrier.* It had been foolish to think Edith would let her simply waltz out of the tent. Wren might be alone, but that didn't mean she was going anywhere.

She slumped back onto her bed in defeat, fingers fussing with the end of her braid. A tidal wave of questions shot through her mind. *Why hasn't Edith taken me this morning? What could possibly have changed?* But then Wren remembered what August had told her the night before.

"I can find a way to convince her to stop. Or at least pause the sessions until Equinox."

Hope surged in Wren's chest.

Maybe he actually did it.

That seedling of hope was instantly snipped when a sudden commotion stole Wren's attention. From one moment to the next, two people materialized at the entrance of the tent—a boy and a girl, the two of them caught in a furious debate. The boy had deep olive-toned skin and buzzed dark hair, a sort of Cheshire cat grin that led Wren to believe he could charm his way out of whatever argument he was having with nothing but his dimpled smile. The girl's bright pink hair brushed her pale freckled shoulders as she shook her head indignantly, scoffing at whatever the boy had been saying before they'd crossed through.

"—absolutely not. Are you insane?" she barked, staring up at him defiantly. She was far shorter than the boy, though Wren had a feeling she could easily take him in a fight. "There is *no* freaking way we stand a chance against them. Either way, they would never set up Silver against Onyx twice in a row—what the hell did you say to him?!"

"Oh, nothing. I just casually insulted his entire bloodline," the boy said with a nonchalant wave of his hand. "But honestly, Callum is *so* sensitive."

The girl's brows creased together. "You're an idiot. You know that, right?"

"But I'm *your* idiot."

"No. You're a pain in my fucking—"

"Uh . . ." Wren cleared her throat. The pair instantly froze, heads turning toward Wren in perfect synchronization. "I'm sorry to interrupt, but who the hell are you?"

"Oh." The girl's face creased in confusion, blinking. "You're awake. I guess the sedative wore off earlier than usual."

Sedative? Wren had wondered if they'd been drugging her, considering how deeply she'd been sleeping. She had found it odd that she'd only ever woken up once Edith was already in the tent waiting for her.

The boy sauntered forward, his limbs moving with an easy grace that made it appear as though he were floating. He placed a hand on his chest and offered a mocking bow. "Arthur Alexander Ellington, but friends call me Artie, which means *you* can call me Arthur. And this here is—" He had begun to gesture to the girl next to her when a sudden wave of recognition swept through Wren.

"Quinn," Wren whispered, staring up at the girl in disbelief. "Quinn Woodrow."

How could she not have recognized her sooner? Quinn had vanished shortly before the Decennial opening ceremony, though everybody knew what her disappearance had actually meant . . . that she'd abandoned Blackwood Academy in favor of the Demien Order.

"Huh." Quinn snorted, crossing her arms. "The great and magnificent Wren Loughty actually recognized me."

"Of course," Wren whispered defensively. "We . . . we had classes together. I was so sad to hear that you—well . . . that you . . ."

"Condemned my soul for all eternity to join the Demien Order?" Quinn supplied with a wry smile.

Wren flushed. "I wasn't going to say that."

"But you were thinking it, weren't you?" Arthur teased with a grin, a slight crinkle appearing at the bridge of his nose.

"Well . . ." Wren looked between them, sighing. "I suppose we should just get it over with."

Quinn raised a brow. "Get *what* over with?"

"I assume you're here to take me to Edith."

"Nope," Arthur said, placing his hand on Wren's back and not-so-gently ushering her forward. "Turns out our benevolent High General has decided to offer you a break."

Wren staggered to a halt.

"A—a break?" Wren glanced between them in confusion, though a part of her already knew why. *August.* She had been right. He must have somehow managed to convince Edith to stop the sessions. But how, and at what cost, Wren wasn't sure. "Why would she do that?"

"Does it matter?" Arthur scoffed. He practically skipped to the entrance of the tent, swiveling on his heels. He wore the same training leathers as Quinn—an armored vest fitted over his torso and laced armguards slipped over the sleeves of his black tunic. Though most of his skin was covered, Wren could still see a sliver of shadows slinking up and down his neck. "Look. The fewer questions you ask, the better. Why don't you just count your lucky stars and follow us."

"But where are we going, then?" Wren asked in bewilderment.

Arthur gestured dramatically to the tent, twiddling his fingers. As soon as he moved, the entrance to the tent appeared.

"It's time for the grand tour."

Wren stilled, waiting for the punch line. "But . . . I'm supposed to be a prisoner."

"You are," Arthur replied. "For the most part. But considering you'll eventually be one of us, we may as well get you acclimated now."

An ember of fury burned in Wren's chest. She crossed her arms, glaring up at Arthur. "I will never be one of you."

Arthur, however, seemed completely unfazed, simply rolling his eyes and saying, "Yeah, whatever, sweetcakes." He dismissed her with a perfunctory wave, strolling through the opening of the tent without a glance back. He called to her over his shoulder, "Just keep up, will you?"

Quinn grabbed Wren firmly by the wrist, nails digging into her flesh. Before Wren could protest, the pink-haired girl gestured to the tent with a tilt of her head. "It's enchanted to keep you in. If you want to cross through, you have to have physical contact with a Demien." She tightened her grip as if to make a point.

Wren groaned and resisted the urge to scream. "Fine. Just . . . *go*."

From one stride to the next, the empty tent became a noxious blur of smoke and leather. A cacophony of noises replaced the chilling quiet—raucous laughter, echoing shouts, the crackle of magic. It was like stepping into a raging current; bodies pushed past Wren, paying her no mind, a stream of Demiens coming and going from all directions. Wren had never seen the main hub of the encampment before. Edith would simply relocate her to the torture sessions, dragging her from one tent to the next. But now she could see that the heart of the encampment was a buzzing hive, the spacious cavern overflowing with bodies. There had to be hundreds of them.

"This way!" Arthur snatched Wren by the wrist, pulling her

forward. "Come on. We can't let the prophesized catalyst of destruction get lost, now, can we?"

They zigzagged through the sea of Demiens, darting past an array of tents occupied by different specialty tradespeople—blacksmiths and leatherworkers—and tents brimming with magical explosives and other volatile potions. Throngs of Demiens gathered around fire pits, the glow of firelight illuminating the unmistakable river of shadows gliding beneath their skin. Woodsmoke and warm pine filled the air, an earthy scent that reminded Wren of walking through the forest in the dead of winter.

As they approached the mouth of a large tunnel carved into the eastern side of the cavern, Quinn and Arthur came to an abrupt halt. They spun around to face Wren, angling themselves closer.

"Listen carefully, because I'm only going to explain this once," Quinn barked, snapping her fingers to get Wren's attention. "The Order is divided into four Units—Silver, Emerald, Sapphire and Onyx."

"Quinn and I are in Silver," Arthur added, pointing to the silver pin clipped to the front of his leather vest. It was fashioned into the shape of a glistening sword with the Demien Order's sigil carved on the hilt. "Which is where we're heading now."

"Silver Unit is solely for new recruits. Those who have recently joined the order but have yet to perform the Reaper's Kiss." Wren didn't miss the slight tic in Quinn's jaw at the mention of the infamous shadow magic spell.

"You take the eastern tunnel to get to our unit," Quinn added, pointing up ahead. "The other units are scattered throughout the encampment. You take the northern tunnel to get to Emerald. The southern for Sapphire. And the western tunnel is for Onyx."

"Though it's best to stay clear of the other units," Arthur muttered.

Wren snapped her gaze toward him. "Why?"

"Well . . ." Arthur peered at Quinn, who lacerated him with a frustrated glare. "The other Units are just . . . different. They've succumbed to the shadows. They're a bit . . . well . . . how do I put this delicately . . ."

"They won't hesitate to rip your throat out if you look at them the wrong way," Quinn interjected curtly. "They won't give a damn that you're the prophesized catalyst of destruction. Not while you're still . . . *you*. Either way, they know you'll eventually heal. So they can carve you open and tear your guts out without worrying about repercussions."

Wren blanched. "But . . . we feel pain."

Arthur patted Wren on the shoulder, guiding her forward. "That's what makes it so fun."

They stepped into the tunnel and Wren followed suit. Flickering torchlight dappled thin slivers of shadows upon the cave walls, illuminating the dimly lit tunnel. A few other Demiens hurried past, most keeping to themselves, though a few greeted Quinn and Arthur with a casual salute.

As the tunnel came to an end, they entered another sprawling cavern carved into the base of the mountain ridge. Dozens of tents stretched out before them, each adorned with a billowing flag marked with the Silver Unit insignia. Despite the absence of wind, the flags rippled as though caught within a breeze—enchanted, no doubt. Fire pits and various campsites dotted the cavern, lanterns suspended in the air, hovering just over their heads.

"Fucking hell," a voice echoed. Wren turned to find the source—a boy sitting on top of a wooden barrel, legs spread, toothpick tucked between his lips. As his eyes landed on Wren, his jaw went slack and the toothpick tumbled out of his mouth and fell to the ground. "The catalyst . . . in the flesh."

As the words left his lips, the other Demiens milling about the cavern came to a halt, eyes falling upon Wren, taking her in with unabashed curiosity. A flurry of whispers rose around her, crescendoing, until all Wren could hear was the grating sound of her own name.

Quinn cursed under her breath, shooting the boy with the toothpick a glare. "Thanks a lot, Jas."

The boy, Jas, chuckled and raised his hands in feigned innocence.

Quinn tightened her grip on Wren, yanking her forward. Arthur scrambled to keep up. "Come on, catalyst. Let's get you out of here."

"Where are we going?" Wren whispered, glancing over her shoulder.

"I don't know," Quinn grumbled. "Your tent, I guess. Edith wants you staying with us for the next couple of days, until Equinox. Lord knows why she'd think it's a good idea—"

"Wait—*what?*" Wren struggled to keep up with Quinn, nearly tripping over her own boots. "I'm staying here? In Silver Unit?"

Quinn bit the inside of her cheek. "Afraid so."

Arthur shot Quinn a wary look. "We should hurry. I think we're about to be—" But Arthur's words were drowned out as a blaring alarm rang throughout the cavern. Wren winced, plugging her ears at the shrill sound.

Thankfully, it didn't last long. A few seconds later, the alarm came to an abrupt stop.

"What the hell was that?" Wren asked, rubbing her ears. She noticed that the Demiens nearby had begun to pour out of their tents, brandishing their weapons as they migrated toward the other side of the cave.

"You have to be kidding me . . ." muttered Quinn, pinching

the bridge of her nose. "Edith cannot truly expect us to bring *her* along." She motioned to Wren with an exasperated wave of her hand.

"What do you mean?" Wren asked, though nobody seemed to hear her. "Bring me where?"

Arthur chuckled. "You have to give Edith credit . . . she's got impeccable timing."

"You think this is *funny*?" Quinn said, seething. "Shall I remind you who we're up against this round? And whose fault it is?"

Wren sighed. "Can someone please—"

"I told you that you should have come to the bonfire with me," Arthur interjected, pointing an accusatory finger at Quinn's chest. "*You* were the one who stayed back! Honestly, you should know by now that I cannot be trusted around Onyx recruits after I've had three glasses of wine!"

Quinn groaned, digging her hands into her hair. "Oh my God. You are a *literal* child!"

And that was all it took for Wren to finally snap.

"CAN SOMEONE TELL ME WHAT THE HELL IS GOING ON?!"

A sweeping hush fell upon Quinn and Arthur as they turned to face her.

It was Arthur who broke the silence with a sigh. "*That* was the battle simulation alarm," he said with a nervous chuckle. "And it looks like you're going to be a part of it."

There was no way in hell Wren could actually participate in a battle simulation without her magic.

And yet there she was. Standing among the other Silver Unit

recruits, attempting to listen to Quinn bark instructions at her despite the persistent ringing in her ears.

"Are you even listening to me?" Quinn snapped her fingers in front of Wren's face, dragging her back into focus.

Wren clenched her teeth. "It's kind of impossible not to listen to you when you're quite literally yelling in my face."

"Then repeat it back. Every word."

"The battle simulation will start as soon as the next alarm sounds," said Wren, echoing the words Quinn had spoken only seconds earlier. "We're competing against Onyx Unit. Our main objective is to capture the black flag on the other side of the domed cave. Our second objective is to protect our own flag from them."

"And what about *you*?" Quinn shoved a firm finger against Wren's chest.

"I try not to get my head chopped off," Wren said with a grim smile.

They were standing at the mouth of another cave, this one hidden deep within the encampment. Around them stood the entire Silver Unit quadrant—a hundred Demiens, at the very least. An electric buzz hummed in the air, a frenzied excitement.

"Here. Take this." Arthur appeared beside Wren, handing her a curved saber. She was surprised to find that the weapon was fairly light in her hands despite its size. "It's not the same as having your magic, but it's still sharp."

Wren flexed her hand over the hilt of the saber. "That's oddly helpful of you. Thanks."

Arthur shrugged. "It's known to happen from time to time."

Quinn, who had unsheathed two finely sharpened scythes from her waist, turned to look at Wren with a withering frown. "Make sure to stay close," she reminded her. "I don't want you wandering."

"Are you sure I can't just sit this one out?" asked Wren. "How are you even sure Edith wants me participating—"

"Because I *know* her," Quinn snapped. The hardness in her stare wavered, a faint prickle of fear reflected in the way she nervously gnawed the inside of her cheek. "She isn't just testing you—she's testing all of us. Silver Unit has a reputation."

"A reputation?" Wren echoed. "Why? Because you haven't done the Reaper's Kiss yet?"

Quinn and Arthur shared a knowing look. Wren had hit a nerve—that much was clear. But before either of them could respond, another blaring alarm echoed throughout the cavern. The bodies surrounding them stirred awake, the sharp *hiss* of blades scraping against their sheaths. Behind Wren, Demiens pushed forward, an unstoppable current guiding her toward the entrance of the cavern. She staggered, nearly losing her footing, but Arthur reached out and grabbed her by the shoulder, holding her steady before she could tumble to the ground.

"Do not leave my side." Quinn was speaking to Wren, but her eyes were fixed forward, locked on the mouth of the cave, as though she were simply repeating a mantra, whispering a prayer beneath her breath. Wren's grip on her saber tightened as she braced herself for whatever she might find inside.

The alarm came to a sudden halt.

Silence.

And then Wren walked forward, wedged between Quinn and Arthur, and entered the cavern.

Red.

It bathed the walls, the rocky floor, the tall domed ceiling. As Wren stepped through, she rubbed her eyes, as though she might be able to clear her vision, but the red remained, engulfing everything in a crimson haze.

"It's not your eyes," whispered Arthur by her ear. "Look up."

Wren glanced upward, catching sight of the glowing red orbs hovering at the center of the domed ceiling. They were the only source of light inside the cavern, and the reason for its blood-red hue.

The cavern was divided into two sides—Silver and Onyx. A maze of stone barricades stood between them, blocking each side from being able to see their opponent's flag. In order to win, you'd have to cross through the rocky maze without getting lost. But even then, it wasn't over. If you made it through the stone barricades, you'd find yourself in your opponents' territory, which meant you'd be faced with two options: sneak your way to the flag . . . or fight.

Around them, Demiens poured in. They scattered, moving in throngs, breaking off into designated groups within the quadrant. Some charged forward, hungry for battle, while others stayed strategically near the entrance, forming a human shield in front of the silver flag that billowed only a few feet in front of Wren.

It didn't take long for the chaos to begin.

In the distance, among the maze of stone barricades, a muffled chorus of shouts rang out, the sharp *clang* of steel against steel.

And then came the cloud of magic.

It was stifling, suffocating. A nauseating scent that made Wren's stomach recoil.

It was an overwhelming mixture. Like smoke rising from charred remains. Like the iron scent of blood. But there was a warmer base layer too, something oddly comforting, like the smell of rainfall in the woods, like damp earth and moss.

Shadow magic.

"We're moving forward," said Quinn, appearing in front of Wren. "Okay?"

Wren nodded and wedged herself between Quinn and Arthur.

They pushed their way into the maze of stone barricades. As they pressed forward, sweat prickled at Wren's brow, her palms itching for her magic, desperate for a way to properly defend herself.

"Where are we going?" she asked warily.

Quinn didn't bother glancing back as she spoke. "To get the flag."

"That's it?" Wren hissed. "That's your big plan?"

"I'm sorry, I don't remember asking for your opinion," Quinn sneered.

"We already have a designated group guarding our own flag," whispered Arthur. "Our main objective is to push forward. To get as close to our opponents' flag as possible."

"But shouldn't we have a strategy?" Wren asked. "Some sort of plan if shit hits the fan?"

Quinn twirled the scythes in her hands and a burst of flames erupted from the blades.

"I *am* the plan."

"Look." Arthur leaned in closer to Wren. "The faster we get that flag, the faster we can get the hell out of this—" He stopped short. Quinn too stood frozen, shoulders rigid as she stared at something up ahead.

Wren nearly crashed into her, taken aback by the sudden pause. "What is it? Why did we stop?"

And that was when she saw what had caught their attention.

Three figures stood in front of them, blocking their path . . . and all three were from Onyx Unit.

The fight broke out instantly.

Quinn slid forward, flames bursting from her scythes, and swung at the attacker closest to her. Before Wren could even attempt to join in, Arthur snatched her backward, throwing her away from the chaos, and charged into battle.

It all happened too fast.

Quinn stumbled out of view, a violent frenzy of steel and magic, disappearing deeper within the cavern as she chased after her opponent. Arthur was caught in his own battle—holding back his attacker with a swirling mass of shadows, gritting his teeth as the partition between them wavered.

But there was still one more fighter from Onyx Unit.

The boy had sharp green eyes, which were currently zeroed in on Wren. When he blinked, shadows swirled behind them, a wicked grin revealing white teeth. He licked his lips in anticipation, head cocked.

"Must be my lucky day."

Arthur's eyes flitted toward Wren. He said nothing, but the message was clear.

Run.

Wren turned and sprinted forward, straight into the heart of the cavern, deeper through the maze of barricades. The stone walls divided her path in various formations, forcing her to turn left and right. She gripped the saber tightly, silently praying she wouldn't go barreling into someone from Onyx.

Which, unfortunately for her, was exactly what happened.

She slammed into another body, nearly colliding to the ground. She looked up and— *No.*

"Miss me?"

Somehow, the same green-eyed boy had found her. Wren's gaze darted to the midnight-black pin clipped on the lapel of his jacket and then back up to meet his venomous stare. He looked *hungry*. Practically ravenous. She staggered backward, tripping on her heels.

"You can't hurt me."

The boy chuckled. He lifted his hand, twirling a bundle of shadows in his palm. In the other, he unveiled a dagger with a serrated blade.

"Why? Because you're our precious catalyst?" He tutted, shaking his head. "No, my dear. You're not our catalyst. Not *yet.* For now . . . you're simply a plaything. A little toy to keep me company."

Wren brandished her weapon. "If Edith finds out . . . she'll destroy you."

The boy's face lit up at the idea. "Then I suppose it'll just have to be our little secret, won't it?"

Wren barely had time to react.

The shadows sprang from his palm without warning, barreling toward Wren. But magic or no magic, Wren was still fast, and she ducked out of the way at the last second, turning on her heel as she darted left and through the maze of stone walls. Behind her, the boy cackled, chasing after her.

He was catching up. His manic laughter grew louder, his footsteps echoing closer and closer. Wren just needed to keep moving, keep moving, *keep—*

One second she was running, and the next there was a hand clamped over her mouth, hard muscles pressed upon her back, warm breath caressing the slope of her ear. Wren writhed, a muffled scream tearing at her throat, but strong arms held her steady in a vise grip. She couldn't see her attacker, but the moment their hand slipped over her mouth, Wren was overcome with a sudden tightness in her chest, a dangerous *pull.*

And then a familiar rasp fluttered behind her, a hoarse whisper. "Don't. Move."

August.

He was holding her against his chest, a cloaking enchantment encasing them in a pale shimmer of blue light. Wren held her breath, panicked. The boy turned the corner, slowly stalking in front of them, searching, his green eyes drifting past them as they remained safely hidden beneath August's cloaking enchantment.

A few seconds later, the boy cursed under his breath, sprinting back the way he'd come. They waited, the two of them shrouded beneath the cloaking enchantment, August's body pressed tightly against Wren's. Once it was clear that the boy wasn't coming back, August dropped his hand and gently pried himself away from her.

"Are you okay?" His voice was rough, his eyes analyzing her face and body with palpable concern. "Are you hurt?"

Wren shook her head. "I'm fine. He just . . ." Wren cleared her throat. "He just scared me. That's all."

A flicker of anger passed over August's face. The muscles in his jaw tightened, breath catching in his throat. Even the shadows running through his veins darkened, as if they had almost expanded in his bloodstream.

When he spoke next, his voice was a lethal blade. "Did he touch you?"

Wren swallowed, shaking her head. "I said I'm fine."

"You need to stay away from Callum," August muttered. "He's stubborn. If he sets his sights on you—"

"I can handle him," Wren interjected.

August scoffed.

"Don't you get it, Loughty?" There was a lilt of frustration in his voice. "You're not on an even playing field anymore. This isn't Blackwood. Demiens . . . they're stronger than you. Even if you had your magic, you wouldn't stand a chance. They can rip out the core of your soul with nothing but a snap of their fingers."

Wren stepped forward.

"So . . . what you're saying is . . . *you* could too." Her words echoed between them, and she didn't miss August's slight flinch. "You could destroy my soul . . . if you wanted to."

August's silver eyes flitted up and down her face. He stepped forward.

"I could."

Wren's breaths quickened as the eye contact between them fused into something charged and heated. Staring into his eyes felt dangerous. She couldn't help but sense the unspoken words threaded through the silence. The hidden meaning that ricocheted in the space between them. But before she could formulate a response, August was stepping even closer, his gaze never once leaving hers.

"But . . ." The word slipped out of him in a hoarse whisper, a slightly breathless quality. "I won't. You know I won't."

Wren couldn't stop her eyes from briefly flicking down to his lips. A heat crept over her neck and onto her cheeks. She fought the urge to blush, but she was helpless to stop it. That was the problem with August. He was the one thing she couldn't control. The one thing that unmoored her.

"I don't know you anymore," Wren whispered.

August tilted his head slightly, his gaze traveling over her face. "Then let me remind you."

Wren wasn't sure if it was the desperation in August's eyes or the pleading strain in his voice, but something about those five words had the last of her restraint snapping. The uncontrollable magnetism between them drawing them closer and closer. But before either of them could decide to do something reckless, another alarm rang out, booming throughout the cavern.

August grimaced as the moment between them fizzled away. He took a rigid step backward, hands flexing by his side.

“What does that alarm mean?” Wren asked once the sound had subsided.

“It’s over,” August explained. “Somebody won.”

A loud chorus of cheers echoed up ahead. The pair followed the sound, walking toward Silver Unit’s side of the cavern. When they got there, they saw a large crowd of Onyx Unit Demiens. They whistled, raucous shouts reverberating within the group as they clapped and cheered.

And standing in the middle of the crowd, dagger twirling in one hand and a black flag tucked within the other, was Callum.

15

EMILIO

Nothing good ever happens in a creepy forest.

Emilio wasn't trying to be a pessimist about the whole thing, but it was difficult not to worry about their impending doom. Maybe it was the eerie trees flanking their path, or maybe it was the impenetrable silence sucking out the air like a vacuum—but whatever it was, Emilio couldn't help but feel . . . off. His skin itched. His stomach churned. And he was certain that if he'd still had a heartbeat, his pulse would have been pounding in his ears, heart thumping against his chest cavity like a wild drum.

Coward, that annoying little voice echoed in the back of his mind.

"Shut up . . ." Emilio mumbled to himself, hand clutching his own wrist like it might run away from him.

"You all right?"

Olivier was peering down at Emilio. How long had he been watching? Emilio flushed, suddenly embarrassed. He *always* felt embarrassed, and Olivier and his stupid dimples weren't helping.

"Just . . ." Emilio's voice trailed away. He shrugged. "You know."

Olivier smiled. His dimples deepened, as if mocking Emilio. "I know."

Emilio shivered, despite the absence of a breeze. He could barely stand the intensity of Olivier's gaze. The unbearable tension radiating between them. Did the others sense it? His flush only deepened at the thought.

It was driving Emilio insane that neither one of them could muster up the courage to act upon their feelings. Emilio didn't blame Olivier—it wasn't like they'd gotten a lot of alone time since being thrust into the world of the Resistance. But their profession of love seemed to perpetually hang between them now, this unspoken *ache* building inside Emilio, and he was certain that if one of them didn't make a change, if one of them didn't close the distance between them, he might just implode.

Emilio sucked in a sharp breath. "Olivier, there's something I need to—"

But his words were drowned out as Catherine came to a sudden halt, calling for the rest of the group to stop. Emilio groaned. *Why do we have the worst timing?* He focused his attention on the front of the group, blinking in confusion when he noticed they were standing at the edge of a clearing, a single tree looming at the center. A willow tree.

Emilio gasped.

The tree from the map.

The willow's twisted trunk was split into dozens of gnarled branches, wispy leaves drooping down like sheets of rain in a storm. Not only was it larger than the surrounding trees of the forest, but it almost appeared older—aged and withered, as if it had been standing there, marking its place, from the beginning of time. Its thick, bulbous roots protruded from the base in haphazard spirals, sprouting from the ground in cresting waves. The strangest part, however, wasn't the ancient tree itself, but what *surrounded* it.

All around the willow stood what appeared to be statues made of bark and vines. Limbs and faces coated in earth and twigs.

Who would have made these? Emilio wondered, approaching the closest one with slow, tentative steps.

"Have you ever seen anything like this?" Masika asked, breaking the piercing silence that had fallen upon the group. She approached another one of the statues—bark and roots fashioned to look like a woman standing with her hand raised to the sky—and gently pressed her fingertips against the statue's cheek.

Catherine shook her head. "Never."

"I don't like this," whispered Dina. The silver-haired girl unsheathed two daggers from the dozen strapped to her thighs. "Something doesn't feel right."

Dina wasn't the only one unmoored by the strange statues. A queasy feeling had erupted in the pit of Emilio's stomach. An unsettling shiver on the back of his neck. Even Benji let out a low whine, burrowing his face into the crook of Emilio's elbow.

Emilio gently brushed his palm against the creature's head. "It's okay, buddy . . ." he whispered, though he hardly believed it himself.

Olivier strode up to one of the statues, squinting in scrutiny.

"Why the hell would someone come all the way out here just to make these?" Olivier asked. "Some weird art project?"

"Better question is . . . if someone *did* make these . . . then who got here before us?" asked Analisa, expression solemn.

"Well. That's not at all ominous," muttered Dina with a snort.

"Does the map indicate where the first clue might be?" asked Olivier.

"No . . . there's just a circle around the willow tree." Catherine unfurled the map, eyes dancing across the page. "It doesn't say anything else."

"Wonderful." Olivier rubbed his face. "Profoundly helpful."

At that same moment, Analisa let out a gasp. The healer's eyes seemed to be focused on the ground; her face was drained of color. Emilio dragged his own eyes down, following her line of sight.

And that's when he noticed the tree root wrapped around Analisa's calf.

It was *moving*. Slowly constricting around her leg like a snake. Panicked, Analisa shot a wave of flames toward the root, but it remained unharmed, as if the fire had been nothing but a light gust of wind.

"What the hell?" Dina choked out, charging toward Analisa. She sliced down on the root with one of her daggers, but the blade simply ricocheted off its surface. At that same moment, another nearby root *jolted* from the ground, wrapping itself around Dina's arm with enough force to knock the dagger out of her hand. Just the way the tree root had latched itself onto Analisa, it began slithering its way around Dina's arm, tightening its grip with every movement.

"Uh . . ." Olivier cleared his throat. "I think we might be in trouble."

Emilio didn't even have time to process what was happening. Without warning, a dozen more roots rose from the ground and launched themselves at the group, taking hold of limbs, until they were all completely trapped where they stood. Both of Emilio's legs had been seized by roots, and a third wrapped tightly around his wrist. He'd accidentally dropped Benji amid the chaos, and now the little creature was pacing back and forth by his feet, anxiously barking at the roots and swatting at them with his paw.

Olivier's panicked eyes flitted to Emilio. His own legs had been completely engulfed by the ravenous roots. They climbed higher and higher at an impressive speed, swallowing his calves and lower thighs. It made it appear as though Olivier's legs were made of plant matter. Almost as if *he* were turning into the roots themselves. Just like . . .

The realization hit Emilio only a second later. "They're not statues," he whispered, voice shaking.

"What?" Dina snapped, furiously attempting to kick her leg away from the tree root that was currently ensnaring her thigh. Another one had coiled itself around her neck, creeping down over her chest.

"They're not statues," Emilio repeated, this time loudly enough for the entire group to hear.

"You mean—" Dina's face fell. The fury in her gaze shifted into panic. "No. *No, no, no.* I am not turning into a freaky tree statue. That is not fucking happening."

"Just stay calm," Catherine snapped. A million thoughts seemed to be reflected in her hazel eyes, emotions coming and going too fast for Emilio to register. "There has to be a way out. Just let me think."

"Why the hell wouldn't there have been anything about this on the map?" Masika stared down at the roots in horror. "Why wouldn't the True Headmaster have warned us?"

Analisa had gone impossibly calm since the tree roots had come to life and trapped them. Her expression remained stoic and serene, not a hint of strain in her muscles. She casually flexed her fingers, observing her situation with detached curiosity.

"I don't sense a natural life-form . . ." the healer whispered softly. "The tree itself isn't alive, despite the intention in its movements. It's almost as though it's doing this against its will. As if someone has programmed it to behave this way."

"I don't give a damn *why* it's doing it, I just need it to *stop*," Dina sneered, scowling down at the roots slithering over her stomach.

At that same moment, a deep rattle echoed a few yards ahead.

A low groan. Emilio's eyes darted in the direction of the noise—*the willow tree.* Something strange was happening to its trunk . . . the edges warping and shifting.

Emilio cocked his head in confusion.

The trunk is moving.

Pieces of bark shifted and fell away, forming what first appeared to be symbols and shapes. Emilio watched in fascination as the jagged shapes slowly morphed into letters, until he could fully understand what was written on the bark.

RUN FROM ME, YET STILL I CLING. THE HEALER OF WOUNDS,
THE SLAYER OF KINGS.
A THIEF, A COLLECTOR, AN ENEMY TO SOME.
THE KEEPER OF THE PAST . . . THE SEER OF WHAT'S TO COME.

"It's a riddle," Catherine remarked, looking around the group. A tree root coiled itself tightly about her waist and she cringed away from it. "That must be the way out. Solving the riddle."

"Any ideas?" asked Analisa with a soft smile.

Dina let out a furious groan and extended her one free arm in front of her. An electrifying jolt of corporeal magic shot out of her arm like a bolt of lightning, bursting against the trunk of the tree.

She dropped her hand, chest heaving.

But the tree remained perfectly intact. Not a blemish to be seen.

Catherine sighed. "Are you done?"

Dina scowled and slumped. "Yes."

As the others continued to bicker about the best way to solve the riddle, Emilio sank into the chaotic void of his own mind. Something about the first part of the riddle stuck out to him. *Run from me, yet still I cling.* And there it was—prickling at the edges of his consciousness. What had they always been running from? What had always continued to chase them, despite how hard they all might have tried to evade it?

The slayer of kings.

The healer of wounds.

Emilio hadn't even meant to whisper the word out loud. It simply tumbled out of him.

"Time."

As soon as the word left his lips, the roots coiling around his body dropped away with a loud thump. They slowly slithered back into the ground, disappearing beneath the dirt. Relief rushing through him, Emilio quickly scooped Benji into his arms. The little creature appeared to be equally relieved, thanking Emilio with a kiss on the nose. But Emilio wasn't the only one who had been freed. The roots trapping Analisa fell away as well.

"Huh . . ." She wiggled her freed hands at the group. "It appears as though we *have* found the way out."

"Well, if that's the case, I suggest we hurry." Olivier gritted his teeth, craning his neck away from the tree root currently attempting to wrap itself around his jaw. "Because I'm afraid we don't have too much time left."

Olivier was right. The roots were doubling in size and speed. His bottom half was completely buried beneath tree roots, and Catherine, Dina and Masika were close behind. If they didn't hurry . . . the ones who remained would be lost to the willow . . . *forever.*

Just as that terrifying thought shot into Emilio's mind, the tree bark began to shift again, revealing the next riddle. This time, Masika read it out loud.

"Reach for me, and I'll hold under strain," she began, her voice echoing throughout the clearing. *"For I fear no phantom, no burden, no pain. Some may forget me, but I'll never stray. For I am your beacon, and here I'll remain."* Silence fell upon the group, the only sound the deep rumble of the roots slowly devouring them.

"*Ugh* . . . I don't know!" Dina let out a throaty groan. Her arms had been tightly pinned to her sides by the roots. "Death? Life? Love?" As the guesses sprang out of her, not only did the tree roots remain coiled around the group, but they suddenly picked up speed, inching faster and faster.

"*Shit—*" Catherine gasped as the roots around her chest doubled in size, completely swallowing her torso.

Masika let out a muffled gasp. "Stop, Dina! It gets worse if you guess incorrectly. We have to be strategic."

"We don't have time to be strategic!" Dina bellowed, terror etched on her features as one of the branches began to slither toward her mouth. "We're not going to make it. We're not going to *fucking—*"

"Wait," whispered Emilio, so softly that the group didn't hear him. Except for Olivier, of course. His green eyes flitted to Emilio instantly. The other boy was always aware of his presence, listening intently.

"What is it?" Olivier whispered back. Though his own body was almost completely engulfed by the roots, his eyes softened the moment he looked at Emilio.

"Some may forget me, but I'll never stray . . ." Emilio's voice was a thready whisper as he met Olivier's gaze. *". . . For I am your beacon, and here I'll remain."*

"You know it," Olivier said. It wasn't a question. His mouth lifted into a soft smile.

Dina let out a furious groan of impatience. "Spit it out, for the love of God!"

Emilio kept his eyes anchored on Olivier as the answer slipped out of him.

"It's *hope*."

And just like that, the tree roots dropped away from Dina and Catherine, freeing them from the willow's clutches. Dina let out a sigh of relief as she scooped up her daggers, peppering kisses up and down the blades. Catherine stretched her neck, wincing. A red welt had blossomed on her neck, though Emilio could see the edges already beginning to heal with every passing second. Despite the flicker of relief at seeing two more members of their group freed, a terrible panic burst through Emilio's chest.

Olivier and Masika.

Not only were the pair still trapped, but the roots had completely swallowed their bodies, only their heads left exposed. Of the two of them, Olivier's condition was worse. One of the roots had already begun to snake over his mouth, making its way higher and higher.

"Shit . . ." Catherine whispered, gaze locked on Masika. Emilio had never seen the girl look so panicked. Her fingers nervously drummed at her sides, as if she was itching to pounce on the tree roots and rip them apart with nothing but her hands. And she probably would have by now, had Dina not already proven that physical attacks against the roots were useless. "We—we need to hurry. I don't think they have a lot of time."

Luckily, the trunk immediately began to shift again, revealing the third, and what Emilio hoped was the final, riddle. He read it out loud, tumbling over every word as he hurried through the riddle.

"I am love's second hand, what follows in its wake. Faded by time, but still, I take. When everything's gone, I'm all you have left—I am the price you must pay, even in death." His mind raced as he scrambled to find the answers.

I am the price you must pay, even in death.

Of course, death had a price. Loss. Pain. Loneliness. Suffering.

But none of those was right. Emilio knew they weren't. And he also knew that if he guessed incorrectly, if the wrong word was spoken out loud . . . then he might lose Olivier and Masika forever.

But there was something about the first part of the riddle that stuck with him.

I am love's second hand, what follows in its wake.

Love's second hand.

And then he saw it. The answer rising inside him like a beacon of light.

"Grief."

He didn't hesitate as he spoke the word. He knew it was the answer. People always saw grief as a terrible, burdensome thing. The lingering darkness preceding death. But Emilio had grown to understand that grief was so much more than that. Grief was the enduring ache of love. Its agonizing reminder. Grief *was* love. It was what tethered them to those they had loved and lost—even in eternity.

Instantly, the roots devouring Masika fell away. She coughed, sputtering, breathing air back into her lungs. Emilio scrambled toward her, wrapping her in his arms, a choked laugh tumbling out of him as he pressed his hand against the back of her head. She was okay. She had made it. And Olivier—

Masika gasped, pulling Emilio's focus. She was staring at something behind Emilio.

Someone.

Emilio spun on his heels . . . and then his entire world came crumbling down around him.

Because Olivier hadn't been freed. He hadn't been saved.

Emilio had solved the riddle, but the tree roots surrounding Olivier hadn't relented. And not only had they remained, but they'd *grown.* In a frenzied panic, Emilio shoved Benji into Masika's arms and scrambled toward Olivier. He brushed a strand of blond hair from the other boy's face. His eyes, *his beautiful green eyes,* were the only thing left of him. The roots were devouring him. Swallowing him completely.

"I don't understand," Dina whispered. Despite her usual bravado, even *she* sounded taken aback, her voice wavering. "He solved the riddle. Shouldn't they *both* have been freed?"

Analisa placed her hands upon her heart. Her bottom lip trembled. "I sense an end."

"No—" Emilio choked out, pointing an accusatory finger toward the healer. "*Don't.* Don't you fucking dare start spouting that nonsense—not about him." He turned his attention back to Olivier, hands cupping what he could of the other boy's face. "Please, Olivier. Not now. Not like this." Panic surged in his chest. He leaned in closer, pressing his forehead against Olivier's with delicate care. "Please, my love. Come back to me. *Come back to me.*"

But still . . . nothing happened. And when Emilio pulled away, staring up at Olivier, he didn't see fear reflected in the other boy's eyes. He didn't see terror or panic or pain.

All he saw was *love.* Heart-wrenching, tender adoration.

Footsteps sounded behind him.

It was Masika. She placed a trembling hand on Emilio's shoulder. "Emilio . . ."

"No." Emilio shook his head. This couldn't be it. This couldn't be their end.

"I don't think . . ." Masika's voice cracked. She reached her other hand toward Olivier's shoulder—her palm pressed against the roots. "I think we might be too—"

But just as the words left her lips . . . the floor rumbled. The tree groaned. And then, as if listening to an unspoken command, the roots dropped from Olivier, collapsing onto the ground with a resounding thump.

Olivier fell to his knees, gasping in a strangled breath. Emilio reached out, grabbing the other boy in his arms, holding him steady. A broken cry escaped Emilio's throat as he cupped Olivier's face delicately in his hands.

"It's okay," he whispered, drawing him closer. "I have you."

Olivier glanced up at him. Tears welled behind his eyes. "My love."

Emilio cocked his head. "What?"

"You called me *my love* . . ." Olivier chuckled, and the sound was the most beautiful thing Emilio had ever heard. "That's my line."

"Olivier Dupont." Emilio bit back his own smile. "Are you *seriously* flirting with me at a time like this?"

Olivier shrugged. "I find that it's *always* a good time to flirt."

Someone cleared their throat.

Emilio glanced to his left to find Masika standing there, smiling, Benji cradled in her arms, with the rest of the group right behind her, staring.

"Oh." Olivier smiled innocently up at the group. "Hello there."

"If you two are done with whatever *this* is," Dina muttered, gesturing toward them with a wave of her hand, "I suggest we keep moving. It looks like we've come through the worst of it, though I'm not hoping to stick around to find out."

"Yeah." Emilio cleared his throat. His cheeks burned. "That's—uh—that's a good idea."

"Hold on." Catherine tightened her grip on the map clutched in her hands. "We can't just leave. It says the first clue is *here.* The willow tree marks the spot where the True Headmaster wanted us to go."

"Yeah, okay, but the willow tree almost just turned us into tree statues for the rest of eternity," Dina snapped back. "I'm starting to think that maybe this *True Headmaster* didn't want his soul to be found."

"It's not that . . ." Analisa whispered. She approached the willow, head tilted. "He *wants* to be found . . . but by the *right* soul."

"What the hell is she on about?" Olivier muttered into Emilio's ear. Emilio tried to pretend the gentle brush of Olivier's breath didn't send a tendril of want up and around his stomach.

He cleared his throat. "Not sure."

Analisa pressed her hand against the willow's trunk.

"It wasn't an attack," she said, turning to face the group. "It was a test. And we passed."

As soon as the words left her lips, the trunk came to life. Analisa took a cautious step away as the willow tree warped and moved, thick chunks of bark falling away, until a gaping hole had formed at the center of the trunk, a perfectly arched compartment. But there was something *inside* the compartment. Something floating inside the heart of the willow.

"Is that . . ." Dina's voice trailed off.

Catherine stepped closer. She reached inside the tree, revealing what lay inside.

A key.

Made of what appeared to be rusted iron, the key burned with a deep emerald-green glow, as if imbued with magic. But something was attached to it, a small note tied with a green ribbon.

"The keys are the answer," whispered Masika, echoing the words etched on the map.

"Well . . ." Dina chuckled, slapping Analisa on the shoulder. "Looks like we found our first key."

Catherine untied the note with shaking hands. She opened it, gently unfolding the weathered old parchment. It didn't take long for Emilio to realize what it was.

Another map.

Catherine's eyes burned with newfound determination as she looked up at the group.

"And our next clue."

16

IRENE

As late afternoon enveloped Blackwood in swirling plumes of fog, the darkening sky painting the grounds in a dusty purple haze, Irene found herself in the Main Yard, tumbling the same question over and over in her mind. No matter how hard she tried to eradicate the question from her consciousness, it remained, latching onto her, demanding an answer.

What the hell is wrong with you?

Irene pressed her head against the stone statue behind her, groaning in frustration. She fussed with the golden ring wrapped snugly around her index finger, spinning it over and over in even circles. She had tried taking it off numerous times since it had first appeared the morning she had taken her place among the Ascended, but whatever magic it was forged with kept it securely fashioned around her finger. That ring was a part of her now . . . forever. Whether she wanted it to be or not.

"Did you miss me?"

Irene yelped in surprise, spinning to find Mateo crouched behind her, a twinkle of amusement in his sparkling blue eyes. But her annoyance was quickly replaced by a surge of panic. If someone saw them . . . if someone saw *him*—

"Relax," Mateo muttered, as if reading her thoughts. "Nobody can see me."

"You don't know that," Irene whispered through gritted teeth. She glanced nervously over her shoulder, half expecting to find someone watching them, but most of Blackwood's students were still in class, and there didn't appear to be any Ascended near the Main Yard. There was nothing but empty benches and burnt-sienna leaves scattered around them. The gentle creak of barren branches swaying in the breeze. In the distance, a few students scurried toward their dormitories, textbooks tucked under their arms and heads lowered. But nobody seemed to notice her.

Or, if they did, they were simply too scared of her to look for more than a few seconds.

"Trust me." Mateo chuckled, leaning back against the stone statue. He stretched his long legs in front of him, twisting a blade of grass between his fingers. His shoulder brushed against Irene's as he settled beside her. "My cloaking enchantments are impenetrable. Nobody is getting through them."

"Not even Silas?" Irene challenged.

Mateo's haughty smirk faltered slightly, though he quickly recovered, eyes sliding toward Irene. "*Especially* Silas."

Irene scoffed. "Your ego will be your downfall."

Mateo shrugged, as if he found her comment more amusing than offensive. As a comfortable silence fell upon them, Irene sensed Mateo's gaze landing on her. There was something about the way he looked at her that made her feel inexplicably naked—as if he were reaching into the innermost parts of her with nothing but a single look.

"I'm sorry I didn't tell you earlier," he whispered suddenly. "About Wren. I needed to be sure you were on our side before I told you."

Irene had assumed he'd bring it up eventually, but the reminder of Wren's involvement in the Demien Order's prophecy still sent a chill down her spine.

"It just doesn't make any sense," she whispered. "You don't know Wren Loughty like I do. She's annoyingly smart and has more talent in her pinky finger than most could hope for in their lifetime, but . . . she's not a Demien. And she most certainly isn't capable of ushering in the destruction of Blackwood."

Mateo's voice was uncharacteristically somber when he spoke next.

"But she will be."

"What does that mean?" Irene asked with a frustrated groan. When Mateo didn't respond right away, she let out a bitter chuckle and added, "Let me guess. It's confidential?"

"It's *complicated*," Mateo corrected with an apologetic smile. As his blue eyes flitted up and down her face, something in his expression changed. "Is everything all right? You seem a bit . . . off."

Irene flinched at the sudden shift in topic. It was almost as if he could sense her thoughts before she had even thought of them. Pick up on her emotions before they had even materialized in her mind.

"I had my first Council test today," Irene replied softly, swallowing. The mere thought of the dungeons was enough to send a wave of nausea up her throat. The stench of blood seemed to follow her everywhere. The howling cries of agony burned into her memory.

Mateo's face hardened. "Ah. I had assumed Everly and Samira's presence this morning had something to do with that."

A gentle breeze drifted between them.

"Did you know about the dungeons?" Irene asked, though a part of her was afraid to know the answer.

A thin rivulet of shadows momentarily flickered beneath the skin of Mateo's exposed forearms. He rarely let the shadows slip out of him anymore—it was clear to Irene that he made an effort to hold them back in front of her. To appear as *normal* as he could. So Irene did her best not to flinch at the sudden reminder of the darkness inside him.

"I've heard of them," Mateo replied, voice hoarse.

Irene tore her gaze away from him, looking out toward the oak trees lining the path to the Main Yard. She watched the gnarled branches shift and move, the crawling vines shiver in the late-afternoon glow.

"I thought Demiens were supposed to be the cruel ones," she whispered. "The ones who had lost their emotions—"

"Some of us have," Mateo interjected. "*Most* of us have."

"Well . . ." Irene let out a bitter chuckle. "It turns out Blackwood and the Demien Order aren't so different after all."

As the words left her lips, Mateo's expression abruptly darkened. He winced, clutching his head, as if a sudden pain had blossomed in his skull. Irene instinctively reached out and placed a hand on his shoulder.

"What is it?" she asked. "Are you all right?"

When Mateo's eyes landed on hers, Irene couldn't stop the gasp that sprang out of her.

Shadows.

His eyes were entirely blotted out by shadows, as if completely submerged in swirling pools of ink. Mateo shut his eyes, grimacing. When his eyelids fluttered back open, the whites of his eyes had returned to normal.

There you are, Irene thought with a sigh of relief. But what she actually managed to say out loud was "What the hell was that?"

"Nothing." Mateo cleared his throat, awkwardly shifting onto his feet. "I just . . . I received a communication from the Order's base. I'm sorry. I have to go."

Irene wanted to pry. She wanted to demand answers. But staring up at Mateo, his face haloed by the approaching silver glow of night, she knew that her interrogation would be pointless. That she would remain unfairly tethered to the sidelines until she proved to the Demien Order that she was *truly* one of them.

"Off on another mysterious excursion that you'll tell me nothing about?" she asked with a teasing lilt.

Mateo's lips lifted into a rueful smile. "Something like that."

And then he vanished, disappearing into the night before Irene could get another word out. There was no puff of smoke. No remnant of a relocation spell. It was simply as if he had blinked out of existence—one moment there, and the next . . . gone.

Irene sat in the Main Yard for a few more minutes, ruminating on her conversation with Mateo. As evening settled upon Blackwood in a shimmering blanket of silver light and feathered clouds of fog, she decided it was time to make her way back to the Ascended Quarters. But as she stood and began walking onto the main path, a sudden noise caused her to stagger to a halt.

A voice.

A deep, familiar voice.

"Apologies for the intrusion."

A strange whirling sensation clutched her skull, a terrible sense of vertigo.

And then it was as though the ground beneath her had slipped away, the world of Blackwood Academy swallowed by darkness. She was falling, plummeting into nothingness, descending deeper and deeper, until—

Irene's eyes snapped open with a gurgled gasp. She was standing in a clearing. A sickening trace of nausea curled around her throat as she gathered her bearings, eyes trailing the dense forest surrounding the perimeter of the clearing.

And standing before her, a coy smile on his face, was Headmaster Silas.

Panic surged through Irene.

He knows.

He knows about Mateo.

Silas stalked forward, rotten yellow leaves crunching beneath his boots. "Hello, Irene."

Irene managed a nonchalant sigh, trying her best to keep her composure. "You couldn't just have called me into your office like a normal person, could you?"

Silas smirked, the thin lines beneath his eyes deepening. *Does he look older?* It wasn't possible, since none of them aged that way in the afterlife, and yet . . . something about him seemed different. It had always been impossible to pinpoint how old the Headmaster of Blackwood Academy was. He looked like he was in his mid-thirties, give or take a few years, with dark, gray-speckled hair and sharp features. But Irene *swore* his appearance had changed. He looked tired. The lines between his brows more marked. But maybe it was simply that she hadn't properly looked at him this way until she'd become an Ascended. Now . . . she saw him. *Truly* saw him.

"Oh . . . but where's the fun in that?" Silas asked with a smirk.

Irene suppressed the urge to throttle him, squeezing her hands into tight fists.

"How can I help you, *Headmaster*?" She made sure to carefully enunciate the formal title. If Silas noticed her subtle jab, he didn't show it. He simply kept his stoic gaze on her, unnervingly still.

"I know this hasn't been easy for you . . ." he said. "Joining the Ascended after what happened to your friends."

Irene stiffened. She hadn't been expecting that. *Is that what he called me here for?*

Her chest tightened at the unwelcome memories attempting to break free. "They . . . they weren't my friends."

"Ah. Right." Silas shifted closer. "What was it that Mr. Dupont had called you all . . . *unfortunate acquaintances,* was it?"

Irene winced at the mere mention of the other nominees. Ever since the conclusion of the final trial, she had done everything in her power to push them out of her mind, to eradicate them from her memory. And either way—what did it matter to her? They had been a nuisance. A terrible affliction. Olivier and his infuriating ego. Wren and her self-righteous philosophy. August and his pathetic yearning. Emilio and his annoying insecurities. Masika and her irritating loyalty. So why should she care? Why should she miss them?

Irene shivered as a crisp breeze blanketed her arms in goose bumps. "Can we just cut to the chase?"

Silas's mouth twitched, the ghost of a smile tugging at his lips. "Very well." He slowly slipped the glove off his right hand, flexing his exposed fingers. Wrapped around his index finger was a ring similar to the one worn by the Ascended, though the golden band was thicker, deep grooves etched upon its surface that burned with a glowing light.

Huh.

Irene had never seen it before.

"Have you ever wondered how far you could stretch the limits of your magic? How deep the well goes?"

Silas raised his hand, and it was as if he had bent the very particles of the air around him, a swirling palette of hazy color dancing beneath his fingertips. He flicked his wrist and the forest around them blurred, shapes and colors moving too quickly for Irene's eyes to process. It was like staring out the window of a speeding train, an indecipherable cloud of color rushing by them.

And then Silas snapped his fingers and the world around them stilled. But they were no longer in the forest.

In fact, from what Irene could gather, they were no longer in purgatory at all.

They were standing in the middle of a park, bathed in the shadow of a willow tree, a glassy lake stretched before them. Leaves rustled in the wind—deep umber, yellow and crisp apple red. An autumnal palette washed in the orange light of sunset. And up ahead, just beyond where they stood, were . . . *people.* Couples and families lounging on picnic blankets. Joggers running around the edge of the lake. Students congregating in the shade.

Silas lifted his hand, tracing the edge of a willow leaf with his fingertips. "Look familiar?"

"Are we—" Irene broke off, her mind struggling to piece together what she was seeing.

Silas stepped forward, gesturing to the park. "Boston," he said. "The Public Garden, to be precise. You liked walking here, didn't you?"

Somewhere in the distance, a chime of laughter rang out, drifting with the wind. Irene couldn't move. Hot tears prickled behind her eyes, chest heaving as she struggled to choke back a sob.

"Is this . . . is this an illusion?" she asked, voice wavering. "We can't . . . we can't *actually* be in Boston."

Silas turned to look at her, eyes burning with something fierce and wild. "What *can* and *can't* be no longer matters, Ms. Bamford. Not when you're with me."

Irene gently lowered herself to the ground, kneeling upon the cool grass. It all felt so *real.* The thin blades of grass slipping between her fingers. The warmth of the sun whispering upon her skin.

"How?" she managed to choke out.

Silas stepped closer. "I've allowed us a temporary visit, if you will."

Irene closed her eyes, angling her face toward the sky. She hadn't realized how much she'd missed the warmth of the sun, how much she'd craved the soft caress of the wind against her skin. Her humanity, long dormant, rose within her, a starved plant reaching for a sliver of sunlight.

Her eyelids fluttered open. The clear water of the pond rippled in the wind. "I never thought I'd see this world again."

Silas hummed. "Did you miss it?"

Irene shivered. "I didn't think I did."

Silas knelt next to her. When he looked at Irene, his eyes had taken on an unfamiliar warmth, a softness. The wickedness in his gaze was gone. The ancient power radiating from his soul had faded.

He looked . . . *human*. Nothing more than a broken man.

"Death doesn't have to be the end for you." Silas reached into the pocket of his waistcoat, searching for something. When he removed his hand, a small golden pocket mirror was nestled in his palm. "This . . . this is just the beginning. A mere taste of what I can offer you. What I can *teach* you."

He opened the pocket mirror and aimed it toward the park, letting it linger there for a moment. A cardinal zipped by, temporarily blotting out the sun. A couple shared a brief kiss by the lake, hands intertwined. A sharp breeze sent a flutter of leaves tumbling by their feet. When Silas angled the mirror back toward Irene, that exact moment replayed over and over within its surface—

the cardinal, the couple, the ruffle of leaves—as though Silas had somehow captured and recorded the moment within the pocket mirror.

"For you," he whispered, gently closing the mirror and placing it in her hand. "Just point it toward the moment you wish to capture and it will be there . . . waiting for you."

Irene shook her head. "I don't understand . . . why are you doing this?"

Silas swallowed, looking out toward the lake. When he smiled, there was an unmistakable sadness behind it.

"I know what you must think of me," he began, his voice low. "That I'm a monster. A tyrant. And . . . perhaps you're right. But I make necessary sacrifices in order to preserve *this*. I was not handed this power—I *claimed* it." He peeled his eyes away from the lake, lowering his gaze toward Irene. "You can understand that . . . can't you, Irene? The desire to fight against your fate. To take what should rightfully be yours."

Irene shivered. *More than you know*, she wanted to whisper back. Her entire life had felt like an unstoppable current she'd been unable to escape. Her mother had made sure of that. Even in death, Irene had been forced to wrestle against the hand of fate, to swim against the vicious tide that threatened to pull her under. And now . . . now she was torn. Split in two. Forced to reckon with two sides that wished to claim her. Mateo offered her freedom—a path to vengeance. With the Demien Order, Irene could rip apart the hand of fate and seize her power. Wasn't it Silas's fault, after all? Wasn't he the one who put them in that godforsaken competition in the first place? The one who lied to them? Who forced Irene to stand back and watch innocent souls perish under the Ether's greed? He was the ringmaster . . . the orchestrator of it all.

And yet . . .

Something inside her faltered. A hesitance. A sickening doubt.

Silas placed his hand upon her shoulder. If he noticed the war being waged inside her, he didn't show it.

"Where to next?" he asked.

Irene closed her palm around the pocket mirror. "Where can we go?"

Silas smiled.

"Anywhere."

17

AUGUST

You idiot.

August stumbled back into his tent, cursing under his breath. He ripped his black cloak off his shoulders and tossed it onto the floor, frantically undoing the first few buttons on his shirt, fingers trembling as he struggled to keep his hands steady. He felt suffocated, like the air around him had begun to solidify, clogging his lungs. He'd squandered yet another opportunity to be alone with Wren. Why did he always say the wrong thing? Why did he always have to ruin *everything*?

August loosened the collar of his shirt, stretching the muscles of his neck.

His eyes drifted toward the full-length mirror in the corner of his tent, involuntarily flinching at what he saw reflected at him. Despite the emotional exhaustion wreaking havoc on his body, he looked . . . strong. As if the shadows swimming beneath his veins had gifted him with a renewed sense of life.

August reached a shaking hand to the collar of his shirt, tugging down, exposing the hard planes of his chest and the shadows that swam beneath. They flowed through his tanned skin in thick streams, twisting up and down as though following an invisible current. He'd had to use more shadow magic than he wanted to during the battle simulation—not to mention the practice duels he'd been forced to participate in afterward. Onyx Unit was proving to be as ruthless and cruel as he had anticipated.

He had to be careful.

If he used too much, he might begin to lose himself even before Equinox.

"You all right there, Augustine?"

As soon as the voice rang out behind him, shadows burst from August's fingertips, ready for a fight. He hadn't even meant to call on them. It was as if they had simply taken over, spurred on by the rise in his emotions. But the person standing behind August didn't look ready for battle. In fact, they looked far from it.

Callum Whitlock exuded lazy arrogance. As he leaned against the tent wall, eyes snaking up and down August's face, his thin lips curled into a crooked smirk. He seemed quite pleased with himself—getting the upper hand over August wasn't easy, and he must have known that, given the smug look on his face.

August snuffed his shadows, though he felt them retaliate inside him.

No, no, no, they seemed to whisper to him. ***Use us, use us, use us.***

"It's General Hughes to you."

"Right." Callum offered a mocking salute. "General Hughes. Of course." He tapped his chin, feigning innocence. "Though . . . I'm not so sure that title is accurate anymore. You know, given the fact that you betrayed your own sister and then came crawling back asking for her forgiveness."

August wasn't in the mood for this. Whatever *this* was. Even though he had spent his time in purgatory safely behind the walls of Blackwood Academy, he had corresponded with Edith and other Demien Order recruits throughout the years. And it hadn't taken long to hear of Callum's infamous reputation.

Callum Whitlock was bloodthirsty and desperate for praise—a dangerous combination.

"What do you want?" August bit out.

"Our catalyst was in the battle simulation." Callum spoke through a calculated smile. "Though I'm sure you knew that already."

August ground his teeth together and prayed he'd have the strength not to rip Callum's soul right out of his chest.

"What's your point?"

Callum looked up, eyes beaming. He was loving this. The tension in the air. The back-and-forth. Honestly, it wouldn't surprise August if Callum got off on it. Some people were drawn to confrontation, in more ways than one, but Callum seemed to crave it.

The other boy pushed himself away from the tent wall, slinking closer to August.

"You know how sound travels in the battle simulation cavern . . . echoes?" He whispered the last word, a conspiratorial glint in his eyes. "At one point, when I was looking for our little catalyst, I *swore* I heard you two talking together."

Shit.

August kept his composure, though the muscles along his neck involuntarily twitched.

"You heard wrong," he muttered casually.

But Callum continued to edge closer, that infuriating teasing glint in his eyes, as though he was savoring every second of discomfort.

"It's funny," he chuckled, rubbing the side of his jaw. "It almost sounded like you were helping her. Or trying to protect her." Callum shook his head, sucking his teeth. "But . . . that would be terribly strange, wouldn't it?"

August didn't take the bait. He knew what Callum wanted—he

was provoking him. But if August's façade was going to waver under anyone's questioning, it wasn't going to be Callum's.

"I'm assuming there's an end to this rambling?" August asked.

Callum came to a halt in front of him.

"I suppose I'm just wondering why you wouldn't eliminate her?" He cocked his head innocently. "She wasn't on our side. She was our competition." Callum tapped his finger against his chin, mouth twisting into a grin. "Unless, of course . . . your feelings for her might have gotten in the way—"

"I don't know what you think you heard," August said, seething, his patience snapping. "But you're sorely mistaken. And if you want to keep that tongue of yours, I'd recommend silencing it before I do everyone a favor and carve it out of your mouth."

"You're awfully defensive, General Hughes." Callum's eyes narrowed, the teasing spark hardening into something far more sinister. "If I didn't know any better, I'd assume you still cared for the girl."

Callum was treading a dangerous line. This was a power play. A desperate attempt at elevating his rank. And August knew what he had to do to end it . . . and to ensure that it would never happen again.

"Listen to me very carefully," August began. "I don't think—" But Callum cut in.

"I mean, I'm not saying I blame you." He chuckled, hand splayed over his chest. "Our little catalyst is a vision. That face . . . and that *body*." He whistled, shaking his head. "I can understand why your loyalty might have . . . wavered." Callum took a step closer. Too close. The next words he spoke were whispered through a sickening grin. "I would have probably betrayed us, too, for the chance to screw her."

August didn't even remember calling upon his shadows. Perhaps he didn't. Perhaps they simply felt his rage and knew what he wanted—what he *needed*. And then two tendrils of shadows were shooting out of him, twisting around Callum's throat, constricting it so tightly that the boy's face was bleached white.

But the shadows weren't done . . . and neither was August.

He flexed his fingers and one of the shadows slithered into Callum's mouth, snaking down his throat, choking him. The other boy tried to rip the shadows away, but August wouldn't let him go that easily. He flicked another set of shadows toward Callum, twining them around his wrists, binding them together.

Callum tried to speak, but his words were muffled. He gagged, retching as he tried to break free, but August only twisted tighter, digging deeper. The power hummed in his veins. An intoxicating feeling that seemed to envelop every inch of his soul. ***Yes, yes, yes,*** the shadows cried. ***More, more, more.*** He hated how good it felt—but *God*, it felt good. It was a power he'd never even known was possible.

August curled his fingers closed and the shadows darkened, shifting from wispy gray to midnight black, trailing down to the floor in a thick current of fog.

He was using too much. He *knew* he was. The rational part of his brain echoed in the background, begging him to stop, that it was enough, but it just felt so damn *good* to watch Callum writhe and squirm under his power.

August stepped forward and gripped Callum's face tightly between his hands, pinching so hard that his fingernails dug into Callum's cheeks, crimson beads of blood dripping from the crescent-moon indents he was leaving behind.

"Listen to me very carefully, Private Whitlock." August barely recognized his own voice, dark and wrong, distorted by the power running through his veins. "I am not someone you want to mess with. Not anymore. The silly boy who clung to his humanity and kept himself hidden away in Blackwood is gone. My sister is cruel, but even she has her limits." August brought his mouth to Callum's ear, unable to stop a smirk from creeping onto his lips as he whispered the next words: "I, however, have none."

Callum coughed, sputtering, eyes rolling back into his head.

"If you ever mention this again—if you ever even *utter* her name in my presence—I will slither my shadows into your soul and tear your bones out, one by one." August's shadows vibrated as the promise left his lips. "You will be unable to speak. Unable to move. And every time your body heals itself, my shadows will resume their duty, deteriorating your insides over and over for the rest of your useless eternity. You will know nothing but the feeling of my shadows coursing through your veins. For once"—August wrenched Callum's head back, forcing the boy's wide, panicked eyes onto his face—"you will know what real agony feels like."

With that, August stepped back, his shadows retreating with him. Callum choked in a rasped breath, clawing at his throat, coughing until the air moved through his lungs. But when Callum glanced back up at August, hands pressed against his knees, it wasn't fear August saw etched upon the boy's face. It wasn't terror. It was something else . . . something far more concerning.

Callum Whitlock looked up at August . . . and *smiled*.

"Well, General Hughes. You've certainly surprised me," he muttered, sauntering back toward the entrance to the tent. He kept his hands shoved in his pockets, eyes locked on August the entire time. "Who knows . . . you might prove to be useful after all."

And then he was gone, waltzing out of the tent without a backward glance, and August was left with the terrible feeling that somehow, despite everything, Callum had gotten exactly what he wanted.

18

MASIKA

Sleep was an elusive beast. It lingered in the periphery of Masika's mind, taunting her with the promise of rest. If she could sleep, she could silence her thoughts, if only for a brief moment. She could slip away from anxiety's pointed claws, hiding from the interminable doubt that plagued her nearly every waking moment. And it wasn't like she hadn't tried—she had. She'd closed her eyes and willed her mind to stop, desperately attempting to convince her body to succumb to the darkness . . . but she couldn't.

She felt too restless.

Too shaken.

It had grown worse since they'd settled for the night, camping just beyond the willow tree. They'd collectively decided to resume their trek toward the next clue the following morning, allowing for the initial shock of the day's events to wear off. It appeared the new map would lead them farther east, snaking a path through the forest, stopping at a strange outcropping marked by what seemed to be a small building.

Masika winced as she recalled the way the tree roots had wrapped themselves around her neck, squeezing the air out of her lungs. The whole thing had left her feeling off-kilter. Not to mention the fact that they'd nearly lost Olivier. She still wasn't sure how he'd managed to get free of the roots. Maybe it had simply been a delayed reaction after the final riddle. But Masika had *sworn* she'd felt something when she'd placed her hand on Olivier's shoulder. A strange jolt. A current.

It was probably nothing.

Just her imagination playing tricks on her.

Now Masika shifted beneath her flimsy blanket, desperate to get comfortable. The ground was hard and uneven, bits of earth digging into her spine. The starless sky provided no light, just a vast blanket of darkness, an empty void. Before retiring, Catherine had lit a small fire, which currently illuminated the slumbering crew in a wispy orange glow.

Emilio and Olivier were curled in toward one another, knuckles brushing, their chests rising and falling in almost perfect synchronization. Next to them, Dina slept with her hands still wrapped around her daggers and Benji cuddled up on her stomach. The healer slept beside her, the ghost of a smile on her lips.

And then there was Catherine.

She was sleeping far away enough that Masika couldn't touch her, but close enough that she could see the details of Catherine's face in the warm haze of the campfire. Her tawny hair, which she usually fashioned into an array of intricate braids, had come undone throughout the day. Now, a few loose strands brushed the delicate skin of her temples, with one particular tendril resting against her lips. Masika resisted the urge to scoot close enough to tuck the loose strand of hair behind Catherine's ear. It was a gesture she normally wouldn't have hesitated to make. But that was before. And now . . . now the mere thought of touching Catherine filled Masika with dizzying fear.

But still, those old memories clung to her, unwilling to let go.

Masika and Catherine were in the Main Yard, lying on a blanket, Masika's head resting on Catherine's lap. They'd just finished a rather grueling psyche exam, and Masika could still feel the stubborn aftereffects coursing through her body, the familiar exhaustion that accompanied mind-focused tests. Catherine seemed equally drained, though Masika couldn't help but notice there was something different about the other girl. A detached, faraway look in her eyes that sent a strange chill down Masika's spine.

"What are you thinking about?" Masika asked, looking up at Catherine. When the other girl answered, her voice barely floated over the gentle whistle of the breeze.

"The past."

Masika tensed. Catherine had never spoken of her past before—it was a decision she vehemently defended. She didn't believe in rehashing what had already happened. In clinging to a life that was no longer hers.

"You mean . . . the past *past?" Masika asked, sitting up on her elbows.*

Catherine nodded.

"The night it happened . . ." she whispered, still staring out into the distance, "it was raining."

Masika held her breath. She'd always hoped Catherine would open up to her about her past, but she also couldn't help but feel as though this sudden decision to bring up her old life had less to do with opening up, and more to do with something troubling.

Something darker.

"You don't have to talk about—" Masika began, but Catherine interrupted, finally tearing her gaze away from the distance and looking down at Masika.

"I want to," she said, a seriousness in her voice.

Masika felt herself nod. "Okay."

Silence stretched between them. Catherine swallowed, fingers nervously fidgeting with a loose thread on the blanket.

"I wasn't sick," she finally whispered after what felt like an eternity of silence.

Masika blinked, taken aback. "What?"

"I know I told you that my death was brought about by sickness," Catherine explained, voice wavering, "but . . . that's not true."

Masika's chest twisted, her breaths quickening. She wasn't sure what it was exactly about Catherine's confession, but it sent a current of panic through her limbs. A part of her couldn't help but feel a slight sting of betrayal. Masika's death had come to her after years of grueling sickness—after years of IV drips and hospital visits and endless rounds of medication. She had connected with Catherine because of their shared suffering. Or at least, she thought she had.

"Go on." Masika nodded encouragingly despite the knot in her throat.

"My life . . . it was . . . it was taken from me." As soon as the words left Catherine's lips, a gasp sprang from Masika's throat. "By someone I trusted. By someone I loved." Catherine's voice wobbled as she regained her composure. "I know I shouldn't have lied to you. But I . . . I couldn't bring myself to tell you."

Masika sat up, fully turning to face Catherine.

"I'm so sorry." Even as she said the words, she knew they weren't enough. Nothing could ever be enough to heal a wound like that.

"Ever since, I've . . . I've felt so out of control," Catherine continued. Tears welled behind her eyes, her chest shuddering as her breaths quickened. "Not only was my life taken from me, but . . . then to end up here? Without a choice? Unable to decide my own fate?" A strange lilt of anger twisted her words, though it faded when her eyes found Masika's again. "And then I met you. And I

just . . . I wanted to be good for you. Happy. Free from those burdens and feelings and just . . . I guess I just wanted to match your light."

Masika gripped Catherine's hand tightly.

"You don't need to hide anything from me," Masika said.

Catherine chuckled, though her eyes remained downcast. "You say that now . . ."

"Catherine," Masika interjected, sitting up. She cupped the other girl's face tenderly in her hands. "Listen to me. There is nothing you could do that would ever change the way I feel about you. Nothing."

Catherine's eyes bored into Masika's. There was something lingering there, something just beyond what Masika could see. Unspoken words. The desire to say more, tempered by something dangerously close to fear.

"My little dove . . ." Catherine smiled. "I truly, truly hope not."

As the present came rushing back in, Masika clamped her hands firmly around her knees, tugging her legs in toward her chest.

Just lie back down, Masika thought, coaxing her body into slumber. *Close your eyes.* But no amount of self-soothing seemed to be enough to still the nervous energy fluttering inside her chest. To eradicate the old memories from her consciousness.

She was about to go for a walk in an effort to calm her mind when she heard a voice.

"Couldn't sleep?"

Masika tensed. She knew who it was, though her eyes remained glued to the fire. It was impossible not to recognize Catherine's voice. Even when they had been apart, even when it had been years since they'd last been together, Masika had often dreamed of Catherine's voice calling out to her, whispering to her in the night. They were more like nightmares, really. She would hear

Catherine's voice, but never find her. Would reach for the ghost of her in the dark.

But this wasn't a dream. Now Catherine was here. And somehow, that terrified Masika more than any nightmare ever could.

"I rarely can these days," Masika replied. With as much courage as she could muster, she allowed herself to tear her eyes away from the fire and look at Catherine. The other girl was still lying in the same position, but her eyes were open, looking up at Masika with a burning intensity.

Catherine dug her hand into the dirt, letting the small grains slip between her fingertips. Masika watched, mesmerized, as the other girl began to draw intricate shapes in the dirt, swirling patterns that reminded Masika of the violet runes used to dismantle illusions.

"For a moment there . . ." Catherine hesitated, her voice shallow, "back at the willow tree . . ." She swallowed, as if the memory pained her. She blinked and cleared her throat. "I thought I'd lost you."

Masika flinched. Something uncomfortable stirred inside her.

"You *did* lose me," she replied, unable to soften the ire in her voice. "A long time ago."

Catherine sat up, pushing the blanket away from her body. "Masika—"

"No," Masika interjected, raising a hand. "You're right. No point in rehashing the past, right? What's done is done. You left. I stayed. There's no changing that."

"I know," Catherine snapped, voice shaking. Her expression, which was usually so composed under the stoic mask she wore, had fractured. A tidal wave of emotions seemed to sweep across her face. "Okay? I know what I did was reprehensible. It was selfish and cruel and I've had to live with it all these years. But I do

not regret leaving you behind at Blackwood. If I hadn't snapped out of it, if the Resistance hadn't saved me, I'd have lost myself completely to the shadows. I'd be plotting to destroy Blackwood, and everybody inside it . . . including *you*."

Masika's chest heaved as she drew in a quivering breath. "But you're not anymore. You made it out. You left—"

"You think it's that simple?" Catherine thrust her arm out, lifting the sleeve of her shirt. Masika gasped when she saw what lay just beneath . . . *shadows*. They ran through her veins, drifting like an ink-soaked river. "*This* is the price I pay. These shadows will never leave me. My humanity is gone. Forever. I am bound to this place. There is no Other Side for me anymore. I have no ending. I am branded. Forced to exist with a constant fucking reminder of the worst decision I've ever made."

Masika opened her mouth, searching for the right words, but came up blank.

"Becoming a Demien isn't a decision you can undo," Catherine continued, pain lacing every word. She scooted closer, looking up at Masika, her own eyes brimming with regret. "I was so ashamed of myself. Not only that I had left you . . . but *why* I had left. To be so weak that I truly thought the only way to take back control of my existence was to leave you and join the Order. I thought . . . I thought you'd think of me differently. That you'd be able to see my humanity missing from my soul. That you'd *hate* me for it."

Masika flinched. Would she have? Would she have seen Catherine any differently? But there was no point in theorizing, not when the answer was already abundantly clear. She'd known the answer the moment she laid eyes on Catherine again.

The confession was a hushed whisper.

"I could never hate you."

Catherine's eyes flitted down to Masika's lips for the briefest moment before returning to her eyes. When she spoke next, her voice was dangerously low. It rumbled inside Masika like thunder. Like waves crashing against a shoreline.

"Even now?"

Silence stretched between them. Masika's breaths quickened. Her hands trembled.

"Does it feel like I hate you?" she whispered.

Catherine hesitated, considering her question. She reached out her hand, the movement tentative, and placed her palm delicately upon Masika's cheek. The moment Catherine's palm made contact with Masika's skin, a rush of warmth coursed through Masika's body. A terrifying need to bottle this moment, to memorize every detail of it.

"I used to be able to look at you and know exactly what you were thinking." Catherine's words echoed between them. Her face was mere inches from Masika's now. So close that Masika could imagine the delicate brush of her lips against her own. "Your wants. Your needs. With just one look."

Masika kept her gaze anchored on Catherine. "And now what do you see?"

Tell me, Masika begged silently. *Please.*

"I see . . ." Catherine gnawed on the inside of her cheek. A battle was erupting inside her—too many emotions for Masika to keep track of. And right when Masika thought she might actually do it, that Catherine might finally heal that festering wound between them, the other girl retracted her hand, placing it upon her lap.

"Nothing," Catherine muttered, her voice even. Unfeeling. "I see nothing."

Masika flinched as if Catherine's words had been a slap across the face.

Nothing.

I see nothing.

Catherine awkwardly shifted onto her feet. She dusted her hands on her pants, staring up at the dark sky.

"I should make some rounds."

Masika chuckled bitterly to herself. "Right."

There was a second of hesitation as Catherine stood there, eyes awkwardly shifting from the looming darkness of the forest back to Masika, and then she was unsheathing her spear and striding off, disappearing into the night.

Masika held her breath, willing the hot tears burning behind her eyes to stay put.

Ever since she'd arrived back at the Resistance, a secret part of Masika, however small, had hoped there would be a way for the two of them to find their way back to one another. A way to take the broken pieces that remained and put them back together into *something* worth saving.

But that secret part of her was destroyed in that moment with one conversation.

One word.

Nothing.

19

WREN

Wren had found the lock of hair on her bedside table. No note. No indication of who might have left it there. It was just . . . *there.*

She brushed the dark strand of hair between her fingers, brows furrowed. Who the hell would have left a lock of hair in her tent? And for what purpose? It made no sense. Was it a message? A threat?

Wren hadn't noticed anything strange when Quinn and Arthur had guided her back to her tent after the battle simulation and the training activities that followed. Wren hadn't participated in the training—given her lack of magic—but she'd been forced to watch. Forced to be in the presence of magic without having a drop in her veins.

Once Wren had entered the tent and Quinn and Arthur had left her for the evening, she'd wandered over to her bed, only to notice the lock of hair in her peripheral vision. And now, here she was, racking her brain for some sort of explanation.

It wasn't her hair, that she was certain of. And it didn't seem to belong to Quinn or Arthur, given that Quinn's hair was a bright shade of pink and Arthur's was shaved close to his scalp.

But it must belong to someone in the encampment.

A Demien.

The realization struck Wren a second later. She gasped, nearly dropping the lock of hair on the floor. A memory flitted into her mind. Something Quinn had said to her earlier that morning.

"It's enchanted to keep you in. If you want to cross through, you have to have physical contact with a Demien."

If this lock of hair belonged to a Demien . . . would it count? Would it be enough to get her through the tent's barrier? If so, the better question wasn't why someone had left this here . . . but who had left it?

Wren pocketed the questions for later, refocusing her attention on the task at hand. She gripped the lock of hair tightly and approached the entrance to the tent, breath held.

Please work.

She shut her eyes and stepped forward.

A delicate breeze. A gentle pressure.

Wren's eyes fluttered open, blinking as her vision readjusted. It took a few seconds for the realization to sink in.

She was standing outside the tent. She had passed through the barrier. It had worked.

It actually fucking worked.

Wren clamped a hand over her mouth to silence the wave of laughter bubbling up in her throat. Getting past the barrier was only the first step, and there was no point in rejoicing when she was still in danger.

Somebody, for whatever reason, had handed her this opportunity.

And now she needed to use it.

Think, Wren. Think. If she was going to figure out a way to remove the cuff and escape the encampment, then she needed to try to uncover high-level security information. She needed to go to the place where she knew Edith and the other generals kept their belongings.

Onyx Unit.

It was a risk. But it also might be her only chance to investigate. *Three days.* That was all she and August had left to try to find a way out. Which meant if Wren was going to do something stupid . . . she had to do it now.

Don't think.

Just move.

Wren sucked in a sharp breath and strode forward. Luckily, it was late enough that most Demiens had retired for the evening, though a few stragglers lingered, chatting by the crackling glow of a bonfire. Wren kept her head bowed and gaze lowered, careful not to make eye contact with anyone around her.

It didn't take long for her to make her way out of Silver Unit and into the heart of the cavern. She thought back on earlier that morning, when Quinn and Arthur had given her the tour of the cavern.

The western tunnel is for Onyx.

Wren pivoted to the right, careful to keep her steps light and hurried. But something caught her attention as she approached the entrance to the western tunnel . . . a hooded black cloak dangling from a post. She reached out her hand, quickly grabbing the cloak and tossing it over her shoulders, tightening the hood around her head. It wasn't the best disguise, but she hoped it would be enough.

She entered the western tunnel, placing the lock of hair inside a pocket in the cloak. As she slowly slid her hand out of the pocket, her knuckles brushed something sharp and cold. *A knife.*

Not exactly the most useful weapon against Demiens, but at least it was something.

With that tiny shred of hope, Wren made her way into Onyx Unit.

It was quiet. Eerily so. Unlike Silver Unit, which was usually bustling with activity and laughter, a dense silence pierced the air of Onyx Unit. No light emanated from any of the dozens of tents, though that didn't surprise her, given how late it was. But there was also a strange pressure in the air. A tension thick enough to drown in. Wren winced as loose earth crunched beneath her boots. Every tiny sound seemed to echo. As if even the soft rattle of her breath might be enough to raise an alarm.

Wren was considering abandoning her plan when a faint noise echoed in the distance.

Her head snapped up. She squinted, attempting to peer through the opaque darkness.

And that was when she saw it. Up ahead, looming near the center of the cavern, was another tent. It was larger than any of the others she had seen—almost like a domed circus tent, though the fabric itself was a midnight black that appeared to shimmer with starlight. She approached the tent cautiously, careful to keep her steps light. Just beyond the entrance, she could hear the deep rumble of voices.

". . . understand your strategy, High General, but isn't it best we resume the sessions as soon as possible?" a muffled voice asked. "The catalyst must be awoken. We are running out of time. We've gotten word that the Resistance has uncovered something . . . concerning. Something that could put them at an advantage."

A resistance? Wren's heart surged. Maybe there *was* hope after all.

"Their silly tactics are of no concern to me." *Edith.* The High

General's smooth voice echoed with authority. "Tell me, Commander, do you not trust in the Soulless One's plan? Do you doubt his timing?"

"Of—of course not!" the other voice sputtered defensively. "I . . . I simply wonder . . . if it would behoove us to—"

"It would behoove *you* to remember your place," Edith cut in, silencing them. "The Soulless One will call upon the girl when she is ready. And I will resume the sessions when I sense that it is necessary."

"Has there been no change?" Another person spoke up. "Nothing at all?"

"Not from what I gather," Edith replied with a sigh. "She remains . . . stagnant. The vision is still concealed."

The vision? Was that what Edith was trying to get Wren to see by forcing her back into the past? Was that what they were waiting for? Wren had stepped closer, desperate to learn more, when a heaviness settled upon the nape of her neck.

A presence.

I'm not alone.

Before Wren could react, a hand was grabbing her by the waist, pulling her backward, another hand clamped tightly over her mouth. She tried to scream, but the sound was muffled in her throat, and then she was being thrown into another tent, swallowed by darkness.

She prepared her body for a fight, but as soon as she stumbled into the tent, her attacker dropped their hands. Using the freedom to her advantage, Wren unsheathed the knife from her cloak and spun on her heels, thrusting the pointed edge of the blade toward her attacker. But before the tip of the knife could make contact with flesh, a hand was wrapped around her wrist, stopping her.

August.

A confusing mix of fear and relief erupted inside Wren.

"What are you doing?" she said, seething, staring up at him defiantly.

"What am *I* doing?" August let out a bitter chuckle, lowering his voice. "What are *you* doing?" His eyes skated to the blade pressed against his neck. Wren wasn't sure if she imagined it, but she swore she saw a flicker of amusement in his silver eyes. "And how the hell did you manage to get a knife?"

"That's none of your business," Wren huffed.

August rolled his eyes. He still hadn't let go of her wrist, though he loosened his grip slightly.

"Where are Quinn and Arthur? They should be watching you."

"First off, I don't need babysitters," Wren shot back. She unearthed the lock of hair from her cloak. "And somebody left this in my tent. It let me bypass the barrier. Was it you?"

August squinted at the lock of hair, brows cinched together. "No," he replied. "It wasn't."

Wren shrugged, shoving it back into the cloak. "Well. It looks like we've got somebody else on our side, then."

August let out a low groan of frustration. "Loughty . . . do you understand how difficult it was for me to convince Edith to stop torturing you? If she finds out you've been sneaking around Onyx Unit . . ." His voice trailed off, teeth digging into his bottom lip. Wren had never seen him look so panicked.

"How did you convince her, anyway?" Wren asked, stepping closer.

"I . . ." August swallowed. He balled his free hand into a tight fist, then stretched out his fingers as he searched for the right words. "I tried to think like her. To suggest something that would appeal to her . . . motivations."

"And what did you suggest?" Wren asked.

August hesitated.

"I told her that your mind might be more . . . malleable . . . if she gave you time to acclimate," he confessed, voice rough. "That if she let you grow comfortable, if she found a way to lower your guard . . . that you'd be easier to break."

Wren shivered. A part of her couldn't help but fear how easily August could tap into his sister's mindset. How seamlessly he fit into their world.

"Good." Wren swallowed back the tight knot in her throat.

"I also told her to wait until after Equinox," August added. "I don't know if she'll listen, but so far it seems to have worked." He let out a sigh, running a hand through his curls. "Which is *exactly* why it's so reckless for you to be investigating alone."

"You're the one who said we needed to find a way out of here!" Wren snapped back.

"I know," August muttered through a sigh of frustration. "I know. But . . . you can't do this alone. If you want to investigate, then *tell me.* We're in this together, Loughty. I'm on your side." Wren's expression must have reflected the conflicting feelings inside her, because as soon as the words left his lips, August's expression shifted. He tilted his head, eyes roaming over her face, before adding a soft and agonized, "You don't trust me, yet . . . do you?"

Wren opened and closed her mouth.

Do I trust him?

She wasn't sure. She wasn't sure of anything anymore.

"I want to," she whispered back, surprised to find that she meant it.

August gave a soft nod in response. His eyes darted back to the knife pressed against his throat. The corner of his mouth lifted a fraction, a hint of a smirk.

"Then how about you start by lowering that knife?"

"Why?" Wren matched his smirk, daring to press the knife an inch closer. "Am I making you nervous?"

"You *do* make me nervous," August admitted, chuckling, "but not because of the knife."

Wren blinked, taken aback. "Do you think I wouldn't do it?"

August shook his head. "No. It's not that. I believe you've made it abundantly clear that you wouldn't hesitate to jam a knife into my back . . ." August craned his neck forward, the edge of the blade just barely piercing his skin. When he spoke next, his voice was lower than before. Deeper. "But I don't care."

Wren flinched. "You don't . . . *care*?"

For a moment, August said nothing. He simply dragged his hand away from Wren's wrist, pausing when it landed on the hilt of the knife. Wren tensed, lips parting in surprise, but didn't back away. She remained rooted to the ground, unwilling to break the eye contact that had fused between them. Instead of pulling the knife away from himself, August dragged it down, stopping only when the pointed edge of the blade was aimed directly at his chest.

"Don't you get it?" August's voice reverberated between them. His smoke-filled eyes locked on her face, unflinching. "You can stab me. Wound me. Carve my bloody heart out. It doesn't matter." The next words he spoke were a whispered confession, his voice hoarse, a desperation burning in his eyes. "I already belong to you. I've *always* belonged to you."

Wren let out a shuddering breath. Her grip on the knife loosened, though she kept the blade aimed at his heart. "I swear to God, Augustine Hughes"—she shook her head, eyes welling with tears—"if you're lying to me . . . if this is all some trick—"

He dropped her wrist, cupping her face gently with his hands. "It's not."

"—I'll *kill* you. I'll kill you ten times over—"

He nodded, thumb gently brushing the edge of her jaw. "Naturally."

"—because . . . because I won't be made to look like a fool again, like some *idiot*—"

August shook his head, drawing her closer. "I wouldn't dare."

"—and I won't fall for it a second time, I promise you that—"

August sighed.

"Wren."

She blinked, dazed.

"What?"

He brushed his thumb against her bottom lip. "If you're quite done threatening to stab me, I'd like to kiss you now"—he smirked, a light flush washing over his neck—"if that's okay with you."

Wren's breaths came in sharp, ragged inhales as she hesitated, eyes locked on his. "August . . ."

His name slipped out of her mouth involuntarily, the faintest hint of a whisper.

The knife clattered to the ground.

And then his lips were on hers.

It wasn't the same kiss they'd shared before the final trial—hungry, desperate, rushed. This was something else entirely. This was slow . . . *torturous.* August took his time, gliding his hands down her back, splaying his palms around her waist. Every place he touched her *burned.* An overwhelming warmth erupted beneath her skin, spreading down her legs, coiling around her stomach.

A soft, involuntary moan escaped Wren's throat when his tongue brushed her bottom lip. She wound her fingers through August's curls, tugging sharply. He hissed, rearing his head back, smiling against her mouth.

"I probably deserved that . . ." he murmured, wincing. "Though . . . if I'm honest with you . . . I kind of liked it."

Wren rolled her eyes, biting back her own smile. "You've always been a bit of a masochist."

"For you?" August whispered. "I'm more than a masochist. I'm a fool. I'm completely and utterly hopeless."

August cupped Wren's face and drew her closer. His lips found her jaw, then her neck, before slowly making their way down to her collarbones. It was agonizing. Feeling his lips against hers. The warm peppermint scent that clung to him enveloping her senses. But it wasn't enough. *Nothing will ever be enough.* August must have sensed Wren's desperation, the way she arched hungrily toward him, begging for more. He let out a low chuckle, smiling through a kiss.

This was a terrible idea. A terrible, stupid, reckless idea.

They were in no position to be doing this—let alone in the middle of Onyx Unit. Not to mention that Wren still found her heart torn between wanting to trust August and knowing that, at any moment, she might lose him forever. The boy she once knew . . . *gone.* Lost to the shadows for the rest of eternity.

"You came back for me," Wren whispered, voice shaking.

August pressed his forehead against hers. "I would have ripped apart the seams of the afterlife looking for you."

August dragged his lips back to her mouth, kissing her with a hunger that made Wren lightheaded. His hands found purchase against her waist, dragging her shirt up higher, brushing the soft curve of her back.

"Come back to my tent with me," Wren pleaded, planting a small kiss along his jaw. "It would be less of a risk in Silver Unit."

August groaned. "I can't. You know I can't."

He was right, but God . . . a part of her didn't care if they were caught. She just wanted more time. More *him.* Wren wound her hands around his neck, pulling him in closer, pressing her lips against his throat. August made a low, breathy sound, and it was enough to send Wren's head spinning.

She needed more. She needed—

Getting into trouble now, are we?

Shock coursed through Wren. August must have felt it too, because he immediately pulled back, eyes roving over her face with concern.

"What is it?" he asked, panicked. "What's wrong?"

"Did you not hear that?" Wren asked. A strange ringing had erupted in her ears. "That voice."

August blinked. His lips were pink and swollen, cheeks tinged with a blush. He listened intently, shaking his head in response.

"I . . . I don't hear anything."

Nobody can hear me but you, my sweet.

Wren gasped, stumbling backward, putting distance between her and August.

Was she going mad?

It was the same voice she had heard earlier that morning. But . . . she had assumed that voice hadn't been real. That it had been nothing more than a lingering by-product of her dreams.

I am no dream, Wren Loughty.

Wren flinched as the voice echoed in her mind once more. She staggered, chest heaving as she struggled to suck in a breath. August extended his arms tentatively, hands reaching for her shoulders, but Wren pulled away before he could touch her again.

"I . . ." She choked out, clearing her throat. "I have to go."

August stared back at her, eyes brimming with worry.

"Wren." He whispered her name softly. "If I . . . if I pushed you too far—"

"*No,*" Wren cut in, mustering up as much reassurance in her voice as she could manage, molding her lips into a tight-lipped smile. "It's . . . it's not you. It's not *this*. I just . . . I need to get back. I'm probably already in trouble."

August scratched the back of his neck. He watched her intently, and Wren shivered at the intensity in his gaze.

"Okay," he murmured. "Are you sure?"

"Positive."

August let out a sigh of resignation, though it was clear he wasn't fully convinced.

"We'll keep investigating tomorrow," he told her. "There has to be a way to find out who made that security cuff." He glanced over his shoulder, lowering his voice. "I'll try to meet with you in Silver, but it might be hard for me to get away. They're . . . keeping tabs on me. Watching me."

"It's okay," Wren replied. "I'll—I'll see what information I can get out of Quinn and Arthur. Something tells me that if there is anyone we can get on our side . . . it might be them."

August tilted his head, unsure. "I wouldn't put your trust in them, Loughty. They're still Demiens."

Wren reached out and cupped August's face gently with her palm.

"So are you."

A pained expression washed over August's features. He lifted his own hand, placing it atop hers, and gave it an affirming squeeze.

Wren wanted to stay . . . to tell him about the voice. But August seemed so determined to get them out of the encampment—to save her—that she couldn't bring herself to. The voice was clearly linked to whatever Edith had been doing to her mind, and if Wren could escape by Equinox, then maybe she wouldn't need saving.

Maybe she could save herself.

"I'll see you soon," Wren assured him.

August nodded. "I'll see you soon."

And then, before she could convince herself not to, Wren turned away from August and hurried into the dark.

When she finally made it back to the Silver Unit cavern, Wren beelined for her tent, hoping and praying that Quinn and Arthur wouldn't be there waiting for her. Luckily, when she stepped over the threshold of her tent, there was nobody there.

There was, however, a note on the bed. Three words scribbled in black ink.

You owe me.

Wren read the words, tracing them with her finger. It was clear that whoever had left the note had also left her the lock of hair. But *who* and *why* were questions she'd simply have to worry about tomorrow.

For a moment, Wren simply stood there. She knew what she had to do, but still . . . it terrified her. But she also knew that sleep wouldn't come to her if she didn't try. If she didn't acknowledge the voice, once and for all.

She inhaled a slow, steadying breath.

"Who are you?"

A part of her already knew the answer, but she needed to ask. She needed to hear it out loud. At first, the only response was the piercing silence of night, and then . . . the voice emerged from the depths of her mind, washing over her.

From my blood she will drink, a debt for a price. A promise of darkness, a last sacrifice. Rotten and broken, his lie comes undone; when the two meet their maker . . . the two become one.

A shudder ran through Wren.

"The Soulless One."

Mmm. The voice chuckled and Wren shivered. ***Is that what they call me these days?***

Panic burst through Wren. No. *No, no, no.* This couldn't be happening. This couldn't be real. This couldn't—

You cannot fight what binds us. You cannot stop what has been set in motion.

Wren winced, staggering. A shooting pain blossomed beneath her temples, a dizzying wave of vertigo that made her stomach lurch. She collapsed onto her knees, hands burrowed in her hair.

"Get out." Wren pulled at her hair, pain stinging her scalp. "Get. Out."

It's almost time, my sweet catalyst. It's almost time.

Something snapped inside Wren. Her last thread of sanity. Her last fiber of restraint.

When she screamed, she barely heard the sound of her own voice.

"GET OUT OF MY FUCKING HEAD!"

Seconds stretched by. Then minutes. Finally, Wren's eyes fluttered open. She swallowed, voice raw from the sheer power of her scream. She searched the depths of her mind, half expecting to feel another presence, but there was no trace of him anymore, no sign of the Soulless One's poisonous voice to be found.

She was alone again.

For now.

Wren fought to stand, pushing herself back onto her feet. She knew that something terrible was happening to her. That her fate was tethered to this prophecy, whether she wanted it to be or not. And though a part of her was desperate to uncover what it was exactly that Edith and the others had been talking about, she couldn't find it inside herself to care. Not when her very sanity seemed to be on the precipice of destruction. Not when she could hardly discern what was real and what wasn't.

But there *was* one thing Wren was certain of.

One thing that was clear.

Her mind was no longer her own.

PART IV

AWAKENING

20

OLIVIER

Olivier was finding it increasingly difficult to pretend he wasn't going mad.

The previous night had been filled with yet another strange vignette of hazy dreams and warped memories. He could remember standing at the edge of a cliff. His feet firmly planted on damp ground. Behind him, a few yards away, were his parents. But their faces were muddled and wrong. First their eyes disappeared, and then their noses, then their mouths. Until the only things staring back at Olivier were two faceless figures, arms extended, reaching out for him with hungry hands.

He'd woken up drenched in his own sweat, chest heaving, unable to shake the terrible feeling that he'd forgotten something.

It had been like that for weeks. That constant back-of-the-mind *itch*. The foggy outline of something he was supposed to remember, but couldn't. He couldn't remember the name of the town he'd grown up in. He couldn't remember the name of his favorite horse, though he could recall its chestnut-brown mane and how the rough hair had felt against his fingers. What terrified him most was knowing there were probably dozens of other details he'd forgotten and didn't even realize. How much longer until his parents vanished along with them? How much longer until he couldn't even remember his own name?

Olivier shivered and wrapped his arms protectively across his chest.

He supposed the terror of the Forgetting did have *one* perk. It was a great distraction from the hours upon hours of monotonous hiking they'd been doing since they'd woken up earlier that morning.

Based on the newer map they'd uncovered, Catherine swore the next clue wasn't far, but Olivier was beginning to worry that she wasn't being entirely truthful. They'd been walking east for hours, inching closer and closer to Blackwood's perimeter, which didn't help quell the nervous flutter building in his chest. Olivier's feet hurt and the air had grown brittle and biting—a cold wind nipping at his nose. It had even begun to snow, tiny, powdery flakes cascading down from the sky, dotting the group in speckles of white.

But perhaps if Olivier hadn't been so preoccupied with the deterioration of his own mind and his aching limbs, he might have noticed that Emilio had been staring at him for the better part of an hour, teeth nervously worrying at his bottom lip. He might have noticed the other boy's mouth opening and closing, as though he was attempting to convince himself to say something. But, as luck would have it, Olivier *hadn't* noticed. So when Emilio did finally manage to pluck up the courage to speak, Olivier nearly face-planted onto the ground from the sheer shock of hearing those five words uttered out loud.

"Why haven't you kissed me?"

Olivier froze midstride. He blinked, swiveling to face Emilio, who appeared just as shocked as Olivier felt. *Did he mean to say that out loud?* The rest of the crew continued forward, completely oblivious to what was happening behind them, and slipped deeper into the forest.

A gentle breeze ruffled the leaves on the crooked branches surrounding them, a light whistle breaking through the silence.

Speak, Olivier berated himself silently. *For the love of God—*

"I'm sorry," Emilio blurted out before Olivier could get a word in. "I just—I didn't mean for it to come out like that. I just . . . I've been thinking about it since we left the manor." He shook his head. "No. That's a lie. I've been thinking about it since *before* that. I've been thinking about it since the first time I saw you, if I'm being completely honest."

"Emilio."

"I know what you're going to say," the other boy muttered, fussing with a loose thread on his sweater, wrapping it around his finger until the tip turned purple. "The timing is terrible. I know that. I—I didn't expect for this . . . for *us* . . . to be a priority right now. We have the balance of the afterlife to worry about. I just thought . . . I thought maybe by now—"

"Emilio."

The boy's mouth clamped shut. He stared at Olivier, eyes wide and cheeks pink. "What is it?"

Olivier stared at him . . . and stared. This was it. This was *the* moment. And yet, despite Olivier's normally unwavering confidence, he found himself unable to move, standing in place like a complete and total idiot. What was he waiting for? What was he so scared of? *You know what you're scared of,* whispered a voice in the back of Olivier's mind. Because what was the point of finally closing the distance between them if they'd only be forced apart in a few short days? What was the point of allowing himself the tiniest glimmer of hope, only to have it ripped away from him? Emilio was already going to be crushed when he learned that Olivier's memories were fading more rapidly, and that he maybe only had a few days left with his sanity still intact. Why cause

Emilio more pain? Why should they make things harder for themselves? Why—

Olivier groaned.

"Fuck it."

And then Olivier grabbed Emilio by the collar and pressed their lips together.

Olivier's mind went utterly, pathetically blank. The entirety of his being was consumed by Emilio, by the feeling of his hands roaming his back, the soft warmth of his breath, the delicate brush of his lips. Emilio sighed against Olivier's mouth and it was enough to leave Olivier breathless, knees buckling as he fought to keep the two of them standing. How had he managed to wait so long to do this? Kissing Emilio felt like the most perfect thing, *the most natural thing,* in Olivier's entire existence. He never wanted it to end. He wanted to exist like this, suspended in this moment, forever.

Let this be my eternity, Olivier prayed.

They parted slowly, reluctantly, their lips remaining inches apart. Emilio's cheeks were even more flushed than usual, his mouth curled into a grin of disbelief. They were both slightly out of breath, chests rising and falling rapidly as they struggled to steady their breathing.

"I'm sorry," Olivier whispered, flushing.

Emilio chuckled, shaking his head. "Whatever for?"

"For not doing that sooner."

Emilio's mouth twisted as he bit back a smile. "You're forgiven."

Olivier had always been naturally greedy, unable to stifle his desires once they'd made themselves known, and now that he'd allowed himself to indulge in Emilio, he was certain he'd never be satiated. He was already longing for more, his lips itching to close the space between them once again.

But he didn't have to.

Emilio pushed forward, cupping the back of Olivier's head with surprising firmness, and placed his lips upon Olivier's once more. There was an intensity to it, a *desperation,* that had Olivier's head spinning. A heat erupting deep within his belly.

Olivier had always known Emilio as softness and comfort and tenderness—but he was quickly realizing that there was more to Emilio. He was also passion and heat and *wanting.* There was an almost bossy quality to Emilio's kisses that had Olivier giggling into his mouth, which only made Emilio deepen his kiss, swiping his tongue over Olivier's bottom lip with surprising assertiveness.

"Emilio Córdova," Olivier whispered hoarsely. He pulled back, just enough to look into Emilio's warm brown eyes. "I thought you were supposed to be a nice boy."

"I *am* nice." Emilio batted his eyelashes with feigned innocence. "I'm *very* nice." He arched a brow before slowly bringing his mouth down onto Olivier's neck. He planted a bruising kiss, teeth scraping against skin. "You don't think I'm nice, *Olivier*?" Emilio spoke Olivier's name as though he were saying something profoundly filthy, with a huskiness that had Olivier praying to whoever was listening that he'd have enough self-control not to pass out right then and there.

"You"—Olivier swallowed, heat rising to his cheeks—"are certainly *something.*"

Emilio chuckled. "You want to know what I am?"

Olivier nodded.

God, yes.

Emilio pulled back. When he met Olivier's eyes, the teasing glint was gone, replaced by something more tender. More sincere.

"I'm yours," he whispered.

Olivier let out a breathy sigh. He was certain that if there was one thing he could never forget, one thing that could withstand the Forgetting's cruel punishment, it was *this* moment. This memory. Those two beautiful words slipping out of Emilio's beautiful lips. He would never forget.

Never.

Olivier had leaned in closer when . . .

"Shit—"

A collection of startled gasps and shrieks of surprise echoed a few yards ahead. Olivier whirled at the sudden commotion, only to find the entire group standing there, eyes wide and mouths agape.

"I'm not looking!" Masika slapped her hands over her eyes. "I can't see anything. I didn't see anything. I don't even know what you two look like."

Dina let out a cackle of laughter. "Oh, I saw *everything*. In vivid detail."

Analisa, who was cradling Benji in her arms, placed her hands over the creature's eyes. "Apologies." She giggled. "We came to fetch you."

Olivier rubbed his face and willed the heat in his cheeks to subside. Next to him, Emilio blushed a deep shade of red and glanced down at his shoes.

"And what, pray tell, was so important that you *all* had to come get us?" Olivier asked with a lilt of impatience.

Catherine stepped forward, map in one hand and her spear in the other.

"We think we found our next clue."

The decrepit house rose from the forest floor like the skeleton of a fallen beast, its gabled roofs piled with powdered snow. It stood at the center of a clearing, surrounded by thick pine trees. Various turrets jutted out from the sides of the house, an array of arched windows adorning the front. But even from where Olivier stood, he could tell that some of the windows were cracked, splintered glass trailing up the surface like a spiderweb. Broken panels dangled from the structure, chunks of dark wood scattered on top of the snow in haphazard piles.

"Let me guess . . ." Dina muttered. "We're supposed to enter the creepy, abandoned building?"

Catherine stared down at the map in her hands, a slight furrow in her brow. "Looks like it."

There wasn't a single part of Olivier that relished the idea of setting foot inside the building. Something about it made his stomach churn with apprehension. It was as if a rope had been fastened around him and somebody was furiously tugging him in the opposite direction, desperate to get him as far away from the building as humanly possible.

Or maybe it was simply that all he could think about was the feeling of Emilio's lips on his.

Analisa took a step closer to the house, eyes trained on the highest turret. She seemed perplexed by something, or perhaps slightly disturbed. She closed her eyes, reaching out her free hand, thin silver threads trickling from her fingers. They sizzled in the air, gently swaying in the breeze before retracting into her palms.

"There is a heaviness here." Her eyelids fluttered back open. "A presence."

Dina pointed an accusatory finger at the healer. "See!"

Catherine rolled her eyes, ushering the group forward. "I don't care if the damn thing is haunted," she muttered, hiking toward the front steps of the house. "We are going in there and getting the next key." There was no dissuading Catherine, that much was clear. And once the rest of the group followed her, Olivier knew there was no turning back.

He stepped forward, Emilio by his side. Masika caught up with them, matching their pace. She wedged herself between them, wrapping her arms around their shoulders.

"Well." Masika cleared her throat, biting back a smile. "I'm sure you two are feeling a bit . . . *distracted*."

Olivier chuckled. "Subtle."

Emilio flushed.

"Hey!" Masika chuckled. "You know I'm your *number one* fan. I've been rooting for you guys from the beginning. Ever since we became friends."

"*Friends*, huh?" Olivier's gaze slid to her, a teasing smirk on his lips.

"Apologies," Masika muttered with mock sincerity. "I meant *unfortunate acquaintances*."

Emilio rolled his eyes. "I think we can call each other friends now."

Masika nudged him playfully with her elbow. "But it doesn't sound as cool, does it?"

"Come on!" Catherine called ahead of the group, impatiently tapping her foot as she placed her hand upon the front door. "No time for chitchat. Let's do this."

Benji growled in Analisa's arms, beady red eyes locked on the door.

"Even the dog doesn't like it here," mumbled Dina, clearly displeased.

Catherine rolled her eyes and opened the door, leading the group inside.

The entryway was small and narrow, barely large enough to fit all six of them. Dark emerald walls surrounded them on all sides, the floorboards beneath their feet old and brittle. A few dust-speckled paintings adorned the walls, some ripped in half, as if someone had taken a knife to them and slashed with all their might.

On the other side of the room was a single door. An inscription was carved over it, the words etched upon the wood in an arch.

Catherine stepped forward and read the words out loud. *"The truth is the way through."*

Dina groaned. "Please don't tell me it's another goddamn riddle."

As the words left Dina's lips, something in the inscription began to change. A deep golden glow emanated from the carving, and then another set of letters formed in the wall, etched below the first line as if with an invisible blade.

CATHERINE CLARKE . . . WHAT ARE YOU MOST AFRAID OF?

Olivier's chest tightened. He glanced around the group in bewilderment, though his eyes snagged on Catherine. She had gone impossibly still, her face pallid as her eyes traced the words over and over.

"How the hell does it know your name?" Dina asked warily.

Catherine swallowed. She gave a weak shake of her head. "I . . . I don't know."

"It's not a riddle," Emilio muttered softly beneath his breath. He placed himself next to Catherine, pointing up at the words. "Look at the original inscription: *The truth is the way through*. This isn't about deciphering some hidden meaning. It's about exposing the truth." He looked around the group, a slight tremor in his bottom lip. "It's about divulging our deepest secrets."

Silence fell upon the foyer, though there was a question threaded through it, something all of them were clearly thinking. Ultimately, it was Masika who dared to speak the question out loud.

"What happens if we lie?"

Analisa hummed, staring up at the inscription with that faraway look in her eyes. "If the truth is the way through . . . then lies will keep us trapped."

Dina groaned. "I do *not* like the sound of that."

"It's fine," Catherine snapped, craning her neck from side to side. "We just . . . speak the truth. Should be easy enough." She cleared her throat, shifting uncomfortably from one foot to the other. "I . . . I'm most afraid of . . ." Her voice trailed off. Olivier's entire body tensed, as if bracing for impact, but then Catherine let out a resigned sigh and whispered, "I'm most afraid of disappointing the ones I love."

Silence stretched by. A collective breath held.

And then the door in front of them creaked open, unveiling another room.

Catherine let out a low huff of air, shoulders slumping in relief, though Olivier didn't miss the way her eyes momentarily drifted to Masika . . . the charged moment sparking between them. But it didn't last long. Dina let out a dramatic sigh and sauntered into the next room, the tension between Catherine and Masika instantly dissolving as the rest of the group followed suit.

The next room wasn't anything special. It looked exactly like the one they had just left behind, though perhaps even smaller. There was, however, a different inscription etched upon the next door.

"Looks like it's forcing us to take turns," Dina grumbled.

Olivier's chest tightened. He desperately hoped that wasn't the case. The last thing he wanted to do was speak *his* fears out loud . . . to expose his darkest secrets. The mere thought sent a shiver down his spine.

Analisa stepped forward and mulled the words over for a prolonged moment. She blinked up at the inscription, a dazed look in her eyes.

"I am most afraid of"—she gnawed on the inside of her cheek before continuing—"the knowledge that there are some pains, some losses, which I cannot fix. Some wounds that cannot be mended by a healer's hand."

A tense beat of silence. A brief moment of doubt.

And then the door was opening, leading them into the next room.

It went on like this for the next few minutes. A name written. A fear spoken out loud. Dina's admission had rattled Olivier, mainly because he hadn't been expecting it. He didn't know the silver-haired girl well, but given her self-assured, brusque demeanor, he'd expected her fear to be something banal, if not obvious. But it appeared there was more to the silver-haired girl than Olivier had originally thought.

"I fear . . ." Dina had whispered, hands nervously fidgeting with her daggers. "I fear the person I could have become, had I not left the Demien Order to join the Resistance. The person I *almost* became."

Masika went up next, though truthfully, her fear hadn't surprised Olivier all that much. He understood Masika well, had grown familiar with her anxious tendencies.

"My biggest fear is my own mind," Masika had admitted with a slight wince. "I'm afraid of losing myself to the anxiety . . . and never resurfacing." As the words left her lips, Olivier reached out his hand and gave her an affirming squeeze on the wrist, which Masika returned with a thankful smile.

The following room was dedicated to Emilio.

Olivier held his breath. Tension pinched Emilio's shoulders as he read the words out loud.

EMILIO CÓRDOVA . . . WHAT ARE YOU MOST AFRAID OF?

Emilio let out a low chuckle. "How much time do we have?"

Olivier dug his nails into the palms of his hands, resisting the urge to wrap his arms around Emilio. He knew this was Emilio's personal form of hell, and he wished, more than anything, that there was a way to relieve him from any further torment.

But before Olivier could even begin to figure out how he might do that, Emilio straightened his shoulders and let out a steadying breath. He kept his chin high and eyes trained on the door as he began to speak.

"I'm afraid of . . . *everything*." Emilio's voice wavered, but he continued. "I'm afraid of pain and loss and not knowing what waits for me on the Other Side. But above all that, what I'm *most* afraid of . . . is knowing that I now have something . . . *someone* . . . I care more about than myself. Someone I can lose."

Olivier's breath hitched in his throat as the door gently creaked open. Emilio glanced over his shoulder, his gaze meeting Olivier's.

As the others made their way into the next room, Olivier scurried forward, grabbing Emilio by the hand before he could cross through.

"Someone you can lose?" Olivier whispered. He didn't miss the trail of goose bumps running down Emilio's neck as the words left his lips. "Do you mind elaborating on who that *someone* might be?"

Emilio bit back a smile, blushing.

"Take a wild guess."

Olivier placed his fingers gently beneath Emilio's chin, angling his face toward him.

"I want to hear you say it out loud."

He hadn't meant for his voice to come out so low and rough, but being this close to Emilio, and with the memory of their kiss still lingering on his lips, Olivier found that he'd seemingly lost control over his vocal cords.

Emilio cleared his throat. His cheeks burned from pink to a deep red. His lips parted, gently, eyes trailing up, higher and higher—

"Olivier!" Masika's voice called from the other room. "You'd better come in here."

Olivier shut his eyes, wincing. He dropped his hand from Emilio's chin, eyes fluttering back open to meet Emilio's startled gaze. The other boy was still flushed, a slightly dazed look in his eyes.

"Hold that thought," Olivier whispered through a shaky breath. Reluctantly, he turned away from Emilio and walked into the next room, eyes scanning the group until they landed on Masika.

"I swear," he muttered. "You have the *worst* timing."

Masika made an exasperated gesture with her hands. "What did *I* do?"

Olivier waved her off. "Nothing."

Olivier snapped his gaze to the next door.

Ah.

That explained the impatience.

OLIVIER DUPONT . . . WHAT ARE YOU MOST AFRAID OF?

Well, he supposed it was inevitable that it would be his turn next. All the others had been forced to speak their truth out loud—why would he be any different? But now that the question had been presented to him, Olivier found the words lodged in the back of his throat, a trembling fear building in the pit of his stomach.

He knew what he was most afraid of.

And he couldn't say it out loud.

Not *now*. Not right after his kiss with Emilio. He'd thought he'd have more time . . . a chance to properly explain it to Emilio.

His eyes anxiously flitted to Emilio. The other boy stared at him, a soft, encouraging smile on his lips. Maybe there was a way around the test . . . a loophole. There were other things, after all, that Olivier was afraid of. Who was he to say what he was *most* afraid of?

Maybe—if he was lucky—there could be more than one truth.

"I'm most afraid of"—Olivier inhaled a sharp breath—"the unknown."

There was a breath of silence. *Please,* Olivier begged silently. *Please be enough.* He waited . . . and waited. But the door remained stubbornly closed. Dread pooled in Olivier's stomach.

Catherine shot him a puzzled look. "Did you lie?"

"I . . . I didn't—" But his words caught in his throat when a deep rumble echoed from somewhere beneath them. The room began to shake. The walls trembled. *An earthquake?* But then it occurred to Olivier that the walls weren't just trembling—but *moving.* Constricting slowly. Shifting toward them, inch by inch.

The room was closing in on them.

"What's happening?!" Dina shouted over the thunderous roar.

"The walls . . ." Analisa whispered, tucking Benji closer to her chest, panic whirling behind her eyes. "They're moving."

"Olivier!" Masika bellowed. "You have to tell the truth!"

Terror twined around Olivier's chest. "I am!"

The walls pushed against them. The group huddled together at the center of the room, the space around them nearly non-existent now.

"We're going to be crushed!" Catherine snapped. "Goddammit, Olivier! Just tell the fucking truth!"

"Fine," Olivier whispered. He closed his eyes, wincing. "*Fine!* I'm . . . I'm afraid of the fact that I only have a few days left, okay?!" The words tumbled out of him before he could second-guess himself. But he kept his eyes shut, unwilling to face Emilio as he spoke the truth out loud. "That my memories have gotten worse since we left the base and that . . . that in a few days . . . the Forgetting will consume me and I'll lose Emilio forever!"

All at once . . . the room stopped moving.

When Olivier opened his eyes, the walls had somehow shifted back to their original positions, as if they hadn't been moments away from crushing the group. As if the room had never moved at all.

The door in front of them groaned open.

Olivier felt Emilio's presence behind him. The searing heat of his stare. But he kept his gaze forward as they entered the new room, terrified to turn back and face the consequences of his actions.

Luckily, what they found on the other side of the door provided enough of a distraction to delay that inevitability. Because floating right at the center of the final room, surrounded by a shimmering deep indigo light, was the second key.

21

WREN

A twisted part of Wren had missed this—the delicate scrape of parchment, the rhythmic tapping of fountain pens against hardwood, the hallowed silence reverberating throughout the tent like a sacred psalm. In a classroom, Wren felt indestructible. Like the power had slithered its way back into her grasp. Here, familiarity snuffed out the stubborn traces of fear, igniting the dormant conviction inside her.

There was, of course, one infinitesimal flaw.

One that was nearly impossible to ignore.

This wasn't a Blackwood Academy classroom.

There were no serpentine threads of ivy to be seen. No arched rose-tinted windows giving way to mist-stippled hills and ornate Gothic structures. Instead, Wren found herself surrounded by the inky walls of a tent, bathed in harsh orange light, the ochre hue emanating from flickering brass lanterns. Around her, Demiens took notes. It seemed almost comical—a bunch of soulless vipers hell-bent on destroying the afterlife, and here they were, scribbling in their journals, noses stuffed in textbooks.

Quinn and Arthur had awoken Wren and dragged her to their first mandatory instruction of the morning—*history class.* Or, more specifically, where Demiens learned about the prophecy.

Where they learned about Wren.

On the walk over, Wren was certain the pair would bring up her late-night escapade. That they'd somehow read the betrayal written on her face. But neither one of them gave any indication that they knew about Wren's trip into Onyx Unit, nor did they seem to have knowledge of the strange lock of hair and the note left behind in her tent.

"Can you stop that?" hissed Quinn, pulling Wren's attention back to the present. The pink-haired girl was seated next to Wren, with Arthur on the other side of her. Wren had been absentmindedly spinning her pen in circles, watching as the black fountain pen blurred into a shapeless vortex of darkness.

"I'm bored," Wren muttered back.

"You know how to read, right?" Quinn shoved the textbook toward Wren. "Then *read*."

Arthur let out a snort, covering his mouth with the back of his hand.

Wren stared down at the book with a grimace of disgust. The Demien Order sigil was carved into the leather cover, an array of symbols and shapes surrounding it. She might have been craving the familiar comfort of a classroom, but that didn't mean she'd stoop to the level of *actually* reading a Demien text.

"You can keep your propaganda," she snapped, shoving it back. She ignored Quinn's searing gaze and leaned back in her chair. "Where is the professor, anyway? Shouldn't they be here by now?"

"It's been five minutes," Quinn said, seething. "And we don't have *professors*. Just generals who act as instructors."

Wren cupped her chin in her hands, blowing a strand of auburn hair away from her face. "Same thing."

The words had barely left her lips when the entrance to the tent fluttered open with a flourish. A figure strode across the room, black cloak billowing behind them in ink-drenched waves. Shock clouding her senses, it took Wren a few moments to register his face, but when he placed himself behind the podium, quicksilver eyes darting up to assess the room, Wren couldn't help but suck in an audible breath.

Of course.

Augustine Hughes stood before the classroom, lips pulled into a scrutinizing frown. His eyes slid over each row, gaze snagging when he spotted Wren seated among the other Demiens. To his credit, he masked his surprise with practiced ease. Most people wouldn't have noticed. But Wren knew August in a way that terrified her. Down to the core of his very soul. So when his eyes widened for a fraction of a second . . . she noticed.

August cleared his throat, flexing his fingers before settling them cautiously upon the podium. The Demiens surrounding Wren leaned in closer, enraptured, breaths held as they awaited further instruction.

"The Equinox Gathering." August's deep voice broke the silence of the tent. "A time of worship. Of remembrance. An opportunity for new recruits to pay respect to the one who will usher us out of darkness and into the light."

Wren shivered at the reverence in August's voice. Nausea curled around her throat, but she swallowed it back, forcing a stoic mask. She knew that the other Demiens were watching her, analyzing her every facial expression, and she refused to hand them any ammunition to use against her.

"The Reaper's Kiss is a sacred tradition," August continued. "And tomorrow evening, you all will be awarded with the opportunity to take part in it. With your offering of blood and shadow, not only will the Soulless One's power be nourished, but *yours* will be too. Your connection will be forged. Your power . . . awakened." Wren shivered at the reminder of their dwindling countdown.

Tomorrow evening. They barely had two full days left to find a way out of the encampment.

August snapped his fingers and the journals around the room slammed open, pages fluttering as they each landed on a blank page. "I want you all to think about what Equinox means by reflecting on your Reaper's Kiss. When you pour your offering of blood and shadows into the fire, there must be a concrete, definitive intention tethering it to the Soulless One. And please remember . . . this is not merely a suggestion. You all know what happens if your Reaper's Kiss is deemed . . . unsatisfactory."

A few people shifted uncomfortably in their seats at his veiled threat, while others immediately grabbed their pens and began writing. Wren glanced over at Quinn, who was focused on her journal, her elegant handwriting creating aesthetically pleasing loops on the aged parchment.

"What happens if your Reaper's Kiss is rejected?" Wren asked in a whisper.

Quinn's eyes narrowed in warning. *"Shh."*

Wren groaned, crossing her arms as she slumped in her chair. She stared down at her own blank page. Even if she wanted to indulge in the assignment, there was no way she could concentrate on anything other than the feeling of August's eyes on her.

Wren snapped her gaze up to meet his. August was staring directly at her, brows furrowed. The tension of their kiss echoed in the air between them. The ghosts of August's hands lingering against Wren's skin.

Despite the tension permeating the air, Wren decided to take a chance, scribbling something in her journal and flipping it toward August.

You sound like a brainwashed idiot.

August let out a sudden cough, a feeble attempt at masking his surprise, though Wren could clearly see that he was biting back laughter. She smiled triumphantly, feeling wholly pleased with herself, which only seemed to frazzle August even more. He spun the silver ring around his index finger, tongue pushed against the roof of his mouth. Eyes still focused on Wren, August took a single step around the podium, though he came to a halt when a voice echoed a couple of rows behind Wren.

"General Hughes?"

Wren glanced over her shoulder, spotting the source of the voice—a boy with reddish-brown hair and a thin line of scar tissue over his lip. He was staring at August with a perplexed expression, brows lifted in a silent question.

August narrowed his gaze. "Yes? Devon, is it?"

The boy nodded apprehensively. "I . . . I was wondering . . . is there a way to ensure that our offering is deemed worthy?" He fidgeted with his pen, eyes nervously flitting around the room. "I mean . . . I know our connection to the Soulless One must be strong, but . . . is there . . . is there a way to ensure that our Reaper's Kiss isn't denied?"

"Well." August chuckled darkly, the sound sending a shiver down Wren's arms. He prowled around the podium, inching closer to the front row. "There is no certainty when it comes to the Soulless One's desires. No manual you can follow. If you open your soul to the shadows . . . if you succumb to them . . . then you should have nothing to worry about. If you don't, however"—August smirked, head tilted—"well, then . . . you most certainly *do* have something to worry about."

The boy swallowed. "Y-yes. Of course."

Silence fell upon them once more as the class resumed their writing, the scraping sound of pens against parchment filling the room. Wren leaned back in her chair, arms crossed, as she met August's gaze once again.

He took a step closer, splaying his palms upon Wren's desk, and leaned in toward her. "I expect you to complete the assignment as well, *catalyst*."

His voice was a deep, threatening whisper. If Wren didn't know any better, she would have believed the venom in his stare. The darkness in his words. But she saw what nobody else could see . . . the slight teasing curl to August's mouth. The unspoken words echoing in his smoke-filled eyes, which seemed to whisper: *Play along.*

Wren straightened in her seat. "I have nothing to say."

August's eyes raked her face. "Insubordination won't get you anywhere. In fact . . . it'll only be to your detriment."

Wren raised her brows.

"Is that a threat?"

August leaned closer.

"It's a *promise*."

Wren bit back the smile creeping onto her lips. *It's a promise.* Only she understood the real meaning behind his words—the covert message threaded between his hollow threats.

I made a promise. And I always keep my promises.

But just as the memory of August's words echoed in Wren's mind, another voice took over, blotting everything else away.

Believing in his promises is a foolish mistake, my sweet.

Wren startled and the pen slipped out of her hands, clattering to the floor.

August's smirk faltered. He tilted his head, barely an inch. "What is it?" he whispered.

But Wren's voice caught in her throat, leaving her unable to utter a single word in response.

He isn't the only one who can break through your defenses. The voice flooded her mind once more, burrowing deeper into her skull like a ravenous parasite. ***He isn't the only one who knows your soul.***

Wren shuddered.

The Soulless One.

A deep, terrible laughter rumbled in Wren's mind, thunderous and menacing.

My dear, I do wish you wouldn't call me that anymore.

Wren jolted onto her feet, chest heaving. She was going to be sick. Her vision blurred, warping at the edges. *No, no, no.* Not here. Not now. Around her, a few curious Demiens looked up, faces muddled in Wren's vision by her terror-induced haze. Quinn reached out, grabbing Wren firmly by the wrist, though her expression didn't match the intensity of her grip. Her eyes were wide and riddled with concern, mouth parted in surprise.

"Are you okay?" Quinn asked under her breath, eyes darting to August, who had seemingly frozen in place, unsure what to do. "What's wrong?"

"I—" Wren winced as a shooting pain erupted in the back of her skull, the voice dripping into her mind once again.

You can't run from me, my sweet catalyst. Our connection grows stronger. You can feel it, can't you?

Wren staggered backward, bumping into the desk behind her. Journals clattered to the floor, a cacophony of startled gasps and fluttering pages. She needed to get out, to get some air, to distance herself—

"Loughty." August's voice echoed, his expression lethal. When he spoke, his words were harsh, though Wren could see the terror in his eyes. "Where the hell do you think you're going?"

Wren shook her head, backing away from her desk, retreating toward the tent's entrance.

"I . . . I have to go. I have to get some air."

Go on. Run, my catalyst. Run.

That was all it took for Wren's legs to move beneath her as she scrambled out of the tent, staggering into the bustling cavern. Everywhere she looked there were too many bodies, too much noise and color. Panic twined around her chest like barbed wire. A crawling heat at the nape of her neck. It was too much. Too much. Too—

"Wren?"

A strong pair of hands gripped her shoulders. Wren swiveled on her heels, coming face to face with Arthur and Quinn. They were standing behind her, both slightly out of breath.

"What the hell was that all about?" Quinn asked. Despite the slight annoyance in her tone, her eyes remained soft, marred with worry. "You can't just run out like that. Are you trying to get yourself thrown into isolation?"

Wren's chest heaved as she fought to steady her breaths. She waited, bracing for the Soulless One's voice to flood her mind, but there were only silence and the feeling of Quinn's and Arthur's patience thinning.

"I'm . . . I'm sorry." Wren rubbed at her temples. "I got a headache."

Arthur's brows knit together in confusion. "Has that been happening to you often?"

Wren shrugged. "I don't know. It's not a big deal."

Quinn scoffed, crossing her arms. "Well, running out on the High General's brother is a pretty big fucking deal."

"I know," Wren muttered back. "I just . . . I wasn't thinking."

Quinn's eyes darted to Arthur, the two of them sharing a silent communication.

"What?" Wren asked through an exasperated sigh.

"Come with us." Quinn grabbed Wren by the wrist and pulled her forward. "There's something we need to show you."

"We're actually going *outside*?"

Wren struggled to keep up with Quinn and Arthur as they scurried forward, beelining toward the entrance of the encampment. They passed hordes of Demiens, all of whom stared curiously at the trio as they made their way through the crowded cavern.

"Don't get too excited," Arthur chuckled. "We're just barely entering Widow's Forest. And there are *plenty* of protective wards in the forest that keep people out—and us in." Wren shivered at the mention of the infamous forest that loomed around the Demien Order's encampment. She'd heard whispers of it, though she had yet to see it with her own eyes.

"Oh, don't look so sad." Quinn's lips lifted into a teasing grin. "At least you're getting some fresh air."

As much as Wren wanted to smack the smirk off her face—Quinn was right. She was *desperate* for fresh air, for the chance to escape the encampment, even if it was just as far as her security cuff would let her go.

An unwanted swell of emotions rose up inside Wren as they approached the main entrance. It had only been a few weeks since she'd last been outside the cavern walls of the encampment, but somehow, it had felt like an eternity. And as they exited the encampment, stepping out into the cool night air, the expanse of purgatory stretching out before them, Wren had to do her best not to let her emotions get the better of her.

The woods surrounding the Demien Order's encampment smelled of earthy pine and damp moss. *Widow's Forest.* Thin rays of pale pink light flitted through the tangled branches of the trees, though the rest of the woods remained bathed in shadows, nestled under the cover of dark, drooping leaves. They were a deep shade of purple, almost black, as if the leaves themselves had been infused with shadows. There was something strange about the forest . . . as if the trees were watching her—daring her to make one wrong move.

They walked a straight path into the forest, a strange chill digging deeper into Wren's bones the farther they ventured. It was perhaps only a minute or two into their journey when Wren began to notice a faint burning sensation under her skin, right where the security cuff was touching her. But before she could mention it to Quinn and Arthur, the duo came to an abrupt halt. They were looking at something, eyes focused straight ahead.

Wren followed their line of sight.

Up ahead, tucked between two pine trees, stood a figure. A billowing darkness. Pointed wings and razor-sharp talons.

The shadow creature.

It looked just like the one that had attacked Wren in the Ether all those weeks ago, though now . . . there were dozens. They drifted between the trees, floating aimlessly, their shadowy forms flickering in and out of vision.

Wren gasped. She staggered backward, but Quinn gripped her firmly by the shoulders, holding her in place.

"Don't move," Quinn whispered, voice stern and level, though Wren could sense the apprehension and panic simmering beneath. "If you're calm, they won't attack you. They don't want to hurt you, but they're programmed to hunger for fear."

Wren shook her head, terror clutching her chest.

"One of them *did* attack me. In the Ether. It chased me into the Shadow Lands and then followed me back to Blackwood."

"It was only following orders," Arthur explained with a grimace. There was a deep line embedded between his brows, a palpable look of anguish muddling his usual sardonic demeanor. He swallowed, hands trembling as he turned to face Wren. "Sometimes . . . Demiens don't acclimate. Despite removing their humanity. Despite joining the Order. They either fail the Reaper's Kiss, or flat-out refuse to perform the spell. And when that happens . . . those Demiens are marked as defected."

A sudden jolt of understanding shot through Wren.

"You're not saying . . ." She trailed off, nausea twisting her insides. But the somber look in Arthur's eyes only confirmed her fears.

"*These* are the defected students," he confessed. "The ones who refused to succumb to the shadows. They're forged into weapons. Brainless shadow creatures who protect the encampment's perimeter. We call them Aberrations."

Wren's head spun. She fought the urge to be sick.

"Why are you showing me this?" she asked, voice thick.

"You need to understand the finality of what it means to become a Demien," Quinn replied, his expression grave. "When we became Demiens, we made a vow. A covenant. We remove our humanity, we use shadow magic . . . and we succumb to it. There are always consequences when vows are broken. The darkest vows, most of all. And *this* is our eternal punishment if we do not bend to the Soulless One's wish."

There are always consequences when vows are broken.

Wren's mind wandered to August. To the covenant now binding him to the Demien Order . . . the unbreakable connection linking him to the Soulless One. If they discovered his betrayal, would he meet the same fate?

"And you agree with this?" Wren asked when she finally found her voice again.

Arthur's eyes drifted to the ground. Was that shame burning in his gaze? Regret? It was impossible to tell. But whatever it was, it gave Wren a glimmer of hope.

Maybe there really *was* someone on her side.

"It doesn't matter what we agree with," Quinn snapped. Her bottom lip trembled, but her gaze remained steady, anchored on the Aberrations in the distance. "Not anymore. This is what the Soulless One demands. This is what is written."

Wren shook her head. "That doesn't answer my question."

Quinn's expression hardened as she peeled her eyes away from the shadow creatures.

"They would never have met this fate if they had simply followed through with their vow." As Quinn spoke, Wren couldn't help but notice the hollowness in her words. There was no conviction. No burning resolve. Just hollow, bitter defeat. "The Soulless One grants us freedom. Power. The promise of a clean slate, cleansed from the corruption planted by Silas." She let out a weighted sigh, glancing up at the canopy of trees. "I don't expect you to understand. Not now, at least."

"I'll *never* understand," Wren replied through gritted teeth.

Arthur shook his head, muttering something under his breath.

He wandered a few feet to the left and crouched down, examining an item on the forest floor. It was a metal rod protruding from the ground. Around it, little filaments of light sparkled and shimmered, a web of shadows twisting inside them.

"What are you doing?" Wren asked, approaching him. "What is that?"

"They form a security barrier around the Aberrations so they can't get too close to the actual encampment," Arthur explained as he fiddled with the side of the contraption. He placed his palm over the top, and one of his shadows slithered from the surface of his skin to the inside of the metal rod, filling the space with renewed shadows. "Keeps them bound to the exterior perimeter."

A searing heat crawled up the back of Wren's neck.

It keeps them bound to the exterior perimeter.

Just like her security cuff kept her bound to the *interior* perimeter.

"Who made these?" Wren asked, careful to keep her tone light. She wasn't sure if she had imagined it, but she swore Arthur's olive-green eyes momentarily shifted to the security cuff on her wrist as the question echoed between them.

"Uh . . . I did." He cleared his throat and returned his attention to his work. "I volunteer in the Defensive Shields tent."

"He has to come out here every few days to reinforce the barrier," Quinn added. "If the shadows aren't replenished, the horde could move too close to the encampment."

"But don't the Aberrations follow the Demien Order's command?" Wren asked.

Arthur scratched his wrist, apprehension clouding his expression.

"They do. Most of the time." He stood up, dusting off his hands.

"But there have been instances in the past where our control on the Aberrations has slipped. It's difficult to explain. Almost like they gain sentience again . . . for a brief moment."

Wren shivered at the thought. If the Aberrations could slip into sentience, even if only for a few seconds, did that mean that their souls were still trapped in there? The defected Demiens who were transformed into the shadow creatures, were they simply shoved into the back of their minds, forced to watch themselves become mindless monsters?

"Either way, that isn't something we have to worry about anymore. The Defensive Shields tent has really made improvements in the security barriers . . ." Arthur's gaze flickered to Wren before awkwardly shifting to Quinn. *Why is he avoiding eye contact with me?* Wren wondered silently.

Another thought burned through her not a second later.

He knows something.

"The security cuffs"—Wren began, and she didn't miss the instant pinch of Arthur's shoulders as the words left her lips—"do you make those, too?"

Arthur swallowed. Quinn watched him carefully. "Yeah," he said. "I've made a few."

Hope sparked inside Wren like a lit match. She scrambled for something else to say, *anything*, but before she could get her mind to conjure up a response, Quinn cleared her throat and interjected.

"Look . . ." she muttered. "I know this is difficult to see, but we needed you to understand the gravity not just of your situation, but of *ours*." Her eyes darkened as she stepped closer. "You're not the only prisoner here."

Wren's throat tightened. Even though she assumed that Quinn

must be referring to the Aberrations, a part of her couldn't help but wonder, couldn't help but *hope,* that perhaps she was referring to herself.

As they headed back to the encampment in silence, a heaviness lingering in the air that wasn't there before, Wren couldn't stop the torrent of thoughts from surging in her mind. The thousands of possibilities. But there was one thought she couldn't silence. One thought rising above it all.

If Arthur can make the security cuff . . . then maybe that means he could destroy it, too.

22

IRENE

Later in the afternoon, once Irene had finished attending to her Ascended duties—assisting in various corporeal and defensive classes, given Birdie's and Russo's continued absence—she received a letter.

Or, rather, a letter nearly smacked her right across the face.

She'd been walking down one of the winding corridors of the Ascended Quarters when the golden envelope had quite literally materialized out of thin air, darting toward her with lightning precision. She'd barely raised her hand in time, snatching the letter out of the air before it could hit her. She'd blinked, stunned, watching as the letter writhed in her hands, as though attempting to yank itself free from her grip. Even when she'd finally managed to rip the envelope open, it continued to flutter in agitation, desperate to be free of her grasp.

The handwriting was thin and elegant, in bloodred ink.

Irene Manette Bamford,

Please meet me promptly in the Opal Chamber.

Sincerely,
Housemaster Marigold

P.S. Apologies for the letter. It can be a bit . . . enthusiastic.

Now, standing beneath the watchful eyes of the gargoyles and grotesques lurking in the upper corners of the Opal Chamber, Irene found her patience dwindling. She was in no mood to deal with Samira's incessant rambling, nor was she particularly interested in enduring Everly's pathetic attempts at intimidation.

"Where the hell is she?" Everly grumbled, tapping her foot against the marble floors. The sound of her maroon Mary Janes echoed throughout the rather empty hall, resounding like a rhythmic drum.

Samira yawned into her palm, glancing up at the ceiling with a dazed look. The whites of her eyes were glassy and red, a strange webbing of veins. Irene leaned in closer, inspecting the girl carefully.

"Are you *high*?"

Samira's eyes widened a fraction. She bit back a smile. "No?"

Irene rolled her eyes. "Christ . . ." She let out a scoff. "How you got chosen as a candidate is beyond me."

The smile dropped from Samira's lips. She leaned in closer, and their sudden proximity sent a jolt of tension through Irene's limbs.

"You really shouldn't underestimate your competition, Irene."

There was something about her words . . . something painfully familiar. Irene could hear a faint chuckle drifting in her mind. A familiar rumble of laughter. The pungent smell of brine. The Ether's intoxicating property. Masika's amber eyes beaming in amusement.

"You're doing it again."

"Doing what?"

"Underestimating everyone else."

Irene blinked, yanking herself out of the memory. Samira was still staring at her, but more with curiosity than hostility. As if she were eager to carve Irene open and see what she might find inside.

"What?" Samira chuckled. "What the hell is that face for?"

"Nothing." Irene swallowed her panic, pushing back the unwanted memories of Masika with it. Luckily, the doors to the Opal Chamber swung open before Samira could utter another word.

Housemaster Marigold entered the room, a long, billowing cloak splayed over her shoulders and cascading to the floor. She offered them a tight-lipped smile as she approached, gesturing for them to follow.

"Come on, girls. I've got something to show you."

They followed after her, silent but watchful as Marigold led them to the back of the Opal Chamber. A particularly strange-looking statue stood against the southern wall—a half-lion, half-dragon creature with glowing yellow eyes. It was there that Marigold came to a halt, spinning to face them.

"Everyone ready?"

"For what?" Everly snapped, annoyed.

Marigold beamed. "I'm glad you asked."

She placed her hand upon the head of the statue and *suddenly*—

Irene screamed. One moment she was standing there, both feet planted firmly on the floor, and the next she was sent flying up in the air, soaring higher and higher over the Opal Chamber. Samira and Everly shrieked, flailing about in a panic. Irene's eyes snapped up and her stomach flipped.

They were heading straight for the ceiling.

She opened her mouth to scream, bracing herself . . . but the collision never came.

Somehow, they had gone *through* the ceiling, as if it had been nothing but an illusion, entering what appeared to be a vertical tunnel. Cold air rushed all around her. The others were still screaming, though Marigold looked simply bored, glancing down at her watch as they rose higher and higher.

And then, just as quickly as it had started, it stopped.

Irene stumbled and jerked backward as her feet hit solid ground, struggling to regain her balance. Samira and Everly appeared beside her, nearly colliding as they came to a sudden halt. Marigold, however, was the picture of grace as she floated to a delicate stop, her feet instantly regaining their forward momentum, as if she'd simply strolled right into the room.

"Welcome to the Guard Tower." Marigold gestured to the odd room they'd found themselves in. One of the rounded walls was made entirely of glass, offering them a vantage point above the grounds and the forest lurking just beyond. An unwanted knot of emotions rose in Irene's throat as she took in the sight of Blackwood Academy laid out before her. Late-afternoon fog swirled between the towering brick buildings and Gothic structures, deep amethyst light encasing the grounds in a dreamlike haze. Candlelight illuminated most of the arched windows, and it was as if she were staring down at the twinkling expanse of the universe.

A shrill voice brought Irene back to the present.

"What—the—*hell*—was—that?"

Everly's pigtails were in complete disarray, her face blanched. She looked like she was about to be sick. Irene stifled a laugh, while Samira let herself break out into a fit of giggles.

"That is how you access the Guard Tower," Marigold explained, feigning innocence with a smile. "It's really just a slightly more complex elemental spell. A manipulation of the airflow through the tunnel—"

"And you couldn't have warned us?!" Everly interjected, aghast.

Marigold shrugged. "I think you'll survive, Ms. Hawthorne." She turned away, leaving Everly to seethe by herself. "All right. Everyone gather around. Come closer." She gestured them toward the glass wall. The three Council candidates approached Marigold, looking out toward Blackwood, breaths held.

Marigold reached into her cloak and produced a small silver coin. It glinted in her palm, and Irene couldn't help but feel a strange twist in her stomach at the sight of it. A need to hold it.

Marigold looked among the three of them. Her eyes snagged on Irene.

"Brace yourselves."

Marigold tossed the coin.

And then Blackwood came to life.

It took a few seconds for Irene to process what she was looking at. The light that exploded around Blackwood was *blinding*, appearing from one moment to the next. Once Irene's vision adjusted, she realized it wasn't just an explosion of magic. It had a shape to it. It was a circle . . . a *dome*. An energetic barrier of crimson light pulsating around the campus. If Irene looked closely, she could see the individual threads of magic that made up the dome, almost like an interconnected web.

She wondered what would happen if she pulled at one of those threads.

Would it all come undone?

"It's beautiful," Samira whispered, awestruck. "Just . . . *beautiful*."

"Are we going to learn how to construct it?" Everly asked with fervid hunger.

"Not yet." Housemaster Marigold tossed the coin, and the dome vanished from their vision, as if someone had reached out and popped it. "That's what this is for. When you join the Council, you receive your own defensive relic coin, which allows you to access the outer wards. You'll get there eventually." She chuckled, slipping the coin into her cloak pocket. "Well, *one* of you will, at least."

Irene's entire body seemed to go numb. She needed to get her hands on that coin. It was her only way to access the outer defensive wards. The only way to achieve her mission and grant the Demien Order access to Blackwood. But what if she wasn't the chosen Council candidate?

What if everything she'd done—all her sacrifices—had been for *nothing*?

She needed to speak to Mateo.

Luckily, Marigold bade them good night shortly after, ushering them back to the main lobby of the Ascended Quarters. Samira and Everly didn't seem to be in the mood for chitchat, the two of them quiet as they parted ways. Irene wasn't surprised. They were probably realizing the same thing she had. Only one of them would get to feel the magnitude of that power.

Only one of them would win.

Irene summoned a relocation spell, tilting her head in confusion when she materialized right outside her room, as opposed to *inside* it. As she pressed her hand upon the door, she felt the rhythmic pulse of a defensive barrier placed around her room—something to deter relocation spells from crossing through. But *she* hadn't crafted it. Only one other person could have.

And then she noticed something else. The soft murmur of voices on the other side of the door. No. Just *one* voice. Mateo's. But who could he be speaking to? Nobody at Blackwood was supposed to know he was here. Was he communicating with someone at the Order again? Was there another Demien in there with him?

Irene pressed her ear to the door. She leaned in closer, attempting to piece together what he might be saying, but all she could hear was the deep rumble of Mateo's voice, the words muffling before she could unravel them. And then—

Irene stumbled forward as the door swung open.

"Hello, Irene."

Mateo stood in front of her, arms crossed, an amused smirk on his face. But Irene didn't bother feeling embarrassed—it was *her* room, after all. If he was having secret meetings in the dead of night, she had a right to know.

"Who the hell were you talking to?" Irene pushed past him and strode across the room. She slammed the door with a flick of her wrist, spinning on her heels to face Mateo, who continued to stare at her with that slightly amused grin.

"No one."

Irene scoffed. "Liar," she shot back. "I heard you. And why did you place a relocation barrier on my room?"

Mateo's eyes raked her face. The self-satisfied smirk on his lips faded. "You have something to tell me."

It wasn't a question. Somehow, he'd sensed it the moment he had looked at her. Irene had to admit, it was a bit unnerving, though a part of her couldn't help but appreciate how well he had come to know her.

"And now we're changing the subject . . ." she muttered with a petulant roll of her eyes.

But Mateo had clearly made the decision to ignore her unrelenting questioning. He stepped closer. His blue eyes seemed to darken as he drank her in.

"You're easy to read," he said. "What is it?"

Irene crossed her arms. She most certainly was *not* easy to read, but she wasn't about to let Mateo know he'd gotten under her skin.

"Housemaster Marigold took us to the Guard Tower."

Mateo raised his brows.

"And?"

"She taught us how the outer wards are crafted."

Mateo's eyes instantly brightened. He closed the distance between them, gently placing his hands upon her shoulders.

"You can dismantle the wards?" He searched her face, waiting. But Irene shook her head and the spark of excitement in Mateo's face instantly deflated.

"It's not that simple," she explained. "There's no bypassing the outer wards without a special defensive relic given to all members of the Council. A coin. But maybe there's a way to steal one. Break into the faculty rooms—"

"No." Mateo dropped his hands, burying them in his hair. He began to pace back and forth, seemingly lost in thought. "If the coin holds that much power, I doubt we'll find it hidden in some office. You'll need your own. You'll need to be chosen."

"That's a gamble," Irene said. Not to mention an awful amount of pressure. "There's no telling if I'll win or not—"

"You'll win," Mateo interjected, coming to a sudden halt. He turned to face Irene. The intensity in his gaze made the hairs on her neck rise. A blanket of goose bumps shivered down her arms. "You will. That's why I chose you, Irene. I could have chosen Everly or Samira or any other student. But I didn't. I chose *you*."

Irene's breaths came to her sharp and ragged.

"Why?" she whispered.

Mateo kept his gaze anchored on her. Irene was desperate to know what he was thinking. He was keeping secrets from her, that much was clear, but there was something else. Every time he looked at her, she saw a painful recognition in his eyes. *Grief.* As if the mere act of looking at Irene was too much for him to bear.

His response finally slipped out of him, shattering the silence.

"You're so much like her."

Irene flinched. "Who?"

Mateo shook his head, as if confused by his own lack of self-restraint. He chuckled, a rough and bitter sound. When he looked back at Irene, the intensity had melted into something tender.

"Nobody," he muttered softly. Irene could see the exact moment Mateo raised the wall between them again. That impenetrable shield he refused to drop. He made his way to the door, stopping when he placed his hand upon the doorknob. Irene didn't miss the way his hands trembled. The tension in his muscles as he turned to look at her.

"You really want to know why I chose you, Irene?" He waited, and Irene felt herself nod, an almost involuntary movement. "I saw your suffering. I saw what the world had done to you. The way it had torn you apart and spat you back out. And yet . . ." He smiled, but there was so much pain behind it. "There you remained. Strong. Resilient. Determined to take what belonged to you. *That* is why I chose you, Irene. Because I knew, when it comes down to it, you'll always put yourself first."

Irene couldn't bring herself to argue with him as he strode out of the room and left her behind. Mateo was right. Irene put herself first. She would *always* put herself first. She was the kind of person who would abandon her friends for the promise of power.

The kind of person who would stomach torture if it meant getting what she wanted in the end.

Irene Manette Bamford was selfish. She was cruel. A heartless, power-hungry bitch.

And she would do whatever it took to survive.

23

EMILIO

Emilio wasn't trying to punish Olivier, but he couldn't bring himself to speak. If he spoke, he'd have to face reality. He'd have to confront the truth he was desperate to run from.

Olivier's memories can't be fixed.

He hadn't said a word since they'd found the second key and map, since they had left the decrepit house and exposed their innermost secrets. And as they'd continued hiking eastward, the awkwardness of the moment had lingered, following Emilio like a nagging fly.

Based on the new map, the third and final key was about a day's hike away, dangerously close to Blackwood's perimeter, and Emilio had committed himself to silence until they got there. Olivier had tried to speak to him, blabbering on and on about Analisa's diagnosis, and how he'd *wanted* to tell him, but had been too scared, and not that it mattered anyway because what good would come out of him knowing . . .

Despite Olivier's ramblings, Emilio refused to believe there wasn't a way out. A way to save Olivier. They'd come too far. They'd fought against the hand of fate and won. And now he was meant to simply let Olivier slip away from him? To let him drift into oblivion?

There was no way. Not in this eternity.

Yet he still couldn't bring himself to break the silence, swept away by the current of his own thoughts. In his defense, Olivier hadn't spoken in a while either, simply trudging along beside Emilio, his gaze anchored to the ground.

It didn't help that the stretch of forest they were walking through sent an ominous chill down Emilio's spine. It was unnerving. An unrelenting fear had blossomed in the back of Emilio's mind, a strange feeling that the trees could hear them, that carved within their gray trunks were a set of eyes watching them, trailing them.

We see you, they seemed to whisper with every flutter of their leaves.

A swell of relief rushed through Emilio as the group stumbled upon a small clearing; he was grateful for the momentary pause from the suffocating greenery. But his relief was short-lived, because it was at that same moment that Olivier came to an abrupt halt, finally breaking the tension between them.

"You can't ignore me forever."

Emilio froze midstride. The rest of the crew continued forward, leaving Olivier and Emilio behind in the clearing as they slipped back into the shadowy depths of the forest. A gentle breeze ruffled the leaves of the crooked branches surrounding them, a light whistle breaking through the silence.

"Say something," Olivier whispered, arms crossed, index finger drumming against his bicep. "Please."

Emilio dug his fingernails into the palm of his hands. He wanted to speak, but the words were trapped, drowned out by the panic and hurt. And truthfully, he was afraid that if he *did* try to speak, if he tried to unravel the complexity of his emotions and say how he felt, he'd only break down in a puddle of tears.

"Fine," Olivier muttered. "If you don't want to talk, then at least listen." He sucked in a sharp breath, wringing his hands as he continued. "I know I shouldn't have lied to you. I know that was wrong. But there was no way I was going to turn around and let you finish the expedition by yourself. If you had gone on without me and something had happened to you . . ." He shook his head, voice wavering. "How the hell would you have expected me to forgive myself?"

Emilio's resolve finally shattered. "And what about *me*?"

Olivier flinched at the harshness in Emilio's words. "I don't . . . I don't understand—"

"You aren't the only one who wants to protect the people he cares about," Emilio snapped, his voice torn and rough. "You aren't the only one who has something to lose." He couldn't stop the words now that they had been released, a splintering crack breaking open into a gaping fissure. "I may not be the strongest of the crew, or the bravest, but I would put my soul on the line if it meant keeping you safe. I wouldn't even have to think about it. You are . . . you *are* my soul. And I decided a long time ago that I have no interest in an eternal existence if it doesn't include you in it."

Olivier stepped toward him, frantic, delicately cupping Emilio's face with his hands. Emilio wanted to lean into his touch, to let himself be held, but his better judgment kept him from listening to his instincts.

"I know," Olivier whispered, nodding. "I know."

"Then answer me," Emilio muttered, fighting back the stubborn tears welling behind his eyes. "How do you expect *me* to forgive myself if something happens to *you*? How do you expect me to—to *breathe*?"

Olivier shook his head, panicked. "I'm not going anywhere."

Emilio cursed. "Olivier. Your memories—"

"—are fading," Olivier interjected, nodding. "I know. But maybe we'll find a way to stop it. Hell, maybe the True Headmaster will know a way to reverse it. The truth is—I don't know. None of us do. But what I do know is that there is nothing in this universe that will keep me from you." Olivier bent down, placing his forehead against Emilio's. *"Nothing."*

Emilio sighed, succumbing to the warmth of Olivier's presence. He stepped closer, placing his hand upon Olivier's chest, balling the fabric of his shirt in his fist. He held him there, the moment stretching between them.

"Must you be so stubborn?" Emilio whispered, the faintest hint of a smile in his voice.

Olivier chuckled, sniffling. "I'm afraid so." He pulled back an inch or so, clearing his throat. His emerald eyes softened, trailing up and down Emilio's face. "You . . . you must know . . . everything I did, everything I've ever done . . . it's all for you."

If Emilio's soul had suddenly ceased to exist in that very moment, he would have drifted into oblivion with a smile on his face.

"No more secrets?"

Olivier looped his pinky around Emilio's. "No more secrets."

As they continued forward, catching up with the others, a thought threaded its way into Emilio's mind. A newfound determination. He knew now, more than ever, that nothing would keep the two of them apart. Even if Olivier found himself swept away by the Forgetting. Even if he was stolen from this world and thrown into another.

Wherever Olivier's soul went—Emilio would follow.

24

AUGUST

If feigning apathy was an art form, then August was a bloody prodigy. Later that night, he sat in silence, eyes trained on the flickering flames of the bonfire, and willed his body not to feel. It came easy to him after a while. Almost effortless. *Feel nothing. Feel nothing. Feel nothing.* He repeated it over and over, the words ringing out in his mind like a dissonant alarm.

Around him, Onyx Unit Demiens spoke in hushed whispers beneath the orange glow of firelight. It was the night before the Equinox Gathering, and already, the atmosphere felt charged. There was an intensity in their movements. An edge to their voices. Luckily, most of the Onyx Unit Demiens left August alone. Whether it was because they detested him for betraying Edith, or simply because they were too afraid of Edith to interfere, the other Demiens barely looked in his direction.

Well, *most* of them.

"Care for a drink?"

Callum sank into the space next to August, a goblet in his hand. He swished the dark liquid, his wine-stained lips curling into a smirk. He was trying to rattle August, *again*, but August remained stoic and expressionless as he turned to face the other boy with practiced indifference.

"I'm fine."

"Ah." Callum hummed, fingers drumming against the goblet. "Right. I should have known that Augustine Hughes would be above such pointless revelry." He took a sip, eyes drilling into August. "Isn't that right, General Hughes?"

August's jaw twitched involuntarily.

"Correct."

Callum let out a snort. He leaned closer, the edge of his elbow pressed against August, who did his best not to flinch at their sudden proximity. Callum's face was inches from his now, those venomous green eyes of his snaking over August's face with bone-chilling hunger.

"You know . . ." Callum's voice was a throaty whisper. "I could tell you liked it."

August exhaled a slow breath.

"Excuse me?" he muttered through gritted teeth.

"Using your shadows," Callum clarified, smiling. He looked at August as though he were something to eat, wine-tarnished teeth gleaming in the darkness. "You should have seen the look in your eyes. The *power*. Honestly . . . you looked ravishing."

Fury dripped into August's veins, though a terrified part of him couldn't help but wonder if Callum might be right. The moment the shadows had erupted out of him, wrapping around Callum's throat, August had felt a suffocating rush of power, a perverse sense of pleasure at seeing the other boy suffer.

He *had* liked it.

And he'd hungered for more.

With every passing hour, with every drop of shadow magic he used, August felt himself change. His anger heightened. His impulsivity a wild animal he could no longer tame. He wondered how long it would be before he could barely control himself. Before he lost himself completely.

Callum let out a deep chuckle.

"It's funny, isn't it? How easily you begin to lose yourself to the shadow?" The warmth of his breath brushed against August's neck. "It's better to just embrace it, my friend. Trust me."

August dug his fingernails into his palms. He wanted to feel pain. To feel *something*. But the sharp sting wasn't enough to numb the terror clawing at his chest.

He slid his eyes toward Callum. "I am not your *friend*."

Callum raised his brows. "Is that so? Then if we're not friends, General Hughes . . . what are we?"

August had opened his mouth to answer when a voice sliced through their conversation.

"Callum, if you're quite done with your pathetic attempts at seducing my brother, I'd kindly ask you to get the hell away from him."

Edith loomed over them, arms crossed and face pinched into a knowing smirk.

Callum hesitated, but only for the briefest moment, before conceding with a sigh and dragging himself away from the bench. He made a dramatic show of curtseying before sauntering away, snatching a fresh goblet of wine out of someone's hand as he strode deeper into the encampment.

Edith sank into the seat next to August. She leaned back, slowly stretching her arms overhead. Her shadows practically purred, vibrating against her skin in delight. August tried not to squirm under her gaze.

"You're scowling."

"I don't scowl," said August, scowling.

"Ah, yes, I forgot that that's simply your natural state of being."

August shifted uncomfortably in his seat. "Do you require my help with something, Edith?"

"Why is it that you assume I want something from you?" Edith asked, a lethal edge to her voice. "God forbid I simply want to spend some time with my little brother."

August flexed the muscles of his neck. He was beginning to lose his patience.

"What do you want?" he asked, each word punching out of him slow and steady.

Edith's eyes gleamed, clearly enjoying August's torment. "I'm resuming my sessions with Wren tomorrow."

Panic settled in August's bones. Even his shadows flinched inside him, stirring with a renewed sense of panic. He sat up straighter, turning to face his sister.

"But I thought you said—"

"You were right," Edith interjected, cutting him off. "About giving Wren a break. Her mind feels more . . . pliable. Her internal defenses have weakened. But I can't afford to wait anymore. I just have this feeling." Edith glanced at the fire, and a wispy shadow floated across the whites of her eyes. "We're close . . . she just needs one final push."

"But why start tomorrow? Wouldn't it be better to wait until after Equinox?" August asked, willing his body to cooperate. He tucked his shaking hands between his knees. "Once the chaos of the gathering has passed?"

At his suggestion, Edith chuckled.

"I know your feelings for her cloud your judgment, Augustine." As the words left her lips, August tried to refute them, but she raised her hand, silencing him. "Either way, it won't be long now.

Come tomorrow, you *will* perform the Reaper's Kiss at Equinox. Whether you want to or not. And once your feelings are stripped from you—once your love for Wren Loughty is ripped away"—her lip twitched, a faint smile spreading onto her mouth—"you'll come to see reason."

August swallowed. He had to remain calm. To still the panic flooding through him.

"That isn't . . ." He cleared his throat. "That isn't what this is about—"

"Do not insult me with more lies, brother," Edith snapped, eyes boring into him. "I am no fool. Your soul still yearns for her. I can feel it." Her eyes roamed down his face, trailing to his forearms . . . to the place where his shadows were exposed. A glimmer of pride burned in her gaze. "But we'll fix that. We will make all those feelings, all of that pain, go away. *That* is my final gift to you, Augustine. My last sisterly act."

August's hands went numb beneath him as his sister's words settled upon him.

Tomorrow was August and Wren's last day to try to find a way to remove the security cuff and get the hell out of the encampment. But if Edith truly intended to force Wren to return to the torture sessions, August would have to try to figure it out without her.

He'd have to save Wren—on his own terms.

Edith stood up. Blanketed by the dimness of the cavern at night, her shadows seemed to melt into their surroundings. As if Edith were *made* of shadows. And perhaps she was. Perhaps that was all that was left of his sister.

Edith turned to face August. Something passed over her expression. A fraction of regret . . . a faint echo of sadness. Or maybe

August was simply seeing things. Clinging to the version of his sister that had died long ago.

"We were bred from darkness, dear brother." Edith's lip twitched and the shadow crown floating above her head darkened. When she spoke next, her eyes bored into August's, branding him. "And to darkness . . . you *will* return."

25

WREN

They were running out of time.

Night had fallen over the encampment, shrouding Silver Unit in a delicate hush, but as Wren readied herself for bed, all she could seem to think about was her conversation with Quinn and Arthur. The way they had looked at her. The shame etched upon their faces. The regret burning in their eyes.

She hadn't imagined it.

There was still hope left for Quinn and Arthur. Remnants of their humanity clawing their way to the surface. She was sure of it. And if she could reach them, if she could find a way to pull them to the light . . . then maybe they would help her.

Maybe *that* was Wren's way out of here.

But time was dwindling. Wren's window was closing—*fast*. Equinox was approaching, the festivities commencing the following evening. Which meant if she was going to try to do something about it . . . she had to act now.

Wren sprang out of bed. She slipped on her boots, fashioning her hair into a simple braid, and fished out the lock of hair she'd hidden beneath her pillow. But as she took a single step toward the tent's entrance . . . something appeared in front of her.

Some*one*.

Edith Hughes materialized at the front of the tent from one

blink to the next. Wren didn't even have time to brace herself. She staggered to a halt, nearly colliding with the other girl, though she managed to stop herself before she could go barreling into her.

But this wasn't the Edith that Wren had come to know since arriving at the encampment.

This . . . this was something else.

This was the version of Edith that Wren had seen in the Ether all those weeks ago. Her teeth were jagged and sharp. Eyes painted black by shadows. Slithering black veins rose from her neck, swallowing her jaw, crawling to her temples.

Edith cocked her head, watching Wren with a sickening grin.

"Hello, Wren." She snapped her fingers and Wren's entire body went rigid, her muscles once again frozen by Edith's curse. "I think it's best we resume our sessions now, don't you?"

Wren Loughty succumbed to the darkness and

fell

back

into

time . . .

She walked among a forest of the dead. The trees, their bark gray and withered, loomed menacingly around her. They seemed to whisper to her, beckoning her forward in their ancient tongue. Beneath her bare feet stretched a path made entirely of charred leaves and sharpened bones. She left a trail of bloody footprints in her wake, a path of crimson gleaming against the ivory floor, and yet . . . she felt no pain.

She felt wonderfully, blissfully nothing.

A perfect circular glade had been carved into the forest. Within the clearing, standing among a graveyard of ruins, was a single statue. A face chiseled from white stone and a pair of sapphires embedded in its eye sockets.

Afternoon light flickered through the naked branches surrounding the glade, illuminating dust particles floating aimlessly in the air. Perched upon one of the trees sat a black-eyed raven. It watched Wren, head tilted, as she ventured deeper into the clearing, approaching the stone statue that sat untarnished among the ruins.

A voice called out to her.

A voice she now knew well.

My sweet destroyer. My fated catalyst. *The Soulless One hummed, deep and grating.* ***I sense your soul awakening . . . our connection growing stronger.***

"How . . ." Wren whispered, voice cracking. "How is this possible? How are you in my mind?"

The Soulless One chuckled.

You, my dear, invited me.

"I—" Wren broke off, shaking her head. "I didn't."

The Soulless One sighed and the ground beneath Wren's feet rumbled.

Oh . . . but you did. With every dip back into your past, with every glimpse of your death, you welcome me in. Can't you feel it? The prophecy stirs inside you. It waits for your command.

Fury surged through Wren, blotting out the fear that remained. She lifted her chin, gaze boring into the statue's crystallized eyes. Throughout the years, Wren had often tried to envision what the ruthless leader of the Demien Order might look like. A beast with pointed claws and sharpened teeth. A celestial monster beyond comprehension. But the face carved into stone, the face staring back at her, was undeniably human. A boy—perhaps only slightly older than Wren. His face, angular and sharp . . . handsome, even.

"I don't care what your stupid prophecy says," she said, seething. "I won't destroy Blackwood. I won't destroy innocent souls."

Innocent? *the Soulless One echoed incredulously.* ***And what of the liar, the thief, the crook? What of the man that wields the book?***

Wren shivered as his words fell over her like a sudden gust of wind.

"I despise Silas as much as you do, but destroying Blackwood doesn't just mean removing Silas from power. It means wiping the slate clean. It means the destruction of all the students who walk those halls."

The voice rumbled in displeasure.

Their loss will not be in vain. They will meet a swift, merciful end. A cleansing.

Wren ground her teeth together.

"You sound just like him."

At this, the voice let out a terrible roar. The trees shrank back, shivering. The curious raven let out a shriek, taking off into the sky. But Wren remained rooted to the ground. She wouldn't quiver beneath his ire.

I am nothing like him. *The Soulless One growled.* ***You understand so little, Wren Loughty. The fate that he steals, the fate that he writes. You have yet to see his virus, his sickness, his blight.***

A pain blossomed behind Wren's temples. A piercing ache.

"Enough riddles," she groaned. "Speak plainly."

But the Soulless One simply laughed.

In time, my sweet catalyst. In time.

Wren opened her mouth to speak, to retaliate, but no sound came out. She felt a pressure in her throat, a slithering current. And then streams of shadows were drifting out of her open mouth, choking her, snuffing out her breath—

Pain.

It welcomed Wren back to reality, twisting her insides, an unrelenting wave of agony coursing through her body. She gasped awake, blinking away the haze of the dream, only to find Edith's scowling face staring back at her.

Clarity washed over her not a second later, a memory from the previous night slithering into her mind.

"I think it's best we resume our sessions now . . . don't you?"

Wren wasn't sure how many times Edith had forced her way into her mind since dragging her back to the tent. She wasn't even sure how long she'd been here. Had it been only a few minutes? Hours? *Days?* She had to assume it was morning now, based on the faint light threaded through the gauzy fabric of the tent. Had Equinox already passed? Had she missed her window? She needed to tell August about the security cuff—about her suspicions that Arthur might be able to help—but how the hell would she get out of here?

She had no way of knowing how long it had been. She'd relived her death more times than she could count, though it was clear that something was beginning to change. In the most recent dip into her mind, Wren hadn't seen her death . . . she'd been in that forest. She'd seen the statue of the Soulless One . . . spoken to him.

What's happening to me? Wren thought, biting back a sob. Maybe the Soulless One was right. Maybe their connection *was* growing stronger. Wren still had no idea how she was meant to become the catalyst—but maybe this was how it started. Slowly losing control of her mind. A terrifying descent into madness.

"Welcome back." Edith stepped closer, hands outstretched, but Wren flinched backward, angling her face away from the other girl's grasp.

"Please." Wren hated how the word tasted in her mouth, cringing at the pleading strain in her voice. She didn't want to grovel, to succumb to her desperation, but the torment of seeing her death—of seeing her *sister's* death—was becoming too much to bear. "Not again. I can't—I can't see it again."

Edith's eyes remained anchored on her face. "There is no other way."

Wren whimpered as Edith stepped closer and pressed her fingertips against Wren's temples. The shadows slithered closer, wrapping around Wren's skull, a terrible anguish dripping into her mind.

Wren choked back a sob. "I'm begging you."

Edith's lip twitched—a small crack in her mask. But if it was disgust or pity, Wren couldn't tell.

"Save your breath," Edith hissed.

The shadows were pulling her under again. Wren could feel her consciousness slipping away, the darkness taking root, tightening its hold on her. Her voice cracked pitifully as she fought to speak.

"Haven't you ever lost someone?"

Wren's vision began to warp, fragmenting. Through the haze, she could see the surprise in Edith's expression, the way her mouth parted, eyes widening slightly. For a brief, fleeting moment, Wren *swore* she saw a flicker of sadness in Edith's dark eyes. A remnant of humanity.

"I know loss well, Wren Loughty. More than you will ever understand."

Searing tendrils of fire coursed through Wren's veins, a never-ending well of pain.

"Edith," Wren choked out. "Please."

And then, for what felt like the hundredth time that day, Wren Loughty fell back into time . . .

26

AUGUST

The screams went on for hours. August had expected them to stop eventually, but they continued to echo through the night and into morning. After a while, the broken sounds seemed to blend in with the encampment's natural symphony. A few Demiens glanced toward the tent, the briefest hint of concern on their faces, but nobody bothered to stop and investigate. Hell, some even looked amused, snickering in delight as they passed the tent.

August had tried everything to distract himself from the sound of Wren's cries. He attended the morning battle simulation. He taught another set of history classes. He tried, with every last shred of restraint he had left, to play the part of the ruthless, unfeeling general. But his façade was slipping with every echo of Wren's hoarse screams. His willpower cracking. He wasn't sure how much longer he could endure this suffering. How much longer he was capable of hearing her scream and not doing something about it.

Not to mention that their window of opportunity had almost closed. In a few hours, the initial festivities for the Equinox Gathering would begin. If August couldn't find a way to get Wren out of that damn tent by nightfall . . . then it would all fall apart. August would be forced to cast the Reaper's Kiss. And Wren's destiny would be solidified—she would be bound to become the catalyst of destruction, once and for all.

Their fates carved into stone.

Forced to meet their ruinous ends.

August was standing outside the tent now, hands clasped behind his back, fingernails biting into the flesh of his palms. Guilt gnawed at his bones. Deep down, he knew it wasn't his fault, that Edith would have tortured Wren with her death even if he hadn't come. But it still felt wrong to simply stand back and listen—to seemingly do *nothing.*

"How is she?" asked a voice behind him.

When August turned to face the source of the voice—Quinn Woodrow—he swallowed back any lingering guilt, contorting his features into that impenetrable mask he made sure to wear around the encampment. A withering scowl. Gray eyes void of emotion. Nothing but stone-cold indifference. Though, truthfully, if he was honest with himself, that façade was becoming easier and easier to slip back into with every drop of shadow magic he used.

"How do you think?" asked August, voice rough.

Quinn's eyes lingered on the entrance to the tent. She seemed . . . torn. Her teeth worried at her bottom lip, fingers drumming against her thighs. It was odd, to see so much palpable emotion written upon a Demien's face. Even those within Silver Unit did their best to mask their stubborn emotions.

"And there hasn't—" Quinn cut herself off, shifting from one foot to the other. "She hasn't . . ."

"No," August supplied sternly, understanding Quinn's unspoken question. "She hasn't transformed into the catalyst yet."

At that moment, another scream echoed from within the tent. The sound felt like a thousand rusted nails scraping against August's skin—a torment beyond anything he had ever endured.

When he glanced at Quinn, he was surprised to find the same terror he felt reflected upon her face.

"But maybe . . ." Her voice trailed off.

"What?"

"Maybe we could find a way to convince Edith to stop."

And that was all it took for August to snap. He reached out, gripping Quinn by the wrist, and dragged her to the side of the tent, away from any prying eyes. Before she could even open her mouth to protest, August was pinning her against the tentpole, holding her in place with his forearm.

"What the hell do you think you're doing?" he hissed. The shadows running through his veins hummed in satisfaction, relishing his anger, but he ignored their call, willing them to stay put.

"What"—Quinn tried to yank herself free, but August held firm—"are you talking about?"

August leaned in closer.

"Your emotions are showing, Private Woodrow." August did his best to seem menacing, his voice a seething whisper. He needed her to be afraid—fear was the only thing that could save her now. "Are you trying to get yourself branded for treason? Marked as *defected*?"

"I'm not . . ." Quinn scoffed, though August didn't miss the slight flicker of panic passing over her eyes. "That isn't what this is about."

"You're doubting the Soulless One." His words were an accusation. "I can see it written all over your face."

Quinn balked.

"That's not—"

"A word of advice," August whispered through gritted teeth, yanking Quinn forward by her wrist. Her face contorted into a scowl, but to her credit—she didn't flinch. She didn't cower under his gaze. "Demiens aren't supposed to care. You're supposed to carve out your humanity and succumb to the shadows. No emotions. No remorse. No feeling." He tilted his head, tutting. "And you're definitely not supposed to become *friends* with the prophesized catalyst."

"She's not my friend," Quinn shot back.

August scanned her face. The realization hit him a moment later.

"But you still care."

"And you don't?"

August blinked, taken aback. "Excuse me?"

Quinn glanced over her shoulder, lowering her voice. "You might have everyone else fooled—hell, you might even have Edith fooled—but not me," she whispered, eyes searing into his with surprising courage. "I was there when you two were in Blackwood. I saw how you were together. How you *looked* at her. That kind of twisted codependence doesn't just vanish—"

"I would think very carefully about what you say next." August inhaled a deep breath and a slithering shadow sprouted from his palm, wrapping around Quinn's wrist. *One more shadow,* August thought. *One more inch closer to the darkness.* Inside him, something stirred . . . fury and rage and something far more rotten. Something he didn't dare acknowledge. "Because it almost sounds like you're accusing me of treason."

"No." Quinn shook her head. "I'm not. But"—she leaned closer—"I *am* saying I would understand."

August flinched. He scanned her face, searching for some flicker of dishonesty, but all he saw was a bone-chilling sincerity etched upon her face. *Can I trust her?* The question echoed in August's mind. It would be a risk, revealing the truth of his motives, trusting anyone but himself.

"You should be more careful," he suggested in a hoarse whisper. "You're supposed to cast the Reaper's Kiss tonight at Equinox. These kinds of thoughts . . . these kinds of doubts . . . they could lead to your ruin."

Quinn's face paled. When she spoke, her voice wavered. "Are you threatening me?"

August stepped closer. "I'm warning you."

Quinn assessed him. She was clearly just as torn as August was—battling her better instincts, confronted with the question of whether or not she could trust him. But she must have read something in August's expression, because she stepped closer, and all at once, her walls came crumbling down.

"We want to help her," she blurted out.

August glanced over his shoulder, paranoia coursing through him, but nobody seemed to be around. Not that that mattered. Anybody could be listening. Watching. He was constantly being monitored and followed by other Onyx Unit Demiens, shadows tailing him that he couldn't shake off.

"Quinn—" August whispered her name through gritted teeth, but she interrupted, eyes welling with heartbreaking desperation.

"No," she muttered, shaking her head. "I can't. I can't keep pretending." Her chest rose and fell with panicked breaths as she continued, the words tumbling out of her, as if she was trying to speak before she could convince herself otherwise. "Artie and I have been trying to plan an escape for her since the beginning. The timing has just been off. We figured if we gave her access to roam the encampment more freely, she'd take it upon herself to investigate—"

"Wait." August cut her off. "The lock of hair. That was *you*?"

"Artie, technically. He snipped it from some sleeping Emerald Unit recruit."

August groaned, rubbing his face with his hands in exasperation. "You shouldn't be telling me this."

"Why?" Quinn snapped. "If you were truly not on our side, you would have thrown me into isolation by now. But I'm still here. Standing. And you're still here. Listening. So why don't we just cut the shit and figure out how to get her the hell out of here."

August dropped his hands from his face. "Why?"

Quinn blinked in surprise. "What?"

"Why would you want to help Wren escape?" August repeated. "What's in it for you?"

Quinn flinched, taken aback. She looked him up and down, brows cinched together. "You really think you're the only one?" she asked, voice trembling. "The only Demien in here who regrets what they've done?" Shame and hurt twisted her words, the sound of it sending a shiver down August's spine. "If Wren stays, she *will* become the catalyst. And once she's awoken . . . then that's it. Blackwood will be in ruins. Hundreds of innocent souls destroyed. Not to mention we have no idea what will happen to the afterlife with that level of corruption. It could all come undone."

"But . . . you chose this." August spoke the words slowly. "You made the decision to join the Order."

Quinn's bottom lip quivered. A flicker of defeat washed over her expression.

"I know," she whispered, voice cracking. "I was so angry. So fucking angry." She shook her head, mumbling something that August couldn't quite hear, her gaze drifting to the ground. She took a breath, as if composing herself, and continued. "I couldn't stomach the thought that my eternity had been chosen for me. That if I didn't prove myself to some stupid institution, then I'd be forced to reap lost souls for the rest of eternity. Lose all my memories? Lose the person I once was?"

August empathized with her—more than she would ever understand. "That's all I have left," Quinn went on. "My memories. My past. I wasn't ready to let that go. But . . . now I realize that I made a mistake. Coming here . . . it doesn't fix anything."

This was August's last opportunity to back out. To solidify the wall between them. He could pretend to be the unfeeling general again. He could stride away from Quinn and continue to work on his own, risking the possibility that he might not have what it would take to get Wren out of the encampment without help. Or . . . he could take a chance—a stupid, reckless chance—and trust Quinn.

August inhaled a sharp breath. He met Quinn's stare.

And then he knew.

He had no choice.

"What do we do?"

Relief washed over Quinn's expression the moment the words left August's lips.

"Artie can remove the security cuff," she said. August couldn't contain the shock that bled over his face. "But our window of opportunity afterward is going to be small. Almost nonexistent. The moment he deactivates it, the internal alarm is going to go off and warn Edith. Which means the *second* that security cuff is removed, we have to get Wren as far away from the encampment as humanly possible. Find somewhere safe to hide her."

Somewhere safe.

August knew *exactly* where. It was the only place left.

"I know somewhere," he whispered back. "It's all the way on the other side of purgatory. Far west, past Blackwood's central location. And truthfully, I'm not sure they'll be thrilled to see me . . . but we can try."

Quinn bit her bottom lip in concentration.

"We'll have to relocate her," she muttered, a faraway look in her eyes, as if she was calculating something. Her face fell. "But you can't relocate normally in the outskirts of purgatory . . . not like you can here or at Blackwood. You'd have to use shadow magic. *A lot* of it."

August shook his head. "I can take care of it."

"No." Quinn's expression hardened. "You're not listening to me." She let out a sigh. "To relocate someone *that* far away . . . it could change you. Not to the extent that casting the Reaper's Kiss would, but . . ." She let out a weighted sigh. "You could succumb to the shadows. It's a risk."

August didn't even hesitate. Screw his soul. Screw his eternity.

He'd damn himself—*destroy* himself—if it meant saving Wren.

"It's a risk I'm willing to take," he replied.

Quinn stared at him for an extended beat. Would she try to convince him otherwise? But she must have seen the determination in his eyes, felt the unwavering resolve burning through him, and decided against it.

"We'll need a distraction," she said simply.

August nodded. "Leave that to me."

They made the decision to meet in a few hours, right before the start of the Equinox Gathering. Quinn would make sure Arthur was ready to remove the security cuff, and August would make sure he had an ironclad distraction.

They'd have to time it perfectly.

But as they whispered their goodbyes and August turned away from Quinn, desperate to put as much distance as possible between him and the sound of Wren's screams, Quinn's voice echoed behind him.

"August." He glanced over his shoulder. Quinn was looking at him with unbridled curiosity, something oddly close to admiration in her eyes. When she spoke next, her voice was soft. "You're really willing to destroy yourself to save her?"

August's breath caught in his throat. He knew what his answer was.

For Wren?

Anything.

"I'll destroy myself," he echoed out loud. His shadows *burned* inside him. "And anybody who stands in my way."

27

MASIKA

A heaviness followed the group on their third day trekking through purgatory. Masika sensed it with every step. Not only were they approaching the third and final key—according to the map they'd discovered after revealing their innermost truths—but they had also begun to venture eerily close to Blackwood. The school's perimeter wasn't far . . . perhaps less than a day's hike away. Masika swore she could even *feel* it. It was something in her chest. A knowing pull in the core of her soul.

Come back, something seemed to whisper inside her. *Come back to us.*

"Seems a bit odd, doesn't it?" Dina remarked, pulling Masika's focus. The silver-haired girl spun one of her many daggers between her fingers. "You know, hiding his soul so close to Blackwood. Every key we find takes us closer and closer to the school's perimeter. You'd figure the True Headmaster would have hidden the damn thing as far away from Silas as possible."

"It doesn't really matter *where* it's hidden," Catherine reminded her. "No keys? No access."

"Yeah, obviously, but . . ." Dina shrugged. "I don't know. Doesn't seem like an entirely logical plan."

Analisa hummed knowingly, staring up at the canopy of trees above them. "Sometimes logic is hidden beneath chaos."

Dina rolled her eyes. "Whatever. My point still stands."

"We're not far," Catherine muttered under her breath, staring down at the map in her hands. "It shouldn't be too much longer."

"What do you think happens once we have all three keys?" Emilio asked. He had Benji cradled in his arms, and the little creature was staring up at Emilio with adoration in his beady red eyes.

"Well, clearly we're going to use them to unlock *something*," Dina mumbled. "Perhaps his resting place requires the keys."

"Or maybe he's sending us on this wild-goose chase for a good laugh." Olivier sighed, kicking a pebble in his path.

"Always the optimist," Masika muttered, elbowing Olivier in the ribs. The boy winced, offering her a shrug. Although his relationship with Emilio had finally blossomed, Masika couldn't help but notice a slight strain in Olivier's face. A palpable concern. She supposed she couldn't blame him—given the dwindling countdown that had begun in his mind.

"You okay?"

Olivier chuckled hoarsely. "Define *okay*."

"He could help you," she whispered. "The True Headmaster. If anyone can . . . it *has* to be him."

Olivier offered her a tight-lipped smile. "I suppose we'll see."

Masika sighed. She was seconds away from making what she hoped would be another encouraging comment when Emilio's voice cut in, echoing just behind the group.

"Uh . . . guys."

Masika whirled on her heels, eyes skating over to where the other boy was looking, and something in her chest surged. The others saw it too. A glowing path had appeared in front of Emilio, like speckles of starlight glittering upon the dirt floor. It was leading them northeast, deeper into the woods.

Analisa walked over to Emilio and bent down. She dug her fingernails into the dirt, the glittering starlight twinkling in her palm.

"Fascinating," she muttered. "It feels . . . warm."

"Should we follow it?" Olivier asked, tentatively approaching the glowing path.

Dina shook her head. "We should follow the map. We have the map for a reason."

"Hold on." Catherine glanced down at the map and then back up to Emilio. She furrowed her brows, clearly piecing something together in her mind. "How did . . . I don't understand . . ."

"What is it?" Masika asked, approaching Catherine.

The other girl shook her head in disbelief. "I swear this wasn't here before."

Catherine angled the map toward her, and Masika saw what the other girl must be referring to. A glowing yellow light now emanated from the map, the same trail that Emilio had discovered reflected upon the map's illustration.

"It wants us to follow the path," Masika whispered. She looked up to find Catherine staring at her intently.

"I think so."

"Well." Dina let out a weighted sigh. "Following a mysterious glowing path would not be my first choice—but *screw it*."

Catherine continued to stare at Masika, as if weighing her options.

Masika shrugged.

"Screw it?"

Catherine sighed.

"Screw it."

They followed the path for what felt like hours. And given the darkening sky stretching out before them, Masika assumed it truly had been hours. She watched as the familiar silver glow of Blackwood washed over the horizon, thin ribbons of mist gliding beneath her feet. They *had* to be close to Blackwood. Dangerously close. Masika nervously drummed her fingers at her sides, willing her body to ignore the strange pull that seemed to be coming from the north, guiding her back toward Blackwood.

Luckily, it was at that same moment that something in the path began to change. The glowing speckles of light widened, veering suddenly right. Catherine's eyes narrowed as she picked up speed and followed the path's new direction, while the others struggled to keep up.

"What's happening?" Emilio asked, scurrying forward.

"Something in the path is changing," Analisa muttered, inspecting the path with wide, curious eyes.

"Hurry!" Dina exclaimed, ushering the rest of the group forward.

They trailed the glowing speckles of light, practically running as the path widened and widened—until finally . . .

The group came to a sudden halt.

Emilio cocked his head. "A door."

The glowing path had abruptly stopped. What lay before them now was a door embedded in the ground, almost like the entrance to a cellar. Without hesitating, Catherine placed her hand upon the doorknob and twisted, opening it with a flourish. There were stairs inside, steps descending into darkness.

Catherine lit a small flame at the base of her palm, igniting the air in a faint orange glow, and turned to face the group. "Stay close."

They ventured forward, slow and cautious. There was no telling what was waiting for them below in the darkness. Each key had come with its fair share of danger, and Masika could only imagine that the final key would be no different. If anything, a part of her feared that the final key might pose an extra challenge—one that, perhaps, they would fail.

But as they reached the bottom of the stairs, entering a small circular room comprised of stone walls and nothing else, confusion settled upon Masika. Because what waited for them at the bottom was no monster or beast or terrifying test. It was far simpler—and far more confusing.

Standing on the other side of the room, a third key tucked in its mouth, was a fox.

Instantly, Benji let out a deep and guttural growl, squirming in Emilio's arms. Emilio did his best to comfort the little creature, shielding him from the fox's line of sight. But the fox didn't seem at all disturbed by Benji's obvious disdain, nor did it seem to care much about the group's presence.

It simply watched them.

Waiting.

"Are you kidding?" Dina barked, gesturing toward the fox with a wave of her hand. "I don't get it. Are we supposed to just walk up and take it?"

Olivier snorted. "I doubt it'll be that easy."

Dina raised a brow at Olivier in a silent challenge. And before anybody could dissuade her, the silver-haired girl gave a determined nod and charged forward, straight toward the fox.

But Olivier had been right.

One moment Dina was standing in front of the fox, hand outstretched toward the key, and the next she was doubling over in pain, a broken cry erupting from her throat. Catherine's eyes widened and she instinctively jolted forward, but when she reached Dina's side, her own face contorted in agony, knees buckling as she clutched her head.

Masika felt her body move, but Catherine extended her hand before Masika could close the distance between them.

"Don't—move." Catherine gritted her teeth. She slowly peeled her eyes away from Masika, seemingly using all her strength to grip Dina by the collar and yank her backward. The second the pair fell a few feet away from the fox, whatever pain had been coursing through them seemingly vanished, and their faces instantly relaxed.

"What . . . the hell . . . was that?" Dina asked through labored breaths. She fought to right herself, swaying as she found her footing.

"It must have some sort of defensive barrier," Analisa commented, inspecting the fox from a distance. "Though I've never seen one quite like *that* before. Defensive barriers usually limit mobility, not cause *pain*."

"Well," Dina huffed. "That thing caused pain, all right. I thought I was dying all over again."

Catherine winced. A sweat-slicked strand of hair clung to her forehead, and Masika resisted the urge to brush it back.

"That must be the final test," Catherine muttered, panting. "Find a way to pass through the defensive barrier and take the key."

Masika eyed her carefully. "Are you okay?" she whispered.

Catherine gave a feeble nod. "I'll be fine."

"Well, how the hell are we supposed to dismantle a defensive barrier we've never encountered before?" Olivier asked, exasperated. He pointed at Analisa. "You! You're a healer! Can't you do one of your—" Olivier wiggled his fingers, making what Masika assumed was a poor attempt at re-creating one of Analisa's famous healing spells.

Analisa sighed. "No. That's not how this works."

The others began to argue back and forth, different theories and ideas being hurled left and right, but Masika could barely hear them. As the room exploded into arguments, Masika felt something stir inside her.

It started at the base of her spine. A faint call. A strange awareness. Masika wondered at first if it was her own voice—her subconscious whispering to her in the back of her mind. But the longer she listened to it, the more she realized that it wasn't her, but someone else.

Some*thing* else.

A voice.

Closer.

She stepped forward. Beside her, Emilio was saying something, though she couldn't quite hear him. It was as if everything in her peripheral vision had melted away. All she saw was the fox and the key tucked in his mouth. Nothing else.

Closer.

Masika gently pushed past Emilio. She felt her arms moving.

Someone was shouting at her. *Stop! Don't!* But Masika could no longer hear them. She continued forward, inching closer and closer to the fox, until she was kneeling right in front of it, peering down at the creature's dark eyes.

She was close enough that the pain of the defensive barrier should have shocked her by now, and yet . . . she felt nothing. No pain. Just complete and total calm. She lifted her hand and scratched the fox gently beneath the chin.

It watched her.

Take it.

Masika reached out her hand. She didn't even have to grab the key. The fox simply leaned forward, opening its narrow jaw, and dropped it onto her palm.

The second it touched her skin, the key came to life. A brilliant deep indigo glow burst out of it, nearly blinding Masika, though she didn't look away. She couldn't even blink. She stared and stared and stared and—

Masika snapped to her senses from one blink to the next, the sound of the others rushing in as though she'd been thrust back into her body. The third key was now tucked in her hand, and the fox . . . it was *gone*. As if it had never existed at all.

"What the hell?" Olivier's brows were pinched in concern, eyes skating over Masika's face as though he was checking her for any signs of injury. Emilio was beside him, staring up at Masika expectantly. "How did you do that?"

Masika blinked, dazed. "I . . . I don't know."

Catherine stepped closer. She inspected Masika with the same tentative concern that Olivier had shown only seconds earlier.

"Did you dismantle the barrier?" she asked carefully.

"Better question is *how* did you dismantle it?" Olivier added.

Masika opened and closed her mouth. What *had* she done? She couldn't remember. All she could remember was feeling as though she wanted—no, *needed* to approach the fox. Had she heard a voice calling to her?

Masika shook her head, clearing away the thoughts. "I don't know, okay? I just . . . grabbed it."

Before the interrogation could go any further, Dina's voice called out to them from a few feet ahead. Masika, too caught up in the dazed feeling that had come over her, hadn't even noticed her and Analisa pushing past them.

"Take a look at this."

A few feet ahead, right behind where the fox had been, now stood a door with three keyholes. It was fairly easy to discern where each key went—corresponding colors were painted over the metal openings. Dark emerald. Ruby red. Deep indigo.

"Is this . . . is this it?" Emilio asked in a shaky whisper. "Is this the resting place?"

"Looks like it," Analisa mumbled. She gestured Catherine forward with an encouraging nod. "Go on."

Catherine turned to face the door, breath held. She inserted the emerald key first. Then, with a steady hand, she placed the red key in its slot. Finally, she turned to face Masika, hand extended.

For a tense beat, Masika remained frozen. She knew she should hand Catherine the third and final key, but she found herself clutching it a bit tighter, holding on to it for a second too long. But before the others could notice, she forced herself to drop it into Catherine's hand, ignoring the hollowness left in its wake.

Catherine slipped the indigo key into the final slot.

She placed her hand upon the door, exhaled a shuddering breath, and pushed.

To Masika's immense relief . . . the door opened.

A small stone chamber greeted them—strange carvings etched into the walls, golden sconces adorning the perimeter of the room. Catherine entered first, with Dina and Analisa on her heels. Masika, Olivier and Emilio entered together, Benji still cradled in Emilio's arms.

Candles lit the chamber in a hazy orange glow, though Masika could tell they were enchanted. They had a dreamlike flicker, an otherworldly shimmer that made the flames appear to be made up of thousands of tiny stars.

And standing at the center, carved from gleaming obsidian, stood a tomb.

But something wasn't right.

The large stone slab on top of the tomb had already been shoved aside.

A panicked thought shot through Masika.

Someone has already been here.

For a moment, nobody moved. Breaths held, they stood there, their minds slowly attempting to piece together what they were seeing. It was Dina who finally snapped out of it, beelining toward the tomb. Behind her, Catherine followed, though she kept her distance.

Dina peered inside, hands pressed carefully on the edge of the tomb. She paused, a hitch in her breath, and then she reached for something, stretching her arm down farther, until finally, she straightened her shoulders, turning back to face them. But when Masika met her gaze, she noticed that Dina's face had gone pallid, her eyes riddled with panic.

"What?" Catherine snapped, eyes wild. "What is it?"

Dina unfurled her palm and revealed a small piece of paper. There was something etched upon the ripped-up parchment. A drawing. "This is the only thing I found."

Catherine's expression hardened. "What do you mean?"

"There's nothing else in there." Dina let out a shuddering breath. "It's empty."

28

IRENE

There weren't many Ascended duties that Irene was fond of, but reformatory watch had to be one of the worst. It was incessantly boring, not to mention an absolute waste of her time and talents. It wasn't like the students in reformatory could leave. A magical barrier surrounded the room, which meant that even if they *wanted* to try to escape, they couldn't. Irene's presence was merely an extra defensive measure.

A stupid one, Irene thought with a grumble.

She crossed her arms and leaned her head against the door. She could hear what sounded like sobbing on the other side, but it was muffled. It didn't matter either way. She'd dealt with reformatory before.

The kid would survive.

As the afternoon ticked by, slow and seemingly endless, Irene's mind wandered to her last conversation with Mateo. She didn't understand why he was being so secretive. Sure, she hadn't *technically* joined the Order yet, but she was quite literally risking her soul to help them infiltrate the school. Shouldn't that be enough reassurance that she was on their side? Shouldn't that be enough to convince them that she was truly one of their—

Irene.

Irene stilled, yanked out of her thoughts. Had someone spoken her name? She glanced left and right, but there was nobody lurking in either of the corridors flanking her. Could it have been the student on the other side?

Irene.

She jumped, startled. Okay. Now she was *certain* she'd heard a voice. It had come from the left, farther down the corridor. *Screw it.* It wasn't like the student in reformatory was going anywhere.

Irene ventured down the corridor, listening intently. Waiting, and waiting, and . . .

Irene.

The voice was right behind her.

She spun on her heels, bracing for a fight, but instead came face to face with her own reflection.

It was a mirror. It was floating, the golden frame hovering in the air.

"Hello?" Irene called out, feeling a bit foolish for talking to her own reflection.

She waited. For a moment, she swore she saw something changing in her reflection, another set of eyes staring back at her, another face lurking in the distance. Irene took a rigid step backward . . . but it was too late.

Irene barely had time to gasp before a pair of hands reached out, gripping her shoulders, and pulled her into the mirror.

She landed on her hands and knees in a rather ungraceful heap. The first thing she noticed was that she recognized the room she'd been thrown into. It was the main hall of Bonestrod. She'd recognize those dark, decrepit floorboards anywhere. And if there was anybody who enjoyed meeting in Bonestrod, anybody who enjoyed dramatic entrances . . .

Irene groaned. "Silas."

The Headmaster's voice echoed not a second after. "Thank you for meeting me here, Irene. Apologies for the abrupt call."

Headmaster Silas was standing by the stone hearth, Samira and Everly waiting by his side. They looked equally frazzled and disheveled, which led Irene to believe they'd been called here in the same unconventional manner.

"Honestly?" Irene pushed herself to her feet, blowing a strand of dark hair away from her face. "I'm starting to get used to it."

"All right. Irene is here." Everly crossed her arms, staring up at Silas with a scowl. "Can you *please* tell us if this is a test now?"

Silas's lips curved into a smirk. "It's . . . *something* like that."

He turned to the fireplace, pulling down on one of the sconces. Instantly, the wall behind them shifted, revealing a hidden room on the other side. Irene balked. Had that always been there? Before any of them could utter another word, Silas guided them forward, ushering them into the room.

Shock coursed through Irene when she saw what waited for them. "Is this . . . an armory?" she asked, bewildered.

It certainly looked like it. Weapons adorned every inch of the walls. Swords. Spears. Daggers. Arrows. There had to be hundreds of objects concealed within the room, an array of defensive equipment.

"As a member of the Council, you are not just a defender of Blackwood." Silas wandered over to the section of the room containing what appeared to be dozens of bows and arrows. He took hold of three arrows, brandishing them. "You are a soldier." He tossed one to each of them, and Irene caught hers with ease, letting the weight of the arrow settle upon her hand. "All of the weapons found here are activated by your loyalty to Blackwood."

"Activated?" Samira echoed. She tapped the pointed edge of the arrowhead. "Don't you just . . . shoot it?"

"These are not ordinary weapons." Silas grabbed a fourth arrow, and the moment he closed his palm around it, a glistening white light erupted from the shaft, nearly blinding Irene. She shielded her eyes. The other girls winced, lowering their gazes as the light exploded all around them. Somewhere beyond the dazzling light, Silas's voice continued to echo. "They hold an ancient magic. One that is activated by true loyalty to Blackwood. Once activated, these weapons hold the ability to rip into the core of someone's soul. Destroy them with nothing but a single arrow to the heart."

The light vanished. Irene blinked, dazed, and noticed that Silas had placed the arrow back in its slot.

"You mean, we can destroy a soul with nothing but an arrow?" Everly asked through a chuckle.

Silas nodded. "If your loyalty is strong—then yes."

Everly rolled her eyes, as if the mere thought of her loyalty being tested was nothing more than a silly nuisance. She wrapped her hand tightly around her arrow and closed her eyes, and Irene watched as a similar light burned through her and into the arrow. Unlike Silas's, Everly's light wasn't blinding. Squinting, Irene could keep her gaze anchored on the other girl, despite the halo of light surrounding her.

"Very nice, Ms. Hawthorne." Silas nodded in approval.

Everly opened her eyes and the light vanished. She turned to Samira with arrogant satisfaction. "Go on. Let's see what yours looks like."

Samira flipped the end of her braid behind her shoulders and took her stance. She gripped her arrow tightly, closing her hands, and exhaled a steadying breath. Irene waited. There was a slight delay, and Everly had already begun to curl her lips into a smug grin when a light suddenly exploded out of Samira's arrow. It was brighter than Everly's, enough that Irene had to shield her eyes, though not nearly bright enough to light up the entire room.

Samira let out a triumphant giggle and opened her eyes. The light vanished only seconds after.

"Wonderful, Ms. Heydari." Silas nodded encouragingly. "Splendid work."

Irene couldn't help but feel a twinge of satisfaction at seeing Everly's smirk falter, though that feeling was instantly squashed when the group turned to look at her and she realized it was her turn.

A thought settled upon Irene without warning.

I'm going to fail.

What loyalty did she truly have to Blackwood? She'd been able to trick the Council into believing she was worth trusting, but could she fake loyalty to Blackwood? And under Silas's watchful gaze?

Her hand shook as she took hold of the arrow. She could feel the grating stares of the others—Samira and Everly watching, a hunger in their expressions. They wanted her to fail. To watch her slip and fall. And then there was Silas. It was difficult to discern what exactly he was thinking, but the intensity of his gaze made Irene's skin crawl.

Just breathe, she told herself. *Focus.*

Irene closed her eyes. She tried to search for a connection to Blackwood, to recall Silas's words back in Boston, but her mind felt fractured. Too many memories flitting in and out of her consciousness. Lately, it had been impossible to figure out where her loyalties truly lay. Could she even say she fully trusted Mateo anymore? It was obvious he was keeping secrets from her. Concealing information. But she still wanted to help him . . . to join the Order.

Didn't she?

Something was stirring inside her. Another voice. Another memory.

"I see . . . the war in you. Your heart . . . is split. Two sides . . ."

Thalia. The words she had spoken to Irene in the dungeons. Right before Irene stood back and watched Thalia's soul disintegrate into nothing.

"I wonder . . . which . . . you will choose."

A face threaded its way through her mind. Amber eyes. Deep brown skin. A small, knowing smile. Irene reached for it, but her fingers came up empty, nothing but wisps of smoke threading through her fingers.

Masika.

The name burned through Irene. And then something snapped.

Irene opened her eyes . . . and the darkness of Bonestrod had shattered.

All around, emanating from the heart of Irene's arrow, exploded a blazing white light. It undulated in shimmering waves, bursting through her and around her, enveloping every corner of the room. There was a heat burrowing into Irene's palm. A power.

She glanced up, hands shaking, and met Silas's gaze. Something was glinting in his eyes. A look that made Irene's chest tighten. A blanket of goose bumps covering every inch of her skin.

Pride.

When Irene dropped the arrow, letting it clatter to the floor, the light vanished, darkness falling upon Bonestrod once again. She didn't understand why it had worked—why *her* arrow had burned the brightest of them all. If the arrows were strengthened by true, unwavering loyalty to Blackwood . . . then did that mean Irene's loyalties had shifted? Whether she was conscious of it or not?

Irene shivered as another question burned its way through her mind. She thought she could ignore it, push it away, force it to the periphery, but there was no escaping it now. It echoed in her mind, unrelenting, demanding an answer.

Whose side am I really on?

Irene was afraid to find out.

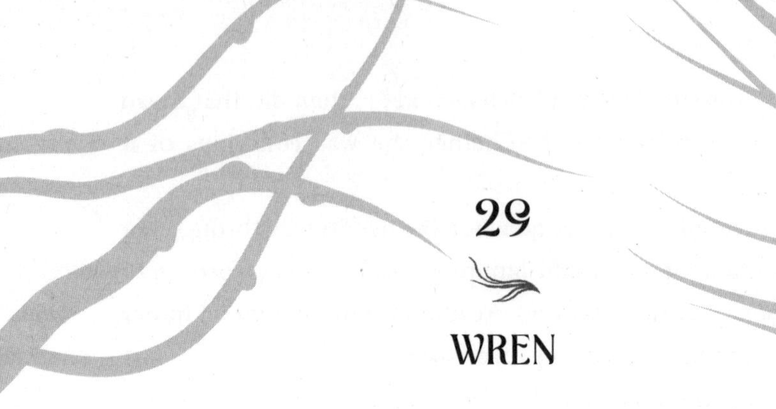

29

WREN

As Wren gasped awake, thrust back into reality, she immediately became aware of three distinct things.

1. She was in a tent she didn't recognize.
2. She was wearing a dress.
3. Callum Whitlock was standing in front of her.

The Demien stared at her as though she were something to eat. His teeth skimmed his bottom lip, his green eyes blazing with hunger as he took in the sight of Wren standing in front of him. Wren's own eyes traveled downward, inspecting her outfit. Silky black waves cascaded down her body, iridescent beads swirling over a tight bodice. Her arms and back were exposed, two thin straps pressed against her shoulders, crisscrossing over her back. The hem of the dress seemed to ripple and move, as if caught in a breeze, candlelight reflecting against the shimmering black fabric. She had no recollection of changing, and the mere thought that somebody had put their hands on her while she'd been unconscious, even if it had been just to dress her, made her want to keel over and vomit.

"Stunning." Callum let out a low whistle and prowled closer. "Just absolutely *stunning*."

"What—" Wren coughed, fighting to find her voice. Her throat felt raw. Swollen. As if she'd been screaming for hours. She probably had been. "What's happening?"

"It's time for Equinox, of course." Callum strode closer, a mocking lilt in his voice. "Oh, come now, Wren. You didn't think we'd leave you out, did you? You're the catalyst! The star of the show. But don't worry, once the festivities are over, you'll go right back to your sessions with Edith."

Wren tried to back away, to run, but her limbs were frozen.

"I can't move," she muttered through clenched teeth.

Callum chuckled.

"That would be my fault." He inched closer, head cocked. "You see . . . I like you better this way." He extended his hand, fingers reaching for her lips, but Wren spat in his face before he could.

"Don't fucking touch me," she said, seething.

Callum wiped his face with eerie calm. When he stared at Wren, she saw a flicker of anger behind his eyes, but there was also a perverse sense of excitement. As if he'd been hoping she'd put up a fight.

"Wren." Callum practically purred her name, lips drooping into a mocking pout. "You wound me. I would never touch you without permission." He inched his face toward her ear, until his lips were practically brushing the side of her face. "Soon, you'll be aching for me. Begging me to touch you and show you what a *real* Demien can do."

Wren wanted to scream. She wanted to tear him apart. She wanted to—

"I can take it from here, Callum."

Wren heard the deep rasp of August's voice before she saw him, and then he was materializing behind Callum, appearing in a plume of shadows. Rage burned behind his silver eyes. He wore an all-black suit with a cloak draped over his shoulders, his dark curls pushed back away from his face. Wren hadn't noticed before, but the shadow-filled veins had begun to snake their way up his neck, inching toward his jaw.

He'd never looked more beautiful.

And he'd never looked more like a Demien.

"General Hughes." Callum's lip twitched as he slowly turned to face August. "I was instructed to fetch the catalyst—"

"And yet here you are, appeasing your ego instead of following orders." August kept his gaze anchored on Callum, and Wren half expected him to tear the other Demien's head clean off his neck. "Edith grew tired of waiting. She asked me to come get her instead."

Callum scoffed. "But—"

"It isn't up for discussion."

August's voice came out warped and distorted, a terrifying sound that sent a chill down Wren's spine. His eyes bled black, but when he blinked, their whites returned. For a fleeting moment, he looked startled.

Did he not mean to do that? Has he already begun to lose control?

Wren's throat grew tight.

There was a tense beat of silence, as if Callum was weighing his options, and then he simply offered a mocking salute, sauntering toward the entrance of the tent. He glanced over his shoulders, shooting Wren one final look.

"Save me a dance, catalyst."

The moment Callum walked out of the tent, leaving the two of them alone, Wren felt her limbs loosen, and she nearly collapsed from sheer relief. But August's hands were on her before she could fall, warm and steadying.

"Are you okay?" he whispered, voice shaking. "I'm so sorry I couldn't get here sooner."

"I'm . . . fine." Wren swallowed and straightened herself. "I just feel a bit . . . foggy."

"That's normal." He nodded, the muscles in his jaw twitching. "You know . . . given what Edith put you through."

"August . . ." Wren's voice cracked. "We're out of time. Equinox is starting . . . We can't . . . we can't leave."

August cupped her chin with his thumb, angling her face toward him.

"I'm not going to let anything happen to you, okay? I promise. We have a plan . . . You're just going to have to trust me."

Wren tensed. "*We?*"

"You were right. There *are* other Demiens who want to help." August's face softened. His thumb drew featherlight circles against the edge of her jaw. "I have a way to get the security cuff off." As he continued to speak, he gently guided them toward the entrance to the tent. "Right before they begin the offerings, there's going to be an explosion. As soon as it goes off, Arthur is going to step behind you and undo the security cuff—"

"Arthur?" Wren's head spun as she tried to piece together everything August was telling her. "You mean . . ."

"He's on your side," August interjected, nodding. "Both of them are. As soon as the security cuff is off, we're going to make a run for it. Quinn is going to construct a temporary defensive barrier in front of the encampment. If there's even a single molecule of the relocation spell left in the air by the time they catch up to us, someone could sense where we went. Ideally, with Quinn's barrier, that won't be an issue. By the time they reach the exterior of the encampment, we'll be gone. And so will our relocation spell."

Wren placed a shaking hand on the security cuff, tracing its cold, sharp edges. "And if it doesn't work?"

There was a silence. August took Wren's face in his hands, drawing her closer. "Do you trust me?"

Wren let out a shuddering breath. "Against my better judgment."

August's lips lifted into a sad smile. He leaned forward and kissed her. It was a torturous kiss—deep and slow, his hands cupping her neck, his body pressing into her. It felt like heaven. Like everything else around them had vanished, blurring away in their peripheral vision.

It felt like . . . goodbye.

As August pulled away and stepped toward the entrance of the tent, Wren felt the way he nervously drummed his fingers against her waist, the tension in his muscles. She wanted to offer him some semblance of comfort, but truthfully, she was just as nervous as he was. This was their last opportunity to make it out. They'd either manage to escape—or they'd lose each other forever.

"With me?" August's voice gently tugged Wren back to the present.

Wren laced her hand through his.

"Always."

And then the two of them inhaled a sharp breath and walked through the tent.

Wren hadn't known what to expect upon entering the Equinox Gathering, but it definitely hadn't been *this*.

A deep crimson fog perfused the spacious cavern, instantly

dulling Wren's senses. Warm light spilled from lanterns strung across the sheer walls of the cave, enchanted string lights glittering like a blanket of stars. At the center of the cavern, bursting from a large black cauldron, roared a fire. The flames crackled with some sort of enchantment, the embers dancing as though caught within an invisible current. A deep, resounding drum echoed in the air, the pounding beat pulsating inside Wren. It was as though her body was drawn to the music, her muscles itching to move along to the drum's rhythm.

The Demiens bustling around the cavern glided in an almost euphoric daze. They all wore gowns and suits as ostentatious as the one Wren had awoken in—a sea of bloodred, royal purple, glistening emerald and ice blue—rich, silky fabrics ebbing and flowing against the darkness of night. Their eyes glistened with hunger. Raucous laugher dripped from their wicked smiles. A few of them carried brass goblets with various glittering liquids bubbling inside, shimmering clouds emanating from the goblets and drifting into the air. They were strange elixirs Wren had never seen before. But whatever they were drinking was clearly having some sort of inebriating effect on their minds. Those carrying the goblets seemed even more intoxicated than the others, a sluggish sway to their movements, a haze draped behind their eyes.

"All the new recruits are forced to drink the elixirs," August explained into her ear as he guided her forward. "It dulls their senses. Makes them more pliable. That way . . . if there are any who have last-minute hesitation about casting the Reaper's Kiss . . ." His voice trailed away, but Wren understood.

"They can't fight back."

August nodded, swallowing.

"We should keep you out of sight," he muttered. "Last thing

we need is Edith spotting you and forcing you to—" But they were too late. A voice cut through August's words. A presence looming behind them.

"Hello, little brother."

They turned and came face to face with Edith Hughes. She swished a goblet in her hands, the deep red liquid sloshing at the edges. Sparkling wisps curled at the elixir's surface, drifting around the goblet in a perfect halo. Edith wore a midnight-blue dress with chain-mail spaulders cascading over her shoulders and down her arms, her shadow crown glinting in the darkness, even more ornate than usual.

"Thank you for escorting our precious catalyst," she said through a piercing smile.

August stiffened beside Wren. His voice was rough and unfeeling as he responded, "Just doing my job."

Edith rolled her eyes with a chuckle. She turned her attention to Wren, extending the goblet in her direction. "Go on." She gestured to the goblet with a tilt of her chin. "Drink."

Wren's heart sank. Her eyes darted to August for a moment, but his gaze was firmly planted on Edith, not an inkling of emotion to be seen on his face. Wren couldn't drink the elixir. Not now. What if she lost herself to the intoxicating properties before she could make a run for it? What if she couldn't follow through with the plan?

Wren gave an indignant shake of her head. "I don't want to. I'm not a new recruit—"

"Listen, Wren." Edith cut her off with a sigh, stepping closer. The goblet brushed Wren's chest. "You can willingly drink it yourself, while still having control of your body, or I can force you to. The decision is yours."

Wren knew what Edith wanted. It was what all the other

Demiens wanted. They wanted Wren weak. Malleable. Nothing but a plaything to be tossed around and to do their bidding. They wanted her *afraid*.

But Wren was done being afraid.

Before she could second-guess herself, Wren wrapped her hand tightly around the goblet, gaze locked with Edith's, and chugged back one swift gulp.

The moment the liquid touched the back of her throat, a disorienting wave of vertigo flooded her body. Her mind grew hazy. Her chest warm. When she blinked, the world around her stuttered, as if her vision was lagging, a disconnect between her eyes and her mind. She swayed, losing her footing.

She'd expected August to catch her. To feel his strong hands against her waist.

But it wasn't August who reached her first.

Edith's hands gripped Wren by the shoulders, holding her steady. Wren's vision blurred and refocused. She fought to keep her eyelids open, and when she finally managed to lock her gaze on Edith, she noticed the shadows blotting out the whites of the High General's eyes. The sinister smile cracking her face in half.

"Welcome to Equinox, catalyst." Edith laughed and a euphoric haze draped itself around Wren. "It's time to have a bit of fun."

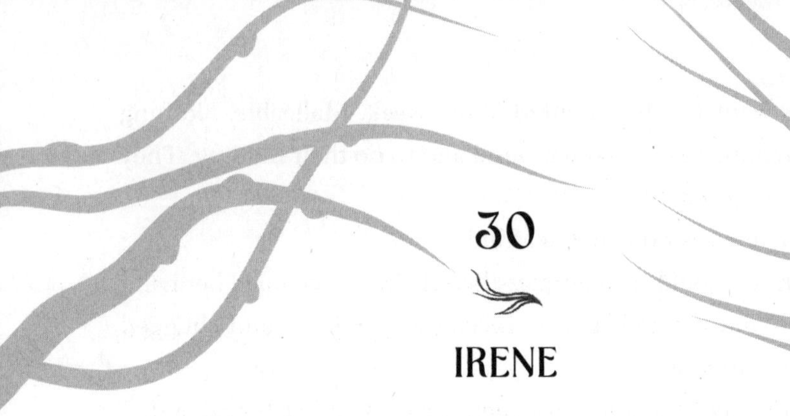

30

IRENE

"You may enter, Ms. Bamford."

Irene tried to ignore the blanket of goose bumps cascading down her arms as she stepped into Headmaster Silas's office. There was nothing otherworldly about the room, nothing outright menacing, but it was still disconcerting, as though the four walls were breathing around her, the air pulsating with power. She tried to mold her expression into one of indifference, overly aware of each sharp breath expanding her lungs.

She'd received the summons later that night, after the weaponry test in Bonestrod, a letter slipped beneath her door.

Upon reading its contents, Irene had been instantly struck by a wave of anxiety. She'd already been left shaken by the demonstration with the arrows—a strange, disconcerting feeling churning in her stomach. She shouldn't feel loyalty toward Blackwood, and yet . . . did she? The arrow seemed to think she did. But perhaps Silas had seen the deceit written upon her face. The doubt.

Maybe he'd called her to his office to expose her lies, once and for all.

But now, as she sat across from Headmaster Silas, she set aside all that apprehension and slipped on her carefully curated mask. She wouldn't cower and plead for mercy. She'd look him straight in the eyes, until the very end.

"What can I help you with, Headmaster?" she asked, tone level.

Silas smiled, though there was a slight edge to it.

"I wanted to see how you were feeling."

Irene cocked her head. That was not what she had been expecting. "I'm . . . fine."

"The Council test period can be rather exhausting," Silas commented, hands clasped in front of him. "It's a lot of pressure."

Irene cleared her throat and shifted in her seat. "I don't mean to be blunt, Headmaster, but you can't expect me to *actually* believe you give a damn about my feelings."

Silas let out a chuckle. He lowered his reading glasses, letting them hang around his neck from a small golden chain. Irene wondered if she'd pushed him too far, but Silas didn't seem rattled by her comment. If anything, he relaxed even further into his leather chair, the strained smile on his lips melting into one of familiarity.

"You make a fair point," he replied. He tapped his fingers against his desk. "I suppose I should just cut to the chase, shouldn't I?"

Irene molded her lips into a rigid smile. "I think that's best."

Silas clasped his hands together. "Tonight . . ." he began, voice low and foreboding, ". . . after this meeting, you and the other Council candidates will enter the woods in search of something."

Irene's throat tightened. "In search of what?"

Silas's dark eyes darted over her face. His expression grew solemn.

"The defensive wards that surround Blackwood don't just protect the school from those who wish to infiltrate the grounds," he explained. "They also warn us when someone is nearby. Almost like a security alarm."

Irene shrugged. "So?"

Headmaster Silas's eyes narrowed, the muscles in his jaw tensing.

"A few minutes ago . . . one of the wards near the outer perimeter alerted us to a disturbance." He stood from his chair, slowly, making his way toward the other side of his office. There, Irene spotted a stone pillar with a small sphere resting on top. Silas gestured her closer. "Please. Join me."

Irene raised herself onto her feet, muscles tense and rigid. She approached Silas tentatively, apprehension in each step. When she finally planted herself beside him and peered down at the pillar, she realized it wasn't actually a sphere resting on the top of the structure. It was a skull.

Irene leaned in closer, examining the alabaster skull with a furrowed brow. "What is this?"

Silas didn't answer. He simply placed his hand on top of the skull; golden light trickled out of his palm, filling the skull's shadowy cracks. Then, to Irene's astonishment, the skull cracked open, revealing a small brass telescope nestled inside.

"The wards can't give us a perfect visual," Silas explained, reaching into the skull and removing the telescope. "But the image is clear enough." He extended his arm, offering the telescope to Irene. "Here. See for yourself."

Irene grabbed the telescope with a shaking hand. She wasn't entirely sure why, but a horrible feeling had begun to unravel in the pit of her stomach. A nauseating sense of dread. She wrapped her fingers around the brass telescope and brought the eyepiece closer.

At first . . . all she saw was darkness.

And then the darkness began to move.

Shapes and figures formed within the shadowy wisps, the vague outline of Blackwood's forest slowly coalescing. There were bodies materializing in the vision too. A group of six. Their forms were clear, especially those who lingered at the back of the group, but there was somebody standing near the front . . . a face Irene would recognize anywhere.

Irene couldn't contain the gasp that sprang out of her.

The telescope toppled out of her hands. Her knees buckled beneath her.

She drew in strangled breaths as she tried to swallow back the panic, to push away the disbelief contorting her insides, and forced her eyes to meet Silas's sobering gaze. The Headmaster of Blackwood Academy was staring at her with an intensity that Irene had never seen before.

"Is that—" She swallowed, shaking her head. "Is that *her*?" She couldn't even bring herself to say her name out loud. Not when she wasn't certain.

Silas picked up the telescope from the floor, placing it back inside the skull.

"I believe so, but . . ." His voice trailed off as the skull slowly closed around the telescope, its splintered cracks mending. "We have to be certain. We have to check."

Irene's heart sank in her chest.

No.

"You . . ." Irene cleared her throat. "You want me to check. You want me to go see if it's her . . . don't you?"

Silas nodded. "You and the other Council candidates will enter the forest and confirm her identity, as well as the others within her group." Silas stepped closer, towering over Irene. "Ms. Bamford . . . you should know . . . this is your final test. Your last chance to show me that you belong here."

This is it.

Despite the silence blanketing the space between them, Irene knew. It was something in the way Silas was staring at her. Something in the dark vortex of his gaze. If Irene agreed to go into the forest, if she swallowed the panic and terror rising up her throat . . . then she would be chosen.

She would join the Council.

"What if we're right?" Irene whispered, voice wavering. "I mean . . . what if it *is* her?"

Silas hesitated. Around him, the air seemed to crackle with electricity, charged with a power Irene could barely fathom. But she wanted to. She wanted to reach out and rip it out of his chest. To seize it for herself.

"If it *is* her . . ." Silas whispered, a solemnness reverberating in his voice, ". . . then you must do what needs to be done."

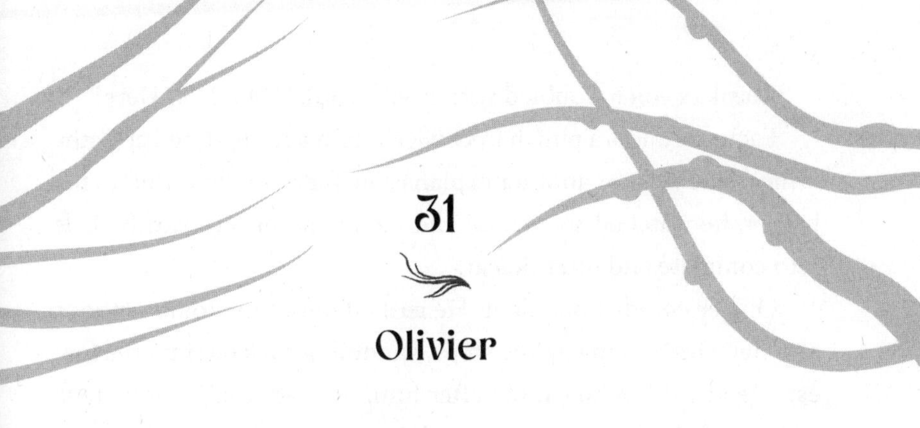

31

Olivier

"What do you mean *it's empty*?" Catherine's voice was a lethal blade, trembling with rage.

"I mean . . ." Dina gestured to the vacant tomb with a defeated wave. "There's nothing in here. No body. No soul. Nothing. Just . . . this." She raised the piece of parchment toward the torchlight.

It was a drawing. The face etched upon the parchment was nothing more than a boy, perhaps only slightly older than Olivier. A sharp, angular face. Impressively blue eyes. Lips pulled into a sullen scowl. It was signed with one letter . . . *V*.

"That isn't possible." Catherine gaped, eyes darting between the group. "We followed the clues. We found the keys." She joined Dina, staring down at the empty tomb with panic burning in her eyes. "This can't be right."

"There *has* to be something else," Olivier agreed, striding up next to her. He searched, frantic. "Maybe—maybe there's another riddle. Something we aren't seeing. The drawing! Maybe the drawing is a clue!"

"Guys." Masika's voice echoed behind them. "He's not here."

Olivier snatched the drawing from Dina's hand. There had to be something they were missing. Something hidden in the tomb.

"Look! Maybe that's a clue! Maybe—"

"Olivier."

Masika's voice wobbled with every word. "He's. Not. Here."

Each word was a punch in Olivier's stomach. He stared at Catherine, searching for another explanation, for *something*. But, to his horror, he watched the denial and panic on her face slowly melt into complete and utter defeat.

Olivier couldn't handle it. He rushed out of the tomb without another word, racing up the steps, stumbling back out into the forest. He heard Emilio calling after him, the patter of his footsteps approaching. The others were only a few paces behind, though it was clear they were giving the two space.

"Olivier."

His name sounded so beautiful tumbling out of Emilio's lips, but he couldn't bring himself to face the other boy. Olivier dug his fingers into his hair, cursing beneath his breath as he paced back and forth.

"Don't you get it?" His voice cracked, unable to temper his own desperation. "He was supposed to fix me. He was supposed to *help*."

"I know."

Emilio reached out a trembling hand, but Olivier backed away.

"No . . . no, you're not listening." Olivier rubbed his face with his hands. The others had emerged from the tomb, and they were watching the scene unfold, silent. "I'm screwed. That's it for me. I'm done. We're not getting our eternity, Emilio. We're barely getting a few days. Hell, without the True Headmaster, we'll be lucky if we have *hours*."

"You don't know that," Emilio said softly.

"Of course I do! I've always known." What had he been thinking, believing in his own happily ever after? In something other than the eternity he'd been handed? "There was no getting out of this. There never was. I was a fool for clinging to hope for as long as I did. For thinking my fate would change just because I *wanted* it to."

"Olivier, please." Analisa's soft voice reverberated behind them. "I could . . . I could still *try*—"

"You said it yourself!" Olivier interjected, pointing an accusatory finger at the healer, who flinched. "I'm a lost cause! You know it. You said you felt it the moment we walked out into purgatory."

"You can't give up," Emilio muttered softly.

Olivier winced. "I'm not . . . I'm not giving up, Emilio. I'm—I'm just accepting it." He wiped the stubborn tears burning behind his eyes with the back of his hand. "It was for you, anyway. The only reason I tried. The only reason I even bothered to hope . . . it was all for you." He shook his head and stumbled backward. "But . . . there's no point in trying. Not anymore."

Analisa stepped forward. "Olivier. I really think that maybe I can—"

It happened so fast.

Too fast.

One second Analisa was speaking, standing there, and the next a gaping hole had been carved into her chest, a golden arrow protruding from the wound.

Somebody screamed. A cry. A broken sound.

Analisa fell to her knees. Catherine and Masika sprinted forward, sinking down next to her. Dina stood there, paralyzed with shock, Benji clutched in her hands. It was as if she had hardened into stone, watching the scene unfold in numb panic.

The healer touched the wound with shaking hands, magic pouring out of her, streams of silver light wrapping around her injury. But the arrow protruding from her torso was keeping the wound from healing, and if she couldn't close it in time . . .

Masika must have noticed the same thing. She summoned

her elemental magic, thrusting her arm out, cerulean ribbons of power wrapping around the arrow. She pulled it out with a grunt and threw it to the ground beside her.

But still, the wound wouldn't close. Analisa's brows creased together in confusion, her magic uselessly swirling within the wound.

She glanced up, eyes wide. "What . . . what's happening to me?"

"The arrow," Catherine choked out, eyes darting to the discarded arrow on the ground. Olivier noticed something strange about it, glowing crimson veins swimming beneath its golden surface. He began to reach out toward it, but Catherine's panicked cry stopped him in his tracks.

"Don't!" she bellowed, frantic. "Don't touch it." She shook her head, a terrifying look of disbelief upon her face. "I think . . . I think it's been infused with some sort of ancient magic. I think it went through the core of her soul."

"*No*," Olivier choked out. He pressed his hands firmly against the wound in Analisa's chest, a desperate attempt to stop the bleeding. "Come on, Analisa. Stay with us. Who's going to annoy the shit out of me if you're gone, huh?" He laughed, but his vision blurred with tears, panic twisting in his chest. Analisa smiled and blood poured from her mouth. "Just—try again, okay? Try your magic."

"I . . ." Analisa lifted her hand and the usual spark of healing magic fizzled and faded, unable to conjure even a single ember. "I can't."

Before Olivier could say anything else, a terrible choking sound erupted from the back of Analisa's throat, blood sputtering onto her lips. And then, as if Olivier had been transported into one of his nightmares, the one where the eliminated nominees haunted him, their disintegrated forms whispering to him in the night, Analisa's soul began to . . . *fade*.

Her skin broke apart. Chunks of flesh melting into ash and dust.

Analisa looked up at Olivier. She tried to open her mouth to speak, to say something, but no sound came out. And from one breath to the next, Analisa came apart, her body splintering into speckles of dust and ash, until she vanished completely, the particles swirling away with the wind.

Nobody had time to react.

Nobody had time to mourn.

Because it was in that same moment that another arrow came hurtling toward them from deep within the woods, nearly hitting Catherine in the shoulder, though she managed to duck away at the last second, rolling back onto her feet.

Olivier's eyes snapped between Emilio and Masika, a silent communication jolting among the trio.

We're under attack.

And then all hell broke loose.

32

WREN

The room is spinning. The thought sliced through Wren's mind as Equinox whirled around her in a haze of colors and shapes. A lovely, bubbling sound echoed in her ears, and it took her a few seconds to realize that it was her own laughter. How long had it been since she'd laughed like that? She wasn't sure, but it poured out of her as the world continued to spin and spin and spin.

Somebody was holding her. Hands pressed against her waist. She realized, then, that it wasn't the world that was spinning, but *her*. There was somebody in front of her. Were they laughing too? But something about their laughter felt different. Colder. Mocking. Yet Wren couldn't bring herself to care. Not when she felt this wholly good and perfect and *free*. The spinning slowed down, the blur of colors and shapes solidifying. And then Callum Whitlock's face came into view.

Wren knew she should feel frightened. Her body seemed to react before her mind—a tension in her muscles that wasn't there before. But despite knowing she *should* be afraid, Wren couldn't bring herself to be. What was so wrong with Callum? He had lovely eyes and hair . . . he was beautiful, really.

Is it warm in here? Wren thought. Callum's face momentarily warped as she blinked and regained her awareness.

"Not particularly," Callum answered with a chuckle. It was only then that Wren realized she must have asked the question out loud. He was holding her hand, swaying in time with the music. It suddenly occurred to her that they were dancing. How long had they been dancing? Wren couldn't remember. But there *was* something she should remember. Something important. Something that could alter her existence forever—

"What's on your mind?" Callum whispered into her ear.

Wren shook her head and it felt like the entire world shook with her.

"Nope." She could practically see the words floating out of her mouth, swirling between them. "*No, no, no.* Nothing that I can tell you."

Callum quirked a brow. "Keeping secrets from me, catalyst?" He pouted and drew her closer. "That's not very nice."

"Well, *you're* not very nice." Wren chuckled. "You're actually quite mean."

"Oh, it's not personal," Callum remarked with a dismissive wave. "I'm like this with everyone."

Run! a voice in the back of Wren's mind screamed. *Find the others.* But where would she run to? And why would she run? She was having fun. For the first time in years—Wren was *actually* having fun.

Callum's eyes darted past Wren's shoulders. He glanced at something behind her.

"Apologies, catalyst." He slipped his hand under hers and brought it up to his lips. "As wonderful as this has been, it appears I'm needed." He brushed a quick kiss against her hand. "The offerings are set to begin soon."

The offerings. Something in Wren stirred. What was it about the offerings that was important? She was about to ask Callum, but then she blinked and he was gone, lost within the chaos.

Around her, bodies continued to move and sway. The pounding beat of the drum echoed deep inside Wren's chest, traveling down her body in a dizzying vibration. Wren wanted to keep dancing. She wanted to dance and dance until her legs gave out beneath her. But just as she was about to find another body to latch onto, she was suddenly tugged backward, pulled through the crowd by a strong set of hands. When the world stopped spinning, she found two familiar faces staring back at her.

Quinn and Arthur peered down at her, arms crossed and faces pinched in concern.

"Wren." Quinn's voice echoed with a dreamlike reverberation. Her light pink hair was pinned back from her face. How had Wren never noticed how blue her eyes were? They were practically glowing. "What are you—" Quinn stopped short, as if she'd realized something. She waved her hand in front of Wren's face and Wren giggled, attempting to catch Quinn's hand with her own.

"It looks like a butterfly," Wren remarked.

Quinn groaned and swatted Wren's hand away. "Great," she muttered under her breath. "She's completely out of it."

Arthur gripped Wren's face in his hands. "Wren . . . how much did you drink?"

"The cup," she announced proudly.

Panic surged behind Quinn's expression. "A whole cup? You *finished* the elixir?"

Wren nodded. "The cup," she echoed.

Arthur's eyes widened. "Wren. You're supposed to drink that over the course of the entire night."

"We need August," Quinn groaned, glancing around the cavern. "Where the hell is he?"

"Okay, Wren." Arthur gave her a light pat on the face, which only made Wren break out into a fit of giggles. "I know it's hard, but I need you to try to sober up, okay? Can you do that for me?"

"But I feel so *goooooood*," Wren whined. And really—why should she? She could barely remember what had happened, but she *could* remember all the bad feelings that had been plaguing her. Sadness. Panic. Grief. And now all those feelings were gone, replaced by the velvety warmth pooling inside her.

"I'm sure you feel *wonderful*," Arthur said, chuckling nervously. "But we need you. The offerings are going to start soon—"

"What happened?"

August's rough voice cut through their conversation, and then he was there, all tall and brooding and *beautiful*. He held Wren's face in his hands, inspecting her with those piercing gray eyes of his. Wren practically melted into his touch.

"Where the hell have you been?" Quinn asked through gritted teeth.

"I had to sneak away from Edith." August didn't even look at Quinn as he spoke, his eyes glued to Wren. "Loughty, darling, can you hear me?"

Wren hummed, nodding her head. "You are . . . insanely good-looking. I've told you that before, right?"

August's mouth twitched. "Once or twice."

"Well," Wren huffed. "I should tell you more often. You are delightful to look at."

"Okay, enough." Quinn waved her hand in exasperation. She pointed a finger at August's chest. "She's your responsibility. Find a way to sober her up—*fast*." And then she gripped Arthur by the wrist and the two of them vanished into the crowd.

"August." Wren practically groaned his name as she clutched his shirt in her fist, drawing him closer. "I don't want to sober up."

August's expression darkened. "You've been drugged, darling. You don't know what you want."

Wren continued to sway to the music, all the while keeping her eyes on August. She raised a brow at him, smirking. "Am I in trouble, General Hughes?"

At this, August's hardened exterior seemed to crack, and he was unable to stifle the slight smirk rising to his lips. He wiped it away with the back of his hand, rolling his eyes as he shook his head in disapproval. "Christ, Loughty . . ." he muttered.

Wren let out a cackle of laughter, grabbing August by the hand, pulling him in closer. "Dance with me."

He shook his head, glancing over his shoulder, eyes searching. "If Edith sees—"

"Then she'll see that I'm a perfectly well-adjusted Demien partaking of all the revelry Equinox has to offer," Wren interjected, spinning them both around and around, nearly tripping over herself. Through the flurry of color and movement, she could see the outline of August's smile, though there was something else contorting his expression, an unmistakable twinge of agony burning behind his storm-gray eyes.

"The offerings are about to begin," August whispered. "We have to be ready for when Quinn detonates the explosion. If you're not near Arthur when that happens—"

"I know, I know." Wren's head whirred, but only for a brief moment. She shook off the sobering wave with a twirl, unwilling to let go of her momentary euphoria. "But in the meantime, we have to blend in, don't we?"

August's body tensed against Wren. The muscles in his jaw tightened. He was clearly clinging to the last remaining threads of restraint. "It's very difficult to say no to you."

Wren gently gripped his hands, guiding them toward her waist. His fingers squeezed, the feeling of him touching her only heightened by the elixir still circulating through her system.

Wren leaned toward him. Her voice was rough and husky when she spoke again. "Then don't."

All at once, August's control slackened. A cautious smile rose to his lips as he tugged her closer, a slight flush sweeping over his cheeks. He swayed in time with the music, muscles relaxing with every thump of the drum. With August beside her, all of Wren's senses doubled. Touch. Smell. *Taste.* August was close enough that she could press her lips against his neck, dragging them down to his collarbone. He arched his head back as she laid a kiss on the soft plane of his neck.

No one noticed. Or, perhaps, they *did* notice, and they simply were too drunk to care. The same intoxication that flowed through Wren permeated every inch of the cavern. Every Demien seemed alight with a glowing euphoria.

But then a voice cut through Wren's haze. Deep. Grating. Demanding to be heard.

Are you having fun, my sweet catalyst?

Wren staggered to a halt.

Around her, everything seemed to vanish. She was aware of the swaying bodies, of August standing in front of her, but the cavern had grown muffled, as though she were miles and miles away from her own body. August was saying something, lips moving, but she couldn't hear him over the sharp ringing in her ears.

"No . . ." Wren choked out, shaking her head. "Not here. Not now."

You didn't think I'd let you slip away from me so easily, did you?

Wren gasped, stumbling backward. Around her, the crowd continued to dance, twirling in time with the music. August was the only one who had stopped. He watched Wren, hands outstretched, calling out to her.

"What is it?" she heard August ask, brows furrowed in concern. "What's wrong?"

I admit, it was a clever plan. But you couldn't possibly have thought that I wouldn't know? That I wouldn't hear those whispered thoughts of yours? That I wouldn't taste the hope rising inside you?

Something was tearing at her ribs. Crawling through her bones. That voice. That terrible, twisted voice was *inside* her. Wren's legs gave out beneath her and she hit the floor hard, collapsing onto her knees. Finally, the others around her seemed to take notice. A few paused their dancing, glancing over with curious eyes. August was pushing through the growing crowd, trying to get to her, calling out her name. Quinn and Arthur stared from their position near the edge of the crowd, brows pinched. They began to move toward her, but Wren knew, with sudden clarity, that it wouldn't make a difference.

"Get out," Wren pleaded, digging her fingers into her hair, tugging at her skull. "I'm not the one you want. I can't be."

You cannot run from your fate, Wren Loughty. I have seen it. I know who you are.

Wren's vision fractured. Darkness pooled over her eyes. She no longer saw the festivities, no longer saw August tearing through the crowd, screaming her name. She was losing her grip on reality, slipping away.

"Please," Wren begged one last time, a whispered plea to anybody who was listening.

But nobody was listening.

Not anymore.

When the darkness came for Wren, she didn't bother putting up a fight.

33

MASIKA

She's gone.

The words rang out in Masika's mind as the chaos broke out around them. *Analisa is gone.* It seemed inconceivable, despite what she had just witnessed with her own two eyes. One step forward, one seemingly inconsequential blip in her timeline and *boom*—Analisa, as they had come to know her, was no more.

Masika spared one final glance at the place where Analisa had been standing moments ago before turning her attention to Olivier and Emilio. Desperation clawed at her chest. She needed to keep them safe. They couldn't meet the same fate, they *couldn't*—

"We need to move!"

Catherine's razor-sharp voice sliced through Masika's panic. She blinked, head whirling, taking in the sight of the others. Catherine and Dina unsheathed their weapons, corporeal magic glistening from their finely sharpened blades. Olivier was still kneeling next to the place Analisa had been only moments before, face torn with disbelief, mouth agape. Emilio was attempting to gather him onto his feet, whispering desperate words of encouragement.

Masika had taken three steps toward Olivier and Emilio, prepared to grab them both by their wrists and drag them the hell out of the clearing, when a fusillade of arrows descended upon them from all directions. Masika ducked, scrambling away from them, barely dodging an arrow that had been aimed directly at her chest.

"Run!" screamed Dina, gesturing them forward with a frantic wave of her hand. "We need to get out of this clearing—*now!*"

There was no logical plan. No order. The group simply sprinted into the dense greenery of the forest as they made their way out of the clearing and back into the cover of the trees. Around them, the forest seemed to spring to life, the sound of quickening footsteps echoing in the distance, the unmistakable *whoosh* of arrows flying over them, crashing into nearby trees with a terrifying crack.

They were being chased. By who? Masika had no clue. But it was clear that whatever magic these arrows were infused with harbored the ability not merely to injure them, but to destroy them. Almost like the arrows held the power to rip through the core of their souls with nothing but a single wound. As if on cue, another arrow flew past Masika's side, causing her to veer right, fumbling away from the group.

They're trying to separate us.

But even as the thought seared through her mind, Masika kept moving forward, putting distance between her and the rest of the group. Maybe if the attackers followed her, she could offer the others a moment to escape.

She could at least save *them*.

Masika sprinted deeper through the forest, breaths ragged and uneven, terror constricting her lungs. Leaves rustled behind her, the crunch of boots snapping against twigs. But she also heard something else, a sickening sound that sent a wave of nausea up her throat . . . *laughter*. Her attackers were mocking her, taunting her.

They're enjoying this.

And they were getting closer.

She had to think, to do something.

An idea blossomed in her mind. She staggered to a halt, stretching her hands out wide, summoning her elemental magic. Green wisps of light emerged within her veins, fluttering out of her fingertips. She twisted her hands, grunting as the exhaustion flooded her body. The trees in front of her shifted and moved, their branches growing larger and thicker, until they had formed a wall of vegetation, a barricade separating Masika from her attackers. She waited, breath held.

Behind the wall, the sound of footsteps echoed, though they quickly faltered, as though they were unsure which direction to go in. To Masika's immense relief, the footsteps veered toward the right, growing fainter, until all she could hear was the whistle of the wind against her ears.

Masika let out a shuddering breath. *It worked. It actually—*

The snap of a twig. A sharp intake of breath.

Masika whirled on her heels.

It took a few seconds for her mind to piece together what she was seeing.

Who she was seeing.

It hadn't been that long since they had last seen one another, only a few weeks, yet somehow, it felt as though everything had changed. The familiarity between them had darkened into something unrecognizable, something rotten and broken. Masika sensed it the moment their eyes locked. The distance between them. The betrayal.

Irene stood a few yards away, bow clutched in her hands, arrow nocked.

Masika couldn't speak. She couldn't even move. She stood

frozen, hands rigid by her side. Irene hadn't moved either, the arrow still tightly nocked, pointed directly at Masika.

Pointed right at her heart.

"Irene."

Masika hadn't meant to say her name out loud, but she couldn't help herself. She needed to say it, to make sure Irene was real. Hearing her name, Irene blinked, as if stirred awake from a trance. As if she hadn't realized it was truly Masika standing before her until she'd heard her name tumble out of her mouth.

Neither one of them looked away. Neither one of them dared.

And then Masika saw it. It was the slightest movement, so faint that perhaps someone else might not have noticed.

Irene lowered the arrow. Not even half a fraction, but still. It was enough.

Hope surged in Masika's chest. She took a step forward, mouth parted. "Irene, we—"

But her voice was cut off by the sound of approaching footsteps, and then two other Ascended were stumbling into view, Everly Hawthorne and another girl Masika didn't quite recognize. At the sight of them, Irene's grip on her bow retightened, the sharp edge of her arrow pointed back toward Masika.

"Look what we have here," giggled Everly. She slung her bow over her shoulder, sauntering closer to Masika. Behind her, the other Ascended—a tall girl with dark hair and a silver streak—kept her own arrow nocked and carefully aimed, her eyes flitting between Irene and Masika, as though she was expecting either one of them to pounce at any second.

"Get back," Masika hissed, sparks of corporeal magic flaring in her palms.

Everly tutted, shaking her head. "Now, be sensible, Masika.

You're cornered. You can try to fight, but the second these arrows pierce your soul . . ." Everly chuckled, a wicked grin spreading over her mousy face. "Well, you saw what happened to your friend back there. I do have to say . . . Irene has *incredible* aim."

Masika's eyes snapped to Irene. *She couldn't have.* But as the thought burned in Masika's mind, she saw the apathy in Irene's glowing eyes, the unwavering determination, and Masika knew that Everly was telling the truth.

"Then go on," Masika challenged, eyes drilling into Irene. "I'm right here. *Do it.*"

Irene said nothing. The wind blew strands of dark hair across her face, her glowing irises peeking through the black waves. Something flashed across her eyes. Whether it was fear or fury, Masika couldn't quite decipher.

"As much as I'd love to watch an arrow plunge straight through your soul," said Everly, prowling closer, "I'm afraid your presence is a bit more . . . valuable." She snapped her fingers and Masika's entire body went rigid, like her limbs had hardened into concrete. She was trapped in her own body, forced to stand there, watching as the trio stepped closer, descending upon her like a pack of feral wolves.

But it was Irene who approached her first. The other two stood back, watching, waiting for a command. Irene inched closer, stopping only a foot or two from her, close enough that Masika could properly take in the other girl's appearance. Despite the power radiating from Irene, the truth was . . . she looked drained. Torn. It gave Masika an inkling of hope, of something other than the helplessness tearing at her insides.

Maybe Irene wasn't completely gone.

Maybe Masika could still reach her.

Irene leaned in closer. Her eyes darkened, brows cinched

together. When she finally spoke, her voice was low and rough, nearly trembling with anger. It was a quality Masika had never heard before—and it sent a shiver down her spine.

"You shouldn't have come here."

And then Masika's best friend swung her arm down, thrusting the tip of her bow against Masika's temple, and knocked her out cold.

34

WREN

First came a voice. It lifted her from the veil of darkness, guiding her toward the light. Wren wriggled her hands and felt damp earth shift beneath her, thin grains of dirt slipping between her fingers. She blinked and came back to her senses. Above her stretched a large expanse—a black sky dotted with brilliant azure stars. They twinkled and glided as if caught in an eternal dance. As if the world were spinning faster than her eyes could comprehend. When she sat up, she noticed she was lying in the same clearing as before . . . the one that had been haunting her in her dreams, calling to her.

The one where the Soulless One had first spoken to her.

A few yards in the distance, flanked by thick greenery and the carcasses of oak trees, stood the same statue. A chiseled, angular face. Sapphire eyes. It seemed to be watching her, an eerie sentience burning behind its eyes.

It's time, my sweet catalyst.

The Soulless One's voice reverberated through her like a dissonant gong. Wren tried to stagger backward, distancing herself from the statue, but when she tried to move, her legs wouldn't budge, as though her muscles had hardened into stone.

"Please," Wren choked out. "I don't want this. I don't—I don't want to be the destroyer of Blackwood."

Oh, but you will. With the truth, you will be reborn.

Wren shook her head. "You're wrong."

The Soulless One hummed. Wren could feel it. It trickled down her limbs, wrapping around the core of her soul. Something was happening to her. She was losing all sense of reality, her vision blurring under an oppressive weight.

Well . . . if you're so sure, then . . . why don't I show you?

Wren opened her mouth to scream, but it

was

too

late . . .

The patter of rain. Tires against asphalt. Static as an old folk song drifted through the radio. The sweet scent of vanilla perfume and the remnants of liquor lingering on minty breath.

Wren's eyes shot open.

She was sitting in the passenger seat of her mother's old Jeep Wrangler, looking down at her hands. The world around her tilted momentarily, blurring and refocusing as she came back to her senses.

"Mom is gonna kill us."

I've been here before.

The thought shot through Wren's mind like a rogue bullet. *I've been here hundreds of times before.* It was the memory of her death. The night she not only lost her own life—but her sister's too. But Edith hadn't been torturing her. She'd been . . . what *had* she been doing? How did she get here?

The Soulless One.

Awareness crept into Wren's consciousness. She remembered now. He had brought her here, dragged her from the depths of her mind. He wanted her to witness something. To see the truth.

Next to her, her sister sat in the driver's seat, fingers drumming against the steering wheel. Wren wanted to tell her to stop, to pull over, but she knew that no matter what she did, the outcome would never change.

"I miss you every day," Wren heard herself say. It wasn't what she was supposed to say, but it didn't matter. No matter what she said, Maeve wouldn't listen. She was stuck playing out the part she was always meant to play.

"Mom," Maeve repeated over the sound of the rain hitting the roof. "She's gonna have our heads for this. There's no way she didn't wake up."

Wren stared at the outline of her sister's face and memorized it one last time. Somehow, she knew this would be her last chance. The last time she'd ever get to see her little sister's face.

"I was always jealous of you," Wren whispered. "You walked through life so effortlessly. Like this constant source of light. And you were oblivious to it. That natural gravitational pull you had. The way people were drawn to you. I always felt . . . dimmer. Not your shadow, necessarily. It was like you were the side of the moon others could see, brilliant and glimmering, and I was the other side . . . the one swallowed in darkness."

Maeve couldn't hear her. She never would. But even so, Wren went on.

"I tried to be better. I tried to be good. For you, Maeve. I tried. But I think something in me is drawn to the darkness. Because even now . . . even in death . . . it's followed me. Even now I can't run from it." Wren choked back a sob as it clawed its way up her throat, and she reached out to touch her sister softly on the wrist. "I just hope that wherever you ended up, wherever you are now . . . that you're happy. That the light inside you is still burning. Because that would be enough for me. That would be enough."

As the last words left Wren's lips, Maeve gasped.

Wren knew what would happen next. She'd look out onto the road, and there, standing before them, would be a deer. Maeve would swerve the car to the left and they'd go rolling down the hill, flipping over a dozen times before skidding to a halt. Maeve would go first. Wren would watch, helpless, as her sister took her last breath. And then, finally, with a soft and merciful hand, death would take Wren.

But when Wren looked out onto the road, it wasn't a deer she saw standing in front of the car.

It was a man.

A man she knew well.

With a sudden jolt, the scene froze. The car halted, as if suspended in motion; Maeve's mouth hung open in terror, unmoving. Wren leaned forward, blinking, as though the man standing before her were simply a speck of dust she could wipe from her eyes. But no matter how hard she blinked, no matter how desperately she rubbed her eyes . . . Headmaster Silas remained.

"I don't understand," Wren choked out. "Why is he here?"

The darkness answered.

Because he* was *there. The Soulless One's voice dripped into her mind. ***He was always there.***

"But—" Wren unbuckled her seat belt, staggering out of the car. She fumbled as she regained her footing, shuffling toward Silas. Her temples throbbed. A dizzying wave seizing her skull. Just like the rest of the scene, Headmaster Silas remained frozen, his eyes focused on the car ahead. "There was a deer. I—I saw it. I remember—"

You remember what he wants you to remember.

Wren's head spun viciously. She placed her hands upon her temples, a tidal wave of memories washing over her. The deer flashed in her mind—dark, beady eyes . . . but *no*. There was never a deer, was there?

Wren gasped as she collapsed onto her knees.

"What are you saying?" she choked out.

There are more lies than what you already know. The Soulless One's voice reverberated in her skull, consuming every inch of her. ***Silas didn't just steal Blackwood from the True Headmaster. He completely rewrote the laws of the afterlife. He changed the balance of Blackwood.***

Around her, the forest changed. Gone were the pine trees and gravel road, replaced by a dark, eerie nothingness. The only thing that remained was Silas. His looming form, cloaked in shadows, those dark eyes staring down at her.

Before Silas took over, the students of Blackwood Academy were selected by the school itself. Their names would appear in its ledger. And upon their death . . . they were given a choice. Admission into Blackwood wasn't a requirement—it was an invitation. The souls who said yes were those who truly wanted to help lost spirits—who wanted a purpose, even in death. And after ten years, they were allowed to cross over to the Other Side. Each and every one of them. But when Silas clawed his way into power, he refused to listen to Blackwood. The school had marked him as Corrupted, and he was vengeful. He tore apart the school's natural order. Instead, he began to choose students himself. He'd pick them when they were still alive and orchestrate a premature death, forcing them into Blackwood on his terms. He didn't give them a choice. He didn't let them leave after ten years. He changed the natural laws that

governed the afterlife. I suppose it simply never occurred to him that eventually, Blackwood would fight back.

Bile rose in Wren's throat. Rattling breaths sputtering out of her. She wanted to scream, to cry, but nothing came out, and then the Soulless One's voice took over, filling her skull once again.

The Ether's discontent. The Forgetting that plagues students and slowly corrodes their mind. All of them are symptoms of Silas's blight. Of his lies and deceit. The afterlife was rotting . . . corrupting under his influence. When it became clear that Silas's control over Blackwood was slipping, he created the Decennial as a desperate attempt to mend the chaos he had caused. But even with his precious sacrifices, he could barely keep things from completely coming apart. And now . . . after this Decennial, after so many of his sacrifices made it out unscathed . . . he knows that his reign has finally come to an end.

Wren glanced up at the frozen figure of Silas standing before her. A fire coursed through her, burning her from the inside out. It was fury like she'd never felt before, an animalistic rage.

Blackwood was always meant to be a choice . . . The Soulless One's voice was softer now, closer. As though he were right behind her, knelt beside her ***. . . and it was never meant to be your eternity.***

Wren wanted to rip her skin off. To free herself from the flames burning her insides. She had never felt such pure hatred, such all-consuming wrath.

"It's because of him . . ." she whispered, voice trembling, ". . . that all of us ended up in Blackwood."

Yes.

"He killed me."

Yes.

"He killed my *sister*."

Yes. There was a slight pause, and then the Soulless One's voice rose again, this time with a trembling ire that matched the wrath Wren felt scorching inside her. ***Your sister was never meant to die on this road. She was meant to live a long, happy life. I saw her fate. What was written upon the stars. Maeve Loughty was going to have a family. She was going to travel to the places she'd always dreamed of going. She was going to die an old woman, blissfully asleep in her bed. But Silas took it all away from her. He took it all away from her so that he could have* you.**

No. No. NO.

Wren screamed and the sound tore the world in half. The image of Silas vanished, ripped apart as if he were nothing but particles of ash. Wren could no longer make sense of her surroundings. It was all just pain and agony and unrelenting torture. The fire was overwhelming now, scorching through her limbs, igniting her insides. She clawed at her chest, unsure what she was even searching for.

"Make it stop!" Wren bellowed. "Just make it stop!"

I know what you're feeling, Wren.

"No . . . you . . . you don't . . ."

We can fix it. We can stop him. No more suffering. No more innocent lives taken too soon.

"I . . . I can't . . ."

Just give in, Wren.

"Please."

JUST. GIVE. IN.

Everything seemed to still. The anger. The rage. The heartache. The memories. It was as though Wren had been suspended against the darkness, a weightless vessel, unburdened by the torment of her past.

Somebody was calling to her. Calling out her name.

Wren. Please, darling. Come back to me.

But the voice was distant, barely audible. It flitted in and out of Wren's consciousness, until it became a meaningless sound that simply drifted into the darkness. A procession of faces flashed in Wren's mind. The ones she'd known in life and in death. Her family. Her friends. The ones that fell somewhere in between. She tried to hold on to them, to find a tangible sense of hope threaded through the images, but her fingers always came up empty. Either way, she couldn't stop the faces once they began.

They flickered in and out like a film reel. One moment there, the next gone.

Wren pressed her hand against her chest. She shut her eyes.

She hoped.

She *hoped.*

And then . . . nothing. Only a never-ending darkness.

A burning fury.

Ultimately, it was her sister's smiling face that Wren saw when she ripped her humanity out and welcomed the Soulless One in.

35

AUGUST

There had been no time to stop it. No time to properly react. One second Wren had been lying on the floor, convulsing, eyes rolling back into her head, and the next, August had been thrown back by an earth-shattering force, crashing down upon the ground a few yards from where he had been standing. Around him, chaos ensued. Voices rose and screams echoed throughout the cavern. An opaque smoke clouded the air, thick enough that August could barely make out his own hands hovering in front of him. He staggered to his feet, searching for Wren, but everything was obscured by the impenetrable cloud of smoke that seemingly filled every inch of the cave.

But it didn't last long.

As quickly as the smoke came, it dissipated. Inch by inch, it parted, drifting up toward the rocky ceiling of the cave. The cacophony settled as the air cleared. August could see the others now—the crowd surrounding him, their faces contorted in confusion. Edith stood only a few feet away, coughing as the last of the smoke vanished.

August had expected to find Wren's body lying on the floor. Her contorted form thrown across the ground, broken and wrong. But when he finally spotted Wren, she wasn't on the floor anymore.

In fact . . . she was awake.

Wren was standing. A serene expression had fallen over her face, a look of pure calm.

For a fleeting moment, relief rushed through August. The tiniest spark of hope.

But it was quickly ripped away when he noticed what was surrounding Wren.

What was pouring out of her.

Shadows.

They were everywhere. Coursing through her veins. Exploding out of her. Dozens upon dozens of shadowy tendrils sprouted from her body, slithering around her limbs with an almost ravenous desperation. Even her dark blue eyes were blotted out by shadows, nothing but two pools of darkness staring back at August, the ghost of a smile curled onto her lips. Wren hadn't simply succumbed to the shadows . . . she had *become* them.

August stumbled forward. He reached for her, hand trembling.

"Darling"—his voice cracked as he fought to speak—"what have you done?"

But Wren—or what was left of her—didn't answer.

He wasn't even sure she had heard him.

Suddenly, Edith stepped forward. She approached Wren tentatively, eyes gleaming with something feral and terrifying. She stopped abruptly, and August stiffened, prepared to throw himself in front of Wren. But Edith didn't draw her weapon. She didn't even call upon her own shadows.

Instead, she did something August had never imagined his sister would do.

She knelt.

The sea of Demiens surrounding them followed suit, knees pressed against the ground and heads bowed in reverence. August watched as, all around him, Demiens fell. Even Quinn and Arthur lowered themselves onto their knees, though August didn't miss the terror reflected in their eyes. The horror.

In the end, only August remained standing.

In front of him, Edith raised her head, meeting Wren's eyes. And this time, when Edith smiled . . . Wren smiled back.

A shudder ran through August. It was a wave of agony that finally brought him to his knees, pushing him to the ground. He kept his eyes locked on Wren the entire time. He couldn't bring himself to look away . . . to avert his eyes from the destruction he had caused. Because this was his doing. His responsibility.

Wren was the cosmos. The very stars themselves.

But Wren was gone.

And now the catalyst had awoken.

PART V

THE REUNION

36

IRENE

Then go on. I'm right here. Do it.

Masika's words echoed in Irene's mind, seared into her memory. Would she have been able to go through with it? Would she even have had another choice?

When Irene spotted Masika in the forest, it had felt like her entire world had jerked to a halt. She'd spent the past few weeks preparing for her friend's demise, convincing herself that she was better off without Masika, that Masika's destruction had always been an inevitability, but all that forced acceptance had gone out the window the moment Irene had laid eyes on Masika again.

Irene had felt it instantly, smacking hard against her chest, unwilling to be ignored.

Relief.

But a tidal wave of other emotions, just as determined to be felt, had risen to the surface. Because Masika's presence didn't change anything. It didn't change the fact that Irene had vowed her allegiance to the Demien Order. That she was meant to play the part of the Ascended to help Mateo secure the defensive ward coin. And, more importantly, it didn't change what Irene wanted.

The promise of power was too intoxicating, too seductive, for Irene to give it up. And she didn't *want* to give it up. But maybe there was a way to meet in the middle. A way to ensure Masika's safety while still following through with the Order's plan. It was Silas, after all, who demanded Masika's destruction. Who needed her soul to be sacrificed. Maybe if Irene spoke with Mateo, he'd be willing to spare her. Masika wasn't technically a Blackwood student anymore, so maybe she didn't *have* to be destroyed when they wiped the slate clean. Especially if they could convince Masika to join their side.

Irene clung to this minuscule sliver of hope as she strode into the dungeons. The damp air of the underground torture chamber filled her lungs, rot and decay overwhelming her senses. She ignored the sound of nails scraping against concrete. The muffled moans of agony that echoed in the shadows. She couldn't stop their suffering.

There was only one soul in here she might stand a chance of helping.

Irene had expected to find Masika curled up on the floor of her cell, terror etched upon her amber eyes. But the girl on the other side of the bars hardly looked afraid. In fact, she looked ready for a fight.

Masika was standing, arms crossed, as if she'd been expecting Irene's arrival.

"Come to finish the job?"

"Of all the places you could have gone . . ." Irene muttered with a sigh. "Why *here*?"

Masika's response was as blunt and vague as Irene had been expecting. "Because we had to."

Irene stepped closer. "And I don't suppose you plan on telling me *what* exactly you were doing out there?"

Masika smirked. "What do you think?"

Irene drummed her index finger against her bicep. "Well . . ."

She let out a small puff of air. "I guess it doesn't matter, does it? You're trapped. You're going to tell us what you know whether you want to or not."

Masika laced her fingers around the iron bars of the cell, leaning in closer. "Is that a threat?"

Irene shrugged. "It's a fact."

A thick hush fell upon them. In the distance, another soul let out a broken cry, though neither of them glanced away. It was as if they had entered a silent battle, eyes locked in an unspoken duel.

Masika pressed her forehead against the bars. A rivulet of dark hair fell over her eyes. "Do you think we could have been sisters in another life?"

Irene flinched. Despite the delicate whisper of her voice, Masika's words made a harsh and grating sound against the impenetrable silence of the dungeons, lacerating Irene's chest.

"What the hell kind of a question is that?" Irene sputtered.

Masika smirked. "Indulge me."

Irene crossed her arms, as if they might protect her from the sting of Masika's words. "What for?"

"*Irene*," Masika pressed. "Just answer the question."

Masika spoke her name with threaded disappointment, like that of a mother chastising her unruly child. Anger flared inside Irene, with a hint of something worse, something bitter and embarrassingly close to shame.

"All right. Fine." Irene scoffed. She paced back and forth, fingers tapping against her arms. "I'll play along. Let's say the answer is *yes*. That we could have been sisters. Then what? You think things would have ended differently for us? That I wouldn't have walked away from you during the third trial? That I wouldn't have made the decision to leave you behind?" Irene's voice rose with every word, trembling with frustration. "I'm still me, Masika. Selfish to my fucking core."

Masika let out a snort of laughter, and Irene flinched, genuinely startled by the sound.

"Oh, spare me the self-indulgent victim complex," Masika chided, which only fueled the ire building in Irene's chest. "You're so much more than that and you know it. You are . . . you are strong. And loyal. Like a terrifying, bloodthirsty golden retriever. You pretend to be selfish, but you're far from it."

Irene balked. How could Masika truly believe that? How could she be so blind to the festering darkness inside Irene?

Irene stopped her pacing, turning back to face the cell. She stepped closer, though she kept her distance, careful not to get close enough that Masika might reach through the iron bars and grab her. Despite whatever of their friendship remained, Masika was still a prisoner, and Irene was still her captor. If it had been Irene behind those bars, she wouldn't have hesitated to strike.

Masika cocked her head. "What is it?"

Irene swallowed. "I left you."

Something flickered beneath the amber gleam of Masika's irises, a fleeting moment of bitterness. *Good,* Irene thought. *Hate me.* But then the bitterness melted away, blotted out by the familiar look of benevolence that made Irene's skin crawl. Because how could Masika possibly look at her that way after everything Irene had done? How could Irene deserve anything less than pure and unfiltered hatred?

Masika gripped the iron bars tightly, eyes locked on Irene's. "You won't hurt me."

Dread settled over Irene upon hearing the certainty in Masika's voice.

"You don't know what I'm capable of."

"Yes," Masika whispered, a startling conviction blazing in her voice. "I do. And despite that . . . you are still my friend."

Irene staggered backward. She clenched her hands into fists, chest heaving as her breaths came quick and ragged.

"Don't."

"Don't *what*?" Masika gripped the bars even tighter. "*Care?* Come on, Irene, would it truly kill you to know that you matter to someone?"

Irene shook her head, distancing herself even further. She wouldn't entertain this. She *couldn't.* Not unless she could guarantee Masika's loyalty, somehow convince her to join the Order. But there was no telling how much time they had left. If Irene wanted to try to explain things to Masika, she'd have to act fast . . . and she'd have to compromise her mission.

Screw it.

Irene extended her arm, constructing a sound barrier around her and the cell. Masika looked on, confusion riddling her features, as the pale blue shield sprouted around them, a sphere of hazy light igniting the air.

"What are you—" But Masika's voice was drowned out as Irene interrupted her, the words tumbling out in a frenzied panic.

"I need you to hear me out before you say no," Irene began, gripping the iron bars of the cage. Masika's eyes darted to Irene's hands for a brief moment before flitting back up toward her face. "I know you think I've betrayed you by joining the Ascended. That I was willing to sacrifice you—all of you—for *this*. But I didn't."

Masika shook her head. "I don't understand—"

"During the Decennial, I was approached by a Demien." As soon as the words left Irene's lips, she saw the glimmer of panic flare behind Masika's eyes, but Irene continued, determined to make her understand. "He wanted me to join him so that I could help him infiltrate Blackwood from the inside. I became an Ascended to go undercover. To learn how to weaken Blackwood's defenses and help the Demien Order take Silas down."

An indecipherable emotion washed over Masika's face. "Why are you telling me this?"

Irene dipped her voice down lower, a pleading strain wavering her words. "You could join us."

Masika shut her eyes, grimacing. "Christ, Irene—"

"He could help you," Irene cut in. She was practically begging, she knew that, but that wouldn't stop her from trying. Not when this might be the last opportunity she had left to save her friend. "I know you hate the Demien Order—I know you think they're all evil and soulless—but they have their reasons. And the Demien I'm working with could spare you from being sacrificed. He could find a way to save you, and the others, but you need to pledge your allegiance to the Order—"

"I don't want to be a fucking Demien!" Masika bellowed without warning, the venom in her voice startling Irene into silence. "Don't you understand what they intend to do when they quote-unquote wipe the slate clean? It's not just Silas they intend to destroy—it's every single student. Every innocent soul."

"But—" Irene grimaced, pushing away her own rising doubt. Whether or not she would ever admit it out loud, the price the Order was willing to pay for justice had always left a sour taste in her mouth. But it didn't change the fact that Blackwood needed to burn for its transgressions. "It's for a greater good. The afterlife is suffering because of what Silas has done. The only way that corruption can be cleansed is if we rip it out at the root."

Masika shuddered, horrified. *There it is.* That was the look Irene had been waiting for.

The real way Masika felt about her.

"God . . ." Masika shook her head. "Maybe Emilio and Olivier were right. Maybe you *are* beyond reach."

Irene winced at hearing their names spoken out loud. When she'd seen them in the forest, when she'd known they might be destroyed by their arrows, Irene had been unable to ignore the current of sorrow that rushed through her chest, warped by the short-lived joy at seeing that they had somehow survived the Decennial.

"They made it . . . you know." Irene noticed the way Masika's eyes lit up for a brief moment, unable to hide her instant relief. "After we brought you back here to the dungeons . . . the others weren't able to find the rest of your group in the forest. I convinced them it was pointless to keep searching."

Masika scoffed. "If you want my thanks, don't hold your breath."

Silence settled over them as Irene met Masika's withering stare. There would be no reasoning with Masika, no convincing her. Not now, at least. But time was ticking, and despite Irene's determination, there was no denying that her window of opportunity was closing, and soon, her only friend would be gone—*forever*.

Suddenly, the clatter of approaching footsteps echoed behind Irene, the familiar rumble of voices bouncing around the walls of the dungeon.

When Irene glanced back at Masika, she saw the panic in the other girl's eyes. The fear she concealed so well. Because as strong as Masika made herself out to be, Irene knew, with unwavering certainty, that she was terrified.

"It's happening," Irene whispered, frantic. She wrapped her hands around the iron bars, dropping her voice even lower. "Whether you want it to or not. The Demien Order will storm the gates of Blackwood Academy, and you'll either be by my side . . . or not."

Masika's chest rose and fell with shaky, panicked breaths. She reached out, placing her hands over Irene's, her movements so quick that Irene barely had time to react, to back away from her.

"I can't."

And that was it. With those two words, Masika had assured her undoing. Her fate was carved into stone, her destruction now a certainty. Irene ripped her hands away from Masika, the feeling of her friend's fingers still echoing upon her hands, as though Masika had left a trace of herself behind.

Irene flicked her wrist and the sound barrier dissipated. Seconds later, three figures emerged from the darkness. At the head of the trio stood Headmaster Silas, navy peacoat upon his shoulders, walking stick in hand. Flanking him were Housemaster Violet and Housemaster Wesley. The pair walked with their hands clasped in front of them, a stoic expression plastered on their faces.

"Ah. *Irene*." Silas's voice rang out, eerily serene. "Reacquainting yourself with your old friend?"

Irene stiffened. Her eyes flitted to Masika, who remained stone-faced.

"I figured I'd try to get ahead of the interrogation," Irene supplied. "See what information I could get out of her."

Silas shifted his gaze to Masika, who sucked in a sharp breath.

"Masika Sallow." He spoke her name slowly, enunciating each syllable. "You've surprised me. Impressed me, even. When I heard you'd been crushed beneath a mountain, I didn't expect you to make it out unscathed." His eyes traced the scar on her face with deliberate precision. "Well, I suppose not *completely* unscathed."

Masika swallowed. To her credit, her gaze remained unflinching. "If you're here to sacrifice me to the Ether—then get on with it."

Silas paused in front of the bars of her cell. They were mere feet apart now, close enough that either could reach out and touch the other, though Irene doubted that Masika would try.

"In time," Silas replied. He watched Masika with a strange glint in his eyes, almost as if he were waiting for something. "You know . . . this really isn't my fault, Ms. Sallow. The Ether has been . . . deteriorating. Almost completely unstable since you all slipped away. If it isn't fed what it craves—"

"*Liar*," Masika spat out, lunging toward him. At the abrupt movement, Violet and Wesley each took a rigid step forward, corporeal magic crackling in their palms, but Silas raised a hand, and the pair instantly stopped in their tracks. "All of this is your fault," Masika said. "The only reason the Ether craves my soul in the first place is because of what *you* did. You're not supposed to be the Headmaster! You never were!"

Violet's lip curled back in disgust. "Shut your mouth, you insolent—"

"It's quite all right," Silas muttered, cutting Violet off. He let out a sigh, slowly slipping off his black gloves. "The girl is right. I *am* a liar. A thief. A crook." He flexed his fingers and his golden ring burned crimson. "I am what I needed to become in order to survive."

Masika's expression hardened.

"Sacrificing me won't change anything," she spat out. "You'll never find the others. And then the Ether will crumble. You'll lose control. You'll lose *everything*."

Silas leaned in closer. He wrapped his own hands around the bars. "And what makes you so sure of that?"

Masika met his gaze, chin lifted high.

"Because I'd rather die a thousand deaths than ever tell you where they are."

At this, Silas smiled. "Well, Ms. Sallow . . . that won't be an issue." He snapped his fingers and Wesley stepped forward, unveiling the same spear they'd used to torture Thalia. "Have you not wondered why we've waited to feed you to the Ether? Why we've bothered to throw you in this cell?" His eyes raked her face slowly.

The realization must have struck Masika at the same time it dawned on Irene, because her expression fell, the defiance in her stare faltering.

Silas chuckled.

"Your presence here isn't just a formality . . . it's a necessity."

Masika staggered backward. A single step.

"You're using me as bait," she whispered, voice cracking. It wasn't a question. "It won't work."

Silas wrapped his hand around the spear. "We'll see about that."

Irene felt like she was going to be sick. She staggered backward, hand clutching her stomach. She just needed some air. A moment to think.

"I . . . I'm going to go check in with Samira and Everly," Irene mumbled. But as she took her first step away from the cell, Headmaster Silas's voice punctured the air, holding her in place.

"Ms. Bamford."

Dread settled upon Irene's shoulders as she spun on her heels, slowly, and turned back to face Silas. The Headmaster had a crooked grin on his lips, an almost mischievous twinkle in his eyes.

"I'd prefer that you stayed," he said. "Observed. After all . . . as a new member of the Council . . ." Silas reached into his coat pocket, unveiling a shiny brass object. It took Irene a few seconds to realize what it was. *A coin.* ". . . it's imperative you learn *all* of our interrogation tactics."

Irene's throat tightened. Even in the dim hazy light of the dungeons, the coin glinted. "What are you saying?"

Silas lifted his lips into a feline grin.

"Congratulations, Ms. Bamford. You are now part of Blackwood Academy's prestigious Council." Silas dangled the coin between his index and middle finger. Instinctively, Irene reached out, desperate to touch it, but before she could grab the coin from Silas, the Headmaster lifted his hand an inch or so, moving it just out of her reach. "You understand what accepting this means, don't you?"

Irene kept her gaze anchored on Silas. She didn't dare look anywhere else. If she allowed herself to face Masika, to see the terror and betrayal in her eyes, then she'd run the risk of falling apart. Her finely honed control fracturing into a million pieces.

There was no fighting this. Not here, at least. If Irene wanted to find a way to save Masika, then she'd have to swallow her shame and face the consequences. She'd have to stand back and watch her friend—*her best friend*—be tortured and ripped apart, all the while knowing it was her doing. Her fault.

My fault.

"Do you understand?" Silas asked again, dragging Irene to the present.

As the question lingered in the air, Irene allowed her gaze to drift to Masika once more. All Irene could hope for was that her friend could see the unspoken words behind her eyes, the tiny flicker of regret carefully concealed behind her apathetic façade.

I'm sorry.

I failed you.

I'm so fucking sorry.

But those words would never be spoken out loud. Lost in the distance between them.

Instead, Irene let her mouth curl into the faintest hint of a smirk. She let her face drop into calculated indifference. And then, with as much apathy as she could muster, Irene turned to the Headmaster of Blackwood Academy and said, "I understand."

37

MASIKA

Masika had promised herself that she wouldn't scream. Even when the inevitable pain came, even when they slithered into her mind and contorted her insides like the strings of a marionette, she refused to give them the satisfaction of hearing her cries.

But Masika was only human.

And once the first scream tore from her lips—she couldn't stop.

38

AUGUST

"*Where is she?*"

August tried to shove the guard out of his way, but two others emerged, forming a barricade at the tent's entrance. They each held curved shadow-drenched sabers in their hands, though their show of force didn't rattle August. He knew that if he called upon his own shadows, he'd rip the three of them apart in a matter of seconds. He'd tear their souls out by their bloody throats. But using shadow magic had to remain his last resort, no matter how tempting.

"Don't make me repeat myself," August warned through gritted teeth.

"High General Hughes has requested the catalyst remain alone for the time being." The guard's top lip curled into a sneer. "No visitors. And that includes *you*."

August stepped closer, peering down at the guard's scornful face.

"I'd like to see you try to stop me."

And there it was. The brief flicker of fear behind the guard's performative act of force.

Go ahead, August challenged with a quirk of his brow. *Fucking try me.*

But the guard must have sensed that he was woefully out of his depth, as he sidestepped out of August's way with a petulant roll of his eyes. "Don't say I didn't warn you," he muttered.

August didn't pay the cautionary remark any mind, pushing past the guard and striding into the tent. But the second he walked inside, he stumbled to a halt. Shock coursed through him when he saw what waited for him.

Wren was standing with her back to him. Silver-encrusted armor adorned her torso, sharpened spaulders placed upon the curves of her shoulders. As August took the first few tentative steps inside, he half expected Wren to face him. He imagined that beautiful smile of hers spreading over her lips. The way she'd run to cross the distance between them and throw herself into his arms.

But she didn't. She didn't do any of that.

"Loughty." August's voice was barely louder than a whisper, but against the piercing silence, it was a thunderous echo. "Are you . . . are you hurt?"

Finally, upon hearing his voice, Wren turned.

But the person staring back at him was almost unrecognizable.

Shadows swam beneath her veins. They poured out of her, enveloping her in a cloak of darkness. The whites of her eyes flickered to black every few seconds—one moment there, the next gone. Inky shadows swam up her neck, crawling over her face, a pulsating energy traveling up and down her skin.

This wasn't Wren. This was something else.

Half shadow. Half human.

"I'm fine." Wren's voice felt like rusted nails. Sharp. Lethal. **"I'm more than fine."**

August stilled. He flexed his fingers by his sides. "What happened to you?"

Wren took a step forward. As she moved, the shadows moved with her.

"I saw the truth," she said simply. **"The betrayal that ties us all together."**

August shook his head. "I don't understand."

"Silas murdered us." As Wren spoke, the shadows trailing beside her morphed, merging to form the vague silhouette of a man. **"He ripped us from our lives. Stripped us of a choice."**

"Loughty." August approached, his movements careful. He wanted nothing more than to take her in his arms. To hold her. But he couldn't bring himself to touch her. "I wasn't killed by Silas. I . . . I died in a fire."

Wren cocked her head, smiling.

"Did you?"

August flinched at the mocking lilt in her voice.

"Yes," he muttered defensively. "My father attacked me. It was an accident. A candle fell, and . . ." August's voice trailed off. Something was tugging at his subconscious. A prickle of doubt. The faded seams of a memory lashing across his mind.

"And . . . *what*?" Wren echoed. The shadows forming the outline of a man ebbed and flowed, and suddenly August was staring at the silhouette of his father's office. A perfect re-creation of the night. **"What happened next, August?"**

"I . . . tried to get up." August choked on his own words. He saw himself in the shadows, his body lying on the floor. Something was rising inside him, tearing through the darkness, breaking free after centuries of restraint. A face. A figure. August watched, horrified, as the shadows formed that same silhouette of a man standing at the doorway of his father's study. The man approached. He placed his hands upon August's chest and held him in place as the fire roared around them.

The memory of his death came rushing back in.

His head slammed against the floorboards, as though he had been knocked to the floor by an invisible weight.

Wren smiled and the shadows around her purred.

"You remember now, don't you?"

A strange pressure built behind August's eyes. A wave of dizziness.

"I don't . . . he couldn't have—" But August saw it then. Clear as day. The figure standing at the doorway. The hands holding him down. Pushing him. *This is where your story ends,* Silas had whispered into his ear. *This is where I set you free.*

His death had never been his choice to make. Silas had made it for him.

August fell to his knees. His hands fought to loosen the top buttons of his shirt, breaths heaving, a strangled sob tearing at his throat. All this time. All these years. How could he not have known? How could he not have remembered?

"We were never meant to go to Blackwood." Wren knelt beside him. **"He violated the natural order. Tore us from our lives and forced us into an eternity that never belonged to us. Even in Blackwood . . . we were never meant to stay here for more than a decade. All of us. We were meant to cross over. We were *always* meant to have a choice."**

August stared up at the monstrous version of Wren. Hot tears burned behind his eyes.

"So *what*?" he sputtered. Even her eyes looked different. Those glacial blue eyes of hers were marked with deadly anger—a primal rage. "Now you're just going to burn it all down? Destroy Blackwood and everyone in it?"

Wren's lip twitched.

"That's *exactly* what I intend to do."

"No." August shook his head. "This—this isn't you, darling. The Soulless One is poisoning you. He's controlling you—"

"Controlling me?" Wren echoed, laughing. She raised her hand and one of her shadows coiled around her wrist, shifting until it had formed a sharpened blade. **"No, my darling. For once in my godforsaken life—*I'm* the one in fucking control."**

August flinched at the venom in her voice.

"No. I know you, Wren Loughty. I know you. And this"—he gestured to the shadows with a defeated wave—"this isn't you." But the moment the words left August's lips, Wren's expression hardened. She raised herself back onto her feet, staring down at August with a leer of disgust.

"Edith is coming." There wasn't an inkling of remorse in her voice. **"Once she arrives, she will know of your betrayal. You'll be marked as defected."** Slowly, she dragged the edge of her blade toward August's neck. **"My last sliver of mercy is this . . . *leave.* Leave the encampment and never come back."**

August remained kneeling. He stared up at Wren.

"I won't leave you."

"I won't offer you this mercy again. This is your last chance to leave with your soul intact."

"Then take it." August splayed his palms over his chest. "Take my soul, Wren. I told you before . . . it's *yours*. Every part of me. My soul. My heart. My eternity. It always belonged to you."

Her expression changed. It was so small, so inconsequential, that August might have missed it. But it *was* there. A morsel of anguish. A tiny glimpse into the emotions he knew were lingering beneath the surface, locked behind the Soulless One's shadows. But Wren swallowed it back, the whites of her eyes blotted out by darkness.

"There is nothing left of the girl you once knew, August." Her voice rumbled, deep and foreboding. **"So *leave.*"**

August reached for her. One last time.

"Wren—"

LEAVE!

The word echoed in his mind with such intensity that he was thrown backward. The voice had been Wren's—but not this twisted, warped version of her voice. It was *her* voice. Desperate. Pleading. In front of him, Wren's shadows had sprung to towering heights, a web of billowing darkness twisting, rupturing with startling violence.

I'm sorry, August whispered into her mind. *Forgive me, darling.*

August gathered himself onto his feet and did the one thing he could think to do.

He ran.

His vision blurred as he strode out of the tent and into the bustling cavern. He paid no mind to the Demiens around him. Their piercing stares and curious whispers were a meaningless speck in his peripheral vision. They didn't matter anymore. *Nothing* mattered anymore. He just kept moving. One foot in front of the other. He needed to leave. To get as far away from the destruction he had caused.

He didn't even notice he was nearing the entrance to the encampment until he was walking out into the cool night air, the expanse of Widow's Forest stretching in front of him.

August had taken the first step toward the forest when a voice rang out.

"Where the hell do you think you're going?"

Quinn was standing behind him, chest heaving as she caught her breath. Had she been following him?

"I'm leaving," August replied. He didn't even recognize the sound of his own voice.

Quinn furrowed her brows. "Leaving? You can't *leave*. What about Wren?"

"That person in there"—August pointed toward the encampment, head shaking—"that *thing* . . . it isn't Wren."

"So that's it, then?" Quinn's accusation was a sharp slap across August's face. "You're just going to leave? You're just going to give up on her?" Shame twisted inside August. He averted his gaze, drawing his eyes back toward the forest.

"I've done enough."

Quinn stepped closer. "She needs you, August."

"I know." God, of course he knew. But what would his presence change? What could he offer Wren other than more damage? "I know she fucking needs me. And I tried. I tried to fix it. But all of this—*all of it*—it's my fault."

A tense beat of silence swept over them. Quinn glanced over her shoulder, searching to see if anybody was approaching. When she turned back to look at him, she lowered her voice.

"Where are you going to go?"

"There's a Resistance . . . in the outskirts." August's eyes drifted to the edge of the forest. "Maybe they can help. Maybe they know how to snap Wren out of it before she destroys Blackwood." He turned back to face Quinn. "You could come with me."

But Quinn's response was instant. "I can't."

August wanted to protest. To find a way to convince Quinn to leave the encampment. She wasn't safe here. Her heart would be her downfall. But he knew it was for that very reason that she'd never leave Wren behind, despite what Wren had become.

"Take care of yourself."

Quinn smiled, but it was hollow. "I'll try."

August turned away from Quinn and stepped toward the forest. He closed his eyes, looking inward. He hadn't used his spacial magic since leaving Blackwood, wasn't even certain it would work. But he had to try.

He scoured his internal map. Searching. Pushing through the dark, ebbing nothingness stretching out before him. And then—deeper and farther than he would have hoped—something familiar lingered. A soul. Multiple souls. He recognized them. August knew, with unwavering clarity—*It's them.*

He'd have to use more shadow magic than he wanted to in order to relocate across such a distance, but it didn't matter. As he called upon his shadows, summoning the relocation spell, he couldn't help but think back on the words that were burned into his memory, etched into his soul. The one thing he had vowed to hold on to until the very end.

Find me. Wherever you are, wherever we end up, don't stop looking for me.

"I'm sorry," he whispered.

And then Augustine Hughes summoned the relocation spell and tore his promise to shreds.

39

WREN?

Wren Loughty no longer knew where the shadows ended and her soul began. She searched for remorse. For remnants of the girl she had once been. But it came up empty. There was nothing left.

Nothing.

So when she banished August and watched him stride out of the tent, leaving her behind, the only thing she felt surging in her heart was fury. The white-hot embers of rage. The desire to rip apart the seams of the afterlife and torch what remained.

It is better this way. The Soulless One's voice leaked into her mind, drifting through her, though this time, it was different. She no longer just heard him—a distant voice lingering in the recess of her mind—but *felt* him, as if he were a part of her, his soul threaded through hers. ***He will never understand.***

Wren stared at her reflection in the mirror. Her eyes were vacant. Her soul hungry.

"I don't want to speak of him."

Very well.

Wren looked into her eyes and it felt as though she were staring *through* herself, into her soul, straight into the Soulless One.

"I do still have one question."

His voice rumbled in the back of her skull.

I'm listening.

Wren flexed her hands and shadows slipped between her fingers.

"Why me?"

The Soulless One hummed, though it felt more like a purr, the sound dripping down Wren's limbs in a vibrating warmth. ***I was wondering when you'd ask.*** The Soulless One paused, a deep sigh fluttering in Wren's mind. ***You see, though Silas had grown to think of himself as a god, he was, and is, nothing more than a man. Flawed. Capable of error. And when he chose your soul—when he forced your death and dragged your soul to Blackwood—he made the greatest mistake of his existence.***

There was a tense beat. A weighted silence.

He hesitated.

Wren cocked her head.

"He . . . *hesitated?*"

When he approached you on the road that night, when he bent down to steal your soul from your dying body and thrust you into Blackwood . . . something in him faltered. Though the doubt didn't last long, it was enough to distract him. And when he cast death's kiss upon you . . . something went wrong. A drop of his magic entered your soul. The tiniest amount. So small he didn't even notice the moment it burrowed into your soul. But it's been there, from the beginning. Waiting inside you.

Wren traced her index finger along one of the jagged black veins marring her forearm.

"I don't see how a fraction of his magic living inside me changes anything."

The Soulless One chuckled—a deep and velvety rumble of laughter.

Patience, sweet catalyst. I'm getting to that.

"Go on, then," Wren instructed. **"Get to the point."**

I am the only one who can wipe the slate clean. The Soulless One's voice grew louder, resounding within her skull. ***Who harbors the power to burn Blackwood to the ground. But I can't do it without you. You are the link. The key.*** There was a strange hesitancy in his voice, something oddly human. ***I . . . require something. A ring. Silas stole it from me—many years ago—and keeps it hidden within a box. The box only opens through his touch . . . through his magic.***

Understanding bolted through Wren.

"And I carry a droplet of his magic in my soul."

You can open the box, Wren. A wretched desire burned beneath the Soulless One's words, an untamed yearning. ***You can unleash my full power. And once you find the ring . . . you must bring it to me.***

"But how?" Wren asked. **"Don't you . . . don't you only exist in my head?"**

The Soulless One exhaled. Wren swore she felt it brush upon the nape of her neck.

No, my sweet catalyst. I have a physical form. But it is fragile. Only a fraction of the power I should wield.

"Then . . . how do I find you?"

I'll be waiting for you in Blackwood. His next words were more of a promise than a warning. **I *will find* you.**

Wren parted her lips to speak, but the entrance to the tent fluttered open without warning, and just like that, she felt her connection to the Soulless One waver. It wasn't severed . . . it would *never* be severed. But he grew dormant. Quiet. Waiting patiently in the shadows of her mind.

Edith strode into the tent, fitted in armor. A chain-mail hood had been placed over her midnight-black hair, shadow crown positioned atop it. A leather cuirass cinched her waist, the Demien Order sigil etched into the hardened black leather. Scalloped trim and rivets accented the front, while a set of buckled straps adorned the sides. As her eyes landed upon Wren, they widened for a fraction of a second, a momentary flash of surprise, though it quickly vanished when her lips curled into a smirk.

"You clean up nice."

Wren rolled her eyes.

"You can save the sweet talk, Edith." Wren sauntered closer, a delicate stream of shadows flowing out of her with every step. **"I harbor no ill will for the torture you put me through. I see now that it was necessary."**

Edith's smirk faltered. A faint crinkle of fear.

"I'm glad," she muttered through a tight-lipped smile. "Though I never doubted you would see reason. Either way, I have a gift for you."

Edith snapped her fingers and two guards entered the tent. But they weren't alone.

"Let go of me!" Quinn cried, kicking her legs uselessly as one guard tossed her in Edith's direction. The High General gripped Quinn by the neck, holding her in place with a shadow blade pointed at her throat.

The other guard had a firm grip on Arthur's wrist, and he kicked Arthur squarely on the back, sending him to his knees. A security cuff had been placed over his wrist. His magic nullified. He couldn't defend himself.

"Ah." Wren stared down at him, head cocked. **"I see. It's our traitors."**

At this accusation, Arthur's head snapped up. He stared at Wren, pleading.

"It was my idea." The words tumbled out of him quickly. "Quinn had nothing to do with it."

"No!" Quinn choked out. She tried to move, but Edith pressed the blade harder, and she froze, sucking in a sharp breath as Edith drew blood. "That—that isn't true."

"I'm the one who knew how to dismantle the security cuff." Arthur slowly pushed himself onto his feet. "I was the one who was going to do it. Not Quinn. *Me.*"

"Artie." Quinn groaned as she fought against Edith's grip. "Don't do this." But Arthur seemed determined. He kept his gaze anchored on Wren.

"Quinn had *nothing* to do with it."

Wren hummed and approached him. She could offer them mercy, but . . .

No, the Soulless One growled. ***No more mercy. No more forgiveness.***

"A price must be paid for your betrayal." Wren traced a finger against Arthur's cheek, and one of her shadows slowly slithered around him. **"For your *insubordination.*"** Arthur shivered as the word echoed between them. **"But what a waste . . . to simply destroy you. Don't you agree?"**

Quinn seemed to understand the true meaning behind Wren's words. She let out a feral scream, clawing at Edith, but the High General's grip remained unchanged. *"No!"* Quinn cried, voice hoarse. "Wren! Please! Stop this!"

Tears welled behind Arthur's eyes. When he spoke, his voice was soft. "Do what you need to do . . . just . . . don't hurt Quinn."

Bravery, Wren thought with a chuckle. *How incredibly foolish.*

"Then . . . let's make you a bit more compliant, shall we?"

Her hands cupped his face. She saw the fear etched in his eyes. The agony.

More, the Soulless One murmured inside her. ***Give me more.***

A broken scream tore from Arthur's throat as the shadows poured in through his mouth, his ears, his eyes, his nose. All at once, they consumed him. Eating away at him. Somewhere in Wren's periphery, Quinn screamed. But her pathetic cries of grief meant nothing to Wren. If anything, they fueled her.

Wren watched, enraptured, as Arthur's face gave way to the shadows bursting inside him. As he *became* the shadows. A vessel for the Soulless One's control. A creature forged from hatred.

Until Arthur Alexander Ellington was no more.

In his place stood Wren's creation.

The Aberration let out a resounding shriek and Quinn howled, a guttural cry that seemed to blend with the creature's roar. *Feel something*, a part of Wren, somewhere deep inside her, begged. *Feel.*

But all Wren felt was the power their suffering provided. The hunger for *more*.

Edith snapped her fingers and a pair of guards picked Quinn up by her elbows, dragging her from the tent as she continued to cry out. Meanwhile, Wren approached the Aberration that was once Arthur with slow, methodical steps. She cocked her head, examining her work with glistening pride.

"Find him." The Aberration blinked in understanding. **"Destroy him."**

The shadow creature curled into itself, its mass of shadows ebbing and flowing until it became a vortex of darkness. From one blink to the next, it vanished. Wren knew where it had gone . . . *who* it was looking for.

Edith approached Wren.

"You sent it after August?"

Wren hummed.

"He's no longer any of your concern."

Edith's brows furrowed.

"But—"

"Unless . . ." Wren interjected, eyes narrowing on Edith, **". . . you're *worried* about him?"**

Edith flinched at the accusation.

"I'm not."

"Because that would be most worrisome to the Soulless One," Wren mused, relishing the way Edith squirmed beneath her gaze. She hadn't been lying—she didn't resent the girl for what she'd put her through—but it was still fun to return the favor. **"We don't want complications due to any pesky lingering . . . feelings."**

To give Edith credit, she didn't break beneath Wren's line of questioning. She molded her face into one of complete indifference, lips curling back into that same careful smirk. Because if there was anything Edith Hughes was good at—it was pretending.

"I can safely say, without a single doubt, that *feelings* won't be an issue here." The muscles in Edith's neck tensed as she continued. "I simply wonder if we made a mistake in letting him go. He knows things. Too much, some would say. What if the Aberration isn't successful?"

The thought had crossed Wren's mind, not that it mattered anymore. She'd made her decision.

"He's too late, either way," she muttered. It was the truth. Nobody could stop her now. **"Whatever plan he has is useless. Futile. It won't help them in the end."**

This seemed to be enough to please Edith. She approached Wren tentatively, pausing only a few feet in front of her.

"The Order is ready." She dropped her voice lower, a gleam of excitement radiating behind her dark eyes. "All of the units are in position. All we need is your command. If the Soulless One says it's time . . . then we strike."

Wren felt him then—the Soulless One's delicate caress. The warmth of his breath.

I am ready.

Wren hummed.

"Good . . . so am I."

Edith's eyes raked her face, confusion furrowing her brow.

"Did the Soulless One . . . say something? Did he speak to you?" There was a reverent quality to her voice, an almost pathetic desperation.

Wren smiled.

"He says it's time."

A blazing exhilaration lit up Edith's face. "So . . . what do you suggest?"

The shadows in Wren's hands ebbed and flowed, twisting until they'd formed a pair of long, jagged swords—two gleaming onyx blades marked by a bloodred hilt. Wren wrapped her hands lazily around the handles, a stream of shadows twirling around the pointed steel. Flames snaked through the shadows—crimson and black intertwined, a vortex of searing power cascading down the swords.

"Well, you know what they say," Wren muttered, and the shadows rose inside her—***more, more, more***. **"When the infection spreads to the root, sometimes there's nothing left to do but to burn the fucker to the ground."**

Edith smiled.

"I couldn't agree more."

40

EMILIO

Emilio felt like a fraud. He'd volunteered to go on this expedition to save innocent souls, to do the right thing for once in his life. Even if he was scared. Even if the voices in the back of his head were screaming at him to run, to retreat to his self-preserving ways. So how on earth could he justify leaving Masika behind?

"Are you *insane*?!" Olivier strode up to Catherine, frantic. "Do you know what they're going to do to her?"

They'd been arguing for the better half of an hour. Catherine and Dina believed that going back to Blackwood would be pointless, and the better course of action would be to head back to the Resistance's base and regroup. The mere suggestion had sent Olivier into a tailspin, and they hadn't stopped arguing since. Emilio understood Olivier's anger . . . he couldn't stomach the thought of leaving Masika behind. But he also knew, deep down, that the others were right. If they were to have any chance of breaking into Blackwood and getting Masika back, they needed backup.

Catherine's jaw clenched. Her voice was low, barely audible. "Of course I do."

"They're going to torture her." Olivier's hands trembled. "They're going to rip her apart. And you want us to simply *let them*?"

"Our main priority needs to be the mission," Catherine said simply, though Emilio could see the anguish in her eyes. As if speaking the words out loud physically pained her. "We have to go back to the base and strategize."

"Then send them a message!" Olivier bellowed, hands tossed in the air.

Catherine pinched the bridge of her nose, eyes shut tight. For a moment, she stood like that, seemingly lost in thought, and then she dropped her hand and met Olivier's prodding gaze.

"Let's say you're right. Let's say she *is* being held prisoner. But if that's true, then what good will it do if we waltz up to Blackwood right now? With no army? We need to go back and get the others. Form a *plan*."

"There's no time for a plan!" Olivier snapped. "Think of what they're doing to her!"

"I am!" Catherine shoved Olivier hard in the chest. He stumbled backward, a momentary flash of surprise passing over his face. "I am thinking about it. Every fucking second since they took her. You don't think I want her back? That I'm not dying on the inside, thinking about the fact that I've failed her—*again*?"

"Guys." Dina's voice echoed behind them, but Emilio ignored her, his attention focused solely on Olivier and Catherine.

"Then why don't you do something about it?!" Olivier shot back incredulously.

"I *am*." Catherine's voice shook with anger. "I'm trying to strategize, instead of barreling in there with no plan!"

Again, Dina's voice echoed, this time more urgent.

"Guys."

Olivier groaned, turning to face her.

"What—" But Dina raised her hand, silencing him. She pointed into the distance, movements slow, index finger pressed tightly to her lips. It took Emilio a few seconds to realize why.

Standing a few yards in front of them, hovering right at the center of their path, was a shadow creature. The same kind that had attacked them in Blackwood all those weeks ago. It was smaller, though that did little to quell the terror building inside Emilio. Long, feathered wings sprouted from its shadowy form, needle-like claws jutting out from its crooked fingers. But though they stood only a few yards away from the creature, it didn't move. In fact, it gave no indication that it saw them.

Dina slowly reached down her thighs, unsheathing two of her daggers. Her movements were steady and measured as she drew the blades, careful not to accidentally brush the handle against her scabbard.

"Cat . . ." she whispered, voice shaking. "Any ideas?"

Catherine shook her head, though the rest of her body remained frozen, perfectly still.

"I'm working on it."

The creature remained fixed in its place. *Is it staring at us?* Emilio wondered. It was nearly impossible to discern whether the creature had a face—they saw nothing but a complex web of undulating shadows.

"Maybe it can't see us," whispered Olivier with a hopeful shrug. "Maybe if we move slowly we can—" But Olivier never finished his sentence, the words dying in his throat as the creature turned suddenly to face them.

There was a second of silence.

And then the creature *pounced.*

Emilio's reaction was instinctual. He gripped Olivier's hand and began to run.

The others jumped into action as well, sprinting away from the creature, though Emilio couldn't quite tell if they were close behind or if they'd run in the opposite direction. It didn't matter. Not when he could hear the creature shrieking and roaring behind him. Not when he could *feel* the creature's presence like a tightening cord around his throat. There was no telling how close it was. If it was mere seconds from catching up, swiping its razor-edged talons across his back.

Lost in the current of panic, Emilio didn't notice the fork in the path until he was already upon it. His hand slipped out of Olivier's as the other boy disappeared on the opposite side of the trees that blocked his path.

"OLIVIER!"

But it was too late. Emilio had lost sight of him, the other boy vanishing into the parallel path. Why hadn't he held on? Why hadn't he tried harder? Emilio cursed, staggering backward. He searched the surrounding trees, desperate for any sign of Olivier, but the darkness of the forest was his only companion, the barren branches looming over him like spindly bones. Emilio choked on a panicked breath. He was lost. And the others . . . there was no way of knowing if they were safe. If they'd been attacked—

Snap.

A twig creaked behind him.

Emilio spun on his heels.

Behind him, only a few yards away, waited the shadow creature.

There was a tense beat of silence as Emilio weighed his options.

Which, to be fair, weren't many.

He started running. He ran faster than he thought possible, chest heaving. He pushed through twisted branches and the web of greenery obstructing his vision. He glanced over his shoulder in the hope that he had somehow managed to outrun the creature, but there it was—*a flash of darkness*. Pointed claws prepared to strike. The shadow creature was catching up, chasing after him, a billowing mass of shadows and talons and razor-sharp teeth.

He needed to find the others. He needed to—

His foot hit something hard. A tree root.

Emilio went flying to the ground, rolling and rolling, only coming to a stop when his back slammed against the base of a tree, a throbbing pain radiating up and down his spine. He let out a hoarse scream. It tore from his throat, desperate and hollow.

He tried to scramble to his feet, but he slipped against the damp earth, hands helplessly clawing at the ground beneath him. Something snapped in front of him. His eyes flitted up, and there it was again . . . the shadow creature.

Emilio hadn't noticed before, but the creature had eyes. Glowing, piercing eyes that were strangely human, despite the animalistic gleam behind them. They were green. Olive green. He couldn't tear his gaze away from them. It was like staring straight into the eyes of the reaper. Into the abyss of death.

"Please," Emilio whimpered, hands raised in surrender. *"Please."*

Then the oddest thing happened. The creature tilted its head. As if it had heard him. As if it had understood him. But it wasn't possible. This thing was nothing more than an abomination of magic. A creature forged from shadows. And yet . . . it continued to watch Emilio. It didn't strike, like Emilio thought it would.

It was waiting . . . but for what?

Emilio never found out.

Suddenly, with a startling force that bent the trees around him and whipped tufts of hair across his face, a supersonic burst of shadows erupted from behind the shadow creature. From one blink to the next, the creature exploded, rupturing into nothing but a noxious cloud of smoke and ash.

Emilio coughed, sputtering. He could barely see. But something was shifting in front of him. Moving behind the curtain of smoke. Not the shadow creature . . . but something else. *Someone* else.

A figure emerged from the mass of smoke. A brilliant force bathed in shadows.

Emilio almost didn't recognize him.

Augustine Hughes stood between two trees like a fallen angel poised for battle. His white button-down was untucked, thick streams of shadows snaking up and down the exposed skin of his chest, crawling over his neck. A cloak lay over his shoulders, cascading down his sides in billowing waves of black.

When his silver-gray eyes fell upon Emilio, there was a moment of hesitation, of complete and utter disbelief, and then Augustine Hughes, notorious traitor and bloodthirsty Demien, broke out into the most brilliant smile Emilio had ever seen.

He took a stumbling step forward.

"Emilio."

Upon hearing his name spoken out loud, with such striking relief, Emilio couldn't help but flush. His body tensed, though he didn't call upon his magic, despite the obvious threat now standing before him.

"August."

Emilio had expected August to approach him, but instead, he did something that Emilio couldn't quite understand. He knelt beside what remained of the shadow creature and placed his hand upon the earth.

"I'm sorry, my friend."

Emillio cocked his head in confusion.

Friend?

But before Emilio could ask what August had meant, Olivier came running up behind him, nearly stumbling to the ground. He managed to right himself, holding on to Emilio's shoulder for stability. The others were only a few paces behind, and then Catherine and Dina were both standing beside Emilio, the entire group wearing identical expressions of bewilderment as they took in the scene. They must have been thinking the same thing Emilio had when he'd first seen August.

It couldn't be real. *He* couldn't be real.

But this wasn't an illusion.

This is real.

August's eyes darted to the right, landing on Olivier. His gray eyes beamed.

"Olivier."

Olivier looked as though he'd seen a ghost. His jaw hung open in shock, eyes wide and brows pinched together. A strangled sound escaped his throat, something between a burst of laughter and a gasp.

Catherine stepped forward. Her grip on her spear tightened.

"August?"

The silver-eyed boy gave a hesitant nod in response.

"Catherine."

A frustrated groan erupted from Dina's throat.

"Well, *fuck*, if we're saying everyone's name . . . Hi. I'm Dina." She splayed her hand over her chest and mockingly bowed her head, nearly dropping Benji in the process. Emilio was instantly relieved to see that the little creature appeared to be unharmed. "We've never properly met, but your reputation precedes you, so no need to give me the whole play-by-play. Now, mind explaining what the hell you're doing here?"

August shifted uncomfortably, tugging at the collar of his white shirt.

"I was actually on my way to find you all," he explained. "Well . . . to find the Resistance. But then I heard Emilio's screams . . ." August trailed off, eyes skating among the group. An awkward current permeated the air. Tension thick enough to drown in.

Catherine thrust the tip of her spear into the ground. A lightning crack of corporeal magic fizzled beneath her feet.

"You were trying to find the Resistance? For *what*?" Catherine stepped closer, head tilted. "To destroy it?"

"No." August flinched at the accusation. "I . . . I was going to ask to join."

Catherine let out a bark of laughter. "You want to *join* us? How stupid do you think we are?"

August sighed. "Look. I know you don't trust me—"

"I tried to get you to join us!" Catherine bellowed, bolts of silver light crackling up and down her spear. "But you said *no*. You refused to leave the Order. You refused to turn your back on the Soulless One."

"Things have changed," August shot back. "*I've* changed."

"I'm sorry, but I have to chime in here," Olivier interjected, stepping forward. "As much as I'd love to believe you're really here to help us—how do you expect me to accept a word out of your mouth when you've essentially spent the past two hundred years plotting to destroy us all?"

August's jaw twitched. When he looked at Olivier, Emilio saw centuries of unspoken words stretching between them. It was a connection that Emilio would never understand. Something forged between two people who had been around long enough to understand the consequences of eternity better than most.

"Olivier." August spoke his name softly. "I know . . . I know I've disappointed you—"

"I'd say *disappointed* is a bit of an understatement," Olivier muttered.

"—and you're right. I *was* on their side. For a long, long time. Longer than I'm proud to admit. But I'm not anymore. The only reason I got rid of my humanity was so that I stood a chance of getting Wren back—"

"Wait." Emilio's world tilted as he processed August's words. "What do you mean *getting Wren back*?" A cautious wave of hope rose inside Emilio. "Didn't she . . . we had all assumed she'd . . ."

August shook his head.

"She wasn't sacrificed," he whispered. With those three words, the hope inside Emilio finally burst open. *Wren had made it.* "Edith took her to the Order's encampment. Held her prisoner there."

"Why?" Olivier asked.

August sucked in a sharp intake of breath.

"Right . . ." He shut his eyes. "You don't know."

"Know what?" Catherine pressed.

And then, with another four words, the hope bursting inside Emilio was extinguished.

"Wren is the catalyst," August muttered, a dark edge to his voice. "The one prophesized to destroy Blackwood."

Olivier let out a cackle. Even Emilio flinched at the sudden outburst. "Fuck off."

August blinked. "Excuse me?"

"There's no way," Olivier muttered through a chuckle of disbelief. "Wren. As in Wren Loughty. As in the same Wren Loughty who once nearly had an aneurysm because she was five minutes late to class? The one who would literally throw a tantrum anytime someone almost beat her top score during reaping assignments? You're telling me *she* is going to destroy Blackwood?"

August didn't hesitate. He didn't even crack a smile. "Yes."

Olivier's face fell. "Oh."

"Last night . . ." August swallowed, voice wavering. "She changed. She had a vision. It . . . transformed her."

"But . . . it's *Wren*," Emilio said. "Can't we just try to talk to her—"

"It's not Wren," August snapped. He shut his eyes, inhaling a quivering breath. "I mean, I think she's still in there . . . somewhere . . . but she didn't just rip her humanity out and succumb to the shadows. It's like she's become an extension of the Soulless One."

A piercing silence fell upon the group.

Catherine reached into her knapsack, unveiling a small amber jar with a strange black liquid inside. The moment she uncorked it, the black liquid rose into the air, billowing until it began to change form, growing larger and larger by the second.

August cocked his head and stepped closer. "What are you doing?"

"I'm sending a message back to the Resistance," Catherine muttered. The inky darkness ebbed and flowed until it had morphed into a perfect oval. But there was something forming inside it. A face. *Catherine's face.* It was like a reflection, as though she were looking into an obsidian mirror. "If the catalyst has truly awoken—then we've run out of time."

She cleared her throat and turned to face the strange mirror.

"This is Catherine Clarke speaking." Her voice shook with

every word, though her gaze remained anchored upon the projection, never once wavering. "The catalyst has awoken. Gather all factions and prepare to storm Blackwood. The time for waiting is over . . . the battle has begun."

She placed her hand upon the mirror and it disintegrated, vanishing beneath her touch.

"Does that mean we can look for Masika?" Olivier asked.

Catherine gave a hesitant nod. "We can try. It might be impossible, and she might not even be there—"

"Masika?" August interjected, stepping forward. "What do you mean *look* for her?"

"We think she was kidnapped by Ascended," Emilio explained softly. He didn't miss the flicker of rage that passed over August's eyes. "We have no way of knowing if she made it, but . . ."

August nodded in understanding. He ran a hand along the back of his neck. "I'll help. We'll find her." He paused, eyes flitting between the group. "What the hell were you all doing out here, anyway?"

Catherine's gaze settled on August with a flicker of distrust. Eventually, she conceded with a sigh. "I suppose if you truly want to join us, then there's a few things you should know."

They caught him up with the events of the past few days. About the map that had been found by Russo and Birdie. About their plan to travel across purgatory and resurrect the True Headmaster. And, more importantly, about how it had all been a colossal waste of time.

When they'd finished, Dina narrowed her eyes at August.

"You don't seem surprised. You *did* hear the part about us trying to resurrect an ancient powerful entity thought to be destroyed for centuries, right?"

August ran a hand through his curls. "Quite frankly, this isn't the most shocking piece of information I've received over the past few weeks."

Dina considered his words with a shrug. "Fair enough."

"Well, what now?" Olivier asked, fidgeting with his hands.

A chilling hush settled over them. Catherine tightened her grip on her spear. "Now . . . we fight. Without the True Headmaster. We fight with everything we have until the very end."

Panic seized Emilio. Olivier wouldn't even meet his gaze. He was staring at the ground, an agonized look of defeat in his eyes. Emilio wanted to go to him. To hold him. But before he could move a muscle, Dina spoke up.

"We'll never make it in time. We can't relocate through purgatory's atmosphere. The only way the others will make it is by using the portal back at the base," Dina whispered softly. "We'd never be able to re-create it. It took *years* to construct that portal. Decades of carefully threaded magic. If we wanted to get to Blackwood now"—Dina swallowed, panic flooding her face—"it would take us *hours*."

"I can get us there," August replied without hesitation.

Dina shook her head. "You're not listening. We can't relocate through purgatory. You'd need an insane source of magic to transport all of us at once. Like, a *massive*, destructive amount of—" Dina's mouth clamped shut when she saw the determination burning behind August's eyes. She gave a quick shake of her head.

"No," she muttered softly. "August. You can't. *Look at you.*" She gestured to the shadow veins crawling over his neck. "You've already used too much."

He shrugged. "What other choice do we have?"

Olivier scrunched his face in confusion. "I'm sorry—what is going on here? What can't August do?"

But neither one of them answered.

"My soul is already ruined," August muttered matter-of-factly. "May as well torch what's left."

"You do understand the consequences of what you're saying, right?" Dina pressed, striding up to him. "If you use that much shadow magic in the state you're already in . . . if you transport *all* of us . . ." Her voice shook with a swell of emotions. "You may as well cast the Reaper's Kiss."

August sighed. "I know."

A gasp sprang out of Emilio as understanding washed over him. "You're going to use shadow magic to take us there?"

August turned to look at him, almost shy. He smirked and Emilio felt his heart splinter into a thousand pieces. "It's the only way."

Catherine stepped forward. "August."

"Oh, cheer up, Catherine." A crooked smile spread over August's face, though Emilio could practically feel the anguish radiating behind his storm-gray eyes. "Once the shadows take me, you'll finally be able to rip my soul out of my chest just like you've always wanted to."

Catherine's bottom lip trembled. She shook her head. "You're a bloody fool."

August shrugged. "I've been called worse."

August brought his hands together. Between them, a cloud of shadows formed.

"How long will you have before . . ." Dina's voice trailed off, but her question was clear.

How long will August have until the shadows consume him?

August shrugged.

"Could be hours. Could be a couple of minutes." Shadows were trickling out of his body, feathering around him, bursting beneath him like a storm cloud. "But when it happens . . . and it *will* happen . . . you cannot hesitate. You strike me down. You put me out before I can hurt anybody else."

Catherine sealed the promise with a nod.

August called upon his shadows.

. . . and they answered.

41

Irene

Irene stumbled into her room and threw up. Her vision blurred, darkening at the edges. She fell to her knees, hands flat against the wooden floors, back curved as her body purged itself of what it could. *Take it all,* she begged. Every memory. Every lingering emotion. Every haunting mistake. She wanted to carve herself open and rip out the rot. That *thing* that made her feel empty. Because she *was* empty, wasn't she? What else could possibly explain the sickness in her mind? The twisted, dark part of her that would let her stand back and watch her best friend be tortured?

She couldn't stop hearing the screams. She couldn't stop them from ringing out in her head, a sickening sound that sent another wave of nausea up her throat. She sucked in a breath, coughing, sputtering, desperate for air in her lungs.

Please. Make it stop. Make it fucking stop.

Irene didn't even know who she was begging to anymore. No one was listening. No one had ever listened. Her pleas were as empty as her soul, careening uselessly around her skull, barely drowning out the memory of Masika's cries. Somehow, she managed to gather herself back onto her feet, stumbling into the washroom. She rinsed her mouth and glared up at her own reflection. She couldn't stand to look at herself. To meet her own reflection and know what she was capable of. What she had been willing to sacrifice to keep her promise to the Order.

Something cold pressed against her palm.

She looked down.

The coin.

She could barely remember the moment Headmaster Silas had placed it in her hand. The memory was already foggy at the edges. Warped by the pain of Masika's cries. *Congratulations, Ms. Bamford.* His voice tore at her mind. Clawed at her insides. *You are now part of Blackwood Academy's prestigious Council.* She'd left the dungeons only moments later, her sanity already fraying at the edges.

She'd let her friend suffer. She'd watched. Complacent. Silent.

And for what? For *this*?

Something tore inside her. A fracture. A splintering crack.

I can't.

She hadn't used the locket Mateo had given her since the Decennial. She hadn't had a reason to. Mateo had always been near, waiting for her. But he wasn't here now. And Irene knew there was something she needed to do.

She unearthed the locket from her nightstand. It hummed in her palm, waiting for her command.

It just needed one word.

One name.

"Mateo."

He appeared before her from one blink to the next. Apprehension pinched his features the moment his gaze fell upon Irene, his brows furrowed in concern. He placed his hands on her shoulders and held her steady.

"What happened?" His voice shook. "What's wrong?"

"Masika." Irene could barely get her name out. It tasted sour on her tongue. "I . . . I watched them torture her. They . . . tore into her *mind.* They entered her soul—" But Mateo's voice sliced through her words.

"What is that?"

Irene blinked up at him.

"What?" she choked out.

Mateo had grown eerily still. His eyes dragged down to Irene's hand. To the coin nestled in her palm. A ravenous hunger flared in his blue eyes . . . something Irene hadn't quite seen before.

"Are you listening to me?" Irene placed her hand against his cheek, angling his gaze back toward her. Mateo blinked, and it was as if he'd snapped out of a daze. "Masika. We have to help her."

"There's nothing we can do," he said solemnly. When Irene opened her mouth to protest, he interjected, cupping her face in his hands. "Irene . . . you knew this would happen. You knew what your loyalty to the Order meant. When the catalyst arrives . . . she will cleanse the corruption at the root. Every single soul that isn't tethered to the Soulless One will be destroyed. And that includes Masika."

"But can't you make an exception?"

Mateo's eyes slowly drifted back to the coin. Again, his expression seemed to change. The tenderness Irene had come to know well—*gone.* As if the humanity had been snatched from his soul.

"Give it to me."

Irene's grip on the coin tightened.

"Please," she begged. "I did what you asked. I've been loyal."

Mateo placed his hand upon Irene's. He didn't try to take the coin, but his grip tightened, almost pleadingly.

"It'll be worth it, in the end." His words tore a hole in Irene's chest. A finality that stole the breath from her lungs. There was no changing his mind. No saving Masika. Irene had made her bed . . . and now she'd have to lie in it. "Just . . . hand it over, Irene. Finish what you started. Join us . . . once and for all."

Irene felt her restraint slipping. The last shred of hope.

She unfurled her fingers.

She watched, helplessly, as Mateo slowly slid the coin into his palm.

"I'll find you." But even as he spoke, his eyes remained glued to the coin. It was as if she weren't even there. As if everything—all the time spent between them—had never happened. "I promise."

When he vanished from the room, Irene didn't stir. She'd expected it. She saw it clearly now. Mateo had gotten what he wanted, and now . . .

An alarm blared in the distance. A sound Irene had never heard at Blackwood.

It was a dissonant gong. A chilling herald.

Then, as if the world had been drenched in the light of a blood-red moon, a scarlet haze floated from the nearby window. Irene staggered to the window. She stared, horrified, at the cost of her greed.

The sky burned crimson. A warning etched into the clouds as the protective dome surrounding Blackwood shattered, piece by piece.

WE ARE COMING.

What have I done? Irene thought, staggering backward. *What have I done?*

There was no fixing this now. She could go to Silas—but then what? He could fill her head with empty, pretty words . . . but was he any different than Mateo? Hadn't they both simply told her what she wanted to hear?

She'd just wanted to be seen. To be heard.

To be fucking appreciated.

Her mother hadn't seen her or appreciated her. She'd tossed Irene away as if she were nothing—and for so long, Irene had believed her. But Mateo and Silas had seen promise in her. The possibility of power. And they'd seen that helpless need inside her and manipulated her like a puppet. Tugging at her strings while she simply stood back and let them.

But not anymore.

Irene Manette Bamford was selfish. She was cruel. A heartless power-hungry bitch.

And she was done believing in the promises of wretched men.

42

WREN

Death danced against her tongue. It swam through her veins, syrupy and warm.

More.

Wren laughed and screams echoed around her. The snap of bones. The crack of skulls fracturing.

More.

She lifted her hand and ripped a soul from existence. They didn't even scream. They didn't have time.

MORE.

Wren stood at the entrance of Blackwood Academy. Around her, chaos reigned. She pressed her palms upon the cold earth and shadows billowed out of her, blanketing the ground, pouring in thick streams. She smiled as the darkness devoured those in her path—flesh torn open . . . souls destroyed. Their cries filled her with ecstasy. Their screams of terror a glorious symphony written just for her.

Wren turned away from her destruction. She wanted to stay . . . to revel in the chaos. But she knew there were other matters that needed her attention. A call she must answer.

Across the grounds, out toward the Library, stood a figure.

Sapphire eyes stared back at her.

A familiar face she'd only seen chiseled from stone.

Despite the distance between them, when the Soulless One spoke, Wren heard his words clear as day ring out inside her.

Hello, my sweet catalyst.

Wren cocked her head. The world was a violent haze of magic and shadows and fire—yet all of that seemed to vanish when she met the Soulless One's gaze across the battlefield.

"Hello," Wren replied with a coy grin.

The Soulless One motioned her forward with two fingers.

It's time.

And then the Soulless One's physical form vanished, drifting away as if he were nothing but a cloud of smoke. A hunger erupted inside Wren at hearing those two words spoken out loud. A ravenous desire. She knew where she needed to go. Her legs seemed to move of their own accord, striding toward her destination with fearsome resolve.

When she finally reached Headmaster Silas's office, the Soulless One's voice echoed inside her again, deep and grating.

He's waiting for you. When you're done . . . meet me outside the gates.

"Don't worry," Wren replied. She flicked her wrist and the door burst open. **"This won't take long."**

She strode into the room, a specter swathed in shadows. Darkness shrouded the office, only the silver glow of night flooding in through the windows, but still, Wren could see the figure seated behind the desk. The dark eyes staring back at her, boring into her soul. The one she had been waiting for.

"Hello, Silas." Wren smiled, pointed teeth gleaming in the darkness. She snapped her fingers and the door slammed behind her with an echoing thud. **"I think you have something that belongs to us."**

43

MASIKA

There was dying, and then there was whatever this was. Maybe there wasn't exactly a word for it. How could Masika even begin to describe the agony of her soul fracturing? Of a thousand hands ripping into her soul, tearing at her insides, tugging at the threads of her sanity in the hope that it would break? That *she* would break?

By some miracle, she'd managed to black out after a while. The pain had lingered, but there was some distance behind it, as if Masika had sunk into her body and watched the whole thing play out as an observer. And now . . . here she was. Where exactly? She wasn't entirely sure. It had to be the same cell, considering she'd been lying on the ground for the past few hours, but the world around her had lost all shape and meaning, nothing but shadows undulating in her peripheral vision.

Somewhere in the distance, there was an explosion. Or, at least, what Masika assumed was an explosion. A thunderous boom rattled the walls of the dungeon, chunks of rock cascading onto the floor, plumes of smoke rising from the ashes. Was that an alarm? A blaring noise echoed above her. Over and over. Screams echoed. Far away, the sizzling crackle of magic reverberated, mixed with something else—a deep, guttural roar that reminded Masika of the moment the mountain had come crashing down around her.

She tried to move, placing her hands against the floor, but her body wouldn't cooperate. A strangled whimper echoed from her throat. Why couldn't she move? Had they broken her legs? Was she *actually* dying?

A shiver of fear cascaded down her spine.

She couldn't help but wonder what was left of her. Maybe her entire soul was broken.

Maybe they'd left nothing behind.

A voice fluttered in front of her. Deep. Warm. Familiar.

"What's wrong, my darling girl?"

Despite the fact that Masika's cheek was still firmly pressed against the cold floor, she managed to drag her eyes upward, facing the source of the voice. Standing above her, scruff on his jaw and a smile on his lips, was her father.

Masika's breaths splintered out of her in shallow huffs. So . . . this was it.

Her ending.

"I'm tired," she managed to choke out.

"Is that so?" Her father squatted down next to her. He reached out his hand, brushing his palm against her forehead, tucking a loose curl behind her ear. It even felt like him. Rough, callused hands tinged with tenderness. "Well. Why don't you close your eyes, then? Take a rest."

Searing heat crawled against Masika's skin. Burning her from the inside out.

"I . . . can't." She breathed and the sound rasped in the back of her throat. "I won't . . . wake back up."

Her father shrugged. "Would that be so bad?"

Masika chuckled. "I suppose not."

Her father smiled down at her. "You've been through so much, my darling girl. You've been so brave. Not just in death, but in life too."

He was right. Her death hadn't been clean and swift. She hadn't gently drifted off into the darkness, welcomed into the afterlife by a merciful hand. Her death had been long . . . arduous. Messy. A sickness that slowly ate away at her. Fluorescent lights and sharp needles jammed into her skin. Endless doctor appointments met with wave after wave of disappointment. Chemicals dripped into her veins. More pills. More pain. More waiting. More hoping.

And what had it all meant in the end? What good had it done?

"Dad . . ." Masika sobbed. "I'm scared. I'm really fucking scared."

Her father's expression changed from one beat to the next. His smile dropped. "Then get the hell up."

Masika flinched. "What?" she croaked.

Her father leaned in closer. "Get. Up."

Masika blinked. Her father's face warped—two versions of him splitting and joining back together. But his features were changing too, molding into another face . . . a face Masika knew well. But it couldn't be real. She was clearly losing her mind, the apparition of her father was proof enough, so there was no conceivable way that what she was seeing was real. That the face staring back at her was—

"I SAID GET THE FUCK UP!"

The voice that shot out of her father's mouth was shrill and familiar, and then suddenly it wasn't her father looming over her but Irene, eyes wide and frantic as she gripped Masika by the shoulders, desperately attempting to drag her onto her feet.

Masika groggily blinked through the haze muddling her senses. "Irene?"

At her name, Irene blinked. A smile crept onto her lips.

"Rise and shine, Masi. It's time to get you the hell out of here."

Masika's mind whirred, nausea licking up her throat. In the distance, more explosions rang out. The screams were deafening. The stench of magic overwhelming her senses. She let out a low groan.

"What's happening?" she muttered.

"Armageddon."

"Oh." Masika let out a soft sigh and her eyes fluttered back closed. "That's nice."

"No—" Irene groaned, cursing under her breath. Masika could feel Irene's hands on her, the desperation radiating from her as she struggled to pick Masika up. Masika wanted to move, but she was just so damn tired. Couldn't she just keep lying there? Couldn't she simply wither away?

"Wake up, Masi." Irene slapped Masika across the face. "Eyes open. Come on."

The sting from Irene's slap was enough for Masika's senses to refocus. She opened her eyes, properly taking in the chaos unraveling in front of her. Soot streaked across Irene's nose, the bottom of her hair slightly singed. Her dress had been ripped at the hem, a deep crimson stain slashed across her knee, though there wasn't a wound in sight.

"You look like shit."

Irene laughed, but there were tears behind her eyes. "Right back at you."

Somehow, despite everything, Masika managed to find a tiny sliver of strength. She pushed herself onto her feet, gripping one of the iron bars of the cell when her leg buckled beneath her.

"Can you move?" Irene asked softly.

Masika shrugged. "Define *move*."

Irene threw Masika's arm over her shoulder, grunting as she helped drag her out of the cell.

"So . . . care to explain what exactly is going on?"

"Well," Irene huffed. "The Demien Order and the Resistance have both stormed the gates of Blackwood, and the school is essentially on the brink of a cataclysmic afterlife war."

Masika opened and shut her mouth. She had a million questions, but all she managed to utter was "Right. And . . . where are *we* going?"

"Uh—" Irene chuckled nervously. "I haven't really thought that through quite yet."

They were turning a corner when the patter of footsteps stopped them in their tracks.

Irene sucked in a sharp breath.

"Shit."

Everly Hawthorne was standing before them, blocking their path.

Her eyes flitted between Irene and Masika, brows furrowed. The brief flicker of confusion in her gaze quickly vanished under sharpened fury. She clenched her hands into fists, flames shooting out of her knuckles. "What are you doing?" Each word slipped out of her with a punch of air. "Put her back in the cell."

Irene placed her arm protectively in front of Masika. "Get out of the way, Everly."

"Oh my God." Everly let out a cackle. "Are you fucking kidding me? Did you honestly think you could get away with this? That Headmaster Silas wouldn't notice? That he wouldn't rip your soul out of your throat for this betrayal?"

"I don't give a damn about Silas," Irene said through gritted teeth. "And if you had even a fraction of a brain cell left in that skull of yours—you wouldn't either."

Everly's nostrils flared. "You filthy traitor—"

She raised her arms, poised to strike.

But Masika moved first.

She hadn't even felt herself summon her magic. It had simply been there, waiting for her.

Masika's arm sliced down in one clean swoop.

Everly stood frozen for a suspended moment, eyes wide, mouth parted.

And then a blossoming line of blood appeared on her neck, severing her head cleanly from her body. It fell to the floor with a sickening thud, rolling over to Irene, who continued to stare at Masika with a strange mixture of shock and admiration.

Masika let out a shaky breath.

"I really, *really* hate that girl."

And then Masika passed out and collapsed into Irene's arms.

44

OLIVIER

Carnage.

That was what greeted Olivier when August's spell transported them back to Blackwood and they materialized near the steps of the Library. For a moment, he let himself revel in the familiarity surrounding him. The thin streams of evening fog drifting beneath his feet. The cool, brisk air whispering against his skin. Large, imposing oak trees flanking his path, their autumnal leaves shivering as they swayed in the breeze.

Blackwood Academy.

He'd never thought he'd miss it.

But before Olivier could allow himself to get *too* sentimental, the stench of violence came rushing back in. Destruction loomed near the southern gates, a sea of black and red cloaks. The Demien Order, Resistance fighters and Ascended clashed. Billowing shadows choked the air, while the Resistance did everything in their power to counter their attacks. But no amount of defensive shields or corporeally infused weaponry seemed to be enough to subdue the power of the Demien Order.

We're not going to win.

Just as the thought echoed in Olivier's mind, a violent blast of shadows shot out from somewhere to his left. Catherine shoved Olivier square on the back before the spell could find its mark, pushing him out of the way at the last second. He stumbled, regaining his footing. Emilio was at his side by the time he reoriented himself.

Olivier could see the source of the attack now. Three bloodthirsty Demiens prowled closer, hands extended, shadows erupting out of them. Their eyes were pools of black ink. A deadly venom in their stares.

And they were heading straight for Olivier and the others.

Catherine jumped into action, unsheathing her glowing spear, a brilliant arch of silver light shooting out of the tip. Beside her, Dina clutched two of her daggers, craning her neck from side to side as she prepared for action.

August cursed beneath his breath. "Shit."

Olivier turned to him. "What is it?"

When Olivier turned to look at August, he saw the cost of his shadow magic written plainly upon his face. The black veins now traveled over his neck and face, pulsating with power. There was also a fury burning behind his eyes—an intensity that made Olivier's stomach churn. But before August could reply, one of the Demiens—the one standing at the head of the trio—called out to them, his voice carrying over the roar of the battle. His hair was blond, though lighter than Olivier's, black veins traveling up and down his pale face, similar to August's. And his sights were fixed on them.

"General Hughes!" The boy spoke August's name with a feral growl. "It appears as though you're on the wrong side of the battle."

August stepped forward, but Olivier didn't miss the slight limp. The way the black veins etched into August's forearms had begun to grow, traveling higher, infecting him more deeply with every second that passed. August winced, grimacing, as if he were battling an unseen war.

"Leave them alone, Callum."

The boy, Callum, raised a single eyebrow. "*Oh?* Is that an order?"

One of the shadows slithering around August's wrist surged downward, extending past his right hand, drawing itself together. It was changing. Coalescing to form what appeared to be a sword. The shadows hardened, less cloudlike, almost solid. August gripped the hilt of the sword, pointing the edge of the blade toward Callum.

"You still have time to retreat."

Callum considered his words, his mouth stretching into a cruel smile as his own shadows were forged into a twin sword. "But where would be the fun in that?"

The Demiens moved as one. Olivier barely had time to react, pulling Emilio closer as a swirling mass of shadows swept past them. Callum and August met at the center of the battle, barreling toward one another. Their swords clashed together. The other two Demiens, the ones who had been flanking Callum, turned their sights on the rest of the group. One of them zeroed in on Emilio.

Olivier tried to jump in front of him, but the Demien was faster, and a spear forged from shadows shot out of his hand before Olivier could even move a muscle. Emilio, however, was ready. Despite cradling Benji in one arm, he lifted his free arm, and a shield spun out of his palm. Just as the spear was seconds away from making contact, it slammed against the golden light of Emilio's shield, disintegrating before it could make contact.

The Demien growled, incensed. He raised his arm, poised to strike. But the attack never came. Instead, the Demien's eyes went wide. His mouth dropped open. It took Olivier a few seconds to notice Housemaster Birdie standing behind the Demien . . . and her arm protruding from his chest.

With a guttural scream, Birdie ripped her arm out, a swirling dark mass clutched in her palm. *His soul,* Olivier realized with a small gasp. The Demien's eyes went unnaturally blank. And then the shadows coursing through his veins seemed to envelop him, swallowing his entire being, until all that was left was a shapeless mass of shadows that vanished into the air.

Olivier offered his former Housemaster a shaky smile. "Thank you."

Birdie wiped the sweat from her brow and chuckled. "Glad I could be of service."

Somewhere to the left of them, Catherine and Dina had been caught up in their own battle, fending off the other Demien with their corporeally infused weaponry. But Catherine had been badly wounded, and Olivier could tell by the blood pooling out of her stomach that she needed a healer—*fast.*

Luckily, it appeared that Housemaster Russo had snuck up on their attacker as well. She plunged her arm into his chest, and Olivier watched as the Demien's soul was obliterated, swallowed by the shadows that burst out of them.

August, however, remained caught in his battle with Callum. The two boys stood face to face, their shadow blades pressed together.

One of them is going to break.

As the thought sliced through Olivier's mind, he watched, breath held, as August suddenly lost his footing. His sword clattered to the ground. Callum didn't waste any time. He raised his sword to deliver the final blow. A wicked grin spread onto his lips.

Olivier opened his mouth to scream. *No.*

But Olivier must have been just as taken aback by August's moment of weakness as Callum had been, because neither of them noticed the secondary shadow blade in August's hand until he was already shoving it straight through Callum's chest. Right into the core of his soul.

Callum's eyes went wide. His mouth twitched, and at first, Olivier assumed it was shock twisting his features. Denial. But as his lips curved higher, it occurred to Olivier that it was something else burning behind the Demien's eyes. Something far more sinister.

Callum smiled . . . proud. And then one word sputtered out of his lips. *"Ravishing."*

The word seemed to snap August out of his stupor. He ripped the shadow blade out and Callum *exploded*—his soul coming apart, dissolving into thousands of infinite specks of ash and shadow.

August remained there, kneeling. His chest rose and fell with panicked breaths. Olivier placed a tentative hand upon the boy's shoulder, and he flinched, staring up at Olivier with shadow-drenched eyes. "It's okay," Olivier whispered, coaxing August back. "It's done." And then August blinked and Olivier watched in relief as the whites of his eyes returned, the familiar icy sheen of his irises coming back into view. But even so, Olivier could still see the internal war being waged inside August. How much effort he was putting into keeping the shadows at bay.

"We've got company!" Russo shouted. A few yards away, a group of Ascended were prowling closer. Despite the shadows of night, their glowing eyes cut through the darkness, a pack of wolves descending on their prey. Birdie had constructed a defensive shield, and though it would keep them safe for now, Olivier knew it wouldn't hold. Next to her, Russo drew a sword, fiery embers coating its blade.

"I'm going to locate a healer." Dina laced Catherine's arm over her shoulder, though Catherine mumbled a protest, something about being *perfectly fine,* which was almost laughable given the fist-sized hole in her stomach.

"Can you take him?" Emilio gestured to Benji, cradled in his arms. "Please."

"Yes, fine." Dina took the creature in her arms, drawing him close to her chest. "Just *go*."

Catherine gripped Olivier tightly by the collar. She tugged him closer.

"Bring her back to me." Her voice shook. Eyes wide and desperate. "Please."

"I will," he whispered in return. "I promise." His promise didn't mean a damn thing, but even knowing that, Catherine let go, slumping back into Dina's arms.

For a moment, Olivier faltered. It suddenly occurred to him that he had no idea where to go. He looked between August and Emilio, and though the latter looked just as perplexed as Olivier felt, the former had set his sights on the towering spiral structure of the Ascended Quarters. It loomed in the darkness, its ivy-draped bricks rising from the ground like a ravenous beast . . . taunting them.

"There." August pointed up to the tower with a tilt of his head. "If they're keeping Masika anywhere, it has to be there."

Olivier hesitated. "Are you certain?"

August nodded. "Go. Find her."

Olivier cocked his head in confusion. "You're not coming with us?"

August grimaced. "You know I can't."

Olivier didn't have to ask him to elaborate. He knew exactly what August meant.

Wren.

Olivier nodded in understanding.

"Good luck."

August smiled, and Olivier felt his heart shatter.

“Right back at you.”

As the three of them took off into the night, August toward Elysium Hall and Olivier and Emilio charging toward the Ascended Quarters, a burning certainty settled in Olivier’s mind.

They might not have what it took to win the war—but he’d be damned if they didn’t get their friends back.

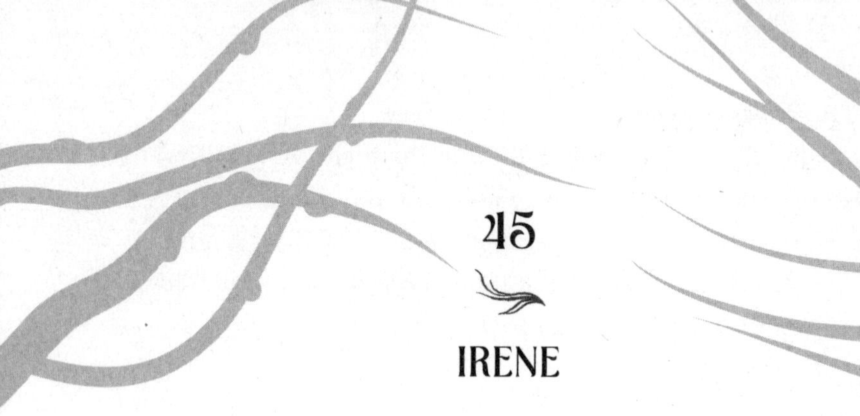

45

IRENE

Thankfully, Irene had managed to wake up Masika with another swift slap across the face. The pair had stumbled out of the dungeons, relocating to the first floor of the Ascended Quarters. But once they were there, neither one of them seemed to know what to do next.

The heart of the battle was still happening near the main gates, though it had begun to slowly trickle deeper north, migrating toward the Library. Irene scurried over to the nearest window and examined the chaos below. Only a few yards away, a horde of Demiens cut across the grounds, the group flanked by billowing shadow creatures. The putrid scent of blood and violence was inescapable. Most of the Blackwood students had been sequestered in their dormitories, though a few had chosen to join the Ascended, determined to protect their sacred halls. Either way, they were vastly outnumbered. Their one advantage was Silas and the Housemasters. Their power rivaled that of the Demiens—teeming with ancient magic capable of destroying their souls with nothing but a flick of their wrists.

"Where do we go?" Masika coughed, shielding her eyes from the cloud of shadow magic that seeped in through the cracks in the windows. Irene winced at the strain in her friend's voice. Her throat was clearly raw from screaming. From hours and hours of torture, suffering under Silas's hand.

While I just stood back and watched.

"Masika."

The word slipped out of Irene's mouth before she could stop herself.

When their eyes met, Masika's face softened. As if she already knew. With just one look.

"You already know I forgive you, so let's just skip over the apologies, okay?"

But that couldn't be it. It wasn't enough. Irene deserved to be hated.

Scream at me. Hit me. Do something.

"I didn't—" Irene shook her head, swallowing. "I should never have . . ." But the words were a tangled heap lodged in the back of her throat. Her gaze fell to the floor. Why couldn't she ever say the right thing? Why couldn't she ever put aside her stupid fucking pride? A hand gently brushed Irene's chin, dragging her gaze forward.

Masika smiled. "I know, Irene. *I know.*"

Forgiveness radiated from Masika's gaze, and it was suffocating. Irene didn't deserve it. Didn't deserve *her*. But she didn't want to push the matter further—truthfully, she wasn't even sure she was physically capable of it—so she simply nodded and swallowed back the knot in her throat.

"I suppose . . ." Irene managed to croak out, "we should go find your friends. The people you were working with."

Masika nodded. "Catherine and Dina should be out there somewhere—"

"Catherine?" Irene's eyes widened a fraction. "*The* Catherine?"

Masika grew unnaturally flustered. "Uh . . . yeah." She flushed and her mouth cracked into a sheepish grin. "*The* Catherine."

Irene had never seen Masika smile like that before, and despite their circumstances, she couldn't help but smile back. She wanted Masika to smile like that more often. For once—she wanted her to have the happiness she deserved.

"Well, then." Irene gave a firm nod. "Let's go find your girl."

But before she could even turn away from Masika, the large double doors that stood at the entrance of the main hall swung open, a billowing gust of wind rushing through the doorway and into the hall.

The rumble of footsteps. A cacophony of startled gasps.

There was a beat of confusion. Of complete and utter disbelief.

"What . . . in the actual hell."

Emilio and Olivier stood at the doorway. The duo seemed equally startled, their faces oscillating between confusion and unbridled joy. And then Emilio and Olivier were running, nearly tripping over themselves as they threw their arms around Masika. They wobbled and swayed in their embrace.

"Oh my God." Emilio pulled back, cupping Masika's face in his hands. "You're actually here. You made it. You"—he stopped short, eyes narrowing as he properly took in her appearance—"look terrible."

Masika chuckled, though Irene didn't miss the tears welling behind her eyes. "Hello to you too."

Olivier practically shoved Emilio aside, gripping Masika tightly by the shoulders as he peppered her forehead with kisses, while Masika let out a stream of giggles and pretended to bat him away.

"You"—*kiss*—"beautiful"—*kiss*—"woman"—*kiss*.

"Okay. *Enough.*" Masika rolled her eyes. "You're obsessed with me. I get it."

Olivier's eyes flitted to Irene. "Hello there." He gave her a genuine, albeit tense smile. "Glad to see you've finally come to your senses."

Irene shifted uncomfortably. "It's . . . uh . . . *good* . . . to see you."

"Careful now, Irene." Olivier chuckled. "Wouldn't want me to accidentally think you *like* me."

Irene scowled. "You know, this is usually the part where you would say: Oh, wow, thank you, Irene, I'm also super glad to see—" Her words snagged in her throat as Emilio stepped forward and pulled her into a hug. Irene's entire body stiffened, though she didn't push him away. In fact, a tiny part of her wanted nothing more than to hug him back. But her limbs couldn't quite allow her to, so she settled for an awkward pat on Emilio's shoulder.

He beamed up at her. "Thank you."

Irene flinched. "I didn't do anything."

"You helped Masika. You saved her."

Irene physically recoiled. "Okay. Don't be dramatic."

Emilio's smile only deepened at her obvious discomfort. "You're a *hero*."

Irene gagged. "All right, enough, or I might just go back to plotting to destroy you all."

Masika looked between the two boys. "I don't understand. How did you get here so quickly?"

"We, uh . . ." Olivier cleared his throat. "We had some help from August."

Irene's eyes widened. *"August?"*

"He's on our side," Emilio explained carefully. "He only gave up his humanity to try to get Wren back. She . . . she was taken by the Demien Order. She's the catalyst. The one who was prophesized to destroy Blackwood."

Masika scoffed. "Fuck off."

Olivier threw his arms in the air. "See! That is *exactly* what I said!"

Irene winced. "Right . . . forgot to mention that."

Masika's eyes widened in her direction. "You knew too? And didn't bother to tell me?"

"There's been a lot going on," Irene muttered defensively.

Olivier cleared his throat, drawing Masika's attention again. "But . . . we're too late. Wren is gone. She's the catalyst now. A vessel for the Soulless One's revenge. August went to go look for her. I think . . . I think he hopes there's still a way to reach her. A way to stop her."

An explosion echoed in the distance. The windows of the hall rattled a warning. Masika, who had been leaning against Olivier for support, looked around among the group. "So." She cleared her throat. "What's our plan?"

"Well." Olivier clasped his hands. "We *had* a plan to resurrect the True Headmaster, though it completely went to shit when we got to his tomb and realized that it was, in fact, empty. So I suppose our next-best bet is to find August and try to help him snap Wren out of it. I believe he went toward Elysium Hall. We could probably meet him there on time if we relocate—"

"I'm sorry. Wait. You were planning to—*what*? Resurrect *who*?" Irene blanched, mind struggling to process what she'd just heard.

"It doesn't matter anymore," Olivier muttered with a dismissive wave of his hand. "We failed. Horrendously. So now we just need to fight."

"Screw that," Irene scoffed. "Let's make a run for it. August can handle Wren. Why do we need to get involved?"

"And go where exactly?" Olivier pressed. "If the Soulless One and his new little puppet get their way, then who knows what will be left of the afterlife? If the Ether's balance is disrupted by Silas's presence alone, think about what would happen if the entirety of Blackwood was wiped away. If *thousands* of students' souls were destroyed."

Shit. He was right. What was the point of running if there was nowhere to run *to*?

"Okay, well . . ." Irene racked her brain, fingers drumming restlessly against her arms. "I still think the journals I have upstairs could be useful. I was working with a Demien—*before*. The bastard lied to me. But maybe there's something in there that can help us. Private Demien Order business that could give us an upper hand.

"His name's Mateo . . ." Irene fished the pocket mirror out of her coat, angling it toward the group. She opened the clasp and summoned the memory, the reflection slowly morphing into an image of Mateo she'd recorded a few days ago, back in the Main Yard. "Silas gave me this enchanted mirror. It can replay memories. Maybe if one of us sees him, we could try to convince him to—"

"Where the hell did you get this?" Olivier snapped, cutting her off.

Irene blinked, taken aback by the sudden hostility in Olivier's voice. "Did you not hear what I said? *Silas* gave me the mirror." But when she looked up, it wasn't just Olivier who seemed suddenly troubled. Emilio was also peering down at the reflection, eyes wide and mouth parted in shock.

"Okay . . ." she muttered. "Why do the two of you look like you've just seen a ghost?"

"You said you *know* him?" Emilio asked, voice wavering.

"Jesus Christ." Irene rolled her eyes, groaning in frustration. "Are you going to make me repeat everything I say? *Yes.* His name is Mateo. He's a Demien. He fucking used me to get information and then abandoned me the second I gave him what he wanted—"

"He isn't a Demien," interjected Olivier. His body had gone impossibly still.

"What are you talking about?" Irene scoffed, panic shooting up her throat. "He is. He showed me. He can harness shadow magic. He has all the Order information. He spoke with the generals on a daily basis."

Olivier shook his head. "He isn't. He can't be."

Irene let out a disgruntled sigh. "What on earth are you talking about?"

Olivier reached into one of his pockets. He unveiled a small, crinkled paper, a torn piece of parchment.

There was a drawing of a face on it.

A face Irene knew well.

"Why the hell do you have a drawing of Mateo?" Irene asked.

"Because this isn't Mateo," Olivier muttered. He held up the drawing next to Irene's mirror, right beside the reflection of Mateo, the two identical faces side by side. "It's the True Headmaster."

"No." Irene staggered backward, shaking her head. *"No."*

"I don't understand," Masika muttered in confusion. "Are you saying . . . are you saying they're the same person?"

Emilio let out a shuddering breath. "It certainly seems like it."

"No," Irene repeated, hand raised. "There's no way. That's not *possible*."

Olivier tucked the paper back into his pocket. "Irene. I know it seems impossible, but you just saw it with your own two eyes . . ." But Irene wasn't listening. Panic whirled inside her as she attempted to scrounge up any possible excuse to dismiss what she had just seen.

"Mateo can't be the True Headmaster," she muttered. "He . . . he can't. I was with him every day. He can access shadow magic. Why would the True Headmaster have given up his humanity? Why would he have convinced me to help him destroy Blackwood's wards so that the Demiens could storm the grounds?"

Olivier scoffed. "The better question is . . . how the *hell* did he manage to resurrect himself?"

"Maybe he didn't," Emilio suggested. "Maybe someone else did."

Irene shivered at the thought.

"Look." Masika let out a calming breath. "None of that matters right now. Wherever he is—*whoever he is*—he's not here. And unless one of us knows how to magically find him, he's the least of our concerns at the present moment."

"Then what do you suggest?" Olivier asked.

"Who is the one person who holds the key to destroying Blackwood? The one person whose presence is essential for the Demiens' plan to work?"

Irene groaned.

"Wren fucking Loughty."

"Then we find her," Masika said. "We find her and stop her."

46

AUGUST

August had no way of knowing if it would work—if there was even anything left linking them together—but he had to try. Back at Blackwood, he'd been able to sense Wren's presence after placing the sliver of his soul inside her, but once Edith had blocked Wren's magic, that connection had fizzled away. But he hadn't tried since Wren had welcomed the Soulless One inside her.

As August sprinted into the main foyer of Elysium Hall, he dipped into his connection with Wren and prayed it would be enough.

Wren. Darling, please. Where are you?

At first . . . only silence. Deep, bottomless silence. But then—almost like a phantom touch reaching out for him—he felt her. The faintest call. An echo of an echo. It wasn't her voice, but . . . it was *something.*

Hidden beneath the darkness. Clawing its way to the surface.

There.

August's eyes shot open.

He'd found her.

47

WREN

The monster that Wren Loughty had become entered Headmaster Silas's office. With each step forward, the old wood beneath her feet blackened and decayed, leaving a river of rot in her wake. But Silas didn't stir. He remained glued behind his desk, watching.

Nestled in his hand was a box.

"This is what you want, isn't it?" His voice carried in the silence. He set the box down on the desk and the darkness inside Wren purred. But before she could reach out and claim it, Silas snatched it back. He stood up, slowly, his eyes never once leaving Wren. There was something blazing in his dark brown eyes. A faint, almost nonexistent part of Wren recognized it. Understood it. But this thing she had become—this parasitic monster—paid it no mind.

"Hand it over."

When Wren spoke, it was her voice and the Soulless One's twined together. A distorted rasp that shook the walls of the office with an unseen force. Silas stared at her, examining her with that *look*—that foul, pathetic look. What was it that was lurking behind his eyes? She knew the word, deep down. And yet . . .

Silas made his way around the desk. The words he spoke next burned her from the inside out.

"What has he done to you?"

Wren cocked her head. When she laughed, the windows rattled.

"The Soulless One didn't do anything. It was *you* who made me this way. Your corruption. Your betrayal."

"Has he sowed his soul so deep into yours that you can no longer see reason?"

"How *dare* you?" Wren spat out. Her shadows billowed out of her, twisting in the air from all directions.

"No . . ." Silas muttered, shaking his head. If he was at all concerned by the display of power in front of him, he gave no indication. "You're right. I am no saint, Wren Loughty. I am far from it. I am a sick man drowning in power. I take, and take, and *take*—and yet . . . it's not enough. It will never be enough." His voice cracked and he inched closer. "Tell me. If you destroy Blackwood . . . what will grow in its place? More destruction? More chaos?"

"Something pure," Wren replied without hesitation. **"Something cleansed of your corruption."**

Silas tilted his head.

"You don't truly believe that . . . do you, Wren?"

The Soulless One's voice bellowed inside her.

BRING IT TO ME.

"Wren." Headmaster Silas extended a pleading hand. "Look at me."

But Wren couldn't tear her eyes away from his *other* hand. From the box clutched in his palm. It called to her. It belonged to her. It belonged to *them*. Silas must have sensed that she was beyond reason. That no amount of pleading and placating would change what Wren had set out to do.

"I saw potential in you . . . was that so wrong?"

At this, Wren's eyes snapped up to his face. Her response was a distorted snarl.

"You took my life from me."

"And I gave you *this*." Silas gestured to the room around him. To the shadows billowing out of Wren. "Magic. Power. A *purpose*." He stepped closer. Close enough that Wren could snatch the box right out of his hands if she could find an opportunity.

"Greatness is born from sacrifice," Silas whispered reverently. "Do you truly regret it? Do you truly wish it would all go away?" Wren pondered his question. A part of her faltered, but she silenced it, pushing it down further. "I know how the magic makes you feel. How it calls to you." Silas splayed his free hand upon his chest. "*I* gave you that, Wren. I gave you that freedom."

Silas was right. Wren had never felt more complete, more wholly herself, than when she first tasted magic. When that first inkling of power had coursed through her veins upon awaking outside the gates of Blackwood Academy. But Silas was *also* wrong. Because though Wren knew that the magic she'd been handed at Blackwood had given her a sense of purpose—she also knew that she would have thrown it all away if it had meant getting her sister back.

"You take, you take, you *take* . . ." Wren whispered, head cocked, **". . . and now it's my turn."**

Her shadows sprang into action. But Silas moved quickly, countering her attack with his own blazing shield of light. They crashed together in a fiery explosion of magic—shadow and light thrusted together, a balancing act on the precipice of destruction.

The Headmaster of Blackwood Academy was strong . . . but the catalyst of destruction was *stronger*.

Wren pushed forward. Her shadows pressed against Silas's shield and a crack splintered down its side. And another. And *another.* With each step forward, his defenses weakened, his power hers for the taking. Her eyes landed on the box and a feral hunger tore through her soul as she pictured the ring nestled inside. With one arm extended, shadows bursting out of her and keeping Silas at bay, Wren snaked another set of shadows to the right, curling around the box and tossing it in her direction.

She caught it with her free hand.

When Silas noticed, a scream tore through him. Eyes widening in terror.

"Don't!"

As soon as the box made contact with Wren's hand . . . she felt it. A connection. A calling. The box knew her soul . . . recognized it. She unclasped the lock, opening it slowly, and dropped the ring into her open palm.

"You have no idea what you're doing!" Silas roared through gritted teeth, desperately pushing against the wave of shadows holding him back.

Wren chuckled. She closed her fist around the ring.

"I think I do."

FINISH HIM.

And she would . . . with pleasure.

But before Wren could shove the shadows through the core of Silas's soul, tearing through his shield once and for all, a voice broke through the chaos, rising above the roaring wind.

A voice she would recognize anywhere.

"WREN!"

August had come barreling into the office, screaming her name, the door thrown open by an explosive blast. And he wasn't alone. Four other students emerged seconds later. Four students she knew well.

Olivier. Emilio. Irene. Masika.

All of them . . . *here.*

But they couldn't be. They shouldn't be.

Something rose inside Wren. A desperate, screaming voice clawing at the back of her skull. *LET ME OUT!* it seemed to scream. But it wasn't the Soulless One. It was . . . who was it? The voice was familiar. She swore she knew it. The words were muffled, drowned out by the shadows swirling inside her, but still, she heard the broken call, the desperation in the words as they echoed helplessly inside her.

Please. Stop this.

And then it dawned on her. This voice. This desperate plea.

It was *her* voice.

"Get out," Wren snarled. She wasn't even sure who she was talking to anymore—whether her words had been addressed to the intruders standing before her, or whether she'd actually meant them for that voice, for that stubborn part of herself that was still clinging to her mind, begging to get out. **"Your actions will only end in more suffering."**

"Jesus . . ." Irene's face fell. She stared at Wren as if seeing her for the first time. "You really *have* lost it."

"Wren." Emilio spoke her name slowly, tentatively, hands raised in appeasement. "We're here to help you."

The Soulless One's voice roared inside her.

DO NOT LISTEN TO THEM.

Wren tore her gaze away from the group with a growl, zeroing in on Silas once again.

"Do you even know what he did?!" Her voice cracked, a dissonant roar threaded through her words. **"He played God with our souls! He's a *murderer*!"**

Finally, Silas's composure fell away. His own face contorted in rage. In fury.

"I gave you all what you wanted! Deep down! You *all* wanted this!"

Something in Wren snapped. A force lurching inside her. That *voice.* It clawed its way to the surface—the faintest fraction of a second—but still, when Wren spoke next, it was her voice that came through. Not the Soulless One.

Just *her.*

"YOU KILLED MY SISTER!"

As the words left her lips, the entire room sprang to life, a swirling vortex of wind bursting into the air. Papers scattered. Books toppled to the floor. Windows burst open, glass shattering. The portrait of Silas that hung behind his desk collapsed to the floor with a deep and resounding thud. Grief rose inside Wren like a phoenix, and when she turned back to look at the others in the doorway, she saw the terror etched upon their faces . . . the horror.

Good.

Fear me.

"He killed all of you," she spat out. **"You weren't chosen for Blackwood. He *forced* you into Blackwood. Your death was orchestrated by his hands, and then he stripped you of the choice you were always meant to have. He deserves to be punished. He deserves to feel our retribution!"**

"You're right," Olivier whispered, voice cracking. "If what you're saying is true, then he *does* deserve to be punished. But not at the expense of the afterlife. Not by destroying hundreds of innocent students."

"How can *you,* of all people, believe that?" Wren seethed. When Olivier furrowed his brows in confusion, Wren stepped forward. **"I sense your time is dwindling, Olivier. Mere hours before you're torn from this plane of existence and thrust into**

the Ether for the rest of your pathetic eternity. And it's because of *him*. He did that to you."

"I know." Olivier's lip trembled, but he held her gaze. "But I'd rather perish than become like him."

Wren chuckled.

"Then you're *weak*."

Masika stepped forward. "*You're* the weak one."

Wren blinked. She snapped her head toward Masika.

"Excuse me?"

"You think *this* makes you strong?" Masika scoffed, gesturing to the destruction scattered across the room. "Power? Your shadows? More chaos and death and hate?" Her voice trembled, but her conviction held, amber eyes blazing.

"You want to know what true weakness is?" Masika asked. "It's turning your back on the people you care about. It's *greed*. It's being blinded by vengeance and retribution." Her eyes raked Wren's face, and something softened. She shook her head in pity. "And the Wren Loughty I know is stronger than all of that. Which is how I know that *this*"—she gestured to Wren with a defeated wave—"isn't her."

Wren's mouth twitched. She narrowed her gaze.

"You don't know me," she growled. **"Not anymore."** One of her shadows slithered away from Silas, slowly trailing toward the group standing by the doorway. **"I'm only going to warn you once more. Leave. Or I won't hesitate to strike you down."** As the shadow approached Masika, Irene stepped forward, placing herself protectively in front of the other girl.

"Go on," Irene chuckled, a smile spread over her lips. Silver shards of light crackled in her palms. "I've always wanted to leave a mark on that pretty face of yours—just give me a reason."

"Enough!" August's voice sliced through the room. When his eyes met Wren's, a piece of her resolve splintered. *Those gray eyes.* Even devoured by the Soulless One's shadows, they stirred something inside her.

She should eliminate him. He was a distraction. A disease.

DO IT.

But she didn't. Wren didn't move.

It was the slightest hesitation. A moment of weakness.

And it was exactly what Silas had been waiting for.

Wren sensed the moment he moved behind her, hand extended, prepared to strike. But luckily, Wren moved fast. Faster than Silas had anticipated. And when she turned to face him, she shot her own arm out, ravenous shadows bursting out of her.

She tried to beat him to it. To move faster than him.

But ultimately, neither of them beat the other.

They moved as one.

NO!!!!

Around her, the world exploded.

Wren glanced down at her hand plunged into Silas's chest, at *his* hand plunged into her own, the two of them connected, shadows and light twisting between them, and she knew, with bone-chilling certainty, that this was her end.

Someone was screaming behind her, but it didn't matter.

They couldn't stop what had already been done.

Wren Loughty met Headmaster Silas's eyes.

"I wonder . . ." she whispered, her voice clear, soft, "when your soul shatters and oblivion finally takes you . . . will you scream?"

Silas smiled.

And then—suddenly—she saw it. That *thing* lurking behind his eyes. The thing she'd seen hidden in his face since the moment she first walked into the office. Engulfed by the shadows, she hadn't been able to recognize it . . . unable to feel the emotion beyond the darkness and hate and anger.

But she saw it now. Clear as day.

Remorse.

"I could ask you the same thing, Wren Loughty."

For a moment, neither of them moved. Eyes locked together. Wren understood him now—the tarnished, broken man withering beneath Silas's façade. The fear. The terror. Silas had never been a god. He was just a man. And as with all men before him, his time had finally run out, his power expired.

Wren smiled back.

And then, together, they ripped each other from existence.

Darkness. Sweet, blissful darkness. The warm embrace of oblivion wrapped around Wren, pulling her deeper, inviting her home. But then . . . something else. A voice. That stubborn, unrelenting voice.

Open your eyes, Wren.

And then she was rising, thrown out of oblivion, thrust back into reality.

Pain.

She felt it all around her. Consuming her. Ripping her apart.

Wren woke up screaming. She was lying on the floor of the office. Above her, August was kneeling, eyes frantic as he spoke her name like a whispered invocation.

Wren, Wren, Wren.

She turned her head, slowly.

Beside her, Silas lay sprawled on the floor, vacant eyes staring up at the ceiling. She reached out, but as her trembling hand touched his cheek, his skin came apart, piece by piece, fragment by fragment, until the Headmaster of Blackwood Academy vanished before her eyes.

Destroyed. Gone.

Finally, *finally* gone.

But why hadn't Wren met the same fate? They'd each ripped the core of the other's soul out. She'd felt it. The moment it happened. The burning flame inside her extinguished. Yet here she was. Her flesh still intact. Her soul . . . *no*. Her soul was barely there. Fading. Hanging on by a thin, almost invisible tether.

But what was that tether? What was holding her in place? What was keeping her from drifting into oblivion? It didn't feel like a part of her soul. Didn't have the familiar essence she had come to recognize.

But it *was* familiar. That anchor. It felt like firm hands holding her. Warm. Tender.

"August."

His name slipped out of her mouth, voice rough and raw. He reached out, cupping her face gently with his hands. "What is it?"

"It's *you*," she whispered back. She was certain of it now. A piece of August's soul. It was inside her, the tiniest sliver, but it held on with all its might, holding her steady, unwilling to let her go.

August cocked his head in confusion.

"What is it, darling?" He brushed strands of damp hair away from her eyes. "What's me?"

Wren laughed, but the sound was wrong and broken.

"Were you . . . ever going to tell me . . . that you put a piece of your soul inside me?"

August's face fell. His bottom lip trembled, tears welling in his eyes.

"I just wanted to save you."

"And you did." She reached out, cupping his face with her hand. "But it can't hold on forever."

From one breath to the next, something rushed inside Wren. A torrential downpour of memories flowed into her. The pain she had caused. The terror she had inflicted. *So many innocent souls.* Destroyed by her hand. Ripped apart. *Arthur.* She'd contorted his soul into a mindless shadow creature. And she had smiled . . . she had laughed.

She had enjoyed every second of it.

NO.

Wren let out an agonized wail, clutching her chest. This pain . . . this was worse than any physical wound. Than any injury she'd endured. This was the pain of knowing there was no fixing the damage she'd left behind. Inside her, the shadows begged to resurface, to numb the memories. She'd managed to push her consciousness back to the surface, but she was weak, and she knew that the moment she lowered her defenses, the darkness would claim her once again.

But there was still one thing she could do. One final act of defiance.

She stretched out her hands toward the pile of ashes beside her—toward what was left of Silas—but she couldn't quite reach, a deep guttural groan emanating from the back of her throat. August looked on, brows furrowed.

"What is it? What do you need?"

"The *ring*," Wren rasped, recoiling as another wave of torment shot through her body, sharpened nails ripping at her insides, tearing at her ligaments. The screams echoed in her mind endlessly. The terror. All her doing. Her fault. "It belongs to the Soulless One. You can't let him put it on. You can't let him unleash what he's hidden inside it."

You think you can stop this, my sweet catalyst? That you can change what you've done?

But Wren ignored the Soulless One's taunting voice. Her fingers finally found the ring beneath the pile of ash. She slowly unfurled her palm. Nestled inside, burning with an emerald glow, was the brass ring marked with the Soulless One's name. August didn't hesitate, taking the ring into his own hand, securing it tightly.

"Go . . ." Wren muttered. "You need to find a way to destroy it."

"I won't leave you."

"You have to. You need to run." Her ribs snapped. Her spine cracked unnaturally. There was no barrier protecting her from the pain anymore. This was her punishment, and the shadows wouldn't relent until she gave herself up once more.

Mmmm. Do you feel my hands tearing at your soul, sweet catalyst? Ripping you apart? Do you feel the torment of your memories? Of your pain? Let me take that away from you, Wren. Let me back in.

Wren let out a hoarse scream as something slithered inside her. She wanted to tear her skin off. To rip herself open and yank that festering darkness out. She wanted—*needed*—the suffering to end.

Panic burned behind August's slate-gray eyes. For a moment, Wren thought she'd managed to convince him, seeing a steady look of determination washing over his face, but then August was tossing the ring into the air, straight toward Irene, who caught it with a strangled gasp of surprise.

"Go." August looked among the four of them. "Find a way to destroy it."

The others hesitated. Their eyes snagged on Wren.

She mustered a strained smile, nodding feebly in encouragement.

"It's okay," she muttered, voice thin and thready. "Go."

And then the four of them were turning away, bolting out of the office and into the chaos of the battle.

I will find them. I will tear them apart.

Wren shuddered. She wouldn't give the Soulless One the satisfaction of answering his call. Instead, she kept her eyes fixed on August. She committed his face to memory—etching every detail into the farthest reaches of her soul. In the place nobody could ever find it. Not even the Soulless One.

"I don't have . . . a lot of time."

August gripped her hands tightly in his, bringing them up to his lips, planting soft kisses on her knuckles.

"Truthfully . . ." August winced, and it was then that Wren realized how haggard he looked. Deep plum-colored bruises stained the skin beneath his eyes. Black veins trailed down his face and disappeared beneath the collar of his shirt. "Neither do I."

Wren tilted her head in confusion, but then understanding struck her hard in the chest.

The shadows . . . they were consuming him. He'd used too much shadow magic.

He'd damned himself.

Wren could only manage one word.

"Why?"

August smiled, but an unmistakable sadness lingered behind his eyes.

"Why do you think?"

Wren bit back a sob. Her insides were alight with an unbearable agony, a searing fire consuming every inch of her soul, yet still . . . she smiled. She raised her hand, fighting the pressure threatening to consume her, and placed her palm upon August's cheek. He shut his eyes, leaning into her touch.

In that moment, Wren was no longer scared. She no longer feared the pointed claws of oblivion. She no longer feared the darkness that awaited her if the shadows finally swallowed them both whole.

Because if this was how her soul fractured, if this was how it all came to an end—staring up at August, *at the boy she loved*—then so be it.

48

MASIKA

"WHERE THE HELL ARE WE GOING?!" Olivier bellowed as they sprinted out of Elysium Hall and into the chaos of night. In the distance, hundreds of Demiens, Ascended and Resistance fighters swarmed across the grounds, all of them caught in a bloody battle. Screams split the night, a pungent cloud of magic stifling the air. Billowing shadow creatures soared over their heads, some of them cradling limp bodies in their talons.

"The base," Masika muttered through labored breaths. "It's the only place that could potentially have something to destroy the ring with. Not to mention it's probably the safest place we could be right now."

"It'll take us days to get there!" Olivier shot back, ducking when a swirling vortex of shadows burst from somewhere to their left. He gripped Emilio roughly by the collar, tugging him closer. "We're never going to make it."

"Well, do you have a better suggestion?" Irene snapped, tossing her hands in frustration.

Olivier hesitated, gnawing the inside of his cheek. His eyes flitted north—out toward the heart of the battle. "Fine." He shook his head, conceding. "Go. But . . . I'm staying here."

"What do you mean you're *staying*?" Masika asked.

"The others"—Olivier gestured toward the Library—"the Resistance needs as many on their side as possible."

Emilio laced his fingers through Olivier's. "If he stays—I'm staying too."

Irene hesitated, weighing her options. Finally, she conceded with a sigh. "Fine . . . go. But we have to move—*now*!"

She was right. Up ahead, only a few yards away, a throng of Demiens were approaching, dark rivers of shadows flanking their path. The group was still focused on the Resistance fighters they were attacking, but it wouldn't be long until they spotted them, and then . . . then they'd have to fight.

Masika lunged forward, wrapping her arms around Olivier and Emilio. She pulled back, looking between the two boys. "Be careful."

Olivier nodded. "Right back at you." He pointed an accusatory finger at Irene, narrowing his eyes. "Watch over our girl. Make sure you bring her back to us in one piece." When Irene rolled her eyes in response, Olivier grinned.

Emilio sniffled, wiping a tear from his eye with the back of his hand. He looked between Masika and Irene with wide, pleading eyes. "See you later?"

The two girls nodded.

"Yeah," Masika assured him. "See you later."

And then Emilio and Olivier vanished, disappearing under the black cloud of Olivier's relocation spell.

For a moment, Masika continued to stand there, staring at the place where the two boys had been only moments earlier. Sorrow struck her like a sharpened blade. They had all just reunited, finally brought back together again, and now they risked losing one another—for good this time.

"We have to go," Irene whispered softly.

Masika nodded. She was right. "Let's go."

Irene grabbed Masika tightly by the hand, and the two of them were swallowed by the crimson haze of Irene's relocation spell, materializing a few yards away from the Blackwood gates.

And then they started running.

There was no telling who might be out here waiting for them. The majority of the fight had shifted deeper into Blackwood, trickling toward the main halls, but there might still be Demiens lurking in the forest—waiting for those who might try to escape.

Masika was about to suggest casting a cloaking enchantment when she noticed that Irene wasn't beside her anymore. She'd stopped a few yards behind, eyes locked on the ring in her hand.

"Irene!" Masika called out to her. "Come on! We have to keep moving."

But Irene remained rooted to the ground. She shook her head, face contorted in confusion. "It's not possible . . ." she muttered softly.

"What?" Masika asked. The battle roared in the distance, and Masika knew they needed to get moving, to put as much distance between them and the fight as possible. "What are you talking about?"

"The ring . . ." Irene whispered, seemingly lost within the depths of her mind. "It belonged to the Soulless One."

"Yes," Masika said, exasperated. "I know. I heard Wren."

Irene finally dragged her gaze away from the ring, eyes falling upon Masika like a guillotine. When she spoke next, her voice was a trembling whisper, disbelief and terror etched upon her face.

"So then why is Mateo's name written on it?"

Masika blinked, taken aback. "What?"

Irene held the ring delicately between her thumb and index finger, holding it out toward Masika. When Masika approached

Irene, reading the words etched into the brass ring, her world tilted.

Mateo Albano.

Masika met Irene's searing gaze. Silence drenched the space between them.

"How is this possible?" Masika whispered.

"Mateo isn't the True Headmaster," Irene replied with a shudder. "And he isn't the Soulless One."

She paused, closing her fist around the ring.

"He's both."

Footsteps. The snap of a twig. A deep, guttural chuckle.

Mateo Albano—the True Headmaster of Blackwood . . . the Soulless One—stood before them, parting the darkness with nothing but his presence. He walked forward and the ground beneath his feet wilted, shriveling into ash and dust and decay. His eyes—a deep shade of sapphire that glowed in the darkness—zeroed in on them. All around him, shadows ebbed and flowed, waiting for his command.

"I told you, Irene." His voice rumbled with power. "If you call me . . . I'll answer."

Masika didn't miss the way Irene's entire body tensed at the sight of him. She'd never seen the other girl look so wounded . . . so afraid.

Mateo snaked his gaze toward Masika. He watched her with chilling curiosity.

"The infamous Masika Sallow. Finally . . . we meet."

Masika held her ground, angling her arm protectively in front of Irene.

"We know who you are," she snapped, hoping she sounded braver than she felt. "Who you *really* are."

Mateo chuckled. "I would expect that much. You know . . . given the ring in Irene's hand."

Irene flinched as her name slipped out of his mouth. "I don't understand," she whispered. "All this time . . . how could you have been the True Headmaster *and* the Soulless One?"

"Those are just names given to me," Mateo replied with a casual shrug. "Titles. Who am I to control what people write in the history books?" He stepped closer, movements slow and deliberate. "I *was* the True Headmaster. Before Silas infiltrated Blackwood and took over. But I had sensed a change cresting on the horizon. An imminent betrayal. So . . . I took action."

"The map," Masika muttered softly. "You left a set of keys meant to unlock a piece of your soul. But it wasn't there."

A sudden silence fell over them. Mateo glanced between Irene and Masika, a solemn expression on his face. When he spoke next, there was a soft smile on his lips . . . a twisted flicker of melancholy.

"Silas was my friend. Did you know that?"

Masika flinched. "What?"

"He didn't just barge into the school and destroy me," Mateo explained. "There's more to the story than what you've been told. More history. He was meticulous. Brilliant, honestly." He let out a deep, bitter chuckle. "Have you noticed the way Silas's appearance seems to . . . *change*? His age often impossible to pinpoint." Next to her, Irene gave an almost indiscernible nod of her head. "That's because of the power he stole. The more he loses control, the more Blackwood takes from him. When I met him . . . all those centuries ago . . . he was just a boy. Just about your age."

A chill ran down Masika's spine. It wasn't possible . . .

Mateo continued, slinking closer.

"I know what the story says. That he simply weaseled his way into Blackwood and took control. But that isn't true . . . not quite. I found Silas, just outside the gates, after he'd managed to drag himself out of the Shadow Lands. I was the Headmaster, after all—I knew everybody who came and went. And I knew, without a doubt, that *he* did not belong." A faraway look had fallen upon Mateo, as if he was lost in the past, stuck in a memory. "I took pity on him. It was foolish, thinking back on it now. But . . . a part of me thought . . . a part of me wondered . . . if perhaps the school had been wrong in marking him as a Corrupted Soul. I thought . . . maybe . . . I could fix him. I could change him."

Mateo let out a sharp exhale and the distant look in his eyes vanished.

"I let him into the school. I enrolled him in Blackwood. I knew it was a mistake from the beginning—could feel the Ether's discontent—but I didn't care. Little by little, Silas gained my trust. We were part of a crew . . . similar to yours, might I add. I trusted him. Saw him like a brother."

His voice cracked at that final word, but he continued.

"When I finally sensed his betrayal . . . it was too late. But I had just enough time to set aside the piece of my soul, hide it in purgatory, and entrust a close friend to resurrect me if Silas was successful in his plan." Mateo's expression darkened. Above them, the crimson clouds began to shift together, a swirling vortex forming in the black sky. "And he *was* successful. But instead of destroying me outright, he thought it would be fitting to let me rot and wither away in the Shadow Lands. His silly need for poetic justice would ultimately lead to his ruin. Because he *didn't* destroy me . . . not completely. And just like he did, I learned to harness the power of the Shadow Lands. I let the corruption seep into my soul. I let it feed on my anger. I let it *consume* me. It gave me enough strength to crawl out of the Shadow Lands and back into purgatory. But what I saw afterward . . . what I discovered . . ."

Mateo's breath hitched in his throat. When he spoke next, there was a deep and grating rasp to his voice, a dark rumble that fluttered the leaves of the trees surrounding them. Even the ground seemed to tremble, as if cowering before his power.

"The person I had entrusted the piece of my soul to had betrayed me as well. I had given her the map that led to the first key, only to discover that she had placed the map right in Silas's hands. She'd *chosen* him." His voice wavered, and Masika *swore* she saw something achingly close to hurt flash across his shadow-drenched eyes. "But ultimately, that irrevocable choice only solidified her destruction. I suppose Silas hadn't wanted any loose ends. Maybe she knew too much . . . or maybe he'd simply known that destroying her would be worse than any fate I could endure."

Irene had gone impossibly still next to Masika, her expression unreadable. Masika wished more than anything that she could reach into Irene's mind and read her thoughts.

"My two closest friends had betrayed me," Mateo said with bone-chilling finality. "And now they were *both* gone. Because Silas wasn't the person I had known . . . the person I *thought* I had known. What was left was an abomination of power." Mateo lifted his hand and a stream of shadows slithered out of his palms, traveling down his forearm. "I understood, then, that there was no point in believing in the balance of the afterlife. Not while Silas was still in charge. I had to leave it all behind if I wanted to find a way to remove him from power. And that included my own soul."

"It was *you*?" Masika asked, voice trembling. "You destroyed the piece of your soul in the tomb?"

"It was a foolish plan," Mateo said, seething. "The plan of a naïve, heartbroken boy who thought he could still save himself . . .

and his friend. I took the final piece of my pure soul and destroyed it, leaving behind the last token I had of the girl who had betrayed me. And I buried it. I let it rot in that tomb forever." *The drawing,* Masika thought. *The one that August showed us. The one signed by the mysterious* V. That must have been the girl who had broken Mateo's heart . . . the one who had chosen Silas.

Mateo continued. "But I soon discovered that without my Headmaster's ring, without my *true* power, I wouldn't stand a chance against Silas. I needed to find a way to get the ring back." He prowled closer, head cocked. "So . . . I ripped my humanity out. I welcomed in the shadows and unleashed an untapped source of magic thought to have been impossible to conquer. As my body succumbed to the shadows, I was plagued with visions . . . a girl with auburn hair who held the ability to open the locked box, take my ring back, and set me free."

Masika's eyes flitted to the ring nestled in Irene's hand.

"But"—Mateo chuckled, a smirk lifting onto his lips—"as luck would have it . . . that girl wouldn't enter the afterlife for a very, *very* long time. I had to wait. Be patient. In the meantime, I'd heard of a group of banished students and Housemasters who had fled deeper into purgatory. Those who had refused to follow Silas as the new Headmaster of Blackwood. And I figured . . . what better way to pass the time than to form an army?"

Irene let out a shuddering breath.

"How could you?" she snapped, drawing Mateo's attention. "I *trusted* you. I thought . . . I thought you cared. Saw potential in me. You tricked me. You—" Irene's voice cracked, and for the first time since Masika had known her, tears welled behind her eyes.

The taunting grin fell away from Mateo's lips.

"If it's any consolation . . ." he muttered softly, ". . . I meant every word of it."

"You lied to me," Irene spat out.

"You're right." Mateo approached her, steps tentative. "But I had to. If I had told you the truth of who I am—*what* I am—would you have trusted me? Would you have opened your heart to me?"

Irene opened her mouth, but no sound came out.

"I can still reward you with what I promised," Mateo continued. Masika didn't miss the way Irene flinched at his words, the faint glimmer of hope rising inside her. "I can still share this power with you, Irene. Offer you what you deserve."

He paused a few feet from them, arm extended.

"Just . . . hand me the ring."

"Don't do it," Masika blurted out. Mateo's eyes snapped to her, rage burning behind them. "He's lying, Irene. You can't believe a word out of his mouth. He told us himself. He's consumed by shadows. He can't be trusted."

But Irene looked lost in thought. Her teeth anxiously gnawed at the inside of her cheek. A palpable desperation in her stare. She couldn't possibly be considering listening to him. She wouldn't betray them again . . . would she?

Irene took a step forward.

Masika let out a strangled gasp.

"Irene. *No.*"

But her friend wasn't listening. Eyes locked on Mateo, Irene approached him, inching closer, the ring remaining tucked in her hand. Would Masika need to strike her down? *Could* she?

"That's it, Irene." Mateo beckoned her closer. "Hand it over. Claim your rightful power."

Irene took another step forward. In front of her, Mateo reached out, fingers trembling, hunger in his eyes. Masika felt her own legs moving beneath her, panic twisting her chest. She readied her magic, reluctantly drawing upon its power.

Please, Irene.

Don't make me do this.

And then, as Irene was moments away from handing the ring over . . . she stopped.

Something in her expression changed.

Her tears continued to fall, but gone was the sorrow that had flooded her face only seconds before.

Her lips curled into a smirk.

Her eyes gleamed with feverish defiance.

And then one simple word tumbled out of her lips.

"No."

Irene slipped the ring onto her own finger.

And then the world erupted.

Bright orange light poured out of Irene, bursting from her chest, consuming her. A swirling gust of wind sent the trees swaying with a violent lurch, leaves lifting around them, a terrible storm splitting open the night sky.

Thunder rumbled. Silver streaks of lightning lit up the sky.

And then Mateo screamed. An inhuman, bellowing sound.

"WHAT . . . DID . . . YOU . . . DO?"

Irene smiled.

"Jealous?"

Mateo's eyes were wild and feral. An empty husk of a man. He was pure violence.

Pure, unadulterated rage.

"You stupid *bitch*."

Irene laughed and blood poured out of her eyes.

"How disappointingly unoriginal."

And then she simply snapped her fingers and ripped Mateo apart.

His chest tore open, a dark stream of shadows bursting out

of him, flowing from the open cavity with a startling force. He screamed and screamed, an animalistic cry filled with fury, with the promise of retribution. But there would be no reckoning tonight. Mateo's face came apart. His bones splintering. His soul nothing but ash and dust.

Mateo was the True Headmaster. The Soulless One.

An ancient entity of magic and darkness and festering corruption.

And Irene had destroyed him with nothing but a snap of her fingers.

Masika shuddered and faced Irene. She was *glowing.* A vibrant light was pouring out of the ring, traveling up her arms, consuming every inch of her body.

"What are you doing?!" Masika bellowed. "Take that thing off!"

Irene glanced over her shoulder. Her lips were curled into a soft smile.

"I can't."

Masika flinched as the two words struck her hard in the chest.

"What do you mean you *can't*?"

"The power has already been activated." Irene's voice was steady. Eerily calm. "If I take it off—it'll only explode outward. It'll consume all of Blackwood. All of purgatory. But . . . if I keep it on . . . I can give it something else to latch onto." She paused and a brilliant bolt of lightning lit up the night sky, streaks of shimmering silver-blue light. "I can let it latch onto *me*."

"You . . . you can't." Masika shook her head. "That'll destroy you."

Irene smiled and a trickle of blood leaked out from her lips.

"That's kind of the point, Masi."

All around them, the forest roared in defiance—trees groaning, ground splitting with a violent lurch. An opaque cloud of smoke and ash poured out from Irene's feet, suffocating plumes bursting into the air.

"Don't—" Masika coughed, sputtering, the swirling clouds of smoke and ash burning the back of her throat. "Irene. Stop. *Please.*"

But Irene didn't stop. The magic burned through her. Igniting her veins. Coursing through her limbs. She stared at Masika, tears welling behind her glowing eyes.

"It's already done."

"No." Masika shook her head. "I can't—I can't do this alone."

"Shut up, Masi." Irene chuckled. "We both know you'll be fine."

Masika cursed furiously beneath her breath.

"I swear to God—"

"To me, then?" Irene smiled, but it was broken and wrong. Blood trickled out of her lips, a thin crimson rivulet dripping down her chin. A fiery glow emanated from her skin, a shimmering golden halo enveloping her limbs.

"Please," Masika begged, her voice muffled by the howling wind. Even the trees groaned in distress, their leaves rustling, as though whispering a warning only they could understand. "I need you."

At this, Irene laughed. The magic burrowed deeper. Her skin burned a deep crimson, licking up her limbs, consuming every piece of her soul, inch by inch. It crept up her neck, infecting her veins, spreading through her like a ravenous virus. Masika watched helplessly as tendrils of shadows erupted from her friend's chest, traveling beneath Irene's skin, intertwining with the burning light, a fearsome web of magic consuming every inch of her soul.

"No." Irene shook her head, a broken sound echoing in her throat. Bloody tears welled behind her eyes. "Don't you get it? You never did. It was *me* who needed *you*."

"I can't handle all this without you." Masika sobbed, shaking her head. "I can't. I won't do it."

Irene's face softened. She tilted her head.

"Yes," she whispered. "You will."

Masika wanted to scream. Maybe she could call upon the others. Maybe one of them could help—

"The others won't make it in time," Irene said, as if she'd read Masika's thoughts. And maybe she *had*. Irene could do anything now. She could rip apart the afterlife with nothing but a snap. She could destroy them all—with nothing but a single thought.

"Look at me, Masi." Irene's voice dragged Masika back to reality. "If anybody can fix this mess, if anybody can make Blackwood what it needs to be, it's you. I think . . . I think I was meant to be here . . . standing in front of you. I think I was meant to do this."

"You weren't meant to be *sacrificed*," Masika spat out in disgust. "How could you even say that?"

Irene rolled her eyes.

"Don't be so melodramatic."

"Irene—"

"I want this." The intensity in Irene's voice sent a shock wave through the air, bending the trees. Irene nodded. Softly. Tenderly. "Just . . . just let me do this, okay? I need to. I'm not going to be the one to let the afterlife crumble. I'm not going to be the one to destroy it all. I'm not going to be like *them*. And for what? For the ambition of men? For their fractured egos and desperate pride?"

"But maybe there's another way—"

"There isn't."

"Dammit, Irene." Masika let out a broken sob. "Why are you choosing to be the hero *now*?"

"I thought . . . for a moment . . . that I had become loyal to Blackwood. That I'd chosen the wrong side," Irene said, voice shaking. “But it wasn’t Blackwood that I chose. It was you. I chose *you*. I choose *you*.”

A sob tore out of Masika’s throat.

“Please,” she begged. “There has to be another way.”

Irene was smiling. It was a tender smile. A sad smile.

It was an apology.

“Years from now . . .” Irene extended her arms, the magic vibrating violently beneath her skin, tearing apart her flesh as if it were nothing but mounds of dust. Her eyes filled with a blazing light, a golden glow that swallowed the whites of her eyes. “. . . when you tell this story . . . make sure to mention how cool I looked, okay?”

Masika stepped forward.

“Irene, DON’T—”

By the time Masika lunged for her—it was too late.

49

IRENE

In the end, Irene Manette Bamford would find exactly what she was searching for. Not power. Not glory. But something intangible—a concept so ridiculous, so nonsensical, that when the magic exploded through her chest, splitting her atoms in two, ripping apart her consciousness, the only thing she could do was stand there . . . smiling.

She understood it clearly now. That thing that had always evaded her. The idea that had always seemed so hazy and out of reach. It wasn't power she craved. It wasn't glory.

It was connection.

It was fucking *love.*

She laughed. Somewhere, a voice called out to her. Warm hands gripped her face.

Irene. Don't do this. Don't you dare leave me.

But that was the thing. Irene wasn't going anywhere. Not really.

Because in that moment, Irene Manette Bamford was the very stars themselves. She was the infinite cosmos. The light of the moon. She was the whisper of the rain. The gentle kiss of wind.

She was—and forever would be—*everything.*

50

MASIKA

Ashes. That was what was left of her best friend. A pile of ashes. Masika burrowed her hands deeper, searching . . . but there was nothing there. Nothing left of Irene. *Come back*, Masika begged, tears blurring her vision, a half scream, half sob tearing out of her throat.

And then she felt it. Nestled beneath. Like a seedling sprouting from the dirt.

The ring felt cold against her hand. Masika raised it higher, lifting it toward the rays of silver light flickering through the branches. As she placed the ring upon her palm, it hummed, a searing current shooting down her forearm and through her limbs.

Fear struck her first. Had Irene's sacrifice been in vain? Had the ring not *actually* been destroyed?

But no . . . this ring was different.

It wasn't Mateo's. And it wasn't Silas's.

Engrained upon the silver band was neither of their names.

Masika Sallow.

She stared at the thin grooves, reading out her name. It couldn't be. It couldn't possibly . . .

A gust of wind blew Masika's curls out of her face. Something surged inside her. It was a million souls reaching for her.

Embracing her. Calling out to her. She felt the seams of the afterlife . . . could practically *see* them.

How had she not seen them before?

The connecting threads that bound them all together. The beating heart of the afterlife.

Masika let out a shuddering breath and stared up at the arched gates of Blackwood Academy. It was as if the ivy-draped halls of the school were speaking to her. Whispering her name.

The wind picked up speed. The ground beneath her shook.

Understanding washed over Masika as a final crackle of lightning lit up the sky.

It all made sense now. The strange connection she'd been feeling toward Blackwood. The way her touch had appeased the unruly willow when it had tried to consume Olivier. Her inexplainable connection to the fox.

This was her right. Her final act of defiance.

Her calling.

Masika slipped the ring on.

It was time for a new Headmaster.

51

AUGUST

August wasn't just going to let her wither away. He refused to simply stand back and watch the light fade from her eyes. So when he lifted Wren back onto her feet, throwing her arm over his shoulder, he ignored the searing current coursing through his limbs, the shadows digging deeper into his veins.

All of his attention, all of his focus, was on Wren.

On finding a way to save her.

He needed to find the Resistance. Maybe there was something they could do. If he could locate one of their healers in the chaos unfolding outside, then maybe they could mend whatever had broken inside Wren's soul.

But the moment August dragged Wren out of Silas's office and into the corridor, he staggered to a halt.

Somebody was waiting for them.

Edith Hughes stood at the center of the narrow corridor. Fury burned behind her eyes.

"It wasn't enough to betray me once, was it?"

"Please, Edith." August raised his hand in surrender. Beside him, Wren let out a groan, head lolling against his shoulder. She was barely conscious, and it was taking all August's strength to keep her standing. "I don't want to hurt you." Not to mention that he was desperate not to use another ounce of shadow magic. He was certain that if he did, if he allowed himself to indulge in his power again, he'd be lost forever. The shadows were intoxicating. He felt them tearing at his insides, begging to consume him.

Edith let out a bitter chuckle.

"*Hurt* me? You think you can hurt me?" Edith lifted her hand and a swirling sphere of shadows hovered over her palm. "That's the point of all of this. Nothing can hurt me anymore. Not you. Not the past. *Nothing.*"

August shook his head.

"I know a part of you still has to care," he muttered through gritted teeth, struggling to keep himself upright with the weight of Wren's limp body in his arms. "You're still my sister."

Edith's scowl only deepened at the accusation.

"I am nothing to you anymore."

August saw with painful clarity the moment Edith called upon her shadows. Everything seemed to slow down. She extended her arm, poised to strike, hand aimed directly at August's heart, and then . . . nothing.

Edith's face twitched. She stared down at her hand in bewilderment, watching as the sphere of shadows in her palms dissipated, vanishing completely. She extended her fingers, but still nothing happened. And then, like the gentle light of the moon breaking through the darkness, the shadows running through her veins began to clear. One by one, they grew fainter, until every single one of the shadows inside Edith had seemingly vanished, even the infamous shadow crown over her head.

Confusion coursed through August as he felt his own body suddenly grow stronger.

The pain in his limbs vanished. The unbearable ache softened, until he barely felt it.

The shadows that had been seconds away from consuming him were seemingly . . . *gone.*

"What is this?" Edith spat out, chest rising and falling with panicked breaths. She fell to her knees. "What's happening?!"

Wren lifted a shaking hand, tracing the edge of August's jaw. He turned to look at her and saw her blue eyes beaming up at him. She blinked, sluggish and slow, as if she were using all the strength she had left to stay awake.

"Your face . . ." She laughed, a brilliant and airy sound. "The shadows . . . they've vanished."

Edith let out an animalistic howl. She writhed and screamed, tearing at her hair, nails digging into her scalp. August gently rested Wren against the closest wall and tentatively approached his sister.

He knelt beside her.

"Edith."

But his sister had seemingly lost control. She looked crazed—eyes wide, wretched sobs bursting out of her as she gripped her hair tightly, pulling and tugging as if she were trying to claw her way through her skull. Tears streamed down her face. A torrential downpour of bottled-up emotions exploding out of her.

"Make it stop!" she bellowed, frantic. "MAKE IT FUCKING STOP!"

August cupped his sister's face in his hands.

"Make *what* stop?"

Edith stared up at him, lips quivering.

"I feel it." She splayed a palm across her chest, fingers clawing at her skin. "All of it."

Understanding washed over August.

Her emotions.

Somehow, by some miracle, their shadows had vanished. Which could only mean that their link to shadow magic had been severed. All those feelings Edith had kept hidden inside her, all the emotions she'd numbed with the help of her shadows, had come rushing back in. There was no more running. No more hiding.

This was her eternal punishment.

"We can figure this out," August whispered encouragingly. "We can—" But his words were cut short when Edith threw a lightning streak of corporeal magic at him, a hoarse scream tearing from her throat.

August dodged it at the last second, sighing in relief when he saw that the spell had barely missed Wren. He whirled back to face his sister, gripping her wrists before she could attempt another spell.

"Stop," August pleaded. "Don't do this."

But Edith wasn't listening. She screamed and screamed, kicking August in the stomach, sending him flying backward. He sensed her next attack—a surge of flames bursting from her palms—and threw his hands up in defense, a shimmering golden shield sprouting from his palms, the light of his shield and Edith's flames meeting in a thunderous crash.

"You did this!" she bellowed. "It's *your* fault! You took the shadows from me! You betrayed me! You—" Somewhere to the left of them, a sudden gust of wind sent Edith flying backward, her words dying in her throat. She hit the wall hard, her flames vanishing as she lost her footing and smacked against the window.

August blinked in confusion, and then Quinn was stumbling into view. Blood stained her pink hair, a streak of it carved against her jaw. She flicked her wrist and a nearby curtain fluttered and moved under her control, jolting toward Edith as it wrapped itself tightly around her torso, pinning her arms by her side.

"I'LL KILL YOU!" Edith screamed, writhing helplessly, legs kicking as she tried to break free. "I SWEAR I'LL—" And then

Quinn snapped her fingers and a strip of the curtain snaked around Edith's mouth, snuffing out her voice.

Quinn let out a weak laugh.

"Much better."

She dusted off her hands and approached August, placing a hand against his shoulder.

"You okay there?"

August shrugged numbly.

"Uh . . . fine. Fine, I think. But—" He sucked in a sharp breath, glancing over his shoulder at Wren. She was still slumped against the wall, shoulders hunched, her eyelids fluttering open and closed as she fought to stay upright.

Quinn's eyes snagged on Wren.

"Is she . . ."

August nodded.

"She's back."

Quinn let out a breath of relief. She walked toward Wren, approaching her tentatively. A tense moment of silence stretched between them as Wren fought to face Quinn, her own eyes brimming with regret.

"I'm . . . I'm sorry." Wren let out a choked cry. "I'm so fucking sorry." Instantly, Wren's knees buckled and Quinn caught her in her arms, brushing Wren's hair away from her face.

"It wasn't you," Quinn whispered, voice wavering. "It wasn't your fault."

Wren shuddered. She wheezed in strangled breaths.

"I—I killed him."

Quinn let out a soft, broken laugh.

"He was already dead."

Wren lifted her eyes to meet Quinn.

"I ruined him," she whispered. "I destroyed him. I turned him into a *monster*. I—"

"Wren." Quinn placed her hands delicately upon Wren's face. The moment Quinn's hands made contact, Wren flinched, as if Quinn's tenderness—her *forgiveness*—pained her more than any physical wound ever could. The next words Quinn spoke were slow and spaced out, each word emphasized carefully. "It. Wasn't. You."

Wren let out a broken sigh. She gave a weak nod of her head, mustering a small smile. When she spoke next, her voice came out thready and wrong.

"He deserved . . . so much better."

Quinn smiled, but her lip quivered as she fought the tears building behind her eyes. "That we can agree on." She turned to face August. "Do we know how this happened?"

August didn't need her to clarify. It was obvious what she was referring to.

He shook his head.

"The shadows just . . . vanished."

"The ring," Wren supplied weakly. "Maybe . . . maybe the others found a way to destroy it."

Next to them, Edith's muffled scream echoed behind the gauzy fabric of the curtain wrapped tightly around her mouth. Quinn stared down at her with a pinch of annoyance.

"Well, I suppose we should do something about her. I'm sure the Resistance will want a chat." Quinn's gaze snaked over to Wren, brows furrowing in concern. "Though I highly advise you to stay inside. She's in no condition to fight."

"We can't." August took Wren gently from Quinn's arms, scooping her into his own. Instantly, Wren lost consciousness, eyes fluttering again as she fought the exhaustion pulling her under. "We have to go find a healer. She isn't going to make it if we don't find someone who can help."

Quinn's face hardened under a wave of determination.

"Then go. I can take care of this."

Wren looked up at Quinn, eyes struggling to stay open.

"Thank you . . ." she whispered. "For everything."

Quinn smiled.

"Just doing my job."

August watched as a tidal wave of conflicting emotions flowed over Wren's face. He knew a part of her wanted to stay, to fight alongside Quinn, to ensure her survival, but they were running out of time. So before either one of them could change their minds, August walked away from Quinn, Wren held delicately in his arms, and ran for their lives.

52

EMILIO

All around them, Demiens scattered. Shrieks of terror echoed like a dissonant symphony. Emilio wasn't entirely sure what had happened, but one moment the shadows had been there, and the next, they were gone.

He'd been standing back to back with Olivier, caught in a rather nasty battle with three Demiens. The pair had constructed a shield around them, but it was breaking. Cracks splitting down the middle as the shadows pushed against them. Emilio had been so certain that it wouldn't hold. That they'd meet their end this way. But then, as if the hands of God had reached down from the heavens and snatched them right out of their veins, the Demiens' shadows had vanished.

It all blurred together after that. Some Demiens fell to their knees, screaming out in agony, as if caught within a current of pain, though Emilio saw no wound. They clawed at their chests. Their faces. Others simply left, running deeper into the forest, though he hadn't the faintest idea where they intended to go.

From the looks of it . . . the Demien Order had fallen apart.

Emilio and Olivier had made their way through the grounds shortly after, eyes frantically searching for a familiar face. They searched through the rubble and carnage. Mounds of dust and ash covered the ivy-speckled buildings—all that was left of the souls that had been destroyed.

It's funny, Emilio had thought. After everything . . . he couldn't tell them apart. Resistance fighters. Demiens. Ascended. Despite their differences, they all looked the same when they had been destroyed.

Nothing but dust.

Eventually, they found what they were searching for. Catherine and Dina were standing near Bonestrod, out by the main gates, surrounded by other Resistance fighters. Emilio had thrown his arms around them the moment he had found them, unwilling to let go even when Catherine blushed fiercely and huffed something unintelligible under her breath. Dina, whose silver hair was now stained red with blood, nearly broke out into a blubbering mess the moment she laid eyes on them.

"You idiots!" she had cried, punching Emilio squarely in the shoulder, which, in Dina's language, was as close to saying *I love you* as she could possibly have gotten. "Where were you?!"

Olivier let out a low chuckle. "How much time do you have?"

He told them everything. About how they'd found Masika and Irene at the Ascended Quarters. How they'd met up with August to stop Wren. The moment Wren and Silas had plunged their hands into each other's soul, ripping each other from existence. The moment the Headmaster of Blackwood Academy was *finally* destroyed.

"But what about the shadows?" asked Olivier now, looking around the group. "They just vanished. How does that even happen?"

"I have no idea." Catherine shook her head. "The shadows are tethered to the Soulless One. So unless he abandoned them, or was destroyed . . ." She shrugged, running a hand through her hair.

"Who cares?" Dina barked through a cackle of laughter. "What's important is that the Demiens are retreating! Their shadows are *gone.* And if you're telling me that Silas was well and truly destroyed . . ." She trailed off, an apprehensive inkling of hope beaming in her eyes. Emilio understood her hesitation. It was almost too good to be true. The Demien Order had seemingly fallen apart only a few moments after Silas had been destroyed.

Which meant—*somehow*—they had won.

The patter of footsteps echoed behind them. August emerged from the darkness, Wren cradled in his arms. She was barely conscious, her eyes fluttering as she struggled to stay awake.

"A healer!" August bellowed, frantic. *"Please!"*

Catherine called out to the group of Resistance fighters congregated a few yards away, and a boy with a golden sash wrapped around his arm approached, running up to Wren and placing his hand on her forehead.

His expression turned grave. "Her soul . . . what happened?"

"Can you fix it?" August's voice trembled.

The healer pressed his fingers against Wren's temples. Silver threads of light trickled from his palm, burrowing through Wren's skin. The healer's face turned grim before he quickly pulled his hands away.

He shook his head.

"I eased her pain a bit. Offered her one last push of strength, but . . . there's nothing else I can do for her. There's nothing I can do to stop her soul from coming undone."

"No." August let out a fragmented breath. "*Please.* There has to be something."

Wren placed a shaking hand on his forearm.

"It's okay," she muttered softly. "August. Look at me." But August couldn't bring himself to face her. Wren groaned, using the last shred of strength offered to her by the healer to gently peel herself from August's grip, standing on her own feet. She swayed, and August held her steady by the shoulders. When their eyes met, Emilio could see the agony and adoration swirling between them.

"It's going . . . to be okay," Wren assured him. "We should . . . we should focus on finding Masika and Irene."

Catherine's head shot up. "Where are they?"

"Last we saw her, Masika had left Blackwood with Irene to find a way to destroy the Soulless One's ring," Emilio explained, watching as panic flickered behind Catherine's eyes. "We have to assume they were successful, but . . . no one has seen them since."

Catherine unsheathed her spear without a beat of hesitation. But before she could charge toward the forest in search of Masika, Dina reached out and grabbed her by the elbow, tugging her back gently.

"Hold on," she muttered. "You can't just go barging into the forest. We all want to find Masika, but they need you here." She gestured to the Resistance fighters gathered behind them with a tilt of her chin. Emilio knew she was right. Though it was clear that the scales had tipped in their favor, it was difficult to discern what was left of the Resistance fighters. Someone needed to pick up the pieces and find a way to put them back together.

Catherine opened her mouth to retort, but Olivier cut in.

"We'll find her," he said. "We'll bring her back to you."

Catherine conceded with a nod, but Emilio could see the apprehension in her eyes. The way it was taking everything in her not to tear herself from Dina's grasp and run into the forest in search of Masika.

"Loughty." August sucked in a breath. "You should stay. Maybe one of the other healers could take a look. Maybe there's something they can do—"

"If it was one of *us* out there . . ." Wren interjected gently, looking between August, Emilio and Olivier, ". . . they would come find us."

"She's right," Emilio muttered. "Masika would have been out there looking for us by now. And Irene . . . well . . . weirdly enough—I think she would be too."

"We'll all go." Olivier threaded his fingers through Emilio's and gave his hand a tight squeeze. "We started this together—and we'll finish it together."

"Then it's settled." Wren's eyes skated among the group. She inhaled a sharp breath, a pallid sheen on her face. "Let's bring them home."

As they set off toward the main gates, determination propelling them forward, Emilio, for once, didn't listen to the doubt and worry building inside him. For once . . . Emilio let himself believe in miracles.

Even if that made him a fool.

53

WREN

They found Masika standing in the forest, only a few yards from the Blackwood gates, a pile of ash beneath her feet. But there was something growing from the ash . . . a seedling. At first, Wren couldn't quite tell what it was about Masika that was different. She'd assumed it was the atmosphere. There was a strange crackle in the air. A thick undercurrent of magic. But when she finally looked at Masika—*properly* looked at her—the realization struck Wren in a staggering blow.

The magic, the power Wren felt, was coming from *her*.

"Masika!" Emilio stumbled toward her, throwing his arms over her shoulders. Wren couldn't tell if he was genuinely oblivious to the power burning through Masika, or if he'd simply chosen to be. "We've been looking everywhere for you! The Demiens . . . their shadow magic isn't working. They've begun to scatter."

Masika didn't seem surprised, only relieved.

"Good," she whispered. "Then it's done."

"What happened?" August asked next to Wren. "And where's Irene?"

Masika's eyes flitted to the ash beneath her feet.

"Gone."

"What do you mean *gone*?" Olivier echoed with a hollow laugh. "Did she leave?"

Masika flexed her right hand. There was a ring on her index finger. A shimmering golden band that glistened with a faint amber glow.

Has she always worn that? Wren wondered silently.

"The corruption has been cleansed," Masika whispered, a waver of sorrow in her voice.

Emilio watched her intently, brows cinched together.

"What are you saying?"

Masika looked between them.

"The Soulless One's ring was destroyed . . . but everything has a price."

The weight of Masika's words barreled into Wren and a strangled gasp escaped her throat. She watched the realization strike the others, one by one. Emilio staggered backward. Olivier shook his head, disbelief creasing his face. August simply stood there, stone-faced, though Wren saw the way he dug his fingernails into the palm of his hand, the indents he left behind.

"No . . ." Emilio's denial was heartbreaking. *"No."*

"That *idiot—*" Olivier choked out. His panicked eyes landed on the pile of ash by Masika's feet. "What . . . what was she *thinking*?"

August's response was a breathless whisper.

"She saved us."

Olivier flinched.

"At the expense of her own soul."

"I didn't say goodbye," Emilio muttered helplessly, though it appeared as though he was speaking to himself, as if it had only now dawned on him.

Olivier strode toward Masika, gripping her by the arms, desperation in his stare.

"There has to be a way to get her back." He searched her face, pleading. "This can't be it . . . she can't be *gone*."

"Her sacrifice is final." Masika's voice cracked. "She's gone."

And then she told them everything. How the True Headmaster and the Soulless One had been connected—one and the same. How Irene had chosen to sacrifice her own soul to save the afterlife, absorbing the ring's power and letting it consume her. And how, in the wake of that destruction, hidden among the rubble and ash, a new Headmaster had been beckoned, chosen by the academy and ushered from the darkness.

Masika.

The Headmaster of Blackwood Academy.

"Holy shit," Olivier muttered, looking Masika up and down. "You mean . . . *you're* the new Headmaster?"

Masika lifted her hand, gesturing to the ring glistening upon her index finger.

"It . . . chose me." Her voice wavered, but she continued. "I don't know why. And I don't expect I ever will, but . . . all I know is that *this* is my duty. What I was called for. What I was born for."

Wren's knees buckled. Just as the words had left Masika's lips, that same searing pain had begun to twist at her insides. Whatever morsel of strength the healer had offered her vanished, and she collapsed onto her knees, though August was next to her by the time she hit the floor, his strong hands holding her steady as he lowered himself beside her.

"What is it?" he asked. "What's wrong?"

The world swayed around her.

"I'm . . . fine."

"You're not." His voice was rough, desperate.

Masika knelt beside Wren. She placed her hand upon Wren's cheek. At her touch, a searing heat crawled through Wren's skin.

A presence. It was Masika. She was in Wren's mind, in the heart of her very soul. And when their eyes met, Wren knew.

This was it.

My time is up.

"What is it?" August looked between them. "What's happening to her?"

"The piece of your soul tethering her to this plane can only hold for so long." Masika dragged her eyes to August. Her expression was solemn. "And once it breaks . . ." Her voice trailed off as she dropped her hand.

August shook his head, indignation building behind his eyes. "Do something."

Masika mulled over his words.

"There's only one thing I can do."

And then she pushed herself back onto her feet and called upon her power.

It cascaded out of her in a brilliant halo, rays of golden light that ebbed and flowed around her. Wren had never seen anything more beautiful. Masika's entire body was alight. Her amber eyes glowing like the heart of the sun.

"I can give her a second chance." Masika's voice reverberated, echoing as if she were all around them. "But just one more."

"Another chance at what?" August asked.

Masika stared down at them. The faintest wisp of a smile curled on her lips.

"Life."

And then Masika brought her hands together and the magic exploded out of her. Wren shielded her eyes, momentarily blinded by the wave of golden light. When her vision finally cleared, she saw the doorway that had appeared before them. Fashioned from stone and vines, the door was propped open, a swirling vortex of color looming on the other side.

Life.

Wren's heart soared as the word echoed in her mind.

"I can live again?" she asked, unable to stifle the hope clinging stubbornly inside her.

"Your soul will be reborn," Masika explained. "But . . . there's a condition. You wouldn't remember anything. You'd forget all about this . . . about *us*."

August didn't hesitate. He turned to Masika, eyes wide and pleading. "Let me go with her."

Masika hesitated. "You could go with her . . . technically speaking. But the same condition would apply to you. Your memories of Blackwood would be gone. Your memories of Wren would be gone."

"I have to go," August replied, his face marked with determination. "I have to try."

But how could she ask that of him? How could she expect him to end his own soul?

"You could stay here, August." Wren managed a weak, hollow smile. "Help rebuild Blackwood. You could live the eternity you've always wanted. Free from your sister. From your duty. You could just . . . exist."

"Don't you get it?" August laughed, but tears welled behind his eyes. "You *are* my eternity, Wren. My soul is yours. In this life and the next."

Wren found herself laughing too, though her own tears prickled the back of her eyes. She reached her hands out and placed them gently on his cheeks. She traced the angular lines of his cheekbones. His jaw. The scar etched beneath his eye. His thick brows. The gentle curl of his raven-black hair.

She needed to remember him. To etch his face into her memory. To find a way to defy the laws of nature. It didn't matter what Masika said—she would remember him.

She would always remember him.

"I will find you." August cupped Wren's face in his hands. Their foreheads touched, gently, reverently. "Wherever we go. Wherever we end up. That is my promise to you, Wren Loughty. I will find you. *I will find you.*"

Their lips met and it was desperate and raw and messy. Wren threaded her hand through his curls, pulling him tighter. She just needed one more second with him. One more kiss. She just needed *more.*

Wren pulled away and they slowly made their way back onto their feet. Behind them, Olivier and Emilio watched, hands interlocked. Olivier cleared his throat, biting back a swell of emotions, while Emilio sobbed freely beside him.

"I would say see you later, though I'm not entirely certain I will," Olivier said.

Wren smiled. "I don't think you will."

Olivier paused, as if considering something. "Then I suppose . . . *have a good life* is appropriate." He looked between Wren and August and let out a shaky breath. "Both of you."

August nodded. His jaw flexed as he managed a feeble smile. "We'll try."

Their eyes landed on Emilio, though the boy seemed completely inconsolable, unable to mutter anything but a soft and nearly incomprehensible "I'll miss you."

Wren felt her heart break in two.

"Don't worry, Emilio." August offered the boy a reassuring smile. "We're really only one door away."

Emilio nodded, sniffling. "Suppose that's true."

"Listen . . ." Masika's voice grew solemn as she looked among them. "There's no way for me to guarantee you'll ever cross paths, let alone be able to recognize one another. I can only usher your souls into a new life. But that's it. It'll be like you never met."

Wren exhaled a thready breath. "I know, but . . . we have to try."

August and Wren turned to look at one another. This was it. There was no going back, no changing their minds, once they crossed through that door. Their souls, as they'd come to know them, would be gone. Ripped from one existence and thrust into another. But it was also their only chance. Their only hope.

And that was the point of life, anyway, wasn't it? To dare to hope? To dare to love?

Wren planted one last kiss against August's lips.

"I'll see you in the next life?" she asked.

August wiped a fallen tear from her cheek. "I'll see you in the next life."

And then Wren Loughty and Augustine Hughes walked through the doorway, hand in hand . . . and ceased to exist.

54

OLIVIER

Olivier had run out of time.

He was certain of it now. As he stood there, watching as August and Wren walked through the doorway, obliterating their souls from existence for the hope of a second chance, he felt the end of his own road approaching. He'd run from the inevitable for longer than most. Tricked fate more times than he could count. But now . . . the time for running was over.

The brilliance of Masika's power was overwhelming. She had always been beautiful, but staring at her now felt *devastating*. It was as if her soul had been infused with starlight. An all-consuming glow burned beneath her skin . . . an awe-inspiring sense of power.

Though, truthfully, she'd always been brilliant.

Lost in the sheer magnitude of Masika's power, Olivier hadn't noticed the moment she'd approached him. Her gaze seemed to drink him in, analyzing something Olivier couldn't quite understand.

"Your mind," she whispered. "I can't reverse it. I can't stop the Forgetting."

Olivier let out a bitter chuckle. "I figured as much."

"But . . ." Masika continued with a tilt of her head, "unlike Wren . . . your soul is intact. It's still tethered to this plane. Which means there's something else I can offer you. Something I can offer you both."

"What?" Emilio asked breathlessly.

"I can relieve both of you of your duties and offer you the choice that should always have been yours."

"What does that mean?" Emilio asked, looking between them. "What choice?"

Olivier met Masika's knowing stare. There was a flash of hope in them . . . a whisper of promise. But there was something else. Something far darker. An ember of sorrow that burned deep inside. An understanding that this choice, this decision, would change the three of them, forever.

"The Other Side." Olivier laced his hand through Emilio's. "She means both of us can cross over."

Emilio's head snapped toward Olivier in confusion.

"B-but . . ." he stammered, brows furrowed. "That's not what you want. You always said you hated the idea of the Other Side."

Olivier couldn't help but laugh. He found that a warm calm had settled over him. He'd never felt more clearheaded. More certain of anything in his entire existence. It was so simple. So wonderfully, blissfully *simple.*

"I want to be with you," he whispered. "It doesn't matter where I am."

"But what if you're right?" Emilio asked in a broken whisper. "What if there's nothing waiting for us?"

Olivier smiled.

"But what if I'm wrong?"

Emilio's chest shuddered. His brown eyes gleamed with tears.

"Are you sure?"

"I used to think there was nothing more terrifying than the unknown," Olivier explained, the words tumbling out of him, almost frantic. "That only a fool would cross over to the Other Side without knowing what was waiting for them. But now I realize that I was wrong. Completely and utterly wrong. It's far more terrifying to *know*. Because now that I know, with utmost certainty, that my heart is yours, there is nothing more terrifying than the thought of existing without you."

Emilio shut his eyes.

"Olivier." He whispered his name and Olivier felt his soul draw him closer, that invisible tether between them tightening. If he closed his eyes, he swore he could feel the echo of his heart daring to beat—daring to *live*.

"I know, my love." Olivier pulled Emilio closer. "I know."

Their lips crashed together. Olivier tasted the universe on Emilio's lips. Felt eternity in his touch. He wanted more. More of Emilio. More of his hands traveling against the length of Emilio's torso. More of his breath brushing against the lines of Emilio's neck. But above all else . . . he wanted more time. He'd never have enough of it. Not here, anyway. But perhaps . . . on the Other Side . . . perhaps they could finally have the afterlife they deserved.

They parted slowly. Reluctantly.

Caught up in the heaven of Emilio's touch, Olivier had nearly forgotten that Masika was still standing there, watching them. She'd turned slightly, offering them privacy, but her presence was nearly impossible to ignore.

Olivier cleared his throat.

"Okay."

Masika turned back to face them.

"Okay?"

"We'll cross over."

Masika let out a breath—a strange mixture of relief and sorrow. She nodded.

"Very well."

She raised her hand and the doorway transformed into another—this one gleaming in gold, a dozen rose-dotted vines wrapped around its edge. A ruby river of velvety petals flowed down its sides, cascading onto the floor.

"This is your stop."

Emilio approached Masika tentatively, a sheepish look in his eyes.

"I trust you'll watch over Benji?"

Masika smiled through her own tears.

"You have my word."

Emilio hesitated, eyes darting over Masika's face, and then he jolted forward, wrapping her in a tight embrace. Masika's expression faltered, a single tear falling down her cheek.

"God, I'm going to miss you," Emilio muttered weakly.

"I'll miss you every second of every day." Masika gently pulled away from Emilio, lifting his chin with her thumb. "But you deserve this. You deserve the eternity you always wanted."

When Masika's eyes landed on Olivier next, he found the breath snatched from his lungs, a sudden rush of panic traveling up his throat. What could he even say? They had quite literally been through hell and back together, seen things, done things that most couldn't even fathom. And now . . . they'd reached their end.

"I'm glad we became friends." Olivier mustered up a smile. "Even if it took us a few decades."

Masika chuckled. She laced Olivier's fingers through hers and gave his hand a squeeze. "Friends, huh? What happened to *unfortunate acquaintances*?"

Olivier shook his head, smiling, but tears burned behind his eyes. "I think I prefer *friends.*" And then a thought occurred to him, and he couldn't help himself, continuing with a sharp intake of breath. "Oh, and by the way, I know you're like the ruler of the afterlife or whatever now—but please . . . do us all a favor and just make up with Catherine already. She's crazy about you."

And then the Headmaster of Blackwood Academy did the unthinkable.

She *blushed.*

Olivier smiled, pleased.

That'll do.

He turned back toward the door, facing it with wild determination.

There was a weighted silence. A moment of hesitation.

"So . . . should we place bets?" Olivier asked casually.

Emilio snorted.

"You want to bet on our souls?"

"I don't know." Olivier laced his fingers through Emilio's, gripping the boy like a lifeline. "It could be fun. We could make it a bit naughty. Loser has to strip naked."

Emilio let out a cackle of laughter.

"Olivier Dupont. You cannot *seriously* be flirting at a time like this."

"Oh, my dear Emilio." Olivier smiled. "It's *always* a good time to flirt."

When the two boys walked through the door, crossing into the unknown, there were no tears to be shed. No sadness. Not even an inkling of fear. There were only smiles on their faces and the promise of *more.* More time. More laughter.

And, most of all, hope.

55

In a sunlit valley, on a warm summer day, Olivier Dupont and Emilio Córdova crossed into eternity.

Together.

56

MASIKA

Masika Sallow, the Headmaster of Blackwood Academy, stood atop Bonestrod and took in the view. Half of Elysium Hall was missing—blown to pieces, as if someone had taken a bite out of its side and spat out the chunks. Blood and ash stained the grounds, fluttering in the air like fallen snow. But that cleanup would be easy. A simple fix.

There were other broken things far more difficult to mend. Things she wasn't quite sure ever would be mended.

Footsteps echoed behind her. Masika recognized their soul like a little pinprick in her chest. She wondered if she'd ever get used to that. The way her mind seemed to be connected to every piece of Blackwood all at once; the beating heart of the school resounding in her chest—*thump, thump, thump.*

"I lied."

Masika turned to face Catherine Clarke. Her braids had come partially undone. Her face was a soot-streaked mess. But she looked beautiful. Broken and wrecked—but beautiful.

"When we spoke the other night." Catherine stepped closer, and it suddenly felt as though they were standing at a precipice, every word tumbling out of Catherine shoving them closer to the edge. "You asked me what I see when I look at you now. Do you remember that?"

A gentle breeze ran through Masika's curls. It felt like laughter. A familiar but lost sound.

"I do."

"I told you I see nothing." Catherine swallowed. Her hands began to shake as she approached Masika. "But that's not true." Silence stretched between them. In the distance, Masika could sense the students of Blackwood Academy emerging from their dormitories to assess the damage. Their precious souls lighting up her own like fireflies beckoning to her in the night.

"Do you want to know what I see when I look at you?" Catherine's voice was soft, almost reverent. For a moment, it sounded like the Catherine whom Masika had once known. The one who had loved her unabashedly—the one who would have stayed. "What I've always seen?"

Masika nodded, and Catherine took her face in her hands.

"My future." Masika felt the dam inside her finally break free. "When I look at you . . . I see my future."

"Everything is going to be different now." Masika's voice wobbled with unshed tears.

"Good." Catherine tucked a loose curl behind Masika's ear. "I like different."

Masika lifted her hand between them. Her ring lit up their faces in its golden sheen.

"I've changed."

Catherine smiled.

"So have I."

Masika's heart soared. It was everything she wanted, everything she needed, yet still—a part of her faltered. It was fear. Fear of losing Catherine again. Fear of knowing she'd already lost so much.

"You can't leave me again."

Catherine's thumb delicately brushed Masika's lip.

"I'm not going anywhere."

I'm not going anywhere. Those four words burned inside Masika, cutting through the fear, wrapping her in a warm embrace. She couldn't do this alone—she didn't *want* to. For once, Masika wanted to believe that she was meant for happiness. That she deserved it.

Masika let out a long-held sigh.

"Okay, then."

Catherine cocked her head. A shy smile spread onto her lips.

"Yeah?"

A soft laugh tumbled out of Masika.

"Yeah."

It was in that moment, standing among the wreckage, staring up at Catherine, that Masika realized how painfully wrong she had been. She'd always assumed that their story had come to an end long ago. That her fate had been written for her the moment she'd awoken at the gates of Blackwood Academy.

But that was the thing about fate. It wasn't some stuck, stagnant thing. It could change.

Masika Sallow had once been destined to love Catherine Clarke and lose her.

But she'd also been destined to love her and love her and love her, forevermore.

THE END . . . ?

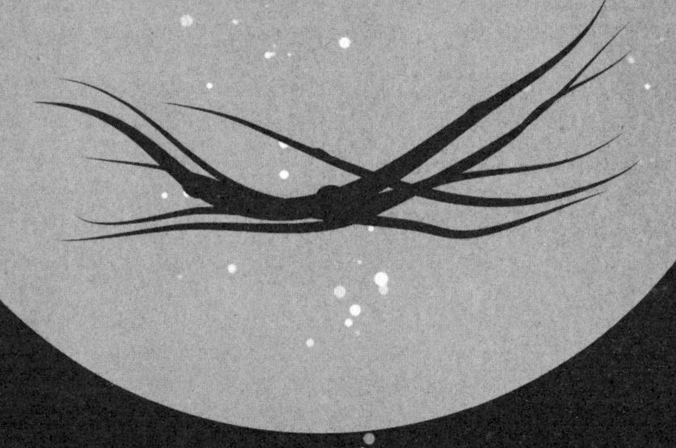

EIGHTEEN YEARS LATER

The Headmaster of Blackwood Academy walked between one world and the next. It had become rather easy for her—traveling from one plane of existence into another. It was just like crossing through a door, after all.

The living never noticed much. Too preoccupied with their mortal concerns. Too caught up with the fleeting complexity of their lives. So, even though they should have seen the strange girl with eyes the color of molten amber and the odd batlike puppy trotting beside her, they didn't. Or, if they did, they simply *thought* they saw her, though when they turned back to check, there was never anything there.

Just a trick of light.

Just a passing shadow.

The Headmaster enjoyed visiting this town. The rhythmic clatter of tourists walking among the cobbled streets. Students bustling nearby, scrambling to get to class on time. It reminded her of another version of herself. Not the one who had belonged to the world of the living, but another. The one who had found her strength in the halls of an academy. The one who had clawed her way to the surface, despite the prickly threads of grief that had attempted to pull her back.

Tonight's visit, however, would be different.

There was business to attend to.

She entered the town in the dead of night. Shadows shrouded the empty streets. A calm, inviting silence drifting in the chill air. It was a Friday night, and a few students scurried in the dark, bundled together, giggling into their hands as they drunkenly waded through mounds of fallen leaves. Pale light shone upon the black asphalt. There was a full moon; the white-laced moon hung high in the night sky, unburdened by the thin gray cloud swimming around it.

The Headmaster glanced down at her watch.

"It's almost time," she whispered out loud. The fluffy creature at her side peered up at her with his beady red eyes. "Shall we?"

The creature sneezed and the Headmaster smiled.

Together, they crossed the street, heading for the small square that sat near the town's university. Full, lush oak trees adorned the perimeter of the courtyard, though the leaves had begun to change as autumn's breath blew upon them, tinged in hues of deep auburn and delicate orange.

At the center of the courtyard stood a fountain surrounded by a stone ledge.

And there, seated upon the stone ledge, beer bottle in hand, was a girl.

Her hair was as auburn as the molting leaves of the trees. Her eyes a pale blue.

The Headmaster looked up at the sky.

"Any second now," she whispered.

Three . . . two . . . one . . .

The boy came into view, entering the courtyard with his hands tucked into his pockets and his gaze fixed forward. His hair was the color of raven's feathers. His eyes a silvery gray. He hummed along to the song blasting from his corded headphones, completely unaware of the girl seated only a few yards away from him.

The Headmaster rolled her eyes.

Must I do everything?

She snapped her fingers and a sudden gust of wind blew through the trees, knocking the boy's headphones out of his ears. He staggered, reaching for them, but the cord slipped right through his fingers, drifting across the ground. He scrambled, chasing after them, though he skidded to a halt when he realized his earbuds had come to a stop right beside the girl's shoes.

He glanced up.

Their eyes met.

The girl reached down, picking up the earbuds. She stood up and faced the boy, dangling them in front of him.

"I'm guessing these are yours."

The boy let out a nervous chuckle. He grabbed them and tucked them into his pocket.

"Yeah. Sorry."

The girl laughed and a cloud of frost billowed from her lips. When she smiled, the boy swore he had seen it a million times before. Swore he could shut his eyes and draw it from memory.

"Do I know you?" the girl asked. She tucked a strand of hair behind her ear and stepped closer.

The boy shook his head. "I don't think so. Maybe."

The girl took a long sip from her beer. Her blue eyes bored into his, that same inkling of familiarity radiating inside them. She stared at him like she knew him—like they'd known each other from the very start.

"Well . . . which is it?" she asked, chuckling.

As the question tumbled out of the girl's lips, a thought crashed into the boy, so wild, so absurd, that he couldn't help but laugh. It was impossible. A silly, ridiculous thought. Because even though he had never seen this girl before, even though they were only now meeting for the first time, he couldn't help but feel as though his entire life—every seemingly inconsequential event—had been leading him to this very moment.

"I'm not sure," he whispered back.

The girl stared and stared. Her brows creased together, mouth parting. The boy could see the same thought crashing through her. The same confusion riddling her features. She laughed, setting the beer bottle down against the stone ledge beside her.

"Maybe it's one of those past life things," she said.

The boy furrowed his brow. "What do you mean?"

"Well," she said, stepping closer. "I've heard that sometimes when you recognize someone but you've never met before, that it's actually your soul recognizing them. That you knew each other in another life."

Something in the boy's chest sang. Calling to him. Beckoning him.

The Headmaster could feel it—the connecting thread. The unbreakable link.

The boy had never given much thought to his soul before. Never paid it any mind. But in that moment, he was certain that if he *did* have a soul, if such a thing existed, that somehow, a part of his belonged to this girl.

"You think we knew each other in another life?" he asked, voice barely audible.

The girl stepped closer. She examined his face, lifting her hand, tracing the edge of the scar etched into the skin beneath his right eye. The boy didn't back away. He didn't move. He simply let her.

"Maybe," she whispered, the warmth of her breath falling upon him.

"Yeah," the boy whispered back, smiling. "Maybe."

The Headmaster sighed, satisfied. She took a step back, retreating into the shadows, watching as the pair continued to speak, drawing closer to one another like two halves of a whole finally reunited.

"Well, Benji. I believe we've done our part."

The little creature barked.

"How about we head back home?"

With a single breath, the Headmaster opened the door to another world, though she paused when she took the first step forward, as if faced with an internal hitch. *Just one more look.* She glanced over her shoulder. The boy and girl were standing side by side, looking at one another, whispering words that the Headmaster would never hear.

A tiny voice in the back of her mind ached to stay, and despite knowing she could never listen to it, she let it linger. She let it *hope.* But deep down, the Headmaster of Blackwood Academy knew this wasn't her world. Not anymore.

There were other souls who needed her attention. Other stories waiting to be told.

And either way . . . this one was just beginning.

ACKNOWLEDGMENTS

WE DID IT! Writing a second book *and* a sequel was an incredibly special—and challenging—experience, but one I would not change for the world. There were many days when I wondered: *What the hell have I gotten myself into?* And though those specific days were filled with doubt and fear and the inevitable imposter syndrome that plagues us authors, there were also days that were filled with inspiration and magic and joy that reminded me: *This* is why I do what I do. This is why I write books.

As always, I have to thank my family first. Mami, Papi, Camila, Andy, Tato, Logan, and the myriad other relatives it would take twenty pages to list . . . los quiero a todos. Gracias por tu apoyo!

Of course, a massive thank-you to my powerhouse agent duo, Ariele Fredman and Gwen Beal, both of whom I would be lost without. I won the agent lotto with you two. Thank you for your endless support, for championing me and fighting for me—go team! And thanks to Elsa Knoke and Graham Weist for your support. Also, many thanks to the team at Curtis Brown UK, notably Steph Thwaites and Grace Robinson, for supporting this book across the pond. And a big thank-you to Savanna Wicks for ensuring the Souls of Blackwood Academy series could be read in so many languages across the globe!

To my INCREDIBLE editor, Lydia Gregovic. I get so emotional when I think of our first call and all the big dreams we had for this series. You believed in this story from the beginning, and I will be eternally grateful for that. To the rest of my amazing publishing team at Random House Children's Books—I am so grateful to have such an incredible group of people working on bringing this series to life. Thank you to Mallory Loehr, Wendy Loggia, Krista Marino, Noreen Herits, Madison Furr, Constance Inglima, Kristin Guy, Gabriella Murdoch, Colleen Fellingham, Barbara Perris, Liz Dresner, Ray Shappell, Tracy Heydweiller, Judith Haut and Gillian Levinson. I truly feel so lucky to have landed a home for the Souls of Blackwood Academy with you all.

Also, a massive thank-you to the Electric Monkey team for all your support in bringing this series to UK readers—especially Lindsey Heaven, Sarah Levison and Aleena Hasan. Another big thanks to Ryan Hammon, Lucy Courtenay, Sophie Porteous, Olivia Carson, Sarah Sleath, Hannah Penny, Ingrid Gilmore and Leah Woods. I truly feel so lucky to have you all in my corner!

To Josh, for your endless support, love and patience. Thank you for making sure I remain fed and sane when I'm on deadline. Life would be a lot duller without you by my side. I love you, mister.

To my incredible friends for always supporting me and cheering me on. To Andrea, for always being one phone call away—even if that's a four-hour FaceTime session. To Dylan, for hearing out my rants, no matter what. To Veronica, for coffee shop writing sessions aka chisme-and-sweet-treat sessions. To Aimee, for still being my friend after the concerning amount of Austin Butler edits I sent you. To Ellie, for being the definition of *we listen and we don't judge*. To Tucker, for being the only person in the world who believes I can eventually do a pull-up. On a serious note, I am nothing without my friends, and every day I count myself eternally lucky that in a world of billions of people, I had the luck of finding you. I love you always.

Thanks, of course, to my dog, Mr. Darcy, for keeping me

company during long writing sessions and yelling at me every time I'm on an important call. Additionally, to Leela Bug—for being the inspiration for Benji.

And last—but most certainly not least—*you*. The readers. Your support since the release of *Immortal Consequences* has been overwhelming in the best way possible. I am so, *so* lucky to have the best community of readers ever. Getting to see your excitement and support has been an endless source of inspiration and motivation for me, and I am so grateful that this book ended up in your hands.

All my love, eternally.

ABOUT THE AUTHOR

I. V. Marie was born to a Peruvian mother and Chilean father in Miami, where she acquired a penchant for afternoon cafecitos and an all-consuming obsession with books. Her writing ambitions began behind her grandparents' computer, where she spent her childhood crafting spooky and fantastical short stories. When she is not writing, you can find her rock climbing or watching atmospheric YouTube videos with her dog, Mr. Darcy. She is the author of *Immortal Consequences* and *Ruinous Ends*.

ivmarie.com